Damaged
LIKE US

KRISTA & BECCA
RITCHIE

CHARACTER LIST

Not all characters in this list will make an appearance in the book, but most will be mentioned.

Ages represent the age of the character at the beginning of the book. Some characters will be older when they're introduced, depending on their birthday.

The Hales

Loren Hale & Lily Calloway
Maximoff - 22
Luna – 17
Xander – 14
Kinney – 12

The Cobalts

Richard Connor Cobalt & Rose Calloway
Jane - 22
Charlie – 19
Beckett – 19
Eliot – 18
Tom – 17
Ben – 15
Audrey – 12

The Meadows

Ryke Meadows & Daisy Calloway

Sullivan - 19

Winona – 13

The Security Team

These are the bodyguards that protect the Hales, Cobalts, and Meadows.

SECURITY FORCE OMEGA

Akara Kitsuwon - 25

Farrow Keene – 27

Quinn Oliveira– 20

Oscar Oliveira - 30

Paul Donnelly – 26

SECURITY FORCE EPSILON

Thatcher Moretti - 27

Banks Moretti – 27

Heidi Smith – 50s

…and more

SECURITY FORCE ALPHA

Price Kepler – 40s

…and more

1

"You can't tell me one thing about him?" I ask for probably the millionth time. I haven't actually been counting. But from Akara's annoyed bite into his blueberry bagel, I'm guessing my question died a bitter death five minutes ago.

Today is doomsday.

The day where my unconventional, strange life becomes *colossally* more complicated. I can handle shit storms while propping up the Earth with one goddamn hand—but I like to be semi-prepared for situations. I have a real switchblade in my fucking pocket, but I want a metaphorical one too.

Akara swallows his bagel. "You want *one* thing?"

"Just one," I affirm.

"He's your new bodyguard."

I slowly blink into a glare. "Thank you for offering the *one* thing that I already fucking know." It's the *one* thing that's been driving me up the wall like a possessed Spider-Man. I've had the same bodyguard for my entire life, and he decided to retire recently.

Just yesterday, I said goodbye to Declan. It's bittersweet. He wants to spend more time with his wife and two kids, not be the 24/7 bodyguard to an internationally famous human being. I get that. Selfishly, I wish he could stay longer.

And when I mean *longer*, I mean *forever*.

Personal bodyguards are like spouses. All of my immediate and extended family have one. They follow us everywhere, eat with us, guard our rooms if we bring home strangers—or in my case, "uncomplicated" hookups. Mind-blowing fucks. One-night stands. All of that is being passed to a new someone.

I've never had to introduce a new bodyguard to the ins-and-outs of my life. It's not just going to be a Day In The Life of Maximoff Hale. It's a permanent position that'll last decades unless he turns out to be an incompetent prick.

This pivotal moment has put me on edge because Akara—the lead bodyguard in Security Force Omega—refuses to share more information about him.

"Like I said an hour ago," Akara tells me, "it's better if you meet in person." Before I can reply, his cellphone pings.

I hope it's my new bodyguard. I check my canvas wristwatch.

He's twenty minutes late, and Akara already assured me that he received the invite.

Location: Superheroes & Scones

Time: 6 a.m. (before the store opens at 8 a.m.)

The homey but *massive* store is empty. I only turned on a few lights since no employees are here yet, the place quiet. Dimly lit. While I wait, I stand behind the bar counter and pour myself an orange juice.

I'm not stealing.

My family owns the two-story hybrid comic book store and coffee shop. With red and blue vinyl booths, stools, and then rows and rows of shelved comics and merch, Superheroes & Scones resembles a retro diner and modern comic store. Eighty-five of them exist throughout the globe, but this one in Philadelphia is the very original.

Since its creation, it's had a few major renovations. The second floor used to be offices for a comics publishing company, which has since moved next door.

Capping the jug of juice, I look to my right. Bright blue stairs twist towards a second-floor loft area. Littered with colorful beanbags, sofas, coffee tables, and mounted televisions that play superhero films nonstop.

If I could rank my favorite places in the world, Superheroes & Scones would be number two. Right behind a pool.

Any pool.

I take a large swig of my OJ, and Akara's phone starts buzzing in quick succession.

I wipe my mouth on my carved bicep and notice the text message boxes lighting up his screen. "Someone's popular." *That better be my tardy bodyguard.*

Akara wipes his fingers on a flimsy napkin. "It's only one person."

I crane my neck to try and see if I can spot a name.

Akara angles the phone towards his chest and scrolls through the messages. "Chill. Eat. Try not to overthink, if that's at all possible for you."

"It's not." I can fucking admit this.

Akara smiles but concentrates on his phone. Pieces of his straight black hair touch his dark eyelashes. His cut muscles could tear through his blue *Studio 9* shirt. There's no uniform for security detail. Bodyguards just typically dress for the occasion.

Like when I attend formal charity events, they'll wear suits and tuxes.

I roll my shoulders backwards, muscles tight. I need to stretch, swim several laps. I check the time on my phone. Then I take another swig of orange juice and watch Akara text.

"You know," I tell him, "I'm not asking for the meaning of life or a planetary map of undiscovered galaxies. You could give me his hair color. Zodiac sign. Maybe a last name—"

"Nice try." Akara's brown eyes lift to mine just to say *you can't bullshit me* before he returns to his cell. "Why don't you finish making your list for him?"

"I already printed it out." It's in the pocket of my jeans. Akara suggested I bullet-point the "rules of my life" for the unknown person.

Like #32: *I take pictures with fans in real time and let them post the pics.* Not all of my cousins or siblings allow this. It gives the public and media a timestamp of where I am. And it's considered dangerous.

A safety threat.

But I've lived my life beneath a spotlight since I was in the womb. I don't give a shit if someone knows where I am at *so-and-so* time. Chances are, paparazzi will find me anyway.

After placing my glass down on the bar, I rake a hand through my disheveled, light brown hair. The strands are dyed from their natural dark-brown hue.

I know that *you* know what I look like. You've seen my face on the front page of tabloids. All while you were checking out two-percent milk, maybe a Kit-Kat bar, hopefully a can of Fizz.

I have forest-green eyes that dagger the souls of those who fuck with my family. Sharp cheekbones that look like knives, and a lean-cut swimmer's build from my competitive swimming days. You may *not* know that Burberry and Calvin Klein scouted me when I was eighteen.

I turned them down.

Akara texts. And texts.

For the past five years, he's been a central part of my life. Even if he isn't my personal bodyguard. As the lead of Security Force Omega, he's in charge of hires, transfers, terminations, and keeping the whole system running. He's the glue.

The constant.

He's twenty-five, Thai-American, MMA-trained but specialized in Muay Thai, and he owns the Studio 9 Boxing & MMA gym down the street. People pack Studio 9 every morning, and evenings are impossible to get into without a referral.

He glances up from his phone. Eyeing me. "You need to relax."

I'm impatient. And I'm overly self-aware. Firmly, I tell him, "If he doesn't show by eight, we have to leave." I can't be here when the store opens. I'll be stuck signing autographs and taking photos for hours on end, and I have a long, *long* list of things I need to get done.

I'm a CEO of a charity organization that raises *millions* annually. And I set a goal to raise $300 million for H.M.C. Philanthropies by December. We're not even halfway yet.

"He knows," is all Akara says. *He knows.*

Who the fuck is he? I straighten up, rigid like I'm seconds from joining the National Guard. "Did you at least choose someone who can keep up with me? He's not going to sputter out after an hour or two?" I constantly drive back-and-forth from my townhouse, to my work offices, and to the gated neighborhood of my childhood home. Where my three younger siblings still live.

"Again, relax." Akara holds out a hand. "I know you. I wouldn't put someone on your detail that can't handle your lifestyle." He pushes back his hair and then fits his baseball cap on backwards.

Akara appears approachable right now. Friendly, even.

But I witnessed him staring down a grown fifty-year-old man. Twice his size. Veins protruding in the man's ripped muscles: a known steroid-user. He was also my cousin Beckett's former bodyguard. And he fucked up. He let a cameraman slip into a public bathroom while my cousin was pissing in a urinal.

Akara laid into the bodyguard. Yelling, scolding—and I just watched this much younger guy make a middle-aged man cry. Tears just *streaming* down his face. Akara made him feel like he committed involuntary manslaughter.

I realized that's why most bodyguards say, "Don't piss off the SFO lead." Pissing off Akara is like putting your ass on death row.

Boom.

Our heads whip to the tinted store windows. Four preteens just ran into the glass, bouncing on their toes. They scream a variety of names, mine included, and they cup their hands to the window. Trying to peer inside.

I smile.

It's funny. If I thought it wasn't, I'd be irritated every minute of every single day. Typically, there's a line outside of the store until closing, so I'm not surprised people are already here before eight.

"One, two, three," they all count together before shrieking, "MAXIMOFF HALE!"

My lips stretch wider.

You, as in the four preteens and also the whole world—you all know me as Maximoff Hale. CEO of a nonprofit charity, one-time philosophy major, competitive swimmer, son of a sex addict mother and recovering alcoholic father, and the steadfast older brother to three and cousin to eleven.

You're obsessed with my perpetual "single" relationship status, and you've never seen me publicly date anyone. On occasion that I wasn't careful enough, you've seen photos of me bringing home random girls or guys.

You know I'm not serious about them.

You know they'll only last one night. Not one damn string attached.

You *don't* know really anything about our bodyguards. Like how they exist in our lives as close as family members. It's their duty to maintain anonymity with the public, and you can't keep an eye on them or *know them* the way that we do.

So you know nothing about Akara Kitsuwon and the rest of Security Force Omega.

Akara grins at the three girls and one boy who can't see us, but we can see them flailing excitedly and taking selfies. "This shit never gets old."

I raise my OJ. "Immortal entertainment." Two homemade signs smack the window.

I read one: *FUCK ME, MAXIMOFF HALE!* She looks twelve, pigtail braids and braces.

My jaw muscle tenses. "Just kidding." That's not fucking funny. It should go without saying, but I'd never have sex with a preteen or teenager or anyone who looks on the cusp of being that young. Jesus… *twelve*. I have a sister that age.

I'm not against hooking up with fans. It's pretty much inevitable, but it has to be a.) consensual and b.) someone of legal age and c.) a one-time thing.

Akara scrutinizes the preteens. "The scary part," he says, "that shit doesn't even faze me anymore." He eyes the lock on the store entrance before returning to his cellphone.

The other sign from her friend: *I WANT TO HAVE YOUR BABIES, XANDER HALE!!*

Xander is my fourteen-year-old brother.

My shoulders square, but I try to brush that sign off without a long thought. Akara resumes texting *again*. I lean forward. Still not able to see his screen.

"Hot date?" I ask.

Akara quickly says, "*No*." Then he removes his elbows off the counter. Sitting up. "It's Sulli."

Sullivan Meadows. My nineteen-year-old cousin.

"Sulli's blowing up your phone?" I give him a look. "Didn't you tell her that you're with me?" I needed a bodyguard just to drive here and meet a *new* bodyguard. The irony. I asked Akara if there was anyone available from Omega, and he offered himself.

"I thought she'd be asleep until nine, at least."

I wait for him to add more.

He stops there.

"Why?" I try not to snap. I swear the whole security team enjoys keeping me out of the loop. I could get twice as much information by just asking my family. But I restrain myself from texting Sulli.

"It doesn't matter," he says evasively and eats another bite of bagel while messaging my cousin.

"It does to me. She's *my* family." She's not a part of security. She's on my side. *Famous.*

Three famous families—the Hales, the Meadows, the Cobalts—are permanently bound together because our moms are sisters. The Calloway sisters, to be exact. And the Calloways, namely my grandfather, founded Fizzle: a soda company so world-renowned that they beat Coca-Cola in sales for the past decade.

Fizzle is part of why we're all famous.

But it's not the whole story.

I add, "I can just text her myself." I reach for my phone, but he caves, nodding to me.

Once he swallows his food, he says, "She kept yawning on our way back from a state park. She didn't get home until three a.m." He sends another text. "I should've known she'd wake up." His eyes flit to me. "She has FOMEFT."

Fear of Missing Every Fucking Thing.

My lips rise.

Sulli coined it herself. The most predictable thing about my younger cousin is the least predictable thing: *sleep.*

I'd think it's strange that Akara knows these details about Sulli, but he's her personal bodyguard. He's been assigned to Sullivan since she was sixteen. If anyone knows her life habits, it's him.

It hits me again. The thought I've been swatting away like a bee: *someone is about to know my life habits that intimately too.*

Great.

I lean on the counter, arms crossed over my green crew-neck shirt. And then my muscles bind as the lock starts to rotate on the tinted-glass door.

Someone is entering. Someone who was given a key.

My new bodyguard.

He's finally here.

2

Dear World, stop fucking with me. Sincerely, an agitated human.

The last person I wanted to see today enters Superheroes & Scones. I refill my glass of orange juice and watch the familiar face open the door.

Towering at six-foot-three, his black V-neck is tucked in black jeans, a leather belt buckled. The hilt of a handgun sticks from his waistband, and his dyed bleach-white hair contrasts his thick brown eyebrows.

Most people find Farrow Redford Keene intimidating at first sight, but I'm immune to most kinds of intimidation.

It's called being a Hale.

I can describe Farrow in three meaningful ways.

1. Frustrating.

2. Aggravating.

3. Piss in my hot tea.

Since he's my mom's bodyguard and she stops by the store frequently, I expect she's not far behind his self-assured, unflustered demeanor.

Farrow carries himself like he owns the world, but amusement constantly rests behind his brown eyes. I sometimes think he's purposefully channeling James Franco circa *Freaks & Geeks*—minus the weed and multiply the Franco *smile* by a billion.

It shouldn't capture my attention.

But it does.

He does.

Like right now, I try to ignore his overwhelming presence, and I slowly cap the juice jug again. My gaze stays on him. No matter how hard I say *look at the juice*.

I've had this problem since I was sixteen. Unfortunately, I've known Farrow for a long, *long* time. I'm talking fledgling teenage years. Before the security team assigned him to my mom, he was just the son of our family's concierge doctor, on-call 24/7 for house visits and medical emergencies.

So when my little sister Kinney broke her ankle in five-inch-heeled boots, Dr. Keene appeared. With his son Farrow in tow.

I tried to tug off Kinney's boot, and Dr. Keene told me, "Move away, Maximoff." Then he gestured Farrow forward. Teaching his son basic first aid. All so he could follow the footsteps of the *many* generations of Keenes before him. A prestigious family of physicians.

Moments like those stoked my competitive nature. If Farrow was pushed to the front, I craved to find a way next to him. If Farrow went fast, I went harder. And he never let up. With *anything*, he was too headstrong to let me pass without a hard-won fight.

Somewhere around my sixteenth birthday, I started crushing on him. Maybe it's because he never just *gives* me the win. Maybe it's that he's five years older and a Yale graduate.

Or that he does thirty pull-ups like it's a damn breeze. Maybe it's all the gray and black tattoos that cover his fair skin, even to his throat. Beautiful inked symmetric wings decorate his neck, crossed swords on his Adam's apple.

Maybe it's his four visible piercings: a hoop on his nostril, bottom lip, and two barbells on his brow.

Maybe it's *all of that* combined together that heats my skin, pools blood south, and attracts me like an idiot. He's made permanent camp in my cerebral cortex and cock, and I don't know how to extract him.

The crush was fine when I was teenager, where I was secretly fantasizing about the hot older guy's lips around my dick. I always knew he was gay, and at eighteen, I told the world I was bisexual. Afterwards I thought there'd be a chance Farrow would look at me with interest.

He didn't.

Then he became my mom's bodyguard. Exactly three years ago.

Whatever attraction I had towards him became more ethically wrong than it already was. I remind myself that he knows *nothing*. I've only told my best friend Jane about my crush and lapse in judgment. And she wouldn't tell a soul.

Farrow enters the store's doorway and takes a big bite of a red apple.

And then his brown eyes latch onto my forest-green. Instantly, he has a *knowing* look.

I attribute it to him being a know-it-all. I must wear my slight irritation because his lips hike upward as he chews and swallows his fruit.

I swig my orange juice before saying, "Look what the wind threw up." I set down my glass.

Farrow raises his apple to his mouth. "You mean *blew in*."

"No," I say firmly, palms on the pearly counter. "I meant threw up."

He rolls his eyes into a humored smile that slowly stretches wider and wider. Then he kicks the door closed. And he locks it shut with his spare key.

I go rigid. "Where's my mom?"

Akara *finally* pockets his cellphone. The one he's been super-glued to since we arrived here. "Lily's bodyguard transfer went through this morning."

Transfer.

Which means…my brain fries, jaw sharpens and breath heavies as I watch Farrow near the vinyl stools, his stride masculine and unconcerned. A kind of confident gait that belongs to people who understand themselves from the core outwards.

Closer, he rests his knee on the stool beside Akara. And he tells me, "I'm your new bodyguard."

I inhale, staying outwardly composed, but my pulse rages at an abnormal speed. *Farrow Redford Keene is my new bodyguard.*

I have trouble adding him to my life *that way.* It's why I'm eerily silent and mentally trying to block out how complicated this'll make everything.

Farrow stares me dead in the eye. "Excited?" he asks with a peeking smile, like he knows I wouldn't be.

Excited that my old crush is going to be a permanent companion to my whole life? And we're ethically bound to remain platonic.

I would choose the words: *sexually frustrated* and *fucking complicated.* But let's go with *excited.* It'll cause the least amount of friction right now.

"That's one word for it," I say and finish off the rest of my drink in one gulp. "What's the actual reasoning behind this?" I gesture at Farrow with my empty glass. The whole security team has good intentions, and I understand that a lot weighs into bodyguard switches.

I can't just demand someone new like an entitled bastard. All the bodyguards work together, and they're *people.* Not plastic action figures. I respect them enough to trust their choices.

And it's not like they knew I used to picture Farrow on his knees.

It's not like they'll *ever* know that.

"The usual," Akara says, "we take into account the location of where you live." *A townhouse in Philly.* "Your lifestyle." *On-the-go.* "Other security variables, and then we match you."

"So it's Bodyguard Grindr without the sex," I quip and try to ignore Farrow, but my eyes involuntarily flit to him.

Farrow raises his brows at me in a self-satisfied wave.

I want to groan and smile. My features, I'm sure, teeter between the two.

"We're not going to promote it like that, but sure…basically," Akara says.

"*Basically,*" Farrow interjects, "Lily wanted me to be your bodyguard." Lily is my mom.

Akara zeroes in on Farrow with an intense but padlocked look. I can only assume that Farrow wasn't supposed to give me that much information.

He even adds, "Word-for-word, she said, *Farrow is the best.*"

"Bullshit," I tell him. "My mom would cross her heart and hope to die before saying *anyone* was better than Garth." Her first ever bodyguard. I'd never seen her so emotional over anyone's departure than when he retired.

Farrow rotates his apple for another spot to bite. "Then she broke a kindergarten oath for me." His matter-of-fact voice is deep and rough, but audibly sensual. Like gravel tied in silk.

My muscles heat from head-to-toe. "Wow," I say, my tone too tight. My head is somewhere else entirely. On this situation.

Our new reality.

Him.

Farrow lowers his apple, and my cheekbones must sharpen because his brown eyes brush my most distinct feature.

I seize his gaze, and in our sudden quiet, a thick tension brews. Both of our lives are going to change from this transfer, and there's an *unknown* factor.

I can't even conceptualize what Farrow as my bodyguard looks like. I sense Akara glancing between us. Gauging how well we're getting along. But his answer is as good as mine.

And I have no answer.

I have no idea what it's like even cultivating a new relationship with a bodyguard. I've had the same one for practically twenty-two years.

Farrow tosses his apple core in a nearby trashcan. Then he drops his knee off the stool, his shoulders noticeably loosened unlike my squared ones. "Let's start with the basics, wolf scout."

"Out of all the things you can call me..." But it never stops Farrow from choosing this. My aunt created the Wolf Scouts as a wilderness & survival scouting organization that includes all genders. It gained national recognition, and yeah, I still help in the summer as a troop captain. "And what *basics?*"

"The basics." He edges up to the lip of the counter. His face only a few inches from my face. "Every time you leave your townhouse, I'll be escorting you. I walk in front of you. I enter rooms before you. I go where you go until you return safely home."

I slowly blink, my skin scorching. Imagining Farrow with me *all day, every day* this quickly is like digesting a gallon milkshake in one gulp. I have a fucking brain freeze. I rub my jaw that's a razorblade.

Farrow tilts his head. "Okay?"

"I'm making a revision."

"To the basics?" He glances at Akara, and they share a look that I can't decipher.

I bypass their exchange and continue, "You walk into places *beside* me—"

"No," Farrow rejects immediately. He runs two hands through his bleach-white hair, combing the strands completely out of his face. Sometimes he does this to give himself more time to answer. Other times, I think it's a sign that he's getting serious.

Akara rests his elbow on the counter. "Moffy, he has to assess the room before you enter. Just like Declan did."

Declan isn't Farrow. My old bodyguard preferred privacy with me, to the point where I can't say I know very much about him personally. I *know* Farrow in a way that I never knew Declan.

It instantaneously changes the bodyguard-client relationship that I'm used to.

"Then when we're on the street," I say to Farrow. "You walk beside me. You don't need to walk in front of me every single time like you're my labradoodle."

"A labradoodle," he repeats, his features balancing on the peak of an eye roll and a laugh. "You couldn't have picked a more docile animal, could you?" Before I can respond, he adds, "I'll consider that, but I can't promise I'll follow through in *every* situation."

That seems fair.

I nod a couple times. "When did you find out about the new assignment?" He looks unaffected, but if he were a superhero in a battle zone, the comic book panel would show Farrow relaxed on a destroyed bench, using his powers to easily survive and make do.

In comparison, I externalize my readiness for shit storms: my back straight, shoulders stringent, and head hoisted.

"I was told last night," he says.

I let this sink in. "So only eight hours more than me."

"Twelve, technically." His lips begin to lift like he beat me at something.

I holster my own smile. "Thank you for that *technical* adjustment."

"Anytime, wolf scout." He eases forward and lowers his voice to the sexiest whisper, "It's good to remember that I'm better than you at most everything."

It takes a lot of effort not to stare at his mouth. "Sounds like an alternate universe."

One corner of his lip quirks, and then he eases back.

Boom.

Our heads whip to the store windows. More people bang against the glass as they try to peer inside, others chatting loudly as they wait for Superheroes & Scones to officially open.

"We need to go," I say the obvious.

It really dawns on me that the *we* in this scenario is me and Farrow. Not me and Akara. Not me and a guy I recently met.

It's just me and him.

And not in a way I fantasized. Farrow is now obligated to protect me, maintain a professional relationship with me, and always keep me safe.

Picturing a polar bear eating Fritos on the moon is easier than imagining Farrow as my bodyguard. I think it's a sign.

That this is about to get fucking strange.

3

MAXIMOFF HALE

Leaving Superheroes & Scones in my red Audi,
I merge onto the freeway. The air is noticeably strained between us since I gave him my eight-page list. While he silently reads in the passenger seat, I concentrate on the road and speed past paparazzi vehicles that attempt to hug me like we're friends.

Farrow glances up and scrutinizes the various SUVs and sedans racing after us. "I really should be the one driving in this relationship."

I stiffen at the word *relationship*. I mentally add in *platonic*, but my sixteen-year-old self with his sophomoric crush would be hard as a rock right now.

Twenty-two-year-old me is still pissed that I put Farrow in my spank bank.

"Number twelve." I nod to the list.

He eyes me for a long moment before focusing on the paper. "It says that you're not used to letting other people behind the wheel." It actually says *I always drive.*

I glance at him once, then back to the road. "I didn't realize that you can't read." I switch lanes.

I can almost feel his smile stretch. "Always a precious smartass." I hear him flip a page. "You have a typo on number thirty-two."

He called me precious. What the fuck does that even mean? *Precious.* I have to let it go, but the word scrolls across my gaze like a tickertape banner. "What typo?"

"You forgot a comma."

I let out an irritated groan. "This isn't a term paper. Don't critique my grammar."

Farrow kicks up one of his shoes on the seat. Balancing his forearm on his knee. Then he bites the staple off and spits it out. I tense and try to watch him and the road simultaneously.

He has a very particular way he moves his hands. They shift with meticulousness and care. A sort of accuracy that belongs to surgeons and someone equipped to disassemble and reassemble a gun blindfolded.

I've imagined those hands *on* me too many times to count. *Don't fucking restart now.* I'm trying not to, but having him this close, the NC-17 fantasies vie to breach the surface. Heat blankets my skin and tries to grip my cock.

Thumbing through the papers, Farrow tells me, "You're about to miss our exit."

"Shit."

He smiles a self-satisfied, entertained smile, but I skillfully veer over three lanes of traffic and dodge more paparazzi. Making the exit ramp safely.

Farrow folds nearly all of the pages and only keeps two sheets.

"What are you doing?" I ask.

He waves the folded stack. "How about you ditch eighty-five percent of your rules and be less of a wolf scout, *wolf scout?*"

"No." I shake my head a few times. Those rules reflect my current way of living. "This is my fucking life, Farrow."

"And you have to make room for me," he says seriously. "We'll find a groove together, but not when you put me in a headlock before the match even starts."

I honestly think he just hates being confined by strict rules that aren't his own. "Declan followed them."

"To your detriment," he says bluntly. "You have a speeding habit. *I* should be driving."

We're on that again.

"I drive," I tell him. "Your options are *endless*. Watch me drive. Watch the other cars. Watch the horizon. Count road signs. Play with the music—"

"Inaccurate." He licks his thumb and flips quickly through the pages before landing on one. "Number ninety-two. *I prefer no music in the car until noon.*" He tilts his head at me. "Because…?"

"I usually have to make business calls. *For charity,*" I emphasize. He knows that I work nonprofit. Every day will be Take Farrow To Work Day. It's weird. What's weirder is that he's currently working right now. He's not just in my car to chat. He's on-the-job.

"Are you planning to make a business call now?" he questions.

"No."

"Then really this should say 'I prefer no music in the car until noon *when I have business calls.*'" He pops open the middle console and finds a pen. He rewrites the rule. "You also have another typo—"

"Shut up about the fucking typos," I say and adjust the air conditioner, my body hot as his smile stretches wider and wider.

To fill the quiet, I switch on the radio and play an EDM station. Heavy bass pumps through the speakers.

"Music before noon," Farrow says. "I've already started loosening his straight-laces."

One hand on the wheel, I use the other to flip him off. "I love how you give yourself credit for the stupid things in life. It's so generous of you."

Farrow almost laughs, but we both suddenly grow quiet and serious. Two paparazzi SUVs flank my sides and abruptly cut me off from a right turn.

"Get off Market Street," Farrow suggests.

"That was my plan." I speed forty over the limit just to pass the SUVs. But they have a Honda friend ahead of me. The blue Honda slams on its brakes. Causing me to slam on mine.

Fuck.

I'm now boxed in. Like a rat in a trap.

I reach into my cup holder for my sunglasses, but Farrow is already handing me my black Ray Bans. Reminding me that he's trained for these situations. He slips on a pair of black aviators.

Arms and cameras stick out of paparazzi's rolled-down windows. I'm forced to drive at their speed, and *flashes* pierce me from nearly every direction. My sunglasses dim the brightness but not my frustration.

Most days, I coexist with paparazzi fine. I'll answer their harmless questions, sign their photographs that they then sell on eBay, and we respect one another enough.

Then they pull stunts like *this* and I question the percentage of decent cameramen to the ones that'd run my family into a ditch for a grand.

"Do you want me to help you?" Farrow asks. "Or would you rather just let them capture photos of you glaring?"

I gesture to the windshield. "There's nothing left to do."

"I'm not Declan." Farrow unbuckles, and he leans over the middle console. Towards me. My breath cages in my lungs, and I watch his arm slide across the back of my seat. With his other hand, he slams the heel of his palm on the wheel's horn.

Blaring into the morning sky.

He extends his body even more over me. While I drive, he's careful not to block my vision of the road, but I'm more concentrated on the fact that his shoulder brushes up against my chest. And one of his knees sits between my legs.

Farrow rolls down the driver's side window. He turns his head, just slightly, our faces literally a breath away. Focusing on the paparazzi, he yells, "Tell the Honda to drive off or I'll shutter Maximoff's windows!" *Shutter*, meaning he'll tape up sheets to block their money-shots.

The cameraman says, "One more minute! Get out of the way!" He makes a *shoo* motion to Farrow.

"Hey! *Now or never*," Farrow threatens, his tone so caustic that I'm not surprised when the cameraman disappears inside his SUV. Moments later, the Honda takes a left.

Freeing the road.

Freeing *us*.

I speed off as quickly as I can. Declan never had that kind of affect on paparazzi. It stuns me silent for a minute.

Farrow eases back in his seat, and I roll up the window. He picks up his papers, and I glance at him, then the road, then back to him.

He arches his brows. "Want to say something?"

"Where'd you learn that?"

Farrow snaps his seatbelt locked. "When you're the bodyguard to the most famous woman in the world, you can't be a passive bystander."

My mom.

My mom is the most famous woman in the world. She's the reason her sisters are famous. The reason I'm famous.

The reason *we're all* famous.

Lily Calloway is the origin to the public scrutiny, the media harassment, the paparazzi invasion in Philadelphia of all cities—but it's not her fault.

It's never her fault.

I wish I could say our fame derived from a pure act of love, of kindness, of rainbows or motherfucking magic—*something* other than what actually happened.

But it was a scandal. Years before I was born.

Someone leaked information when she was only twenty-years-old.

Lily Calloway, the heiress of Fizzle soda empire, is a confirmed sex addict. The headline about her addiction rocked the globe. A salacious, shocking headline—that's all it took. The news caused every Calloway sister to go from rich obscurity to instant notoriety.

Our fame burns. And burns. None of us need to stoke the flames for it to stay lit.

And me—fame is my friend and foe. It's a part of me. A tangible thing that lives inside of me. This is the only life I've ever lived.

It's the only life I know.

These days, I currently reside with Jane in an old, historic Victorian townhouse that's just shy of 900 square feet. All hardwood floors. Interior brick walls. And a kitchen so cramped that a third person has to play Indiana Jones and scale the counters to fit.

I'd live a more minimalistic lifestyle if I could. I don't need much.

And I'd say the three-bedroom, one-bath is extremely modest for someone with my bank account, but I'm well aware that living in Philadelphia's Rittenhouse-Fitler Historic District isn't cheap for most people.

I may be obnoxiously wealthy, but I try my best to understand what I have, what I can give, and what others need.

I drive into a three-car garage, which is a real luxury in this Philly area, and I park next to Jane's baby blue Volkswagen Beetle.

My car clock blinks 8:12 a.m. before I shut off the ignition. Farrow already unclips his seatbelt and tucks the folded papers into his back pocket. He acts like he's just visiting, but my bodyguard is *moving in*.

That's right.

This isn't a *welcome to my life* sitcom. This is a *you've joined my life* drama or possibly, a horror story.

It's too soon to tell which.

At least we're not about to be roommates. Above this garage are *two* identical townhouses that sit side-by-side and share an adjoining door on the first floor. All for easy access.

Security stays in the right townhouse.

Jane and I stay in the left one.

Farrow barely even takes a second to digest his surroundings. I know that *he* knows he's moving in—there are two suitcases and a black duffel in my trunk to prove it.

I unbuckle. "Do you need anything else? I can pick up something for you at the store." I almost groan at myself. Why the hell am I asking Farrow this? I'm on automatic and someone needs to switch me to manual, quick.

He pauses, his hand on the door handle. As he glances at me, his lips rise. "That's cute that you're pretending you can go to the store without me."

"I wasn't pretending." I pocket my keys and push open my door. "I just omitted the fact." For my own sanity. I'm highly aware that Farrow is now obligated to follow me everywhere. *Highly aware.* I can't exactly pretend that this twenty-seven-year-old tattooed guy is some random barnacle that attached itself to my ship.

He's my fucking co-captain right now.

And I'm not thrilled.

In case I didn't make that vitally clear.

We climb out of the Audi and shut our doors in unison. I pop the trunk, and while I grab his largest suitcase, I tell him, "I retract my offer."

"That's too bad," Farrow says in a serious tone, slinging his duffel on his shoulder, "I forgot shampoo and conditioner."

"You can borrow mine—Jesus fucking Christ," I growl at myself, wanting to be an asshat to him for at least two seconds.

Farrow laughs like he won. "I just now remember. I have shampoo and conditioner."

I glare and remove his second suitcase while holding the other. "You're an asshole."

"You're pure of heart. What else is still the same?" Farrow tries to take the larger suitcase from me.

I tug it out of his grip. "I can carry it for you."

He gives me a look. "You're not earning a *valor* merit badge. I can carry my own shit." He adjusts the strap of his duffel. "But to be kind, I'll let you roll in the little one."

"Oh thanks," I say dryly and then I shove the *little one* in his chest and keep the larger one.

We're two alpha males, and it becomes extremely apparent during these pointless fights. Where we want to carry the heavier suitcase.

I'm just used to helping out, especially since I have a large extended family and I'm the oldest guy. And Farrow—his whole job, his whole upbringing has been about *duty* and aid towards others. We're like lightning and thunder, inherently different but alike enough to share the same sky.

Farrow doesn't argue for the larger suitcase.

So I shut my trunk. "You remember which is which?" I nod to the two entrances. He's been here before as my mom's bodyguard.

Farrow keeps his gaze on mine. "Left door goes to Azkaban. Right to Mordor."

I stare at him like he just grew antlers. I'm the one who cracks the pop culture references. Farrow doesn't even like fantasy.

He tolerates it like someone who hates mayo and eats it on a turkey sandwich.

"You've been hanging around my mom too long?" I question. I have comic-book-loving, pop-culture-obsessed parents. *The coolest.* I'm sure the two Meadows girls and the seven Cobalt children would protest and say their parents are cool, but there's no comparison.

Hands down, mine are the goddamn best.

Farrow slowly licks his bottom lip into a smile. My muscles contract, and I try to focus on his eyes and not his mouth. *Not his mouth.*

"No," he says. "It's an inside joke with the whole security team."

I'm surprised he's sharing this with me. "Seriously?"

He nods, and we head to the right door. What he called *Mordor.* "I was told that this one started with your little brother. His bodyguard repeated the joke to another bodyguard, and it spread."

I could see Xander making a comment about *Harry Potter* and *Lord of the Rings.* Easily.

We head up the few stairs, and I wait on one below him and place the suitcase on its wheels.

Farrow searches for his key in his pocket. "Declan didn't talk to you that often, did he?"

I go still, my apprehension filling the garage. In hindsight, I wonder if I was supposed to make a greater effort to know my bodyguard personally. Was I being rude? What if all that time, he wanted me to pry into his fucking life, and I thought I was just respecting his space.

Declan knew everything about me. The world knows *most* everything about me. And I only knew the names of his kids and wife.

Almost nothing else.

Farrow peeks back at me and assesses my features. "It's okay if he didn't."

I remember the origin of his question. "He didn't spill any security team secrets, if that's what you're asking."

Farrow finds his key, but he rotates fully to face me. "Let's deal with this, Moffy—"

"*Maximoff*," I correct, my voice firm like solid marble. All of my family calls me Moffy, but when he uses the nickname, I flashback to childhood where he called me that. It makes our five-year age-gap more apparent, and when I imagine my young, teenage self *in bed* with him (which only happened in my fantasies), it's cringe-worthy.

So he's not allowed to call me Moffy.

Done and done.

"Maximoff," he says like I'm being a stick-in-the-mud prick.

"What are we dealing with exactly?" I put the train back on the tracks before he catches my actual reasons.

"What I share with you—they're not *secrets*. At least half of us don't consider them secrets. The other half are so uptight they could be mistaken for the Queen's Guard outside Buckingham Palace."

"So you're pretty much like a *rebel* in the security team." I give him a blatant once-over, eyeing his tattoos, the black wardrobe, the piercings. "All this time, I had no idea."

Farrow lets out a short laugh into an agitated, amused smile, nodding a few times. I think *smartass* sits on his tongue, and then his gaze falls to my lips—for the briefest second.

Before I even process what that means, he acts like nothing transpired. And he starts to unlock the door.

It could've just been in my head.

I'm prone to fantasizing. What's to say I didn't invent that out of the horny recesses of my sexually frustrated brain?

I need to go out and find a one-night stand tonight.

It's my first thought. My second jarring thought slaps me cold: *Farrow has to come with me.*

I can't escape him. For pretty much all of eternity.

4

Luggage in hand, I lead the way up two flights
of narrow wooden stairs. Much to Maximoff's chagrin. I'm certain he'd
love to be the one *leading* the nonexistent pack, but he has to be second-
place to me this time.

And really, every time as far as I'm concerned.

It's not just me being pompous or arbitrarily arrogant. For his safety,
he has to learn to let me lead.

Thick silence stretches while we both ascend the stairs. I'm not used
to uncomfortable tension, and I doubt he is either.

See, I didn't *ask* to be his bodyguard. I didn't apply for the position or
submit an application. I fell into the role at his mom's request.

I like change.

I *welcome* change. But when one of my favorite pastimes is pissing off
Maximoff Hale—I'm not so sure I'd have volunteered for this job.

Another tense beat passes between us before Moffy warns me, "Your
room is small."

I end up smiling because I've been in these two townhouses multiple
times. They're identical. Second floor has two bedrooms and the only
bath. Third floor is an attic bedroom. Everything else is crammed on the
first floor.

Maximoff lives in the third-floor attic inside the other townhouse. A room barely big enough for a full-sized bed, a bookshelf, and a dresser.

I'm about to live in the identical version of *that* same attic room. "I can manage. It's the same size as yours." I glance back at him.

Only two stairs below me, one of the most beloved celebrities stands confident and agitated at my heels.

And he has my fifty-pound suitcase easily hoisted on his shoulders like a soldier carrying a rucksack. He's not flaunting his strength. With Moffy, he's just being *efficient*. Giving himself more room to walk up the narrowest staircase imaginable.

His carved biceps stretch the fabric of his green tee.

I smile. I'm sure most people would faint at his feet right now. Possibly stammer. Maybe try to seduce him. Say all the right things in the right way.

Instead, he has me.

"If only your grammar were as good as your weight lifting skills," I tell him, "you'd be a real contender."

"If only your wit was actually funny, I'd be laughing."

I smile wider. "I wasn't trying to make you laugh, wolf scout."

Moffy groans out his irritation, but his lips slowly rise. He scrunches his face until his features set in a scowl.

"Feel better?" I ask and keep ascending the stairs.

He'd flip me off if he had use of his hands, but he never falters with the suitcase. Never struggles. Many tabloids rank Maximoff Hale as the number one *hottest celeb*.

It's accurate.

He has eyes like blades of grass, a jawline just as sharp—features so striking that he's already a treasured, marble relic before adding his statuesque, out-of-this-fucking-world body.

And he's entered my thoughts in ways that Disney wouldn't permit. It started three years ago. During his first semester of college.

I'd just become his mom's personal bodyguard, and she attended one of his swim meets. I sat on the bleachers and watched as he pulled himself out of the collegiate pool, Ivy League banners hanging overhead. Latin insignias scrawled on free wall space.

His muscles flexed when he stood straight and confident at six-foot-two. Pulling his goggles to his head, water dripped down the ridges of his tanned skin. His legs were more muscular. Shoulders broader. He looked older.

I remember thinking, *Maximoff Hale is a man.*

After that, his image basically invaded my mind during "personal" moments. Being his mom's bodyguard didn't really stop me from envisioning Maximoff naked and bent over a bed. Things happen. People pop into your head when you're rubbing one out.

I'm just glad I have good taste.

When I discovered that I was assigned to his security detail, I didn't fixate on the fact that I'm attracted to him. It's irrelevant.

I could have a framed photograph of him that I jack off to every night (I don't), and I'd still do my job at 100%.

I'm a damned good bodyguard.

One of the best, and nothing and no one will change the fact that I'm going to protect him.

While silence blankets us again, I reach the top of the staircase where a single door lies. I enter my new room with Maximoff close behind.

I let out a long whistle. "You decided to warn me that it's small but not *hot* and *musty*?" I toss my luggage beside my full-bed and test the springs with my boot. Ah, it'll do. Nothing but a mattress and box springs.

Moffy drops my suitcase by the door. "I'll check the AC."

"You don't need to." I rub my mouth, my lip piercing cold. Of course saying *it's hot* would make him want to fix the temperature. "I appreciate the concern, but this is where you have to stop treating me like a guest or a sibling or really, anyone you feel the need to coddle and protect." I hold his strong gaze. "And heat rises. We're in an attic."

"I've never known that before," he says dryly. "I've just been living in the other attic for three years thinking, *why the fuck does it feel like hell's sauna?* Thank God you're here to share this unfound wisdom."

I have to lean on the brick wall, my smile killing me.

Sarcasm is just written in his DNA. Equipped with verbal pitchforks at birth.

I gesture him onward with my hand. "Keep going."

"I'm done."

I roll my eyes before standing off the interior brick wall. They're all brick, I realize. No mold, luckily, but the wooden ceiling rafters look like they haven't been dusted in a decade.

I waft my shirt from my chest. It must be ninety degrees in here. It's August in Philly, summer heat still present, but with the AC cranked low, downstairs is a freezer in comparison to the attic.

I'm about to open the only window, but Moffy already aims for the windowsill. Completely ignoring my earlier speech.

I tilt my head upward, restraining another eye-roll.

He has no idea that I spent six hours being debriefed this morning about *him* and the entrances, exits, and windows of the two townhouses.

Omega's recommendation: *try to keep him away from windows.* I'm not in a gated neighborhood anymore. Windows face public streets. Which means anyone can whip out a camera, point a lens upwards, and try to film him.

Moffy's 44th rule: *I open my own windows.*

And there lies the discord. His mom welcomed all the airbags that kept her safe, but Moffy would rather live his life as unrestricted as possible.

It's considered dangerous.

See, a very small space exists between freedom and safety for celebrities. I fight to give that middle-ground to a client. Especially for someone like Maximoff who wants that freedom. But the more he tries to protect *himself*, the more we're going to have a problem.

He can't be his own bodyguard.

It's impossible.

"For every one window you open, I get two," I tell him.

He pauses by the windowsill. "Why the hell would I agree to a lop-sided ratio that's in your favor?"

"Because one-to-two is better than one-to-three."

He licks his lips. "How about one-to-one?"

I swing my head from side-to-side, considering for less than a second. "No."

"Yes."

"Fine," I concede early, surprising him, but I really just need him to let me in somewhere. One-to-one is better than one-to-zero.

My job is about split-second choices that affect his life. And I subtly and quickly weigh risks. My window faces an overgrown magnolia tree that obstructs the street view. Also, if he cared about being caught on camera, he wouldn't actively go for the window right now.

Conclusion:

Risk = low.

Window = have at it, Moffy.

I keep an attentive eye on him and remove my black sheets and bedding from my duffel.

Maximoff wrenches the crusted window open, muscles flexed. The old wood screeches as it reaches the top.

When he returns to my mattress, he cracks his knuckles. Moffy scans my bedding, his phone buzzing in his jean's pocket, but it's been vibrating since I first saw him today.

Earlier, I deduced that he's ignoring his texts. "Do you need a minute?" I ask.

"For what?" He's rigid, but he always stands at attention like he's one breath from sprinting into a fight to save his family.

I nearly smile. "A minute to let this sink in."

He inhales a strong breath. "Sure. Just change that *minute* to a *century*, and I'm good."

I rest my knee on the mattress, my hand slipping in my pocket. "If I give you a century, you'll be dead."

"Great. You can guard my corpse."

My brows hike. "That's really adorable that you think I'll outlive you."

"Who says you won't?"

"I'm five years older than you." I find a piece of gum in my pocket and peel the foil. "And I'm still taller than you too." *By one inch.*

"I forgot that in your fucked-up alternate universe, *height* determines one's life expectancy."

I laugh a short laugh and pop my gum in my mouth.

We stand still on either side of my bed, and neither of us really moves. I skim his wardrobe, just a green T-shirt, jeans, and a cheap canvas watch. He looks like he's worth twenty bucks, not over a billion.

His quiet humility makes him seem even older.

My eyes flit up to his, and he visibly tenses.

One of us needs to speak. Not jokingly. No humor. I rarely have serious conversations with him, and to be his bodyguard, our serious talks need to outweigh all the others.

I rake both of my hands through my hair for the third time today. Pushing the strands back. "What are your plans for tonight?"

My words must wash over him like a bucket of ice water. He cringes, looks away and shakes his head a few times. "This is too fucking weird."

I slowly chew my gum, thinking of how to approach this. I'm attaching myself to his life. Not the other way around. I'd be just as irked if our positions were reversed.

"Help me make my bed," I say.

Maximoff easily takes the detour, and he motions for me to give him the corner of the sheet. I do.

He'd never reject someone's request for help. I can't even remember the last time I asked him to help me with anything.

Most likely never.

We both hook my fitted sheet onto the corners of the mattress, and then I toss him a pillow and the black pillowcase.

I stare at him for a long moment, and his daggered green eyes lift to my brown. We slow down, and neither of us needs to speak to be aware of the taut air.

I know the source.

He knows the source.

It's *sex*. Sex is the untouched topic.

Maximoff Hale is the most eligible bachelor in the country. It's public knowledge that he frequents nightclubs and bars. It's my job to *hide* how many one-night stands he has from the media.

The security team gossips, but Declan never shared with anyone how many people Maximoff fucks. I'm now supposed to safeguard that mystery. And whoever he wants to sleep with, I have the distinct responsibility of not only meeting them.

But interrogating them.

I'll get them to sign a Non-Disclosure Agreement. I'll stand guard at his bedroom door in case something bad happens. I'll be there until they leave. I'll even escort them out of his townhouse.

I'm the one who has to protect his cock. And his heart.

"You can trust me," I tell him.

He shakes my pillow into its case. "I *have* to trust you. There's a fucking difference."

I pop a bubble and tilt my head back and forth, considering both statements. "You'll *see* that you can trust me sooner rather than later. I work for you now. Not your mom."

Those words loosen his shoulders a fraction. The whole security team often refers back to the parents since most of the Hale, Meadows, and Cobalt children are still underage. Out of fear of parental wrath and subsequent termination, many bodyguards would snitch on Maximoff in a heartbeat.

I won't.

I fear none of the parents or the possibility of being fired. Three years, nearly 24-hours a day protecting his mom was no joke. She's shy, a sex addict, and her gangly build and soft features make her look perpetually young: round cheeks, shoulder-length brown hair, and green eyes like Moffy. Hecklers see her as an easy target.

I've been spit in the face numerous times. I've taken right hooks to the jaw, uppercuts to the ribs—all meant for her. I've broken a fucker's cheekbone and was subsequently *sued*. Though, he was the one who tried to reach beneath her dress.

I've disarmed gunmen, knife-carriers, and hecklers wielding plastic water pistols, bags of glitter, *dildos*—any hard projectiles. I've driven Lily out of passionate crowds that rocked her car. I've cleared thousands of rooms and bathrooms before she entered. I've made sure no one in the fucking world would put a hand on her.

I live by my actions, and my actions say: *I'm the best at whatever I do.*

And if someone really wants to fire me, they would've done it years ago whenever I turn off my comms and leave blanks in my daily "where did you go" and "what did you do" write-ups. That standard practice serves more to ignite gossip in the security team than to protect my client.

Maximoff tosses my pillow down. "So what is this, a promotion or demotion for you?"

I tuck in my black comforter. "It's a *transfer*. Everyone on security earns the same amount of money. Except you make more if you're a lead of a Force." I wipe sweat off my forehead with my bicep, the heat not dying down.

Moffy uses the hem of his shirt to rub his own forehead. Revealing his cut abs. *Damn.* I casually avert my eyes.

I pop another bubble with my gum. "But this little housing situation is a definite *demotion*." I look up and smile as he uses his middle finger to point at the door.

"There's the exit if you can't handle it."

"I can handle anything, Maximoff." I bite my gum into a wider smile. "I'm stating a fact. This townhouse is old and small. Where I lived before was brand new and a mansion." The Hales, Cobalts, and Meadows families live on the same street in a rich gated neighborhood. Not far from here.

Philadelphia suburbs.

One street over in that same neighborhood, they bought two eight-bedroom mansions just to house the 24/7 bodyguards. Security Force Alpha and Epsilon all currently room there; basically the ones who protect the parents and the underage kids.

Omega, those of us who protect the eighteen-and-older children, are the ones spread out.

Our movements mimic our clients. We don't choose where we live. We just live wherever our clients do, and bodyguard shuffles happen.

Someone quits to start a family or concentrate on their kids. Someone is fired for incompetence. Someone wants a life-change. Whatever the case, the three security leads will shift many of us once a vacancy appears.

That person just happened to be me this time.

I never became a part of the "cliques" of Security Force Alpha. Because I hate cliques. And I was too much of a maverick to be accepted by the older, regimented bodyguards. Now that I'm a part of Omega, I'll see Alpha less, which is perfectly fine with me.

Moffy tucks in the last corner of my comforter. "So when security found out you'd be my bodyguard, no one sent you condolence cards or told you that you'd be better off rocketing to the fucking moon?"

He's fishing for information on how security perceives him—because Declan obviously told him shit. "No one had time to send me cards," I say. "But if they did, most would say *good luck trying to steer that ship.*"

"Sounds about right," he says. "Is that it?"

Wow, he knows nothing. If I came face-to-face with Declan today, I'd shake his hand and say, *you're a fucking asshole.* But I'd have to do that with two-thirds of the security team. We all have different relationships with our clients.

I prefer the mutual kind.

"No one would pity me." I slide my empty duffel beneath my bed. "It's not like when Oscar was transferred to Charlie's detail. We all threw him a funeral." I raise my brows in a wave at Moffy.

He smiles a bit and shakes his head a couple times. "Charlie."

Charlie Cobalt, his nineteen-year-old cousin and the oldest Cobalt boy, is notoriously difficult to follow around. One day he'll be in Ibiza, the next Paris, then Japan—he's spontaneous, unpredictable, and out of all the kids, his frank tweets and comments go viral the most.

Only a second passes and Moffy's lips start to downturn, his cheek-bones sharpening. I've heard rumors from security that Moffy and Charlie don't get along.

I've even seen them argue before. If he rarely hangs out with Charlie, then I'll rarely see Oscar.

That's how this works.

Maximoff checks his buzzing texts, but soon after, he slips his phone back into his pocket. "So today, I'll have lunch at my place. You can settle in here, whatever you need to do, and I'll go to my office in Center City about two. I'll text you when I'm in the garage."

"I need your number."

His brows pinch. "We've never exchanged numbers?"

I chew slowly again. "We've never needed to, wolf scout." When we were younger, I only saw him when I had to tag along my dad's on-call appointments or the holidays the Hales invited us to. Labor Day cookouts, some birthdays. It's not like Moffy and I were friends.

He was only fifteen when I was twenty. I was in college with friends my own age.

I tilt my head, watching him stare off into space. I wave my hand at Maximoff. "Did I lose you?"

He moves my hand away, mentally present, and then he reaches out. "Pass me your phone. I'll put my number in your contacts."

"Or you could just hand me yours."

"No."

I roll my eyes at the firm *no*, but I decide to just comply and give him my cell for now. It's not an argument I need to win. "What about after your work ends?"

He types his number on my cell and hands it back. "Dinner plans are up in the air. I'll let you know if I'm going to a restaurant."

"Are you in for the night after dinner?"

Before answering, Maximoff pulls his damp shirt off his head and balls the fabric in a fist.

My brows hike at his sculpted body, broad swimmer shoulders, and lean torso that gleams with sweat. Photograph-worthy, a money-shot for paparazzi. Certain clients want money-shots "blocked" from cameramen. Some post money-shots on Instagram so they're worthless for paparazzi to sell. Others don't care.

His Rule #67: *don't worry about money-shots. It's not important.*

I eye the curvature of his long arms. "Is the gym a constant pit stop? Because your mom was a certified couch potato." I used to spend my *tiny* free time at Studio 9 or passed-out asleep.

Maximoff rubs his damp forehead with his bicep. "The pool."

"Just the pool?"

"Yep."

I scratch my throat where my tattooed swords lie. "I can count eight places on your body that say you're full of shit." I casually point at his abs.

Maximoff scrutinizes me. "You look unimpressed."

He's used to people outwardly fawning. I begin to smile. "Because mine are better, wolf scout."

He huffs, then glares and motions to me. "Take off your shirt and we'll find out."

I pop my gum. "I love a dare." I pull my V-neck off my head and then toss my shirt on the mattress.

His gaze sweeps the black ink on my chest, ribs and abs—almost everywhere. My fair skin is a mosaic of skulls, crossbones, swords, rough swelling water and sailing ships. Colorful sparrows and swallows intersperse the gray scale pirate imagery.

I follow his eyes as they descend. All the way to the hem of my black pants.

Normally I'd think he was checking me out, but Maximoff has more ethical boundaries than a football field stacked on top of a tennis court stacked on top of a hockey rink. I bet he'd drive a sword through his heart before he broke his morality.

"Mine are better," he retorts.

"We're going to need an unbiased judge."

Moffy glances at the door. "Janie isn't home yet."

"I said *unbiased.*"

"Find someone who doesn't know me, and then we'll talk." He's aware that's impossible. Then he asks, "Is my list still in your back pocket?"

"Yeah."

"You'll want to take it out and write this down."

His list was thorough, but he definitely left out significant details concerning *sex*. I didn't even see any mention of NDA's on the paper, but he has to have those if he wants to fuck strangers and not have his underwear stolen.

I say, "I can memorize whatever you have to tell me." I've already memorized his 132 rules in the car, and I briefly skimmed the eight pages. Steady hands, sharp mind—I graduated top of my class at medical school, which enraged half the faculty. I didn't "look" the part. I heard "take out your piercings" and "cover your tattoos" daily.

And they nearly shit themselves when I got neck and hand tattoos my second year. Still, I graduated in the top one-percent.

Maximoff doesn't prod me to grab a piece of paper. He barrels ahead. "At some point," he says, "not tonight because I'm still digesting this new arrangement—"

"Relationship," I correct, and his shoulders instantly lock. It definitely annoys the fuck out of him that we're attached somehow.

He steps over my comment. "Soon I'll go out to a nightclub, and I'll find someone to fuck. It's just about sex, NSA"—*no strings attached*—"a one-night stand, and I need you to remember this next part."

"What?"

"You can't tell me *no*."

My nose flares, and my eyes roll in the slowest wave. "You can't be serious?" His glare says he is. "Moffy—"

"Maximoff," he corrects, which makes me shake my head and almost roll my eyes for the thousandth time. Everyone in his family and security uses his nickname. No one but the media and public stick solely to calling him *Maximoff*. I assume he's lumping me in with *tabloids* to try and piss me off.

He motions to me. "For a guy who has such a great memory, you forget to call me by my full name a hell of a lot."

"*Maximoff*," I say with extra flair, and he flips me off with both hands. I barrel ahead with the real issue. "All security would tell you *no* if they sensed someone with ill-intent wanting to sleep with you. And I'd tell you *be smarter than that*."

He's a billionaire celebrity. Half the population either wants his money, fame, or dick. Most of the time, all three, and some are willing to cross lines for it. Someone could drug him. I could overhear shit-talk that he doesn't hear.

The list is endless.

He considers my words for barely half a second. "You have to trust my instincts like Declan did."

My gum is stale in my mouth. "I'll trust your instincts until they fail you. How about that?"

"Fine. Because they won't fail me." He heads to the door and leaves my room.

5

One hand on the wheel, I drive towards a grocery store. I raise my phone to my lips with the other and speak into a notes app. "Laundry detergent, eggs, dish soap—"

"*Lawndo egg soup*," the automated voice reads back.

Are you fucking kidding me? I glare at my phone.

Farrow's amusement is palpable in the passenger seat. "Brake."

"Dammit." I slam on my brakes before I bulldoze into a white sedan. Two days of Farrow as my bodyguard and I'm already feeling the effects.

Scatterbrained.

Rattled.

Sexually tensed up.

I haven't had sex in 48 hours. I masturbated in the shower this morning, and I tried so goddamn hard not to imagine *him*. Hot water pelted my squared shoulders, my head dipped forward while warmth doused my brown hair. My left hand was closed into a white-knuckled fist against the tiled wall. My right hand stroked my throbbing cock that stood at hard attention.

Begging for a release.

One fantasy plays on a loop, no matter how much I say *off. Turn off.* Farrow enters the shower right behind me. Fog steams the glass doors. Layering the stifling heat.

His commanding, assertive presence pushes up against my muscular back. Then his strong arm extends around my build, and his large palm encases my white-knuckled hand on the tiled wall.

He holds tight. Water cascading over the sharp planes and valleys of his muscles. My gaze travels along his inked skin. His soft lips skim the base of my neck. To my ear.

Where he whispers in the deepest, most gravelly voice he owns.

"Maximoff." Farrow snaps his fingers at my face—*shit.*

I yank myself out of a fantasy. Coming to the present where I'm driving. Where I'm gripping my phone way too tightly in one hand. Where Farrow is staring at me like I've just flown to an unknown dimension. How did I even fall into that shower scene again?

I was just trying to remind myself to *forget it.* Forever.

Farrow opens his mouth, and before he asks where I mentally departed, I beat him to the punch.

"I was thinking about Janie." *What the fuck is wrong with me? Jane, really?* I restrain the urge to cringe. She may be my best friend, but she's also my cousin. Swiftly, I add, "You know, I'm on my way to see her." At the grocery. That part is true. We do almost everything together.

Farrow studies me for an even longer moment, not saying anything. I fix the air conditioning. My muscles constricted, body hot. At least I didn't sweat through my gray crew-neck. At least I didn't get hard.

He extends his arm towards me.

My brows knot at him.

Farrow leaves his arm on the back of my seat. "Do you need a second?"

"For what?" I go absolutely rigid, but my gaze spends half its time on him and half its time on the road. I think he's about to make a jerking motion with his hand.

His lips slowly rise, and he scratches his brow where his barbell piercings lie. "You seem distracted," is all he says.

"I'm *fine.*" I grip the steering wheel ten times harder, and I keep licking my lips like I'm about to say something else. I have nothing to offer except *fuck me.*

He's your bodyguard. Yeah, well when I give him that title, it's starting to make him *more* attractive. I didn't think that'd be possible. But when he's not following me around, I picture him with me. My brain refuses to detach my bodyguard for a single moment of Farrow-free peace.

"Give it." Farrow motions to my hand.

My phone? "What?"

"Since you won't let me drive, I can do the bare minimum and type out your grocery list."

I should let go of this task, but I hesitate to pass it off to Farrow. I enjoy doing shit myself. "You're not my assistant."

"I'm the guy trying to ensure you don't run us both off the road. You obviously need two hands on the wheel, so…" He waves me to release the phone, and in my silence, he adds, "Or you can pull over and let me drive—"

I drop my phone on his lap.

"You really don't want me to drive." He puts his boot on his seat, elbow to his bent knee, and he cups my phone. "The day when I finally drive you around will just be much more gratifying."

"The day," I say dryly. "You mean *the day* that's never happening? That one?" I spot the roll of his eyes before I point at my phone. "Is it unlocked?"

"I'm already in your notes." He fixes the spelling errors made by the app.

"Janie texted me stuff she needs." I switch lanes. Two paparazzi vans trail me now, so I constantly check my rearview mirror. "Her text thread should be the top one."

He lets out a long whistle. "One hundred *unread* text messages." I sense his surprise as he says, "You're actually breaking your moral code."

I glare and then go for the phone.

He retracts it out of my reach. "*Thou shall not ignore thy family.*"

"You think you're so damn smart." I effortlessly weave between two pick-up trucks and bypass the paparazzi. "Those texts are just from today, Sherlock." I flick off my blinker.

"You're serious?"

"Yep. I'm in twelve group chats with different family members." I have *eleven* cousins alone. That's not including my siblings and my parents. Or my aunts and uncles. We all talk. "If I can't answer during the day, I go through my texts at night."

He scrolls through Jane's thread. "If someone has an emergency, what do you do?"

"I'll glance at the texts in case someone's freaking out, but most of the time, they'll call if it's serious." I strangely have an easy time freeing these facts. Ones that I generally keep to myself.

I trust him.

It helps that he's been a part of my world long before he was a bodyguard. It's also the *issue*, but that's another thing entirely.

As quiet descends, he types on my notes app and says, "Jane is asking for chocolate turtles, pretzels, tampons, and lemonade packets." He adjusts the air vents and points the ice-cold at me.

I glance from him to the road. "You cold?" I can adjust the air for him.

He types on my notepad app. "You looked hot."

How the fuck can he tell? "I'm not," I refute and crank the air to a warmer temperature.

Farrow scrolls through his phone, too. "I still have time to call the store. I can get someone to fill a cart with all the items on your list." It's a safe route.

So shoppers won't bombard me in aisles. Alpha is known to go one step further and shut down the grocery store. Giving my parents, aunts and uncles privacy and secure exits and entrances.

"No," I say firmly. "I'd rather just get the groceries myself." It takes me two hours, but I don't like the idea of being waited on and taking up someone else's time.

"Okay." He sounds genuinely *okay* with that scenario.

I was expecting a two-minute argument. My strained muscles ease a fraction. "Fair warning," I tell him, "paparazzi will bum-rush me when I leave the store. They'll get up close to take shots of my bags."

He listens carefully.

"I don't care if they can see what I bought, so don't worry about pushing them back. I just need to be able to get out in a reasonable amount of time."

"I'll get you out." His staunch certainty heats my core. He raises my phone. "Anything else you need?"

"Ground beef, chips, taco seasoning, everything-bagels, oatmeal, protein bars and shakes—" *I need condoms. And more lube.* Fuck.

At my abrupt stop, I sense his confusion brewing, but he finishes typing those items.

I shouldn't be censoring myself around him.

At some point, I'm going to have a one-night stand. He may hear me orgasm through the fucking door or wall. I've also tried not to make sex a taboo subject in my life. With people I trust, I try to speak about it as easily as the weather. My parents raised me to see sex in a positive light.

That's continuing. Until I'm a dead, lifeless corpse.

"What else?" Farrow looks over at me.

I change my grip on the steering wheel. "At least three boxes of condoms and water-based lube," I say, my edged voice more like a serrated knife right now. Ready to butcher him. *Calm down.* I'm high-strung.

I get that.

Farrow drops his foot to the car mat. Sitting straighter. He types on my phone, the silence thickening. I can't read his reaction. Not while I concentrate on the evening traffic and a van that almost touches my bumper.

I've been trying to drive only fifteen over the limit. To show him it's not a "speeding habit" but a choice that I can control. A choice I make.

But it's hard not revving to thirty-over when paparazzi latch *this* close.

I speed.

Just to pass a Mustang and switch lanes. Putting distance between me and the paparazzi. As I decelerate, Farrow drops his arm to the middle console.

Done typing, he says, "Silicone-based lube feels better than water-based."

I glance at him. Just once. "I've never tried it."

He keeps his hand to his mouth. *What does that mean?*

I start glancing to the road. To him, the road, him, and I realize—he's smiling. When I catch his expression, he lets his hand fall, his lips stretched so wide, and he shifts in his seat and hunches forward as he types out something on my phone.

"What are you doing?"

He turns his head to me, and bleach-white strands of hair slip to his lashes. "Writing down my favorite lube for you, wolf scout."

I flex my abs to stop from hardening. *Dear World, I hate you. Worst regards, a human being who's trying not to bust a nut.*

"Cool," I say as he passes me my phone. Yeah, so cool. Let my childhood-crush-also-turned-bodyguard pick out my lube for me. That will make not fantasizing about him *so* much easier.

So smart of me.

Genius.

Maybe I shouldn't have dropped out of Harvard.

6

MAXIMOFF HALE

Six months ago, Jane Cobalt rushed into my room at midnight. Face covered in an avocado mask. Brunette hair twisted in a pink towel.

"Moffy?" she whispered.

I hadn't fallen asleep yet. At the spike of her breezy voice, I flipped on my lamp fast. And Janie saw the girl nestled beneath my covers. Bucknaked. Both of us.

Jane winced. "Désolée. Ça n'a pas d'importance." *So sorry. It doesn't matter.* She started to leave.

I whispered with urgency, "Attends." *Wait.* I hurried out of bed and tugged on boxer-briefs. "Jane." I sprinted to the door, and my one-night stand groggily said my name. I assured her, "I'll be right back."

I left my door ajar so she'd be less inclined to take pictures of my bedroom.

Jane waited for me in the middle of the staircase. At the top, Declan played a game on his cellphone—he'd been guarding my room that night. My bodyguard gave me a colossal amount of figurative space. Barely acknowledging me.

"Jane?" I stopped one stair above hers.

"*Go back,*" she emphasized. "I didn't mean to interrupt you. I just had a sudden…" With two hands, she motioned to her body and outward. Jane was rarely lost for words.

DAMAGED LIKE US **45**

My brows knotted and I shook my head repeatedly. "You had a creature come loose through your small intestines?" Alright, I wasn't used to Janie miming.

Her tiny smile pulled at her avocado mask. "And you still question why you're never picked first for charades."

Alright, that too.

She inhaled. "I had a sudden...épiphanie." *Epiphany.*

"About what?" I stood like a stone statue. *She's moving out.* My sudden guess stabbed my lungs.

We'd been together since birth. Inseparable as kids and teenagers. In Philly, there weren't laundry lists of actors and celebrities to shirk attention from ourselves. We weren't in LA or New York. Our families were the only shiny toys in the window. The only animals in the zoo.

Growing up in the public eye here, we related to very few people. So we naturally stuck together. As an adult, it always felt like we were *supposed* to move on somehow—but I never understood why that meant we had to move on from each other.

I wanted Janie in my world. And she was the one who said those three months we separated at college—I went to Harvard, she went to Princeton—were the "darkest, most miserable days" of her life.

After a quick glance at my cracked door, she murmured, "An epiphany about my future. Midnight life contemplations, you know those."

I did. When we were sixteen, we used to sneak into the Meadows girls' treehouse at night and talk for hours about our identities. Our role in the world.

Who we were. Inside. And out.

Our attention drifted as two calico kittens skulked up the stairs. She picked up Walrus and let his brother Carpenter scamper away. Jane owned five cats: Walrus, Carpenter, Toodles, Ophelia, and Lady Macbeth. I never minded them or even the strays she sometimes housed.

They made Janie happy.

"I can't do philanthropy for much longer," she said after a short pause. *That.*

Too many emotions hit me at once, so I knocked them aside. And a heavy nothingness weighed me down.

Since she was eighteen, Jane had been the temporary CFO for H.M.C. Philanthropies. I tried to prepare myself for the day she'd leave, but I let the idea wither and die in my brain.

She'd be by my side forever.

Except forever always ends.

"It's almost been three years, Moffy." She tried to kiss Walrus without avocado-ing his calico fur. Then he sprung out of her arms. "Charity work is just supposed to be my pit stop. It's what you're good at. It's what you desperately *love*." She said the word *love* from her core. "But me—"

"You don't have to convince me. I know it's not your thing." I wish it could've been, but I wouldn't selfishly *beg* her to stay.

Because out of loyalty, she would. And I wasn't going to trap my best friend.

Jane lowered her voice to another whisper. "We're all incredibly privileged, and the thought of wasting a moment or any opportunity we've been given feels like eternal failure."

"No," I snapped, concerned about where this was headed.

"It's true." She tried hard not to scratch her face. But her mask must've itched because she kept crinkling her nose. She tilted her chin up and looked me right in the eye. "I can't sit idly by and be the woman *no one* hoped I'd be."

My jaw tensed. "You put *way* too much fucking pressure on yourself." All of the girls I was surrounded by did, and it had a lot, in part, to do with the media placing impossible ideals on them.

Before they even hit puberty, they were supposed to be role models, advocates, successful, beautiful, fierce, strong, humble, and sweet—when all I ever wanted for each of them was to be *happy*.

"Let me preface," Jane said, "my epiphany has nothing to do with math."

"Good."

Jane loved math as a child. Even joined mathletes as a teenager, and people fantasized about Janie having a career in the field. But she never meant for it to be a *lifelong* passion. Still, people on Twitter, Tumblr, all social medias—they created an entire life for Jane off a favorite childhood school subject.

It was a lot of pressure for a *kid.*

Fear of disappointing your parents—that's one tough thing. Fear of disappointing fans, the world—that's a massive, indestructible wall that many people I love keep running into.

I've even met that wall before.

Jane took the largest breath. The crux was coming. "I realized tonight," she said, "that I've spent nearly all four years of my 'college experience' ambitionless. Lackluster. I need drive." She clenched her fist like she channeled Joan of Arc into her soul. "A challenge." Her eyes lit with fire. "My parents live by ambition, and my tank is dry. Empty. *Caput.*"

"You're not ambitionless. You're in Princeton." In anyone else's world, that would be considered a success. For the Cobalt family, attending an Ivy League was just expected.

"Online courses," she corrected. "And I only have three semesters left. I'm setting a goal. A challenge. I *have* to find a career path by the time I graduate. No floundering like a dead fish. I'm born from lions."

There it was.

The biggest truth.

Her parents had their shit figured out in the womb. Her mom created her own fashion company at *fifteen*. Her dad ran a multi-billion-dollar paint, magnet, and diamond business called Cobalt Inc. by *twenty-four*.

In Jane's mind, she wasn't even the tortoise lagging behind. She hadn't put herself in the fucking race yet.

Ambition. She wanted it.

I vowed to help her, and we've been doing random activities together ever since. Just to ignite a modicum of inspiration. Flight lessons, roller derby, and most recently, *cake decorating*.

Bells ding as Farrow holds a door open to a

polished city bakery. I was a centimeter away from grabbing the knob first.

"I'm just faster than you," Farrow says, near-laughter as my scowl deepens.

On land maybe. "And so much more humble too." I know he only lets me enter the bakery before him because it's empty. Bought-out for a couple hours by Jane.

A few weeks ago, her bodyguard retired too, and Akara assigned a new face to Jane. Twenty-year-old Quinn Oliveira is the youngest bodyguard in the team, and he's earning his stripes by starting on Jane's detail.

I don't know him that well. Just that he's a former pro-boxer, Brazilian-American, and his older brother is another bodyguard on SFO. Quinn's inexperience doesn't bother me. Everyone has to start somewhere, but I do find it strange that they're letting Farrow train him. Christ, Farrow practically threw out my rules on *day one*. He's not the ideal bodyguard role model.

Quinn looms by the bakery's sprinkle rack. Right near the store window for optimum *entrance security.*

And where there's a Quinn, there has to be a Jane.

I leave Farrow at the bakery-front. Attempting my best to glance back only one time. Not half a million. Farrow rests his knee on a stubby wooden stool and quietly talks to Quinn. My bodyguard motions towards the entrances and exits, probably giving him tips or something.

I walk deeper into the bakery. And my smile forms the instant I spot my best friend.

Hands perched on her wide hips, Jane surveys the artistic chalkboard menu as though this one decision will determine her whole future.

Pale blue cat-eye sunglasses perch on long, frizzy brunette hair. Jane's as unique as her style: mint-green pants, frilly Victorian sleeves beneath a Zebra-print sweater, mismatched sequined heels, and a watermelon-shaped purse—no one can duplicate or clone this girl.

She's patented one-of-a-kind, and I'm not letting go of her. Not anytime or day or year. I love her too damn much.

Approaching fast, I steal her gaze and watch her own smile take shape.

In seamless French, I say, "Bonsoir, ma moitié." *Good evening, my other half.* I kiss both of her freckled cheeks.

Her long lashes shade poised, blistering blue eyes. "It's just you and me, old chap."

Nearly at the same time, her arms wrap around my waist and mine slide around her shoulders. I draw her into a warm hug.

My muscles start to loosen like I'm home.

You know Jane Eleanor Cobalt as the oldest Cobalt child out of seven. The twenty-two-year-old pastel-loving, cat-hoarding girl who invites you into her life like a friend. You've seen Instagram videos of her burning French toast, trying on a new pair of pants, and reading passages of old literature.

You also pressure her to become a math professor and to advocate for women in STEM. And you pry about who she's dating or not dating—but you're not sure if it's "serious" between them.

I know her as Janie.

My best friend, ma moitié. One month apart in age, but she's a million light-years smarter. A girl who breathes loyalty like it's a third lung. Who will sacrifice every day, minute, and second for the people she loves.

Fair warning: I'll break both of your kneecaps and stake your head on a pitchfork if you fuck with her. Glad we have that covered.

Jane rests her chin on my chest. And she looks up. "Just us. *Except* for the two very strapping bodyguards, the bakery employees, and your three siblings that'll arrive at seven."

I invited my two sisters and my brother to join us later. "Thanks for calling the bakery in advance," I say seriously. No sarcasm. When I asked Jane if my little brother could join, her first response: *I'll buy-out the bakery for a couple hours.*

The two of us—Jane and me—we don't typically shutdown stores for ourselves. We can handle media and public attention. But Jane knew that Xander wouldn't come if people were around. Instead of saying, *just leave him back*, she was the first to help include him.

"Avec plaisir," she says silkily. *With pleasure.*

So I'm fluent in two foreign languages for *very* different reasons. I'm not going into the rabbit hole of the second one, but the first, French—Jane and I taught ourselves more than we learned in prep school. We picked it up quickly since her parents are fluent.

My arm stays around her shoulders while we face the menu. Sketches of different shaped cakes are scrawled in pink chalk.

Boom.

My head whips to the storefront. Hoards of young *excitable* girls push against the glass door. I'm talking enough bodies to flood the sidewalk and trickle into street parking.

I stand up, muscles constricted. "Our location got leaked." *Already.* Jane and I don't draw crowds like we're a band at Coachella unless people post about us.

Janie starts scrolling through a Twitter feed. "…it looks like a fan tweeted that they saw the paparazzi outside the bakery."

"Did they post the address?"

"Oui." *Yes.*

"Great," I say dryly, and I take my phone out of my pocket. A few cameramen flocked the area when I first parked my car. I don't mention them every time I see one. It's like pointing out the grass, cement, or the damn sky. They're scenery to my world. Always there. Always present.

And sometimes fucking up my day.

"Back up!" Farrow shouts through the glass. Girls keep trying to yank open the locked door. Some pound on the windows. For as severe as his voice sounds, Farrow looks unconcerned by the growing masses. He grips the handle to keep the door from jerking against the lock.

Quinn yells at the fans to *leave* too. But my gaze is tethered to Farrow. I sweep his relaxed six-foot-three build, his supreme composure—all in the face of a high-stress situation.

Farrow turns slightly, keeping his hand on the door. And with one quick glance, his eyes touch my eyes.

Before he reads my expression, I rotate completely. I rub my sharpened jaw.

My phone vibrates in my palm. I see the names *Luna* and *Kinney*, my two sisters, and I read the incoming texts.

Moffy!!!!!! Xander won't leave the house :'(((— **Luna**

I told him nothin' bad will happen, but he saw his name trending on Twitter — **Kinney**

And #PhillyBakery — **Luna**

I text: it's not that crowded here.

Don't lie. — **Xander**

I rapidly text: I'll be by your side when you walk in. I promise. I won't let anyone touch you.

No response yet.

I look up. Farrow is watching me. I follow his precise fingers that touch a small, slender mic attached to his black V-neck collar. The microphone's wire runs up to his earpiece and then down to a radio that's clipped on his waistband.

All security wear comms, but if he's touching the mic, it means he's actively talking to other bodyguards right now.

"Are they bailing?" Jane asks as she sidles next to me.

"Probably." If Xander stays at home, it means his anxiety is through the roof. Luna and Kinney will want to keep him company.

I try one last thing and text: I'll distract the crowds when you come. I want to add that I'd kill for him. I'd move mountains and rip through stone. I'd do *anything* to ensure my little brother's safety. So I type: I'll take a bullet for you. I'll do any fucking thing. Just get here.

I press send.

After a long pause, my phone buzzes.

It won't work. It never works. — **Xander**

My muscles bind. I flash the text to Janie. "This'll be two weeks that he hasn't left the house." My parents try not to hound him about the isolation unless it reaches one month. *It adds to his anxiety*, they say. But staying cooped up for weeks on end isn't goddamn healthy either.

Jane frowns. "Next time, we should pick him up first."

I nod in agreement.

7

"Alpha to Farrow." A strict male voice blares in my eardrum. I scrape late-night scrambled eggs out of my pan and into a ceramic bowl. In the kitchen of my townhouse, I toss the frying pan into the sink, lagging on replying to Price. The forty-something stern Alpha lead keeps acting like I'm still a part of SFA.

I'm on SFO.

And I don't take orders from anyone. What I will do: listen to Akara's orders and decide whether I want to follow them or not.

"Alpha to Farrow," Price snaps.

I lean on the counter and eat my eggs at a leisurely but naturally quick speed. The oven clock blinks *11:23 p.m.*—I've been home for less than twenty minutes. Enough time to piss, shower, and crack a few eggs. Three weeks into my new role and I'm already used to Maximoff's fast-paced lifestyle.

He jam-packs his days, and his plans constantly change depending on paparazzi, family in need, and the hundred employees he manages at H.M.C. Philanthropies. Most security on his detail would be whiplashed, but his high-stress, hectic schedule reminds me of doing rounds at the ER.

I eat and breathe every second like it's candy.

What surprises me the most: he hasn't gone to a single nightclub or bar yet. He was the one who said it'd be happening "soon" but he's been stalling. I don't ask why because I'd rather not pressure him to fuck someone. When he's ready, he'll be ready—and I'll have to keep him safe.

It's what I focus on.

"Alpha to Farrow, *Alpha to Farrow*," Price repeats harshly a few more times.

I should only be hearing *Omega to Farrow*. I touch my mic. "Farrow." Let's hear what he has to say. I eat a scoop of eggs, alone in the kitchen since my only roommate is sleeping. Jane's bodyguard, Quinn, hasn't grown accustomed to the strange hours yet. As soon as Jane headed in for the night, he practically passed out upstairs—despite my best effort to suggest grabbing a quick meal first.

Bodyguard 101: *eat when you have a free second 'cause you never know when you'll find another chance.*

Through my earpiece, Price says, "You need to ask Moffy about the annual Charity Camp-Away. We've heard rumors that he plans to open the event to the public this year, and the security team needs confirmation. Don't take long." The radio quiets.

Opening a controlled, private event to the public creates major security risks. Ones that I'd never ignore. But Maximoff has the power to do whatever he wants with the Charity Camp-Away. Not only as the CEO, but *he* built the highly praised and promoted December event years ago.

Wealthy donors will buy expensive tickets to the three-day camp retreat with him and several family members. They basically pay to huddle around a campfire with celebrities. And only extremely affable people can afford the tickets.

I've overheard many of his phone calls in the car, and he's never mentioned a change in the Camp-Away's format.

I click my mic. "Farrow to Alpha, where'd you hear these rumors?" Carrying my bowl, I pass through the archway into my living room. The wooden door beside the brick fireplace connects my townhouse to Maximoff's.

"SFA traced the word *public* from his assistant's email," Price tells me. "We need more intel from Moffy. Respond with an affirmative." When security hacks emails, it's in favor of the families. Yet, I see the irony. We protect them, but in doing so, we strip away their privacy.

I can't change that fact.

Alpha, Omega, and Epsilon have a motto: *stay ahead of the media.* It's impossible to stop tabloids, but we have to be aware of everything that could potentially hit the press and cause harm.

Before I grab the doorknob, I click my mic again. "I'll get back to you." The second I open the door to Maximoff's living room, a calico kitten darts past my ankles.

I swiftly turn and catch Jane's pet. Walrus claws the hardwood, but I lift the little thing and raise the kitten's face to my face. "Naughty, naughty."

The kitten paws my nose. I smile and tell the cat, "You're not allowed to escape, you little bastard."

Walrus meows.

Jane stressed, *"Do not let the little kittens in security's townhouse. It's not kitten-proof. They'll wedge themselves in nooks and crannies."* I'm not about to lose a kitten.

Once I enter the adjoining living room, I release Walrus and he darts beneath the rocking chair. No one's on the first floor. I kick the door shut, and voices echo down the narrow staircase.

I lean on the brick wall, eat my eggs, and scan the cramped area. The decorated version of my bare place: a pale pink Victorian loveseat, frilled pillows, a rocking chair, pastel blankets, glass teacart, two-person café table by the kitchen archway, and at least twenty family photos on the mantel.

The ugly granny style screams Jane Cobalt.

Their house also has a distinct smell of brewed coffee, tea, floral candles, and *cat.*

Stairs creak, and Jane emerges first, dressed in pale-blue silk pajama shorts and tank top. She carries a bottle of oil and only notices me when she steps off the last stair.

"Farrow." She smiles and gives me a curious once-over. As though she's the one who caught me with a bottle of oil.

"Jane," I greet, eating another scoop of eggs. If she had a "guy friend" in the house, I'd already know about him. She has no time to respond. Maximoff skips two stairs at a time, coming in hot.

He pulls his white shirt off his head, his hair disheveled, body ripped, and his gray drawstring pants hang low on his waist.

My lips rise and rise. He hasn't seen me yet, and he's going to flip the fuck out the moment he does. I eat my eggs like popcorn.

Jane watches me really keenly, but I have nothing to hide. I'm unapologetically me. Every day, all day.

"Ready, Janie?" he asks, combing his hair back with a quick hand. Then he looks up. And sees me. He solidifies, his jaw tensing and eyes widening.

"I missed you too," I quip and finish off my eggs. My smile growing as his irritation scrunches his features and daggers his eyes.

Maximoff drops onto the first floor. "It's been two minutes since I last saw you."

"Thirty-three," I correct and watch Jane plop down on the loveseat and unscrew the bottle of sweet almond oil. I have a feeling I know its use. I focus on Moffy. "Security wants more information about the Camp-Away."

Realization hits him, and he nods. "You'll have to wait. I promised Janie a massage, and she comes first."

"Giving or receiving?" I ask.

His brows jump, and he licks his lips, turning his head slightly. He rubs his sharp jaw.

I smile, my body tightening, but I ignore the feeling. "The massage, wolf scout. Are you giving or receiving it?"

"Receiving," he says more easily. "Jane's trying out massage therapy."

She ties her wavy hair into a low pony. "If you two need to talk about the Camp-Away, I can wait—"

"No." Maximoff shakes his head repeatedly. "I'm focusing on you right now. Your ambition, your goal, remember?"

Jane nods and reads the ingredients on the back of the oil. Her blue eyes lift to me. "I can give you one after Moffy."

"Let's see how this one goes, first." I set my empty bowl on the nearby café table.

Maximoff gestures to the rocking chair. "Take a seat." He orders me mostly because he has to sit down, and he hates when I tower above him.

"I'll stand." I pass between him and the rocking chair to reach the fireplace mantle.

"And you think I'm the stubborn one?" He sits next to Jane, and she kneels on the cushion behind him.

I skim his family photos. "I never said you had a monopoly on stubbornness." I pick up a framed picture of Maximoff doing a backflip off the Hale's yacht, Jane in the corner pointing at him with a pretend-surprised face. I flash the photo at him. "Whatever you can do, I can do better."

"Such fighting words," Jane says, squirting oil on her palms. "As the third, unbiased participant in the room, I volunteer myself to be judge of any competitions."

"I think you mean *biased* participant." I set the photo back. The two of them are together in nearly every picture on the mantle.

"I can be unbiased," Jane says, and she begins to knead Maximoff's *tight* deltoids. He grips the back of the uncomfortable Victorian couch for support.

I watch him while I ask Jane, "Who's better at boxing?"

Jane pauses and opens her mouth, but no sound comes out.

I help her, "F-A-R—"

"M-O-F-F-Y," she spells rapidly and exhales a breath like she escaped death by betrayal. "Aunt Lily says *the truth will set you free*, and I couldn't agree more. I feel so much better." She focuses on the massage again, using her knuckles on his back.

Maximoff smiles at me. Like he one-upped me.

"I don't know why you're so happy. She just proved she's partial to you."

Maximoff gives me a look. "You can't, even for a second, admit that *maybe*, just maybe, I'm better than you at your own sport."

It'd take great effort to tear my gaze off his. "Your humility is waning."

"Your superiority is worsening."

I break into a huge smile, but my lips lower as Maximoff bears on his teeth, almost wincing. He glances briefly at Jane and tries to peer at her knuckles that edge towards his spine. His shoulders stay in their usual rigid, locked position.

"Try to relax," I suggest, nearing the loveseat. "Or do you need *how to* instructions?"

He glowers. "The only instructions I need are how to make you shut the fuck up..." he trails off and stifles another wince. Jane can't see his expression.

"You're too close to his spine," I tell Jane, and I reach out to her wrist. "Can I?"

"Please."

I shift her hands to his traps, muscles lateral to his shoulder blades. I close her fingers, oiling my hands, and as soon as she starts kneading his muscles again, she asks, "Better, Moffy?"

"Yep." His collar is tight, and when he glances at me, then intakes a sharp breath, I realize that my closeness is the cause.

I sweep his stringent posture: Maximoff Hale, shirtless, muscles oiled, and being massaged beneath novice hands.

He'd feel better beneath mine.

He winces, "*Fuck*. Jane." She pinched his nerve.

She raises her oiled hands. "Sorry." Jane searches for something. "Merde," she says *shit* in French. "Hold on, Moffy. I'm going to pop up the video again." She nods to me, then the coffee table where her phone lies. "Farrow, would you mind?"

I wipe my oiled hands on my black pants and then I grab the phone, cased in a blue zebra-print hard-shell. "How serious are you about being a masseuse?"

She elbows a piece of hair off her freckled cheek. "If I really enjoy it, then I'll research how to become a professional masseuse and go from there." She nods to the phone. "The video should be in my 'recently watched' list on YouTube."

I wait to unlock her cell. "And what happens when you have a customer who wants a 'happy ending' from the famous Jane Cobalt?"

Maximoff glances at Jane, exchanging a look like they've both discussed the safety risks before.

Whenever I scroll through social media for security threats, the ones surrounding Jane Cobalt range from disgusting, plain creepy to *violent*. They're both also aware of how some people perceive them. All it takes is a Twitter account:

I'd spank the fuck out of Jane Cobalt. I wanna see her cry.

Tie that bitch up and choke her good #JaneCobalt

Jane Cobalt likes it just like her mom. Ridden rough & hard, put away wettttttttt!!!

I'm gonna bang Connor Cobalt's daughter until she can't walk straight.

Omega is very protective of Jane without her realizing. In the past three weeks, we've intercepted her mail since a sick little shit keeps sending her ball gags. I'll never broadcast this to Jane either. Security wants all of them to live without constant fear.

I agree.

We read and deal with all the fucked-up, demented shit so they don't have to.

Jane shrugs and squirts more oil on her hands. "I'd have to screen my customers. It comes with the territory."

"Of being famous," I say.

"Of being the daughter to Rose and Connor Cobalt," she clarifies. "Everyone watches me through the lens of my parents."

Maximoff cracks a crick in his neck and mutters, "For better and for worse."

I understand.

Their fame derives from their parents. Not from themselves. Rose and Connor Cobalt just happen to be notorious for having sex tapes leaked to the media. Specifically BDSM. Therefore, the public assumes their oldest daughter is just like her mother.

The security team has an intimate, inside perspective. Really, the truth. And I know Jane isn't into BDSM.

Jane places her palms on Maximoff's back but waits for the video. "YouTube," she reminds me, and as our eyes meet, she adds, "I'm already lucky that I have the opportunity to take this time to find a passion. And I'm lucky that I can even *consider* the idea of being a masseuse. If I find what I truly love, I can't let my fame stand in the way."

I glance at Maximoff.

His jaw is a razorblade. He's concerned about security risks, too. He's seen those tweets. And I have a feeling that he's just indulging her ambition for the moment and is banking on Jane landing on something safe.

I swipe into her phone too easily. *Jane.* "Where's your passcode?" I ask, my tone very *kind* considering two-thirds of the security team would scold her like she's a kid right now.

"I don't have one," she says. "They're infuriating, and if I lose my phone, I'll wipe the data clean immediately. Plus, I have nothing incriminating. I delete all my texts, and I upload most of my photos and videos to Instagram already. There's nothing anyone can steal."

Maximoff smiles, proud of his friend.

Her preparation reminds me of something the security team says about Jane. That she acts carefree, but her whole life is outlined and planned to her liking, and she juggles just as much, if not more, than Maximoff Hale.

While I find the video, I tell Jane, "Lightly rub his shoulder blades, and you won't hurt him."

Maximoff grips the back of the loveseat harder, and he licks his lips again. I find myself watching him, and as I near the armrest, closest to his chest, he's more eye-level with my belt.

Maximoff stares off into space. *Where'd you go, Moffy?* I wave my hand at him, but he's lost in his head.

"Farrow." Jane's blue eyes twinkle. "How many massages have you given before? And why?"

Alpha also calls her Jane "Curiosity Killed the Cat" Cobalt.

I scroll through her YouTube "recently watched" feed. "Too many, and look up the main purpose of a massage and you have your answer." I discover the video and whistle. *"How To Give An Amazing, Super, Fantastic Massage."* I press play and find a blurry image of two high school girls. "No." I shut if off. "Let me show you."

Maximoff wakes up, glaring at me. "No."

"Welcome back, space cadet."

He flips me off and repeats harshly, *"No."*

Jane shakes out her arms, tired already.

"You have to use your whole body," I tell her, and to him, I say, "Let me demonstrate so she can copy me." I'd *love* to give him a massage for more reasons than just to help Jane.

Maximoff gestures to my chest. "You don't know how to give a massage."

"And you really missed the part where I just said I've given massages before." I place Jane's phone on the coffee table. "I know how to do a lot of things better than average. I'm good with my hands."

"Great." He's being more headstrong over something I thought he'd forfeit for Jane. I hone in on his stiff posture and the way his Adam's apple bobs as he swallows.

"Maybe Farrow is right," Jane says, "maybe I could use a real live demonstration."

"Maybe Farrow is full of shit," Moffy replies.

"Maybe Maximoff is scared of getting a massage from me," I refute.

"You're wrong." He stands, facing me with as much self-confidence as Atlas bracing the world. He crosses his arms over his bare chest. "So what now?" He's agreeing to a massage.

I use my boot and push the coffee table away from the couch. Then I throw a pillow onto the ground. "Lie down, wolf scout. Let me change your world."

8

MAXIMOFF HALE

I'm so fucked.

I breathe through my nose. Suppressing whatever tries to heat my veins and disorient my head. Lust? Irritation? *Infatuation?*

I stare him directly in the eye. Unabashed, but I keep thinking, *never in my goddamn life have I wanted to accept an order like that one as badly as I do now.*

I'm highly aware that I've always been drawn to alpha males. The kind of men who want to top me as much as I want to top them. I get my way *almost* every time, but just toying with the vulnerability of being with someone just as strong, just as dominant, lights me up to the fucking max.

Imagining that person while I stand here, right now, I realize that Farrow Redford Keene is the penultimate match.

He's your bodyguard. Thank you, moral conscience. It's why I refuse to let my gaze slip down to his mouth or his six-foot-three build. I don't even let him read my reaction for long.

I retie my loose drawstring pants. And then I kneel on the rug before lying on my stomach. A position I rarely find myself in.

I prop myself on my elbows. And crane my neck over my shoulder. Keeping a narrowed eye on Farrow. He removes his silver rings. One-by-one.

Christ. His fingers—*those fingers are going to be on me.* The back of my neck is boiling hot.

His brown eyes travel languidly along my back muscles—ones that showcase my diehard love of swimming. And proficiency in the butterfly stroke.

After he pockets his rings, Janie hands him a bottle of oil. "A dreadfully bad idea or good one to film this for reference material?"

"Bad," I say, for no other reason but this one, "if it leaks somehow, people will start asking who's my amateur masseuse."

Farrow rolls his eyes at the word *amateur*, but he also agrees, "Don't record."

We both know people would fixate on Farrow in this hypothetical video recording. Because he's a.) fully-tattooed, b.) the kind of attractive that makes you crave a "happy ending" and c.) his hands would be on me.

It'd make him famous.

Famous people can't protect famous people. Or else I'd be the bodyguard to my own siblings. And once a bodyguard *needs* a bodyguard to protect themselves, they're worthless to security.

Farrow would lose his job.

Jane lounges on the loveseat. "I'll watch attentively then and take mental notes." Lady Macbeth, an old black cat, springs onto her lap and collapses, purring. Janie kisses the cat's fur and scratches behind her ears.

That damn cat better not distract Jane. I'm not about to repeat this massage.

"Cela n'arrivera pas deux fois," I tell her. *It will not happen twice.*

She strokes Lady Macbeth, her bright blue eyes on me knowingly. "Je regarde. Profite du massage, Moffy." *I'm watching. Enjoy the massage, Moffy.*

I stay propped on my forearms and glance over my shoulder again. Standing, Farrow oils his palms, so damn confident. His smile stretches at the sight of me watching, his bottom lip piercing too hot.

Everything about Farrow is lightning cracking the night sky.

He lowers.

Fuck—here we go.

He rests his knee beside my waist, and the sole of his boot is on my other side. Straddling me without touching me. Not yet, at least.

"All the way down, Maximoff," he says in that deep, gravel voice. "Arms flat by your sides."

My pulse pounds in my neck. I tensely extend my arms by my waist. Which forces me to look away from Farrow. I'd rather hide my face, so I put my forehead on the decorative pillow. Concealed, but also staring at *nothing*.

"Don't kill me," I snap.

He leans forward, his lips near my ear. "Hurting you is the antithesis of my job description."

Right.

"Trust me," he breathes. "Relax." The silky part of his voice soothes me from head-to-toe like stepping into a steaming sauna.

Fuck.

Me.

My normally bound shoulders want to unlock, and I force my arms to stay still and not bring them to the pillow. My whole back is exposed. And only the gray fabric of my drawstring pants lies between Farrow and my bare ass.

I'm not wearing any boxer-briefs.

He can probably tell.

I shut my eyes. Breathing stronger. The anticipation killing me.

And then his warmed, oiled hands start at my tailbone. *Holy shit.* Using the weight of his body to dig deep, he runs his thumbs and palms up the length of my back. Reaching the base of my neck and kneading circles around my broad shoulders.

A sharp breath catches in the pit of my throat. *Holyshitholyshit.*

His fingers and hands create hypnotic movements up and down my back, shoulders, and even my biceps and forearms. Every time he anchors his weight to knead and rub my body, I imagine his pelvis near my ass—I grit down.

Tighten my eyes shut more. I can't get hard.

"Relax," he breathes, his thumbs running up the back of my neck. *That feels too fucking good.*

He leans nearer to my body as his large hands travel down my build and then veer to my waist. Teasing against the band of my drawstring pants.

Don't fantasize.

Don't fantasize.

I breathe through my nose again. If I rotate and sit up—would we kiss? *Stop thinking.* When he leans closer again, I picture his lips beside my jaw. Nipping my ear before sucking, then I turn and we—*no.*

Yes.

Hell yes.

I'm still lying on the ground. He's still massaging my tight shoulders that refuse to unwind. His lips do brush my ear, and he actually, realistically whispers, "Let go."

I can't.

The moment I let go, I'll cross a line that can't be crossed.

He kneads my traps harder, deeper, almost bringing me somewhere I can't ignore. To a state of euphoria. My eyes open but nearly roll back, my mouth slightly agape. *Fucking...*

I grab his wrist.

Suddenly. Instinctively. And he freezes, his palms on my lower back. Without releasing him, I use my other arm to prop my body. My chest rises in a heavy, ragged breath.

I glance at him.

Farrow breathes just as heavily, his eyes searching mine for reasons as to why I stopped him. I imagine shifting his hand lower. To my waistband. Beneath the fabric.

Do it.

I blink once—remembering that Jane is here. And then I think: *that shouldn't be the only reason why I stop.*

He's my fucking bodyguard.

I let go of his wrist.

The old loveseat squeaks as Jane sits up. "I can leave you two alone if you'd like—"

"No," I say firmly and stare hard at Farrow, waiting for him to reject that offer with me.

Farrow sweeps my body with a heady gaze, practically saying, *I would've said yes.* And then he stands up off of me.

I have no real time to think.

My phone rings on the coffee table. An incoming call. Not a text. I quickly stand and grab my phone. I see the caller ID: my little sister, and I become laser-eyed.

Colossally focused.

I concentrate on the here and now. Everything else behind me.

I put the phone to my ear. "Luna?" Strange breathing filters through the speaker. I frown. "Luna?"

Farrow stares faraway like someone is speaking into his earpiece. He walks towards the front door. Jane springs to her feet and checks her cell for any texts or information.

"Luna, *answer me.*" My cheekbones sharpen. I listen fixatedly, my grip tightened on the phone. She's never done this before, but she's also an oddball.

You know Luna Hale as the seventeen-year-old alien devotee who posts inarticulate ramblings on Twitter and believes UFOs are real. You rudely nicknamed her Secondhand Embarrassment. Some of you even call her "drunk" when she's 100% sober, and you question the sanity of anyone who'd date her.

I know her as my little sister. A girl who stays true to herself amid constant ridicule. Someone I admire and love unconditionally.

Fair warning: I'll kill you if you so much as breathe on her wrong. Simple as that.

Over the phone, Luna sighs so softly. I almost miss the sound.

"Talk to me, sis—" The call drops. What the fuck is going on? I turn to Janie. "Did you text your brothers?" Luna's best friends are two of Jane's younger brothers.

"Oui." Janie texts rapidly. "Eliot and Tom keep sending me devil emojis."

I shake my head, pissed. There are *five* Cobalt boys, and my little sister had to befriend the two that lit Jane's dollhouse on fire and laughed while it burned. They were ten years old back then, but at eighteen and seventeen, they still dance in chaos.

By the door, Farrow speaks into his mic. "Garage is full. You need to drop her off or park on the street. I can meet her at the car." Farrow gestures me over, but I'm already approaching him.

My phone vibrates.

A text.

I'm on my way to you. Can't talk :(— Luna

"Luna's on her way here," I tell Janie, who continues to text, and I stop only a foot from Farrow. "What do you know?"

He clicks his mic and says to the security team, "Okay." His gaze clasps mine as he tells me, "Luna asked her bodyguard to drive her here. She also requested that he remain inside his vehicle, which means—"

"She doesn't want him to overhear her," I finish, nodding to myself.

Janie collects the rest of the facts. "She must be hiding something from her parents, and she's afraid her bodyguard will tattle." He would. She's underage.

It's not the first time my siblings have come to me. When they fuck-up, my reaction is the lukewarm version of our over-protective dad. They say I go three-fourths Loren Hale. Sometimes I think they test their wrongdoings out on me just to build the courage to confront him.

Farrow looks at the outdoor security cams on his phone. When he catches me staring, I expect him to turn his back.

Instead, he clasps my wrist and draws me to his side. Our shoulders almost touch. "This is the street view," he says.

The screen shows a few paparazzi loitering on the sidewalk.

Farrow explains, "When Luna's car reaches the curb, I'm going to open her car door and escort her into the house."

I cross my arms and nod. I want to be the one to lead my sister safely inside my house, but I'd make the situation worse.

With paparazzi constantly camped out, exiting my front door is like purposefully stomping on an anthill. Considering I'm *deathly* allergic to fire ants, that's not something I'd do. I typically just leave in a car. Right through the garage.

Jane pulls the coffee table to its original place. "Luna can spend the night. I'll make the bed in the guest room. We can even watch her favorite movie." Janie tosses the decorative pillow on the loveseat. "I haven't seen *Guardians of the Galaxy* in ages."

"Yeah," I say dryly, "how about we postpone baking my sister cookies and rolling out a fucking red carpet until we know what happened? She could've flunked twelfth grade for all we know." Last week, she had detention for vaping in the girl's bathroom. She's been apathetic towards school since the bullying started in kindergarten.

I wish I'd been in her grade.

So I could've been there more than I was. I could've stopped the harassment. Somehow. But I'm *five* years older. By the time she hit freshman year, I was gone.

Farrow clicks into another security camera.

Jane nears us, her features soft and empathetic. She reaches out for my hand.

I keep my arms crossed.

"Moffy," she says tentatively. "I know you'd rather believe Luna screwed up somehow because the alternative is painful, but you need to consider the other possibility."

That something bad could've happened to my sister. And she's coming to me for help.

I lock all my emotion in an iron-tight trunk. Nothing crosses my face. "I'm aware."

Farrow scrutinizes me for a quick second, and then he hands me his phone. "I'll be right back." He slips out the front door, kicks it closed, and nearly the exact moment a black Escalade pulls onto the curb.

Declan would've never given me his phone. I realize that I can watch my sister from Farrow's cell. He knew I'd want to be outside with him, but to actually keep Luna safe—from media attention, from rabid paparazzi—this is as close as I can get.

And he gave me a better view than any bodyguard ever has.

9

FARROW KEENE

Street lamps and rapid camera flashes illuminate the idling black Escalade. I tune out the security team in my right ear, and I easily walk through the frenzied paparazzi.

About five men swarm the car, pressing their lenses to the tinted windows. Others pace back and forth on the sidewalk and call their colleagues hurriedly.

"Get here now!"

"We think it's a Hale kid, hopefully Xander."

Two men crowd the rear door, and I storm ahead. My threatening stride and appearance is like a gunshot. They stumble backwards, and I grip the handle to the Escalade. I mime opening the car door to rid the over-zealous idiots.

One man rushes up and knocks into my hard back. I shoot him a brief, scathing glare.

Brief, because they don't need to think I care about them. Some paparazzi want a fight for footage or insurance payout (I hurt them, they sue), and then most hecklers want a fight for fame or because they're morons. And my job is to avoid confrontations.

Not start them.

When I really open the door, I fit my body in the free space. Not letting the cameramen see Luna yet.

I'm not surprised by what I find. A gangly seventeen-year-old girl is sprawled on the leather seat like a starfish. And she's dressed in a full-body Spider-Man costume. Mask and all.

It's an easy ploy so people avoid snagging a money-shot.

She looks at me upside-down.

I won't smile during pandemonium, but Luna always manages to make life interesting. Out of all the Hale kids, I'd say I'm closest to her. For my twenty-fifth birthday, she wrote me an *Avengers* fanfic where Bucky Barnes and Captain America weren't merely *just* friends. It was entertaining as shit.

"Luna, you ready to go?" I ask.

The driver rotates. It's her three-hundred-pound bodyguard who's been blowing my eardrum out for the past ten minutes. I'm not close to anyone on Epsilon since the SFE lead calls me a "liability" when really, *he* could audition for the role of hall monitor.

Thankfully her bodyguard *isn't* the lead of Epsilon. I dodged that headache.

"She won't talk," he snaps at me.

"She doesn't need to talk to climb out of a car." I extend my hand. She grabs hold, sitting up and sliding across the seat.

Paparazzi scream, "WHO IS IT?! WHO'S IN THE CAR?! IS THAT YOU, XANDER?!"

As soon as she drops onto the cement and lets go of my hand, I slam the door shut. I push ahead to clear a path, and I make sure she stays right behind me.

I keep an eye in front and constantly glance back at Luna. She's not one of the kids who fear the paparazzi. She seems fine, but with her Spider-Man costume hiding her face, it's hard to tell why she's here and what happened.

When no more paparazzi lie ahead, I fall behind Luna and protect her from the back. We reach the brick stoop, and the door already flies open.

Maximoff pulls his little sister safely inside.

Squatting down, I rummage through

Maximoff's bathroom cupboard beneath the sink. I hit my elbow on the nearby toilet a few times. There's no space in here, not even for a tub. Just a small shower stall.

I push aside Jane's baskets of nail polish, and Maximoff bends down next to me and searches through the cupboard too. He has this intrinsic need to *help*, and he's been in big-brother, over-protective mode for the past twenty minutes.

His love for his siblings toughens him, not softens.

And a guy being so protective over the people he loves, I find extremely fucking sexy.

I grab the first-aid kit in the very back. "The mouthwash needs to be alcohol-free," I tell him, and when he finds a bottle, we both stand up. I pop open the kit to see what else I need.

Maximoff watches me. "How up-to-date is your medical knowledge?"

"I know more than you," I say since he tried to diagnose Luna downstairs until I butted in, "and I'm the one who gradated medical school at Yale."

"But your undergrad only took two years—"

"Because I passed the requirements faster than the average person, Harvard Dropout."

"Really?" he deadpans. "Maybe you just sucked."

I roll my eyes and laugh. "That's not how that works." I sift through the kit's items. Gloves, cotton balls, a plastic syringe, thermometer, but I'm still missing something.

"Farrow," he says seriously, "if you're not sure—"

"Maximoff." I look right at him. "I'm *one-hundred* percent sure that she has an infection from a really shit tongue piercing. If you don't trust me, then go Web M.D. her symptoms. It'll tell you that I'm right."

He cracks a knuckle. "I trust you. I'm just"—he gestures to his head—"processing that my sister stuck a sewing needle in her tongue a week ago, and it's still bleeding and she may have a low-grade fever. You know, the usual Friday night."

I take out my supplies and shut the first-aid kit. "It's a good Friday night when no one's crying or dead."

"Which is exactly why she didn't want to tell my parents yet." He rotates his stiff shoulders. "My dad will fucking die, and my mom will cry out of worry." He keeps shaking his head, thinking about something else. "*Fuck.*"

"I need to make a saline solution, so take your *fucks* downstairs with me, wolf scout."

He carries the mouthwash while I have the rest of the supplies. Once downstairs, we bypass the living room where Luna and Jane talk quietly on the loveseat.

Not even a foot into the kitchen and Maximoff already fills a pot with water and sets it on the stove. I smile and place my supplies on the counter. He slides salt to me and ropes my gaze tenfold.

"You know saline solution is just distilled water and salt," I realize. "Where'd you learn that? Wolf Scout Training?"

"Common sense."

Who knew common sense could be so fucking attractive? The heat ratchets up.

I end up saying, "Common sense is a good look on you." I pass him to grab a cup out of a cabinet, and my shoulder slides against his bare skin. Barely any room for two bodies in this cramped kitchen.

He tenses, breathing shallow, and he looks back at me.

He's still only dressed in drawstring pants, his ass literal perfection in them. I've never wanted to touch, hold and fuck someone as much as I want to touch, hold and *fuck* him. And even though I just massaged Maximoff, it still feels like not enough.

Not nearly enough.

Still, he said *no*, and when a guy says *no*, I'm at full-stop.

Maximoff pours the distilled water into a glass, and I mix salt and then I measure a small amount of mouthwash into another cup. Our biceps and forearms keep crossing and skimming.

His breath audibly catches a few times, husky, and he clears his throat.

My muscles burn—if he does that again, I may harden. "What was eating at you from before?" I ask, referring to his earlier exclamation of *fuck*.

Maximoff glances at the archway, then to me. "My little sister pierced her *tongue*. So I'm thinking about what other people think of tongue piercings, and what they'll say about her, how it'll affect her, the media, and the subsequent headline: *Luna Hale Gets Tongue Piercing, She Likes to Give Head.*"

I can't say I'm surprised. "We've officially established that you think way too much about what other people are thinking."

"I have to," he refutes. "People judge my family every damn day, and if there's any way I can save my siblings and cousins from harassment— then I'm taking it."

Using the syringe, I suck up the saline solution. His parents pay people to predict headlines, soften fallouts, and obsess so he doesn't have to. They're called publicists, but Moffy tries to be everything for everyone.

The quality that I like the best about him may also be his worst trait. He's too caring.

"Most likely," I say, "your sister isn't that worried about other people's judgment."

Maximoff shakes his head, skeptical.

"Do you see me?" I ask, motioning to my facial piercings. My left ear is also pierced, but I took out my earring last month for a change. And a barbell is hooked through my right nipple. "Those of us who get piercings and tattoos generally don't give a flying shit what people think of said piercings and tattoos."

Maximoff rests his elbow on the counter and faces me. "Generally, most people aren't the kind of famous where internet trolls Photoshop your head on two humping rabbits."

That happened to his mom. Not Luna.

Slowly, I put on the white latex gloves. "You should remember that your sister is used to ridicule."

He lets this sink in for a second. Luna isn't defenseless against cruel headlines. She has a bit of grit that her brother doesn't take into account.

"And realistically"—I snap my last glove up to my wrist—"she could've picked a tongue piercing with oral in mind."

He grimaces. "No."

"Little sisters can like giving blow jobs," I say and laugh as his scowl appears.

"Because you have so many little sisters." He knows that I have zero little sisters, zero brothers, and one much older stepsister. Sibling relationships are uncharted territory for me, but I like seeing his and how much they all mean to each other.

It's endearing.

Maximoff leans closer and lowers his voice. "As far as I know, she's never been kissed." He pauses, thinking. "Wouldn't the security team know if she's been with anyone?"

"Epsilon would know," I correct, "and if I radioed them to ask, they'd tell me to fuck off." I'm not interested in Luna's sexual history enough to extend an olive branch to SFE. On the list of important things, it's very, very low.

While Moffy contemplates this, I shout, "Luna!"

Spider-Man mask now off, Luna waves and trudges into the small kitchen, and Maximoff jumps on the counter by the toaster. Sitting up high so she has room to stand next to me. Her features are a mix of her mom and dad: soft round face, amber eyes, and long light-brown hair.

Luna slurs a little as she says, "If I die from this, please tell the world that I got into a fight with a space alien and the alien won."

Maximoff says certainly, "You're not dying, sis."

She takes a deep, relieved inhale, happy about being alive.

I hand her the cup with mouthwash and saline solution mix. "Swish and spit."

Luna swishes and winces, and she tries to say *dammit* with a mouthful of salt water. Saliva drips down her chin. I guide her to the sink.

"Spit."

She does, and bloody salt water hits the metal sink basin. "That stings so badly," she breathes, clutching the edge of the sink.

"It's happening again," I warn her. "Stick your tongue out."

Luna winces already. "Right now?" She wipes her forehead with her arm, her cheeks beet-red. I need to take her temperature.

Maximoff glares. "You plan on going somewhere, Luna? What else are we doing?"

"Jane promised a movie night, and we could always watch the movie, then come back." She shimmies her shoulders awkwardly. "Yeah?" She gives me a thumbs-up.

"Stick your tongue out," I say.

Luna frowns. "Moffy is supposed to be the hardass."

I roll my eyes. "I was a hardass first, and then he copied me."

Maximoff interjects, "Sounds like fan fiction."

"Man, I was born before your parents even officially started dating." I give him a look. "Five years older, ten times smarter."

He shoots me a middle finger.

I smile and focus on his sister. "Luna."

She reluctantly extends her tongue. Red streaks run from the silver ball to the tip of her tongue, a little swollen. At least she bought an actual barbell. I leave the jewelry in place to avoid an infection closing inside the wound.

Luna leans slightly over the sink, and I use the syringe to wash near the piercing, places that just swishing wouldn't reach. When I finish, she spits into the sink again.

"Done?" she asks.

"Not yet." I dunk a cotton ball in saline solution. "Hold this against your tongue." She looks ashen, and her forehead glistens with a sheen of sweat. While I stick an ear thermometer in her right ear, I go over shit that I know.

"No kissing or oral sex until the infection is clear."

She nods, but her brother cuts in, "Have you been kissed before?" No one said Maximoff Hale isn't just as blunt as me.

Luna says, "Uh-huh."

"What?" His jaw lowers. "By who?"

She takes the cotton ball out of her mouth. "Guy at school. You don't know him. He bought me a sandwich afterwards." She starts laughing at Maximoff's furrowed brows and hard confusion.

"You're totally fucking with me." He pauses. "Right?"

I can't tell what's real or fiction with Luna Hale anymore than he can.

Luna just laughs again, followed by a wince. She touches her mouth.

"Luna." His edged voice deepens, more serious. "Why'd you even choose your tongue? You could've pierced your ear—"

"I already have pierced ears." She rubs her arm across her sweaty forehead. "I just like how tongue piercings look, and I thought it'd be easy to do myself." She glances between us. "Anyway, I heard it doesn't do much for pleasure."

"It doesn't do a lot," Maximoff confirms, admitting to being sucked off by someone with a tongue piercing.

I look at him. "They have to be good at using the piercing for you to feel something."

He licks his lips. "Experience or are you just bullshitting?"

"My last ex-boyfriend had a tongue piercing." The thermometer beeps, filling a sudden dead silence. I take the thermometer out of her ear and read the temp: *101 Fahrenheit*. Shit.

"You have an ex?" Maximoff's voice is tight.

I raise my brows at him and reach for my phone in my pocket. "Four exes. Long gone." I scroll through my list of contacts.

Luna rests her elbows on the sink. "Moffy's never dated anyone." The world knows that he doesn't publicly date, but I wasn't sure if he'd found a way to date privately in the past.

"You've never dated anyone?" I ask, pausing on my phone.

"No."

I can't help but smile. "Your purity is showing." I return to my phone.

"Pretty sure I've had more sex than you."

Luna seems unsurprised that he's had sex at all, and since he trusts his family, I'm sure he's less guarded around them.

"That's something neither of us knows for sure, wolf scout." I find the contact in my phone. "And secondly, you don't win a prize for fucking around. Just like I don't win one for being in relationships. Thirdly, you're still *pure*."

He groans.

I almost smile again, but I need to call someone that I'm not thrilled to call. Before Maximoff asks, I explain what I'm doing. "Luna needs antibiotics. I can give her over-the-counter medication to combat the fever, but to get rid of the infection, she's going to need a prescription."

He eyes my phone and the contact screen that says *DAD*. His gaze lifts to mine. "You're a doctor. Can't you just prescribe the meds yourself?"

"I never did my year internship, so I'm not medically licensed." I may have an MD beside my name, but it's practically useless without finishing my internship and taking a board.

"Now you tell me."

I roll my eyes again. "I know everything that a doctor does, I just can't do shit without being sued."

Luna mumbles, "I'm gonna go lie down."

Maximoff concentrates on his sister. "Stay with Janie just in case you need anything."

Luna nods and puts the soaked cotton ball back on her tongue. Right when she leaves, Maximoff jumps to the floor and then takes my phone out of my hand.

"It'll be faster if I call your dad," he says.

It reminds me that everyone—the entire security team *and* all of the families—know that I'm on the worst terms with my father. He accepted every single tattoo, every piercing, every means of self-expression, but the day that I quit medicine, he looked right at me in front of these famous families, in front of the giant security team on a hot Labor Day vacation, and he said loudly and clearly, "You're a disappointment."

If I call him right now about medicine, there's a chance he may hang up on me.

I nod to Maximoff and let him talk to my father. I stay during the conversation, but it lasts maybe three minutes, prescription ordered, and he hands back my phone.

"You're in for the night?" I ask.

"Yeah."

"Okay." My ticket out of his townhouse has always been the information Price wanted. About the Camp-Away event. I feel like my time is up, and I have to board a train to an undesirable destination. I'd rather stay here, but duty calls. "I just need to know your plans for December's Charity Camp-Away."

Maximoff crosses his arms over his bare chest. "You can tell the security team that the plans are the same except for the entry process."

I shift my weight. "What do you mean?"

"There won't be hellishly expensive tickets to purchase in October. Instead, there'll be a raffle."

"A raffle," I repeat flatly.

"My team projected we'd earn fifty million with the Camp-Away with either entry process—and I recognize the higher security risk with a raffle—but I want to give people who can't afford the tickets an opportunity to experience the event." He explains, "So for every one dollar donated, a person enters their name to the raffle. One week before the event in December, we'll randomly pick the attendees out of the pool."

I cement in place. "Basically, you're opening your three-day camping trip to anyone who has a dollar." *The public.* I raise a hand, my pulse pounding against my throat. "How many attendees will be chosen through the raffle?"

"All of them. So three-hundred."

Three-hundred. Security is going to have to background check *three-hundred* people in seven days. And if anyone with mal-intent slips through the cracks, Maximoff will be put directly in harm's way.

10

FARROW KEENE

Sweat dripping down my temples, I jab a red punching bag and finish my combination with a right hook and hard left kick. 4:23 a.m.

Not even five hours after I radioed security about the raffle, Akara called a mandatory and "emergency" Omega meeting at the Studio 9 gym.

See, I recognize the danger of the raffle, but if I can't even convince Maximoff to let me drive his Audi, then I highly doubt *anyone* can convince him to alter a charity event that he's poured months and months of work and thought into.

And I warned Maximoff that the entire security team would overreact about his Camp-Away changes. He just said, "I'll speak to the Tri-Force and comply wherever necessary, but the raffle is staying."

Not many people ever volunteer to speak to all three lead bodyguards at once. Price Kepler of Alpha, Akara Kitsuwon of Omega, and the bane of my career, Thatcher Moretti of Epsilon, are all at the peak of the security hierarchy.

The Tri-Force.

My gaze travels to the closed door; the silver plaque reads: *office.*

Maximoff has been in there with the Tri-Force for fifteen minutes already. The three leads think they can "further illuminate" the risks to him, but Moffy contemplates too much. Whatever they have to tell him, he's definitely already considered.

In short, they're wasting their time.

I peel off my black boxing gloves, my chest rising and falling heavily. Three rows of red boxing bags line the right side of the gym, where I stand. The left houses the boxing ring, racks of weights, and other gym equipment.

There are only five bodyguards in Omega. We're all young compared to the other Forces, and that's by design. The Hales, Meadows, and Cobalts hired us on to last a couple decades in this career, not just a couple years. Being closer in age to our clients, it's more likely we'll stick around for the long-haul.

While we wait for Akara to leave the office, the four of us squeeze in a workout, but we all slow around the twenty-minute mark.

Oscar tugs off his blue gloves, his damp, curly brown hair hanging over a bandana. "You guys hear that Luna pierced an 'unmentionable' place?"

I'm used to news traveling fast within the security team. Bodyguards gossip like family, but we never leak info to the public. Not even accidentally. Everyone's too careful.

Quinn pauses his sit-ups on his punching bag. "What...like her...?" He gestures to his crotch.

I roll my eyes and unravel my black hand-wraps.

Donnelly tosses his towel over his shoulder. "Her clit? It's not a big bad word."

Oscar butts in, "Everyone lay off Quinn—alright, my little bro is young, impressionable, and still has his innocence and virtue; whereas the rest of us have lost our ever-loving minds."

Quinn chucks his green boxing glove at his older brother, ten years apart in age. "Bro, I can say *clit* every day easily. *Clit, clit, clit, clit—*"

"We get it," I say, dropping my hand-wraps on the mats.

Quinn scratches his unshaven jaw, sweat built on his golden-brown skin, and a tiny scar sits beneath his eye. Likewise, his nose is a little crooked from a short stint and bad blow in a pro-boxing circuit. Oscar has similar lasting marks. Security jokes that no matter how many punches Oscar and Quinn have taken as pro-boxers in the past, they'll always be handsome motherfuckers.

"I purposefully censored myself," Quinn clarifies. "I wasn't about to mention a teenage girl's...you know."

"Clit," Donnelly says.

"Jelly bean," Oscar adds.

"Magic button." Donnelly smirks.

Quinn shakes his head like we're all the fucked-up ones.

My brows spike. "You're the one who assumed 'clitoris piercing' at the word 'unmentionable'." I tilt my head at him. "And weren't you *like* a teenager *like* one year ago?"

Oscar and Donnelly laugh loudly, and Quinn gives me a faint death-glare. He needs to work on his "intimidation" a bit—he's very green: brand new to security detail, and at twenty, he's the youngest bodyguard in the whole team. If he screws up, that falls onto Omega's shoulders, but really, it'll weigh on mine.

Akara texts me every day:

if Quinn needs anything, help him

check in with Quinn

keep Quinn in the loop

When I left Alpha and joined Omega, Akara told me straight up, "Don't go rogue on me. I need you to help the new guy." Because I'm around Quinn as much as Maximoff hangs around Jane.

Which is literally every hour.

Inadvertently, it's made me Quinn's unofficial mentor, and I'd never call myself a teacher. I like to do shit on my own.

Oscar should fill this role, but the Oliveira brothers requested to be separated to avoid "family in-fighting". Probably because they almost stopped talking a few years ago when Oscar trained Quinn as a boxer.

No one ever talks about the old rift. I can barely tell it existed.

Quinn grabs his nearby water bottle. "What'd Luna really pierce then?"

"I think belly button," Oscar says.

Donnelly hangs onto his punching bag, a colorful tattoo sleeve covering his fair skin. He's a chestnut haired, blue-eyed shameless twenty-six-year-old from South Philly. "Real or rumor, Farrow?"

"Why would you know?" Quinn asks me like I've withheld information from him. Technically, I did.

"Because I'm closer to the Hales than all of you combined." They're each a 24/7 bodyguard to a Cobalt, and at the end of the day, we're all partisan to the families we protect. The Hales, Cobalts, and Meadows love one another to the very death, and they'd prefer that we love all three equally too.

But spending day-in, day-out with one specific family, we grow attached.

Oscar reties his bandana. "You'll see, little bro. Soon you'll be taking European vacations with Jane and the rest of the Cobalt Empire—while Farrow, here, will be stuck at comic book conventions with the geek squad."

I smile. "You mean you'll be *trapped* on a private jet with seven Cobalts, their mom and dad, and fast-paced banter that'll give you a permanent migraine thirty-thousand feet in the air."

Donnelly points his water bottle at me. "Pokin' at our lion's den, Farrow, you're gonna get bit."

My lips stretch wider, my allegiances always clear. The Hales are known for being welcoming to oddballs and black sheep, very fandom-loving, and all-around laidback and cool. The first day I guarded Lily, she asked me, *"What house are you in?"*

She meant a *Harry Potter* house. When I told her I'd never read the books, she bought all seven for me and post-noted her favorite parts.

The Hales are a bunch of dorks. For me, they're instantly lovable.

But I respect the other two families, too. The Cobalt Empire is the largest, known for their regal poise, intellectual prowess, and fierce commitment to one another. Each Cobalt is prideful and passionately unique, but when push comes to shove, they'll band together like an army of one.

Quinn asks us, "Where do the Meadows go for family trips?"

"Costa Rica," we all say together.

Quinn chucks his other glove down the aisle of bags. "Akara is one lucky bastard."

Bodyguards *vie* to protect the two Meadows girls. The family of four is wild, adventurous, and they spend more than half the year outdoors. Since Akara protects Sullivan Meadows, the oldest daughter, he's backpacked around South America, swam with sharks in the Keys, and last summer, he was backstage when she won four Olympic golds for swimming.

Donnelly nods to me. "Real or rumor? You thought I forgot you didn't answer?"

"Rumor," I tell him easily, having nothing to hide. The truth is better than letting security make far-fetched assumptions. So I add, "She pierced her *tongue* herself."

Oscar rests an elbow on his bag, not at all caught off guard. His features say, *I've seen everything; I'm unshakable.* "Epsilon shouldn't nark on the kids," he says. "If she trusted her bodyguard, he could've taken her to a piercing shop without her parents knowing."

"That's allowed?" Quinn asks, but no one answers that loaded question. Is it allowed? Not really, but the best bodyguards go to the grave for their clients.

I will.

I turn to Oscar. "Luna's eighteenth birthday is in three months. If she wanted, she could've waited until November to get a professional to pierce her tongue."

Oscar cocks his head. "So piercing herself has nothing to do with secrecy?" He raises his arms. "Then *why?*"

"Because she wanted to." I notice the office's doorknob slightly rotating.

Donnelly lowers to the mats and sits against his bag. "I must've been about her age when I pierced my cartilage myself." He wags his fingers. "Four safety pins."

Oscar swigs his water. "Using yourself as an example, Donnelly, goes on the *cons* side automatically."

Donnelly blows him a middle-finger kiss.

Finally, the office door opens, and four men emerge. My gaze instantly hooks onto Maximoff. He stands stoically, assuredly, not shrinking among the Tri-Force's authoritative presence.

Damn.

The corners of my mouth begin to lift, but they lower at one irritating thought: I'm not leaving with Maximoff. Thatcher and Price said they'd escort Moffy to his townhouse. That way I could be a part of Omega's meeting.

I'd rather be the one to lead him out.

Maximoff says goodbye to Akara. As Price and Thatcher walk ahead of Moffy towards the gym's exit, he abnormally hangs back for a second. His forest-greens search the gym.

And then they land on me. *He was looking for me.*

My smile stretches, and my brows rise knowingly.

He licks his lips and eyes my damp hair and black shirt that suctions to my muscles. He calls out, "Already beat after a five minute workout?"

"Twenty minutes," I correct, "and never forget, I last longer than you."

Maximoff touches his heart mockingly and then shoots me a middle finger on his exit. The door thuds closed behind him.

Oscar rests his bodyweight on his bag, still staring at the exit. "Photos don't even do that guy justice."

I rub my bottom lip, my piercing cold beneath my thumb. I've known Oscar is bi since I met him at Yale. He was a science major, too, only his focus was on kinesiology. So we shared a couple of the same courses, and on Friday nights we went to gay bars together because 1.) Oscar is fun 2.) watching him hit on guys is amusing as shit; no one has simultaneously the best *and* worst pickup lines.

I read into his words. "You think Moffy's hot?"

"Everyone thinks Moffy's hot." Oscar rotates to me. "It'd be near impossible to find someone who says less than that. You see him. On a scale of one to ten, he's—"

"Out of your league," I say matter-of-factly. Trying not to appear territorial. My muscles contract, almost flexed, but Oscar can't tell.

"More like, he's way, way *off-limits*."

Maybe.

Akara approaches all four of us, standing well over six feet. "Hey, everyone take a seat."

Oscar and I lower to the mats where Donnelly and Quinn already sit. As soon as we're on the ground, Oscar sticks his hand into a Doritos bag.

Shit, with Oliveira, he could've packed the whole snack aisle in his gym bag. The guy is always hungry.

"First things first, if you plan to recommend your gym buddies as security detail, *ask* where they're from. It's not that hard. Like this, *hey, Donnelly*."

"Hey, boss."

"Where were you born and raised?"

"South Philly." He pats his chest. *South* sounds like *sow-philly* out of his mouth.

Akara gestures to the Oliveira brothers. "Oscar and Quinn, where were you born and raised?"

"Northeast Philly," they say with deep pride.

Akara nods to me.

"Northwest Philly, two streets over from you." We grew up in an affluent neighborhood and attended the same high school. Really, we were acquaintances. We became friends when Akara opened this gym, and I was one of the first to walk through the door.

"See, easy," Akara says right at Oscar, calling him out. Tri-Force only hires new bodyguards who were born in Philly. They want people on the team who can navigate the city blindfolded.

Oscar raises a hand. "I thought Reynolds was from here. He had that annoying South Philly lilt, sounded like Donnelly trying to order breakfast at Lucky's Diner—kept saying *beggles* and *wooder*."

We all laugh.

Most everyone has a mild to no dialect, but the South Philly guys carry a much thicker Philly accent.

"Again," Akara smiles, "just *ask* where they're from. Saves me time." He finally takes a seat on the mats and closes the circle. Looking around to each of us, his lips fall in a serious line. "You're going to hate what I have to say about the charity event, but you get a grand total of five fucking minutes to complain. Then you're done. I don't want to hear anyone whining over the comms for the next three months. Don't be that guy."

Quinn nods repeatedly. *Akara should've been his mentor.*

I hang my arm casually on my knee. "Too bad Oscar's already that guy."

"Get back to me when you've been assigned to Charlie Cobalt. You'd start bitching if your client chose to experiment with hallucinogenics at a metal concert, and not even a day later, he takes an eighteen-hour flight to volunteer for the Red Cross on another *continent.* I've never even seen him tired or even yawn."

"I'm sure he's grown tired of you, Oliveira," I say.

Everyone laughs again.

Quinn nods to his older brother. "You shouldn't bitch about your client to Jo. All yesterday, she said *I can protect Charlie better than Oscar.*"

Oscar sighs in annoyance. Their younger sister Joana isn't a part of security, and I've only met her once or twice around the gym. She just started boxing professionally this year, and the Oliveira brothers don't want her to quit.

For as much as Oscar complains, there's no one that could do his job. Many have tried. He's tactically strategic, and the perfect fit for Charlie Cobalt. It's why he's been on his detail for three years and counting.

Akara snaps his fingers to his palm. "You all ready for the news?"

Donnelly nods. "Lay it on us."

Akara starts, "Moffy was really clear that he's not allowing any of his siblings or cousins under eighteen to attend."

"Epsilon is out," Oscar says since SFE protects the young kids.

Akara shakes his head and pushes back his black hair. "Most of them will be at the event for extra security."

I stretch out my legs and bare feet, my muscles cramped. We've never needed extra security for the Camp-Away, and that fact hoists dead silence in the air.

"We asked Moffy for more than seven days to background check the attendees. Which means that he'd have to close the raffle more than a week before the event," Akara mentions the largest point of contention for security. "Moffy agreed to give us more time, but he printed out twelve pages of stats that Jane had calculated."

I shake my head, my smiling forming. *Wolf scout.* I know what he did before Akara explains the rest.

"He predicted the profit loss for every extra week that we'd hypothetically close the raffle early. If we were to take fourteen days to background check the attendees, the event would lose about ten million."

That's not a little sum of money.

"Their lives are priceless," Donnelly says. "Did you tell them that?"

"I did," Akara says to all of us, "but you know Moffy."

"He's stubborn," Oscar says.

"Selfless," I add. "H.M.C. Philanthropies helps people."

Quinn's brows knit together. "Don't the families just contribute their wealth to the foundation? Raising more money is chump change in comparison. He could even cancel the event and it'd be fine—"

"No," the rest of us say in unison.

Akara leans towards Quinn. "All of the H.M.C. money is allocated to four areas: education, environment, LGBTQ issues, and mental health. Within those categories, Moffy built specific programs and initiatives, and not every one is given the same sum. Some programs rely completely on these events."

"Like the Camp-Away," I chime in. "All of the earnings go to One More Day." Everyone knows the program Maximoff created. One More Day provides aid to low-income individuals in need of addiction rehab.

Oscar swishes his water. "Do we really want to deny people-in-need ten million? Just to have an extra week to weed out the hecklers, glitter-and-flour-bombers—possible murderers and rapists?"

Donnelly wants the extra week to ensure everyone's safety, but I'm ready to tackle "murderers" and "rapists" every day, every hour.

"Tri-Force already made a decision," Akara says, "and we agreed to Moffy's terms. Seven days for a background check."

Donnelly groans.

Oscar curses.

Quinn falls into deep contemplation.

I'm smiling.

Akara leans back on his hands. "It's not the end of the fucking world. Any threats that get into the event, we'll detect and isolate there. The Hales, Cobalts, and Meadows trust us for a reason. We make few mistakes, and we never fail."

Before they talked to Maximoff, the Tri-Force was *adamant* about changing the raffle. Now they're gleefully content with his plans.

The guy has a way with people. I'm so impressed, my cock actually pulses.

11

Declan left his replacement—which turned

out to be *me*—a short note. I hadn't thought hard about Declan's words, his *warning*, until the end of September. Until today.

Until Maximoff invited his three siblings and five of his cousins to mini-golf. Until everyone except Jane cancelled when they saw social media: paparazzi and crowds amassed, jumping onto the putt-putt green, like they caught sight of rock stars or English dignitary.

And then Maximoff firmly and concisely said, "We need to leave."

We'd only been there for a half hour, and he'd spent the prior *three* hours coordinating the mini-golf outing for his family.

Being forced to drop set-plans that quickly would piss off most people.

Maximoff just pivoted and created a new one in seconds. He signed the golf balls and putters for the mini-golf facility to sell, and then he spent the next hour taking selfies with fans and Jane. I spent that time detaching overwhelmed, sobbing girls and guys off his waist.

When we finally climbed into his Audi, I expected Maximoff to sigh in exhaustion. Maybe express frustration. His mom would've been tired, a little upset.

Instead, he seemed just as prepared for anything, and he said, "Let's find a pub. Jane will meet us."

Declan should've written: *Maximoff Hale will barrel through every circle of hell and come out unscathed.*

He actually wrote: *everything in Moffy's life is short-lived.*

9:12 p.m. we shake off paparazzi and discover a hole-in-the-wall Irish pub around South Philly. After I ensure the place is safe, we order our food and drinks at the bar. They say they'll bring it to us shortly.

We claim a low wooden table in the very back. Cigarette smoke clouds the cramped, dimly lit area, and a soccer game airs on the only TV. Engrossing several old bearded men at a high-top table, plus the bartender.

I lean back on two legs of my chair and casually examine our surroundings, but I find myself looking at him.

Maximoff reads a text. "Jane and Quinn are still fifteen minutes away."

I open my mouth to reply, but a voice infiltrates my right ear. "Omega to Farrow." I drop on all four legs of my chair and press my mic. "Farrow." My eyes lift to Maximoff who watches intently. Like he's never even overheard his old bodyguard speak to security before.

Maybe he hasn't.

I'm not about to excuse myself from the table to speak to Akara. I don't care if Moffy listens to a conversation that's *about* him.

In fact—I pop my earpiece out, hang the cord over my shoulder, and then I swivel the volume knob on my radio. Increasing the sound.

His brows furrow, confused.

My smile stretches. *Just wait, wolf scout.*

Akara's voice crackles over the earpiece speaker, audible to me and Maximoff. "I need to know if Moffy plans to go to a drugstore or grocery within the next week. We'll have to put extra security on him." With the Camp-Away approaching and its annual popularity, he's been in entertainment news almost nightly.

"And?" I ask Maximoff. He knows that Akara can't hear me unless I touch the microphone.

He leans forward, forearms on the table. "Tell him *no.*"

I click the mic. "No, not anytime soon."

Akara says, "Thanks." The line goes quiet after that.

Taking a deep breath, Moffy straightens up, and neither of us unfastens our strong gazes.

"Did you like that?" I ask, my lips lifting.

"So badly it hurts," he says dryly, but a real smile crests his mouth. "Would you be willing to do that for me all the time?"

"Would you want me to?"

I love giving him things that no one else can. For a guy who has the world at his fingertips, you'd think there's nothing left to offer Maximoff. But he's been denied some simple pleasures and human rights.

Like the ability to drive safely down a fucking highway.

Maximoff cracks his knuckles. "Actually, no. Security will kill you."

"Now you care if I die? What happened to shoving me out of the car and backing up over my body?"

"Give me five minutes," Maximoff says, "we'll be back to your death."

I roll my eyes into a wider smile, and my tattooed fingers rotate a saltshaker like it's a coin. I catch Maximoff staring at my fingers for two long beats. *He's in love with my fingers.* I try to seize his gaze.

He purposefully glances behind me.

I follow his attention to the bar, and I run my tongue over my molars, my smile slowing hardening. A guy about my age sits on a tattered leather stool, dressed in a black beanie and graphic T-shirt.

My jaw muscle twitches. I look between them, and the guy gives Maximoff a suggestive *I-want-your-ass* once-over.

Maximoff begins to smile back.

I can't tell if he's just being nice or if there's real interest. My narrowed gaze pings from him to the guy, my muscles burning the longer they scrutinize one another.

I shouldn't care.

I set my elbow to the table and put my hand to my mouth. I spin a saltshaker with my free fingers while a million replies grind at me.

He's not good enough for you.

You could do better.

You really like that dickhole?

You're here with me.

Don't flirt with him.

Don't fuck him.

The saltshaker falls on its side.

Moffy glances at me while I upright the salt.

Jealousy. I'm jealous of a nameless, beanie-wearing dickhole on a barstool. My ex-boyfriends would laugh at me for caring this much about a twenty-two-year-old celebrity.

I unwrap a piece of gum, and as soon as I peel the foil, Maximoff asks, "What's your favorite color?"

The corners of my mouth curve upward. "My favorite color?" I repeat like he asked me a kindergarten question. Which he did. But I keep thinking, *he's not interested in that other guy anymore.*

He's more interested in me.

Maximoff crosses his arms. "What kind of high school names someone *valedictorian* when they can't even answer their favorite color?"

I lean forward and whisper lowly, "Says someone who doesn't know what it's like to be valedictorian."

"Just admit it," he says, "you don't have a favorite color. It's sad."

"It's silver," I retort.

He nods a couple times, his own smile appearing, and just as he goes to speak, the waitress brings out two Fizz Lifes, a plate of loaded potato skins, and basket of French fries.

He stares off for a long second, lost in his head.

I wad a straw's paper and toss the tiny ball at his face. It hits him square in the forehead, and he wakes up to glare at me.

He asks, "Do you know mine?" *His favorite color.*

"Orange."

"You actually Google-searched me," he says it like he caught me jacking off.

I almost laugh. "Man, you have a *mom* who buys orange plastic silverware and plates for any Maximoff-Hale-related event." I count off my fingers, starting with my thumb. "Which includes your sixteenth birthday party, your prep school graduation—"

"Alright." He cringes. "You knew me when I was sixteen. I get it. The world gets it—"

"The world doesn't care that I was at your sixteenth birthday."

He flips me off with one hand and grabs a potato skin with his other. He gestures at me with the potato skin. "Eat. Stop staring at me."

"Not until you admit that I know you better than a Google search."

Maximoff pauses eating, just to quiz me, "Why don't I date anyone, Farrow?" That's not a fact available on the web, and it's also something he's kept private from me.

"You're not into relationships," I guess.

"Not because I wouldn't want to be. I just can't."

I shake my head. "I don't follow."

"I'll never be in a relationship," he tells me flat-out. "I'll *never* experience any kind of romance beyond a one-time hookup. Because once I date someone in public, media will hound them to the point of intrusion, vulnerability—I won't ever subject someone to an extreme loss of privacy that they'll never get back. I've accepted that this is my life, and I'm satisfied with that."

My brows ratchet up. "You're *not* satisfied. You're just resigned." Before he protests, I ask, "Have you ever wondered what it's like to hold someone's hand romantically? To see them in your bed two nights in a row? Cook breakfast the next day, share clothes, wake them up before work? You've never imagined that?"

Maximoff shakes his head once. "I can't."

"*That's* sad." Because he wants to desire those things, but he's not even allowing himself that.

And no one else among the Hales, Cobalts, or Meadows would sacrifice the possibility of a relationship just to protect their significant other from the media.

Only him.

"What about dating privately?" I ask.

"No. If I can find someone to trust for longer than one night, they'd be all over the news every time I was spotted with them. Especially if I let them meet my siblings."

I'm the exception to that. Our eyes meet, and that fact passes between us. He clears his throat and reaches for his Fizz Life, the world's most popular diet soda.

"Give it here." I gesture for the glass. He has a rule about ordering drinks. #45: *sip all my drinks first. I don't trust bartenders.*

He slides over his Fizz Life and takes a moment to eat another potato skin.

I swig his drink. *No alcohol.* "It's good." I slide the Fizz Life back.

Maximoff Hale doesn't drink alcohol. He never has. It's public knowledge that alcoholism runs in his family, and he chose to be sober. Bartenders sometimes purposefully spike his drink. Hell, some people *pay* the bartender to do it.

Just to see a celebrity break sobriety.

Maximoff washes down his food with Fizz Life. Then he motions to me. "What's your favorite childhood memory?"

I smile and eat a fry. "What's with the twenty questions?"

"You can Google me. I can't Google you." He wants to be on equal footing.

Okay. I swig my own drink. "My favorite childhood memory is the only memory I have of my mother." He's aware that she died from breast cancer when I was four.

Maximoff holds my gaze strongly.

"I can't distinguish her features, but I can hear her silky voice as she says my name. That's all, just my name."

Farrow.

She named me. And she could've picked Edward Nathaniel Keene after my father, my grandfather, my great-grandfather, all the men in a long legacy before me, but she chose differently. Apparently she loved the old film version of *The Great Gatsby*, and she named me after the two lead actors.

Mia Farrow.

Robert Redford.

And I'm a Keene.

I recognize how special and unique Maximoff's name is too. His parents also named him after something they love, and it's why neither of us ever use our names in banter—and why I'm trying to honor whatever the hell he wants me to call him.

He nods a couple times, appreciative that I told him that story.

I dunk a fry in mustard. "Anything else?"

"If I asked about medical school, you'd tell me...?"

"That you have to be more specific." I pop a fry in my mouth.

"For someone who completed all four years, you have to like medicine at least a little bit, right?"

"There are people who suffered through med school, but I wasn't one of them." I slide the mustard aside and grab the glass ketchup bottle. "I enjoyed medicine, just not like my family."

"What do you mean?" He uses a straw to push the ice in his soda.

I unscrew the bottle. "It's not just about medicine for them. My father, my grandfather, great-grandfather, great-*great* grandfather all share the same name and the same profession." I pour ketchup in the French fry basket. "There's status and pride in continuing this legacy and obtaining the MD. And I really couldn't care less about honoring a generational tradition."

"Why not just be a doctor for you and say *fuck them*?"

"That's why I finished medical school." I wipe my hands on a napkin. "I genuinely wanted to help people. But every day I thought about how I was another Keene falling obediently in line, and I just couldn't breathe. I remember doing rounds in med school and feeling wrong. Like out-of-body." I rake my fingers through my hair. "Like I was experiencing someone else's life that wasn't supposed to be mine."

Maximoff nods. He's a good listener; he always looks interested in what people have to say. At least when he's not staring off into space.

"There's a possibility," I tell him, "that I only liked medicine because it's all I knew; it's what I was conditioned to do. And I can honestly say it's the only thing that's ever terrified me."

He thinks for a second before asking, "So how'd you decide that security detail was the right fit?"

"I'd been taking MMA classes for years at Studio 9. Akara suggested I try security training. I liked it."

Maximoff is quiet for an even longer moment.

"You can say it. I'm not easily offended."

He leans forward some. "So you like the fame without being famous: the fine-dining, the yacht trips—"

"Me?" I give him a look. "I was born to an aristocratic lineage of pretentious *assholes*; I didn't need to guard a celebrity to get a five-star meal."

He begins to smile. "Then why do you like it? What'd you tell me yesterday about security work?"

"This profession is notorious for inducing three things."

Maximoff nods, remembering what I said. "Sobriety, celibacy, and sleeplessness." He gestures to my chest. "Why put up with the weird hours, isolation, inconsistent days and sleepless nights?"

"For your life," I say. "I'm here to protect you, and I love being put in high-stress situations and coming out on top. Wearing a white coat isn't the only way to impact a life. My father never understood that."

He's speechless.

Maximoff keeps swallowing, and he turns his head, a smile forming.

"You're grinning," I point out.

"Shut up," he says flatly and then rubs his jaw, looking right at me. "We're so different."

"I know." He has enough siblings and cousins to create their own flag football team. I have one older stepsister who lives halfway across the country. I see her maybe once every three years. If that. And it's something deeper.

It's how his family is a life force that keeps him breathing and waking up in the morning. Mine was suffocating me. I made a career decision at the cost of hurting my father.

Maximoff would probably sooner fall to his death than betray his.

Where I go rogue, he stays loyal.

I recall a brief conversation we had a few days ago. He told me that he didn't go through with a Batman tattoo because it'd kill his dad. Everyone knows that Loren Hale is a diehard Marvel fanboy, and Maximoff *cares* about hurting him.

Over a tattoo.

"I don't know how you can care so emphatically about your parents," I tell him.

Maximoff outstretches his arm. "They've given me everything. I don't feel *indebted* to them, but I feel like it's my duty to pay it forward somehow. Some damn way."

I lean back on my chair legs again. "Like taking over your family's companies?" Fizzle, Hale Co., Cobalt Inc. are multi-billion dollar family businesses that their parents inherited. Then they created their own conglomerations: Calloway Couture, Halway Comics, Superheroes & Scones, Cobalt Diamonds, Camp Calloway—the list goes on and on.

The Hale-related businesses could one day be passed down to Maximoff, and that'd be his life.

"If I could take over Hale Co., I would in a heartbeat," he says, "but my dad, for whatever reason, says *no* on a daily basis."

Good.

Loren Hale is keeping Moffy twenty-two and not aging him to fifty, and since Maximoff collects responsibility like it's his favorite toy, I doubt he'd recognize that.

Maximoff sits up straighter, and I hone in on his confident demeanor that hoists his body like he's ready to go. For a run, a fight, a competition, mind-blowing sex—*anything*. It's not manufactured resolve or tenacity; it's palpable.

24/7.

I lower my chair legs and shift forward. Shit.

I'm ensnared without a fucking trap even being set.

"So let's rewind," he says. "Say that you hypothetically finished your year internship and started your residency, where would you've wanted to end up? Surgery or—"

"Emergency medicine." I fiddle with the saltshaker again. "But I didn't have a choice."

His brows knot. "What do you mean?"

I frown. "You really don't know?" By his sheer confusion, I realize that he never figured it out. I edge forward, arms on the table. "Maximoff...I was going to become your concierge doctor."

12

MAXIMOFF HALE

I stiffen, my face padlocked of emotion. Except for my sharpened cheekbones. My first thought: *avoiding Farrow was always going to be unavoidable. In every alternate universe, I'm stuck with him.*

My second thought makes me cringe.

"What?" Farrow asks, his fingers absentmindedly nudging his silver rings. He notices how I'm eyeing his hands. His know-it-all smile fucking kills me, and I swear he's one second from saying, *do you like that?*

And I think, *too damn much.*

I'm not sharing the intimate details of my second thought. How his *father* checked up on me when I was eleven and had a rash on my dick. From chlorine irritation. Imagine if that Dr. Keene had actually been *Farrow*—cringe with me.

I gesture to him. "I had a mild stroke at the thought of you being my doctor." I feign surprise. "If only you were my doctor, you could actually save me right now." My mouth falls. "What an idea."

"You wouldn't be talking if you had a stroke."

I wear my irritation, and he laughs on cue, *loving* to pop whatever humor I cast into the world. It shouldn't turn me on, but most people just placate me. Farrow does the opposite.

When his laughter fades, he stares at me with a peeking smile.

I bite into an ice cube, my stomach tossing in a weird way. Almost *excited.* "What?" I ask now.

"You want me to save you?" His brows rise with his barbells.

"I'd rather die," I say instinctively.

"Maximoff." He stretches closer to me. Over the table, and his voice drops to the deep, rough octave that strokes my cock. "As your body-guard, I can't let that happen."

My gaze latches intensely onto his. And his brown eyes plaster onto my green. So strongly that I'm drop-dead positive we're forcing ourselves not to look lower. Not to our lips, not to our bodies. Not to any forbidden place that'd cause disaster.

I try to master restraint, but my eyes say what my mouth can't.

Kiss me.

He reads them.

I know he reads them, and our chests collapse and rise in heavy unison. *Jesus Christ.*

I can't.

We can't.

But I think, *fucking kiss me.*

Just do it.

Farrow moves his hand. To put his earpiece back in, and then he sits his ass down. "They're coming inside, behind you."

I turn my stiff neck, and sure enough, Janie walks through the entrance with Quinn out in front. Headed towards the table. She wears a pastel purple tulle skirt and a striped top that put her on *Celebrity Crush's* Worst Dressed list this morning. She didn't care.

I blink once, and they've already reached us. Jane collapses on the chair beside me, and I wrap my arm around the back of hers. I push beyond whatever the hell just happened with Farrow. I have no other choice but to move forward.

Janie very subtly glances between Farrow and me, but thankfully says nothing about any lingering tension. "Dis-moi qu'ils ont du café," she whispers, hands in prayer formation. *Please tell me they have coffee.*

"Je ne sais pas." *I don't know.*

Quinn takes a seat beside Farrow and says, "Another reminder that I really need to read that French textbook Akara gave me."

Jane's eyes glimmer with curiosity and she places her chin on her fist, elbow to the table. "And how is that going?"

"Bien." *Good.* Quinn shrugs. "It'd be easier if you two just switched to Portuguese."

I'd tell Quinn that we don't know Portuguese like him, but I'm superglued to the fact that he's actually learning French. I look at Farrow. "Did Akara give you a French textbook, too?"

"No. Because he knew it'd go straight into the dumpster."

"I'm glad we've found the location of your apathy," I tell him.

Farrow laughs. He tosses a fry in the basket and then eyes me, mostly. My neck is on fire, and I keep rubbing my jaw.

Quinn scans the table for food. His stomach audibly grumbles. I slide the basket of fries away from Farrow and to Quinn. Farrow makes a face at me. Like I just passed his cellphone off to a stranger.

"Do you not know what sharing looks like?" I ask.

Farrow slides the fries back between me and him. "Quinn needs to learn how to order his own food."

Quinn doesn't let Farrow bother him. "Where's the waitress?" he asks.

"Yes, please, *coffee coffee,*" Jane says. "One sugar, dollop of cream, and strapped to an IV."

"You have to order at the bar," I tell her.

"Merde." Her head slumps on my shoulder. She's exhausted from today's putt-putt debacle.

"I'll go for you." Just as I'm about to stand, Quinn and Farrow motion for me to stay seated.

"I can go alone," Quinn tells Farrow while I sit back down. "She's my client."

"Akara would want you to stay with her," Farrow says.

Quinn considers this for half a second, and then we all look over at the six-foot bearded bartender who approaches. He stops and towers over the table. Nearer Janie than to me. He fingers his gnarled beard and appraises the length of her body.

Hovering on her chest.

I'm on edge. Anyone who appraises us like we're cattle—I don't trust. From experience, they'd rather hurt my family than make cute small talk.

Likewise, Quinn's guard seems to rise tenfold. He angles his body towards Jane. Sitting straighter. More menacing. Like a boxer about to face off an opponent. If I didn't know, it'd be hard to tell that he's new to the team.

"Hi," Jane starts, but the bartender cuts her off with, "You're Jane Cobalt."

"Yes." Janie's voice is stiffer than usual. "You wouldn't happen to have coffee—?"

"Your mom is hotter."

I glower. "What the fuck did you just say?" I see blood red, and I'm already halfway out of my seat. Our bodyguards are right behind me. Where Farrow has an *at ease* demeanor, as if this is just another normal day, Quinn's eyes widen and darken. Horrified.

Pissed.

He probably hasn't gotten used to hearing the vitriol people sling at Janie.

I wish it was something you didn't have to get used to.

The bartender doesn't balk. "I said *Rose Calloway* is a hotter piece of ass than that chubby bitch."

I charge forward, venom in the back of my throat, but chairs clatter, more than just me shooting up completely from their seats. I instinctively stand in front of Janie. In my peripheral, I notice her hand gripping her watermelon purse.

Where pepper spray and a pink switchblade lie.

I may've cut off Jane, but Farrow cuts off my path, his hand on my chest. He says something to me that I don't hear. I stare past him, hawkeyed on the bartender who watches Jane's reaction.

"Fuck you," I sneer, trying to steal his attention away from Jane.

The bartender laughs at me and then says to her. "You can't cry if it's the truth."

Jane isn't crying. She sighs into an angry growl and tries to ignore him. "I ask for coffee, and instead receive an unsolicited opinion on my *looks*. Disastrously unequal and a complete nightmare—Moffy." Fear spikes her voice, grabbing my wrist when I try to step towards the bartender.

Farrow and Quinn break our hands as they shift around us. The bartender opens his mouth to speak again, and I hear the beginnings of the word *slut* and Quinn growls, "Fuck off."

Farrow raises a hand to him, and I hear him hiss, "Cool down. Just focus on getting her out of here."

Quinn's nose flares and he nods. Quickly, Quinn begins to lead my cousin safely out of the pub. I hear Jane protesting and shouting, "I leave no one behind!"

Farrow rests a strong hand on my shoulder. Trying to steer me towards the exit.

With one move, I tear out of his hold. I'm seething from the inside out. My skin is crawling. Our eyes meet for a heated second. Both of us are headstrong. And I'm not *moving* on his accord.

Farrow warns beneath his breath, "Don't jump out in front of me." He rotates, protectively shielding me from the bartender. Using his body as a barrier between me and that bastard.

Bodyguards are required to deescalate aggressive situations. Calm them. Stop them.

Not fuel or even win fights.

In case you aren't already aware: I make that difficult.

I should leave right now. I should forget the bartender's crude gaze. And malicious intent. *I should.* And Janie won't leave until I do. Even if Quinn drags her out, she'll dig her feet into hardwood or pavement and claw herself towards me.

I want her somewhere safe. Far away from here.

So I open my wallet and toss money on the table. Unable to leave without paying. Even if I'm paying a fucking douchebag.

"And you're Maximoff Hale," the bartender says. *Don't engage,* my parents always tells me. *Ignore the hecklers,* they say. *They're trying to incite you,* they remind me.

They want to fight you.

No shit.

I can handle overwhelmed, overzealous fans. I can handle competitive paparazzi. I can handle the tears and the autographs and the selfies. I can even handle tonight. The fucked-up part of fame.

The sick hatred. Chipping bit by bit at our humanity.

You want to know what the few other people in the pub are doing? They're *filming.* With their cellphones. Like I'm the star of a fucked-up drama. And the title is This Is My Life.

Welcome. Take a seat.

I put my wallet in my jean's pocket.

"How does it feel," the bartender starts up again, "knowing a thousand-plus dicks have been inside your mom? She must've been stretched out when she had you. Bet you just fell out of her vagina." He laughs right at my face.

I have tunnel vision. I see red. I see the bartender.

I see how devastated my mom would be if she heard someone say this shit to me. She'd cry herself to sleep—and you know what that does to me? It makes me want to fucking scream and throw my knuckles at a face. And by *a* face, I mean *his fucking face.*

I charge.

Farrow restrains me, gripping my fist in his palm, and forcing my hand to my side. He walks me backwards. "Look at me, Maximoff."

I'm glaring beyond Farrow. At the bartender.

His lips are against my ear. "He's not worth your attention."

I've said all those words before: *be the bigger person. Walk away. You're feeding into their bullshit. Violence solves nothing. You're the CEO of a nonprofit. Stop.*

Stop.

Breathe.

Leave.

I let about fifteen feet divide me and the bartender. Backing up. Backing away, all the while he's talking shit. "What about your sister," he laughs mockingly. "Luna Hale—another wet slut. Bet she puts out twice as much as your mom. Is she a little sex addict too?"

I taste acid on my tongue, but words burn the back of my throat. Dying inside of me.

And Farrow can't provoke the bartender. If these insults eat at him, he can't show me either. I'm in a thundering boat of *one*.

Trying to steer myself towards the door. I almost get there.

And then he says, "I hope she locks her doors at night."

I go rigid.

Motionless and still faced towards him. "What'd you say?"

He laughs. "I hope she keeps her doors locked. You know how many men would break through just to taste her—"

I lose it. Tearing out of Farrow's hold, I take a few lengthy strides. And I swing. The *instant* my knuckles crack the bridge of his nose, Farrow cuts off my path and then he thrusts back three men who spring up from the barstools.

Blood gushes out of the man's nostrils, and he shouts the word, *sue*.

"Go ahead and fucking sue me." I turn around with rage in my eyes, leaving the mess I burst behind. I forget that Farrow isn't Declan. My old bodyguard would've stayed to cool down the pub. Instead, Farrow sprints and reaches my side.

Step-for-step with me, and I glance at him. His hard gaze holds a raw understanding that says *you're not alone*. And as we face forward, his hand falls to my wrist, then my palm—he's holding my hand for a strong but brief moment.

No one has ever held my hand like that.

He lets go, and we both push through the pub doors. Walking side-by-side towards my Audi parked on the city street. Philly lit up at night.

Paparazzi are here.

I glance at my phone that says:

I saw you leave. I'm in the car, driving home. I'm safe. Text me as soon as you are. — Janie

I text quickly: I'm on my way home.

While I find my keys in my pocket, three cameramen near with their lenses. Asking the same question, "Why are your knuckles bloody?!"

"Did you get in a fight, Maximoff?!"

Farrow pushes a camera aside. "Get out of his face."

"Sorry," the paparazzi apologizes, pretty sincere. He takes more than a few steps backwards.

Silent, I unlock my car, and I climb into the driver's seat.

Farrow is in the passenger, doors locked, and I drive out onto the highway. Like it's just another day of my life.

I move forward.

I don't look back.

Flicking on my blinker, I switch to the left lane. Speeding ahead of trailing paparazzi that race after my car.

Farrow reaches across my body. I stiffen, my eyes flitting from him to the road. He seizes the silver buckle by my shoulder and pulls the strap over my chest. Clicking the belt in by my ass.

"You're not dying today," Farrow reminds me. "Let me see your hand."

I grip the wheel with both hands. Skin busted on a few of my knuckles. "I thought we've been through this. You're not my damn doctor; you're not my assistant. Not a caped crusader or a fortuneteller or my friendly neighborhood Spider-Man. You're just…"

Farrow.

I swallow a lump in my throat and then I take a chance and look at him. He wears only the same understanding.

So I say, "It'd break my mom's heart to hear what he said. You know that?"

"I know." Farrow was around my mom for three years. *He knows.* "But it'd break her heart more to see her son get jumped by four men twice his age." I watch the road as he says, "You don't want anyone to help you, *but* you're willing to put your life at risk for—*fuck*." He pops his earpiece out completely and unclips his radio from his waistband.

Hunching forward, he tinkers with the comms.

By the tic of his jaw muscle, I can tell he bites hard on his teeth. "What's wrong?" I ask.

"My radio just died."

"Well you can't save everyone," I say, which makes him smile.

And he tilts his head towards me, pieces of his bleach-white hair falling in his eyes. "Still a precious smartass."

I nearly smile too, but both of our phones start incessantly buzzing. Family, for me. Security team, for him. It's going to be a long night of rehashing the same story over and over.

We both reach for our phones.

I'm ready for it.

13

For seven consecutive nights, Maximoff buries his time in charity work. I'd think it's penance for the pub fight, but he's drowning himself in work to avoid his old nightclub routine. Where he "finds someone to fuck". He's been delaying that since I became his bodyguard.

Except for tonight.

Tonight is the first night. I'm at a darkly lit nightclub. Lights blink and flash, music thudding the floor.

See, I'm a damned good bodyguard. The best of the best. But I'm teetering between doing my job and being a prick. Maximoff is going to ask me to vet whatever stranger he wants to fuck, and my first instinct is to lie.

To tell Maximoff that the stranger is a dipshit.

A liar.

A psychopath or murderer.

Whatever I need to say to terminate the subsequent events.

All night, I've been silently convincing myself not to go that route. Not to be a jealous prick. *Do your motherfucking job, Farrow.*

It's never been difficult. Not like this.

"Farrow, you can sit beside me," Maximoff says. "They're not going anywhere." He gestures to the three men in black suits that guard the VIP couch, their hands cupped and eyes alert.

I made a phone call to Tidal Wave, the two-story nightclub, before we arrived. I let the managers know Maximoff Hale would be dropping by and he'd need extra security.

It's been the easiest part of tonight. Seeing him entertain girls and guys with the sole purpose of getting laid—let's just say I've chewed my gum stale.

I focus on the task at hand. Tidal Wave has decent security, but even with the additional manpower, drunk men and women try to snap photos and hop the VIP ropes.

All eyes are on Maximoff.

That, I'm used to. He has an endless sea of people to choose from. Yet, he's now hiding out on the leather sofa and listening to the alt-rock band one story below.

Heavy bass booming, the metal floor thumps beneath my black boots. I stand above Maximoff, and I rest a hand on the couch by his shoulder.

Leaning closer to him, I say, "You trust *them* more than you trust me?" I motion with my head to the club's security. "Or does this position just really bother you? Me, standing. You, sitting."

He blinks slowly into wide, sarcastic eyes.

My smile stretches, and I laugh while I chew my stale gum. Easing back a little bit.

"You should've been a psychologist!" he shouts over the music. "That way you'd get a certificate or cash or something for psychoanalyzing me other than *this!*" He gives me two middle fingers.

I roll my eyes, my smile fucking killing me, and I decide to sit on the armrest next to him because he asked. Soft chatter echoes through my earpiece, but it's not for me.

I tune most out and scan the crowds that keenly fixate on Maximoff. Most people point at him from the neon-lit bar. Then I steal a glance at Moffy, our eyes catching. "Is this position better for you?!" I ask.

His lips pull upward, and a small smile overtakes his agitation. "When I asked you to sit beside me, I meant *next* to me!" He gestures with both hands to the available cushion.

Since I'm on the armrest, I'm sitting taller than him. Which pisses him off a little bit, but he gets handed things easily. I like making him work a little harder.

As the alt-rock song hits a crescendo, I shout, "I'm technically still next to you!"

"You love your technicalities!" Maximoff tosses his phone from hand-to-hand, his shoulders taut and eyes as alert as the club's security.

I watch other people fawn over him from afar. Taking photos, gushing with their friends, making *come hither* signals for him to join. I turn to him, wondering if he will.

Maximoff stays still, his dyed light brown hair thick and unruly.

I chew my gum, trying not to smile that much while I study him. He did an extreme close shave; his jaw smooth like cut, polished marble, and his scent is always chlorine and citrus.

Like summer.

He clicks into his phone, and his brows pinch in firm irritation.

I slide down onto the cushion beside him and spot the pink *Celebrity Crush* logo. Closer, I can speak without shouting. "I thought you don't actively check tabloids."

"That was before I *busted* my knuckles open and had thousands of people threatening to refund their dollar raffle entries." Now October, the raffle for the Camp-Away went live this week, and the publicity has been uncontrollable. I doubt a fistfight will seriously hurt the hype.

Because it's definitely not the first time he's been caught publicly in one. All to defend his family.

Sometimes the fights are even nastier. He gets hit. Things get broken. Someone ends up sued, either him or the bodyguard. The fact that we evaded all those scenarios makes it a success.

The security team critiqued the video footage from the pub, and the only criticism they could scramble together was Quinn's sudden outburst.

But I don't blame him. The first time I heard the shit people said about Lily Calloway—to her face—I almost blew it.

We're told all the time about the constant harassment these families receive, but until you meet it head-on, it doesn't seem real.

Glancing at the phone, I say, "You're trying to see how much damage the fight caused?"

He nods and scrolls through *Celebrity Crush.*

I take constant surveillance of his environment and him, splitting my attention between the two. "Even if you have several refunds, more people will enter the raffle." I try to steal his gaze. "You're overthinking."

"I always overthink. It keeps me..." Color just drains out of his face, eyes plastered to his phone.

My muscles bind. "Maximoff?" I lean into him, his shoulder taut and firm. Quickly, I skim the screen.

25 REASONS WHY
MAXIMOFF HALE IS LIKE RYKE MEADOWS!

He slowly scrolls down to the first bullet point, and I see words:

> Maximoff Hale fights with his fists first and talks later. Exactly like Ryke! Compare the most recent video of Maximoff losing his cool at a Philly pub with this old video of his Uncle Ryke Meadows outside a diner.

Maximoff plays the video of his uncle and increases the volume, barely audible in the club.

Ryke must be no older than twenty-five in the footage. Unshaven, tan from the sun, brooding, tabloids like to call him an aggressive jackass.

Ryke grabs his helmet off his black Ducati.

"How's that Calloway pussy, Ryke Meadows?!" A preppy-dressed man snickers, jumping up on the curb near Ryke.

"Go fuck yourself," he growls, hardened to stone and white-knuckling his helmet. He cements to that one spot, zeroed in on the man like a predator to prey. The look in Ryke's eyes *feels* the same as the look that was in Moffy's.

The man snickers. "If you don't tell me how Calloway pussy tastes, then I'll just find out myself. Starting with the youngest one—"

Ryke lunges and swings—

Maximoff abruptly clicks off his phone. The screen blinks to black. Taking a huge breath, he asks me, "Did that video remind you of me?" He stares me dead in the eye. Building defenses against my upcoming response.

I want to be transparent with him. No hoarding secrets, no doling out lies, but this truth will hurt him a little. I suck in a breath through my teeth. Pinching my fingers, I say, "Seventy-five percent."

Maximoff digests this silently and then he eyes my fingers, obsessed with my hands for some precious reason. "Your seventy-five percent looks a hell of a lot like two-percent."

I smile, and as the music booms, I have to raise my voice. "Then you're not looking closely enough!"

"Purposefully!" he shouts back, gripping his cellphone in a tight fist.

I chew my gum, assessing his tense state. Turning my head into his neck, my lips a breath from his ear, I say, "Lean back with me."

"What?" He stiffens.

I raise my brows. "He's never relaxed on a couch." I let out a long whistle. "The new things I'm showing him."

Maximoff realizes what I mean. He pockets his phone like he's accepting a bet, and then he slides back until his spine hits the leather. His shoulders unwind, somewhat.

After a short, silent beat, he says, "Thanks for being honest with me. I mean it."

I hear the deep sincerity in his voice. "Anytime, wolf scout."

Our arms touch unconsciously, and when our heads turn towards one another, our faces are only a couple inches apart.

The air seems to crack with that familiar, hard-to-breathe tension that I felt weeks ago when I massaged him. Our gazes grip securely.

In my head, I can be his bodyguard and sleep with him.

I'm that good. And it's that simple.

In *his* head, I'm not sure what's going on up there.

He inhales strongly, his chest rising, and his gaze bores into mine, searching for a sign. Mine caress his like the stroke of flesh against flesh. I want to slide nearer. I want to wrap my arm across his shoulders and close the two-inch distance.

My muscles tighten as I stay still, pulse pounding. And the next look he wears, I know that look. The look that melts his forest-green eyes and softly and forcefully begs, *kiss me*.

I breathe, my body doused with kerosene. Lit on fire, and just before I make a move, a sound, a clearer, more visible acknowledgement for him, his gaze just drops.

Off of me completely. To the ground, then the bar where girls start squealing in *glee* at the eye contact he gives them.

I grit down, pained like someone ripped out a rib. I comb my hands through my hair, and Maximoff stands up.

I stand not a millisecond after. "Where are you going?" I ask tensely.

"I don't know," he mutters, and then shakes his head like he's trying to catch his bearings.

"We need to talk," I say, but he can't hear me over the sudden switch in songs, a hardcore rock anthem blasting. He's already leaving the VIP area.

I follow. Step-for-step beside him, and a stool instantly opens at the crowded bar. Maximoff smiles at a short brunette in a sequined mini-dress. "You can sit!" he tells her. "Don't get up for me!"

I restrain an eye roll.

She giggles.

He flags down the bartender and orders drinks.

For his safety, I have no other choice but to do my job. I stand behind him like an intimidating authority, someone that says *don't fuck with him*. Since he wants to be approached tonight, I shouldn't be scowling this hard.

I'm out of the way, but in the way. Unseen, but seen. All of those oxymorons are killing me tonight.

She gasps and says, "No way!" a thousand times.

Moffy leans down, cups his hand by her ear, and whispers for a full two minutes. Her eyes glow like she hit a jackpot, and she nods repeatedly.

I can only imagine that he's telling her he wants to fuck her. In a subtler way but still blunt. Upfront. *Sex only.*

I spit my gum into my wrapper, my jaw aching. I pocket the thing, and then the girl hops off the barstool and heads for the bathroom.

Maximoff stays by the bar, and since this is my first time being his bodyguard while he's trying to get ass, I'm somewhat in the dark. It's not like he listed this in his rules.

He faces me. "We need to talk!" He has one-hundred percent padlocked his feelings. I glare, his face so impassive, so inexpressive— you'd think he's channeling Connor Cobalt. His uncle who can will away emotion whenever he likes.

I hate it.

I step towards him and whisper in the pit of his ear. "Are we discussing your flirting techniques?" I unwrap a new piece of gum while he struggles to hide his feelings.

Let it out, wolf scout.

He gestures to me. "I assume you're asking for advice."

I smile and pop gum in my mouth. "That's funny, I assumed you wanted advice from me."

"You should look up the word *joke* because I don't think you know the definition of funny."

I whistle. "You're just on a fucking roll today, aren't you?" He can't answer. A server swoops in with his earlier drink order. Club soda for him and a cocktail for the girl. She sets the cocktail on the bar, and I grab the club soda off the tray.

I pause before I put my lips to the rim. "You've never taken a sip of alcohol," I say to Moffy, "which means you don't know what it tastes like."

He stares at me, blank faced. "Is there a question in there or are you just Nancy Drew-ing shit out loud?"

"I'm more of a Hardy Boy, but nice try." Our eyes lock, more headily, all the while I put my lips to the glass and sip.

Sharp alcohol bites my tongue. "It's spiked with vodka." I look for the server.

"Just let it go. It's not a big deal." When he sees me searching for a server, he adds, "Farrow, it's fine."

He refuses to complain, but he can send back a spiked drink. And if the act makes him feel like an asshole, I'll fucking do it for him.

Maximoff tells me, "Declan would just drop it."

"I'm not Declan," I remind him for the forty-fourth time this week. I catch a server's attention. "I need a bottled water, *sealed.*" I give her a fifty-dollar bill.

"Right away." She darts behind the bar, scoots beside the bartender, and then tosses me a bottled water. When I turn around to Maximoff, he looks stunned.

He licks his lips, emotion raising his carriage.

"Take it." I pass the water.

He holds the bottled water like he's never seen Evian before.

"It's just water."

Maximoff is frozen still. "You didn't have to do that." He means get him the water.

"Okay, but I did." It's not the first time he's been like this after I helped him. I step closer. "Don't you see, Maximoff? There's a cement wall in front of you, and you've just been told to be *satisfied* with staring at it." He listens intently. "And so you just stand there, not able to see the other side." The wall is paparazzi.

The wall is the people who spike his drink.

The wall is hecklers and his lack of privacy.

Screw it all.

"What's the alternative?" he combats. "Me hating my life?"

"No!" I shout as chatter escalates around us. "It's my job to help you over the wall! Declan may've told you to accept the shit in your life, but I'm going to give you what you've never been given!"

Like a bottled *water*, for one.

That's a solution that Declan never thought of. Or maybe he just listened to Maximoff stubbornly say *just let it go.*

Maximoff opens his mouth to speak, but the brunette slips up beside him. Yanking his attention to the left, and he tells her, "Give me one more second! Your drink is on the bar!"

"Take your time! I'll be waiting!" She bites her bottom lip and slides onto her stool.

My pulse is wedged in my esophagus.

Maximoff whispers in my ear, "The talk I wanted to have with you..." His voice is noticeably tight. "I can't have her in my car unless she signs an NDA. So you'll need to take her to the VIP section while I hang around the club's security."

This is really happening. I don't blink.

Do your motherfucking job, Farrow.

Shit.

I have to stay professional. I have to give him what he wants, and if this is it...

I ask him, "You don't want to be around for that conversation?"

He shakes his head. "My presence usually pressures them, and I want her to sign the NDA on her own terms."

I have no real ability to nod or to even force a smile. My body refuses, but I'm able to lean back from him. A painfully cold acceptance mortars my features like brick on brick. This is about to be hell. A hell that I'm obligated to walk through, and really, it's my fault.

For liking him in the first place.

In the briefest second, our eyes touch, but I'm the one who bails on the moment this time. My head swerves towards the bar. "Okay!" I yell back at Moffy.

On my way to the girl, I lower my volume on my radio, the soft chatter grating on me all of a sudden. Just when I look up at the brunette, a strong hand grabs my bicep from behind.

"Farrow, wait." His voice is right against my ear.

Slowly, I turn to face him, and he breathes like he ran five miles to reach me.

I tilt my head, still hesitant about the direction this all may go. *What do you want, Maximoff?* Stopped in place, I bear hard on my teeth.

And then I freeze. I watch him subtly check out my features: my cheeks, my piercings, the freckle on my jaw, and he finally allows his gaze to drop to my lips.

"Maximoff—"

"I can't do this."

A pit wedges in my ribs. "Be more specific."

"I'm going home." He gestures to the exit with his water bottle. "I'm leaving right now after I tell her goodbye." He takes a half a second to kindly say goodbye to the girl. Then his focus is on me.

Heaviness hoists off my chest, my lips beginning to upturn.

A night listening to him fuck someone else averted. And I didn't even have to be a prick.

I move to lead him out. "I'm walking in front of you." He's already trying to push *ahead* of my stride, but he stops himself short.

And he says, "Walk beside me."

I do. We move with equally strong, determined gaits, but we're both sitting on the beginning of something unknown. And we carry our familiar tension like a third companion and a bomb.

14

Neither of us breaks the silence while I drive

home. Compounding and compounding in each untouched second. Every moment weighs down. Sunken in eternal slow-mo.

Farrow reaches for the air vents. Languid, sensual—his tattooed fingers slide the vent open. Cold air gushes out. But it does absolutely jack shit to temper the heat brewing against my skin.

I lick my lips for the thousandth fucking time. My cock *throbs*, aching to harden. To be stroked. To be fucked and to fuck.

I force my gaze to the highway. Gripping the leather steering wheel in an iron-tight vice. His hot gaze shifts from the road where paparazzi trail after my Audi—to me. Over and over.

Road, then me. Road, then me.

I'm watched and observed all the time. By strangers. By cameramen. By *people*. And never, *never* have I come undone. Until now, until his eyes feel like hands, and I want them all over me.

"Brake," he says deeply.

I slow the car at the last second. Hitting bumper-to-bumper traffic. Now the car is unbearably still. I feel like my Audi has shrunk into a compact.

Too small.

The middle console barely divides his body from mine. And my body from his. Do I even want a divide anymore? *No.* And *yes.* He's my bodyguard—that's not changing.

It's not.

But I can't even *think* about anyone else. He hasn't just pitched a tent in my brain and dick. He's built a fucking stone castle that no wolf can ever blow down.

What am I supposed to say to him? *My cock only wants you. My brain only wants you. I didn't pick up that girl because I only want you.*

Or: *if I fucked someone else tonight, it would've made me sick.*

None of that extinguishes this one cold fact: it's ethically wrong to be with my bodyguard.

"Maximoff," Farrow says, my name slicing the dense air like dropping a guillotine.

I steal a quick glance at him.

He rubs his bottom, pierced lip with his thumb, and his brows rise. "Ready to talk about this?"

"*This,*" I say, imagining my hands ripping his shirt off his head. Muscle against muscle, lips against lips—I blink. "*This* traffic is fucking terrible."

"*This* as in *you* and *me.*" He pauses. "Us."

Headlights glare in my rearview. My stringent posture contracts my shoulders, my deltoids, my whole body. And I switch lanes fast. Windows of a nearby SUV roll down, a Canon pointing at my car.

Great.

I drive thirty-over just to desert the SUV. Farrow keeps an eye on neighboring vehicles while he says, "I know talking about this isn't easy. In any other situation, I'd just kiss you."

Fuck. I lick my lips again. Muscles flexing.

I *harden* beneath my jeans and boxer-briefs. "You sure I wouldn't be the one to kiss you?" I counter.

I can feel his lips lifting. For how close we are, the space between us couldn't feel farther away. Whoever makes the first move will have to cross miles, scale mountains, ferry oceans to reach the other side.

I glance at him.

And his amused smile stretches wider. "In your dreams, maybe you'd kiss me first." Talk of my dreams reminds me of how long I've crushed on him.

Since I was *sixteen*.

I start to padlock my emotion with a thousand iron keys.

His smile slowly falls. "Did I say something wrong?"

"No," I say instinctively, and then, "I don't know." *Beware: he's your bodyguard!* scrolls across my vision like a tickertape warning. For Christ's sake, we can't even *kiss* without having a conversation beforehand. It's all so elementary.

Kissing.

I want to do more. I *want* more. In a way that I've never even had before, and is that what's being offered? Is it even possible?

"What are you thinking?" he asks. "Because I don't know where you stand. You have so many boundaries, you're practically a walking-talking *Don't Enter* sign."

"Like you don't have any?" I combat.

He laughs into a grin. "I consider some boundaries like cautionary tales. Proceed with caution, but you know, still go on ahead." He flashes me the hottest smile I've ever seen, and I bear on my molars, my erection wanting pressure. A mouth, a hand, an ass.

His mouth, *his* hand.

His ass.

I find myself shaking my head.

"What?" he asks.

I have to tell him my biggest roadblock. As though it's not in-his-face-obvious enough. "I value self-awareness." I take a colossal breath. "The *ability* to understand and perceive every facet of my own weird existence. In Greek ethics, it's said only the self-aware understand what is right, and therefore will have the knowledge to do what is good."

I want to do what is right. To do *good*.

To be good.

Farrow taps the middle console, his thumb ring clicking against leather. His hand is an inch from my arm. He nods, understanding. "And you see being with your bodyguard as *wrong*. And wrong leads to bad; and bad equals unhappy in your philosophically-bound head. You realize that not everyone thinks that way, Maximoff?"

My brows knot. "In what universe does *wrong* lead to rays of fucking sunshine and happily-ever-afters, Farrow? Please, enlighten me."

"How about rewinding and asking yourself, *is it really wrong?* Or how about this one: *what is ethical to begin with?* Who decided on these moral rights?" He leans back, boot on his seat. "Or what about what Thoreau said?"

I frown. "You've read Thoreau?"

"I took philosophy and lit during undergrad."

I give him a brief look like he's flown off this planet. "That was over *seven* years ago." And I doubt he reads in his spare time. While my shelves are stacked and stacked with comics, graphic novels, and philosophy texts—his one small bedroom bookshelf is *bare*.

"I remember everything I skim," he says, not even lying about "skimming" texts.

One right turn and I drive onto our street.

We go silent.

I pass rows and rows of townhouses, both of our homes in view. Then I pull onto the short driveway. He clicks the garage button. And I park next to Jane's baby blue Beetle. After shutting off the ignition, the garage door grinds closed.

We stay right here. Inside my three-car garage, sheltered from the Philly noise.

Quiet. Alone.

In one single breath, Farrow turns towards me. His arm extends over the back of my leather seat. My muscles burn and tighten like rubber bands that beg to snap. I want him even *closer*. But I hold still, marbleized.

His other arm rests on the middle console. His hand one move away from my leg.

Farrow caresses my gaze as he says, "Thoreau said, '*Do not be too moral. You may cheat yourself out of much life. So aim above morality. Be not simply good; be good for something.*'"

His deep voice and Thoreau's words pour through me like liquid honesty. "*Be not simply good.*" Self-perfection has its limits. Being moral, making moral choices—it all means nothing in comparison to doing good for others. I don't need to be the perfect picture of morality in order to help someone in need.

I'd rather be good for something.

For someone.

So I look at him.

I'm talking a *real* look. Like I'm excavating his every thought and desire. My eyes bore into his eyes, and then my gaze melts in a carnal wave against his gaze.

Farrow returns the aroused, taut sentiment. Our short breaths are the only true noise.

The headiest exchange of my life. Undeniable.

He leans forward, his lips an inch from mine. And very deeply, very huskily, he whispers, "What do you want, Maximoff?"

In an instant, I close the distance.

My lips meet his lips, and the tension explodes. We thrust forward together. An invisible divide detonates, blown to pieces.

He deepens the strong kiss. Our tongues wrestling, breath caught in my lungs. I clutch the back of his head. With firm, possessive passion. Wanting *more* of him.

His muscular arm falls to my broad swimmer's shoulders. His fingers skim lightly, teasingly against my burning neck. Rising through my thick hair.

Fucking Christ.

A low groan sticks in my throat while we kiss. His smile grows against my stinging lips.

I want closer, but the middle console is in our fucking way. I untuck the black shirt from his pants. My hand slips beneath. Discovering the warm ridges of his abs that flex against my large palm.

My other hand shifts to his jaw, his skin rough from a less-than-close shave. His masculinity pumps blood in my dick, turning me on inside out. I like men that can bench press as much if not more than me. The kind that tries to steer my ship in bed and then relents, ultimately.

The kind that kisses like a fiend but becomes a pleasured puddle while we're fucking.

Farrow pulls me nearer to his six-foot-three build. Finding extra room to move. He breaks the kiss, only for his mouth to travel down my sharp jaw. To my neck.

Fuck me.

I twist his shirt in my fist and then I climb between the seats. Heading into the back, I pull Farrow in this direction behind me. He follows. Our asses hit the stretched leather seat. No physical objects in our way.

We breathe heavily. Sprinting towards something we've never chased.

I yank the shirt over his head. And he tugs off mine. Hot skin against hot skin, tattooed chest to bare chest—I pin him to the side door; his head gently touches the window.

He grins, panting for two breaths. "So it's like that then?" His fingers hook in my waistband.

I need his hands on my cock. I grind forward, shifting his hand lower. His brown eyes pool with intrigue. And arousal.

"It's like what?" I ask deeply.

One corner of his mouth curves. "You're bossy every place, every-where. It's like that." And then Farrow uses his strength and hooks his arms beneath mine. Swiftly, he turns me, my spine meeting the interior car door. Our positions reversed. The back of my head meets the window.

And his knee presses on the leather between my legs. Closer, he clasps my hand. He sucks my ear before whispering, "So am I."

"Fuck," I pant, oxygen barely leaving my lips. I'm fucking breathless. Lightning has been striking me on repeat.

I've never felt breathless in my life.

I've never been with anyone I've known. Not like this. Never have I had real feelings beyond physical attraction. Not until him.

Merging the two—the feelings with the physical, it catapults me to a new plane of existence. Farrow lets go of my hand to clutch my jaw. His fingers—on my face.

My neck arches back against the window, my eyes almost rolling but they fasten into a daggered look. *Fuck.* I need him lower.

When I train my piercing gaze on him, I see how he drinks in my pleasure. Getting off by my expression. He kisses outside of my lips, and I kiss him more fully. Tongues tangled.

He grabs my neck, our pelvises digging closer. Erections bound beneath fabric but fucking dying to meet.

I fist his hair. Tugging. Sitting up more to be at equal height. The handle-bar protrudes into my back, but I wrench Farrow harder to my chest.

His lips part into a gruff groan.

I can't wait anymore. I draw his hand *lower.* To my zipper. *Unzip me, man.* I want jeans off, boxer-briefs off.

Farrow palms my cock, then squeezes above the fabric with the perfect pressure—*fuck me.* Swiftly, he fishes my button through, unzips—and on instinct, I lift his head back up. To kiss me again. Farrow seizes my jaw in a strong but affectionate grip.

Ensuring that I stay still.

So he likes control. Not a new fact, but I wonder if he'd let go, just in bed. And then I wonder if he's thinking the same thing about me.

The second our lips break, I put a firm hand on his chest. And I guide his back to the bottom of the leather seat. Until he lies supine.

His ravenous gaze swallows me whole.

I expect him to protest about the new position, but he clutches my shoulder and pulls me down on top. Our movements quicken, feverishly. Our legs intertwining. Our dicks grind before I stroke the outline of his length, rock-hard. *Fuck.*

Me.

I unbutton his black pants. He yanks my jeans halfway down my thighs, revealing my green boxer-briefs. We exchange hard, rough kisses in every free second.

His lip piercing no longer cold but warm against my mouth. I unzip him—we stop.

We suddenly freeze as my phone vibrates in my pocket. Loudly. Incessantly.

Someone's calling me. Our chests visibly rise and fall. His lips reddened from my force, and before I tell him I have to answer, he's already digging into my jean's pocket. Retrieving my phone.

He remembers that calls are more important than texts. I never ignore phone calls. I can't. Not if family may be in trouble.

I just realize his earpiece is out. And also his radio. He left both on the passenger seat up front.

Checking the caller ID, Farrow says, "It's your dad."

15

My dad is calling me. Greaaaat.
I sit up off Farrow, and he sits up with me. Turned towards one another still, our arms are on the back of the same seat.

I steady my breath. Used to the *worst timing* for most things.

Farrow presses the green *accept call* button and hands me the phone. Basically saying, *I'm okay with you talking to your dad, wolf scout. Do what you need to do.*

"Hey, Dad," I say, putting the call on speaker for Farrow.

Almost subconsciously. Throughout the years—but also while he's been my bodyguard—he earned my trust, and now I can reciprocate. In my life, that's monumental.

Farrow combs a casual hand through the just-tugged strands of his white hair. His lips quirk when he catches me staring longer.

I made out with my bodyguard.

Officially.

I'm in the no-takebacks fly zone. While I hover here, I just want to do so much fucking more. My brain is zeroed in on him.

And as far as I can tell, he's just as honed in on me.

"Hey, Moffy." My dad's naturally sharp-edged voice fills the car, but he can't see anything. Thank God. "I'm the bearer of shitty news tonight."

My brows knot. "How shitty?"

"Hold on…" He must pull the phone away, his voice harder to hear. "What are you doing awake—no, never mind. Bed. Now."

"Dad." I know that voice and her serious tone like he's unconscionably destroying her favorite pair of boots and gothic makeup. It's my little sister Kinney. "You don't understand. The witching hour is at 3 a.m.—I need to commune with my people."

"Wait…are you dead? Did I forget to print an obituary of my own thirteen-year-old daughter? Let me think about this." My dad's dry voice definitively says *I'm not thinking about this*. His thick sarcasm makes Farrow's lips upturn even more towards me. Knowing exactly where mine originates.

"Dad," she huffs.

"Kinney Hale," he refutes, "I banished ghosts from this house millenniums ago. They're all afraid of me. You're wasting your time. So *bed*. Now. You have school tomorrow." He must put the phone to his ear. To me, he sighs, "Kids." Just to piss her off.

"I'm not a kid, you troll." I can actually hear her stomping away.

My dad laughs. "I love you, little Slytherin!" he shouts after her. And to me, he asks, "Sorry, where was I?"

"Shitty news," I say, hesitant to pull off my jeans in case I need to go home for whatever reason. Farrow stays as motionless as me.

"Are you in your car?"

"Yeah. You're on speaker by the way."

"Farrow, is he speeding? If he is, you have my full permission to ground him. Take away his phone. He hates that."

Farrow is smiling like a Cheshire cat. *Loving* this too much. I glare and flip him off. He clasps my hand. "He's only five-over," he says easily, still smiling. I bring our hands down, examining his tattooed fingers that spell *k.n.o.t.*, the other hand reads: *t.a.m.e.* in black ink. Farrow watches me fixatedly but adds to my dad, "Let's blame traffic."

It's more than a good lie. It's one that's meant to help me first and foremost. Not my parents. Not the security team. *Me*.

He's on my side.

"Steal his keys next time," my dad says.

I glance at the phone. "How about you not order my bodyguard around? That's my job."

Farrow grins and mouths to me, *you wish.*

I almost groan. I just want to fuck him.

Before my dad talks about my mom worrying about me behind the wheel, I say, "I can't talk long. What's the shit news?"

"We're gonna have to reschedule our lunch tomorrow. Your Uncle Connor and Uncle Ryke have parent-teacher meetings."

I read the texts earlier this morning—and the pictures have been going viral since noon. My little cousins Winona Meadows and Ben Cobalt spray-painted Dalton Academy's science lab with the words: *frog killers!*

Those two always send me memorandums on environmental objectives that H.M.C. Philanthropies should complete. They're thirteen and fifteen. And they get in trouble together monthly.

"Let me know the new day for lunch; I'll be there," I tell him. I look forward to lunches with my dad and my uncles, but if one of us can't make it, we just reschedule to a day later in the week. It's shitty, but it's not the worst.

"Drive safe, Moffy," my dad says, his tone serious.

"I will. Night."

"Love you, bud." He hangs up.

I pocket my phone and stare off. Thinking. My dad's voice lingers in my ears. Being with my *bodyguard*—there are consequences packed on top of consequences. If I can, I want to avoid all of them.

I train my gaze on Farrow.

He rests his knuckles to his lips, brows raised at me. "Listening to Socrates and Plato again?"

I force an irritated smile. "No." I lift my jeans to my waist, but I don't button or zip yet.

Farrow eyes my movements. "What's wrong?"

I stay near him. Not adding distance or space. "What happens between us—it has to stay secret. All of it. If you want to do *anything* with me, you can't treat this rule like it's flexible or meant to be broken."

Farrow smiles. "I agree."

"We agree?" I say, disbelieving. *What alternate universe am I in?*

"I love my job." He holds my gaze. "And if the security team or your family finds out that I crossed a line and broke their trust, I'm gone. Someone will replace me as your bodyguard. Which means that the new bodyguard will spend more time with *you* than I do, and that's just...not happening." His voice falls to a husky whisper. "You need to know that I only do exclusive. No fucking around. You want me, you only get me, and vice versa."

Exclusive.

A relationship.

A secret relationship.

I've never had any of those. I wish I could be happy that he only wants me. I wish that I could accept the truth: that I only want him. But I'm concerned about the little annoying details that slip between these facts.

I look straight at him. "You have no idea what you're getting yourself into. You can't know."

He never breaks eye contact. "Then tell me, Maximoff."

I don't falter. "I genuinely love sex," I say the truth I've always hidden. "I have a really high fucking sex drive." It sounds so simple. *It's not.* "I've never spoken publicly about how much sex I have. Sharing those details—it's a heavy responsibility that I carry very prudently. For one, my mom is a sex addict." *He knows.*

I'm used to this fact too, but the depth that I still need to go pins my tongue down. I pause.

I turn slightly and crack my knuckles. People usually ask *isn't it so awkward that you know your mom's sexual history?* I can handle the awkward.

I can handle everything.

Even the cruelty towards her, but it'll always boil my blood. If you're going to attack someone, come at me.

Farrow shifts his arm that's on the back of the seat. So his forearm lies on top of my forearm. Almost comfortingly.

I stare at the way his fingers clutch my elbow, and then I look up at him. "There's not enough information or research to claim that sex addiction is hereditary. But if I publicly share how much sex I have, the media will start calling me an addict. Then they'll say it's *hereditary*. Then they'll start harassing my siblings about sex more than they already do. So I stay quiet."

The frequency someone has sex is *not* enough to determine a sex addiction—but it won't matter to the media. They'll cling like fucking koalas to the detail and never let go.

"And it's not the only reason I stay quiet about my sex life," I tell him. "I war with a stereotype that I know I fall into, something I feel an obligation to break."

He sucks in a breath through his teeth. "*Maximoff.* That's not your cross to bear."

I'm not surprised that he knows what I'm talking about. "It is, Farrow. When I came out as bisexual to the world, I knew people would look at me as a role model for something. I have a fucking duty not to reinforce harmful stereotypes: like *bisexuals are over-sexual*—that we all just fuck around and fuck a lot." I rake my right hand through my hair. "You know the minute that I told the world I like guys and girls, a lot of people *assumed* that meant I like threesomes—that's not fucking okay." Quickly, I add, "To clarify, I'm *not* into threesomes."

His lips tic upward. "I grasped that by your vitriol." He tilts his head. "In short, you're saying that you have a lot of sex, but no one can know. And I'm sure you were always safe since you're *you*."

"Thank you," I say dryly, not mentioning that I've been checked out every week and that I'm clean. I also don't add how I go to my concierge doctor for the screenings and tests.

And by *doctor*, I mean *his dad*.

Thank God for doctor-patient confidentiality.

Farrow's know-it-all smile starts expanding inch by inch.

My eyes narrow. "What?"

"You jumped from *exclusivity* to announcing that you have a lot of sex."

I don't follow his logic. "Your smile is going to fall off your fucking face."

He practically overflows with amusement. "You don't think I can satisfy you?"

My brows jump. Huh.

By his sheer confidence, he clearly knows he can.

Our eyes trail over each other, and my cock throbs again. A groan scrapes my throat. "More like," I whisper lowly, "I was warning you. In case you didn't want sex every day, multiple times a night. I try not to assume what people are into."

Farrow opens his mouth, but loud voices filter through his earpiece on the front seat. He stretches towards the middle console but glances back to say, "I'm into *you*. If I couldn't keep up, I wouldn't be your bodyguard." He grabs the radio and connecting earpiece. Turning up the volume, Akara's voice floods the car.

"...find Farrow. He needs to check in."

His jaw muscle tics, and he hooks his radio to his waistband. Whoever was chosen to "find Farrow" can't find me with him. Not bare-chested, hair askew, lips reddened, dicks stiff—*no*.

I toss his black shirt at his tattooed chest. I'm used to abrupt endings and constant *rain checks*, but this one is hard. Pun abso-fucking-lutely intended.

I pull my green shirt over my head and open the door. "Thanks for the blue balls."

He fits his earpiece in. "You'll thank me more when I take all of you in my mouth."

My muscles clench, blood heating at the visual. I look back at Farrow.

His lips rise. "You're easily hot and bothered."

"And you're not?" I combat.

"I conceal mine better. Comes with the territory." He motions to his radio. "Don't look so sad, wolf scout. You can't be the best at everything."

I wear *zero* sadness. I'm glaring. "Have fun with your hand. Dream of me." I climb out and shut the door. In the garage. I leave with the last word but feel his amusement as I go.

Despite all the risks, the new territory, I find myself grinning.

16

MAXIMOFF HALE

Out of my whole family, Connor Cobalt has the best office, the best view—hands down. Whenever I'm in the sleek city high-rise of Cobalt Inc., I either lose myself gazing out the window, a breathtaking Philly skyline, or I focus on the memorabilia my uncle shelves and hangs.

Rain pelts the glass and thunder roars. I'm not fixated on the storm. I'm currently staring hard at a framed *National Geographic* magazine on the navy-blue wall.

The cover shows a rugged, dark-haired man in his late thirties, skin tanned from the sun. With the horizon bleeding orange and yellow, he grips a rock face from at least four-hundred feet high. Using only his right fingertips. Legs hanging off, left arm dangling.

No harness.

No rope.

The sun rises behind him.

I read the title of the magazine:

FROM SUCH GREAT HEIGHTS:
THE BEST FREE-SOLO CLIMBER IN THE WORLD.
RYKE MEADOWS.

My uncle.

My dad's half-brother.

He's in his forties now, and he still climbs. He still makes the front pages of magazines, and he has about five different sponsorships and ad campaigns.

Usually I would stare at this with admiration and be proud to know Ryke. I am. But I'm stuck here. Looking harder. Staring longer.

I see his dark, disheveled hair, his thick eyebrows, golden tan, and the way his body is cut and ripped and lean—and I see me. Or at least what I look like without the constant light-brown hair dye.

I inherited my sharp cheekbones from my dad, but that's it. At the end of the day, I look more like Ryke Meadows than I do Loren Hale.

"He hates that one," Uncle Connor says.

I rotate.

My intelligent, polished uncle watches me from behind his desk. Jane's dad has blue eyes, wavy brown hair, and he wears a tailored suit with as much confidence as he's worth. Billions. Like my dad and Uncle Ryke, he's in his forties, and they're all still lauded for their good looks.

Connor Cobalt has been *People's* Sexiest Man Alive three times in the past decade alone.

We're waiting for Ryke and my dad to show. I typically meet them at public restaurants. But since the media frenzy about my fight and the Camp-Away, they all three decreed "office lunch" before I could protest.

And Connor was the one who reinstated the cancelled lunch. This morning he called Dalton Academy and smooth-talked the administration. No parent-teacher meeting, so here I am.

Trying not to remember about last night in my Audi.

With Farrow. I'll start smiling like an idiot, and he'd totally call me out if he were here. The high-rise has secure entrances. So Farrow is allowed to leave and eat at the food court below, drive my Audi around—pretty much whatever he wants.

I have no clue what he chose to do, and we don't really text. We're both too smart to get caught by a phone or email hack.

I study the magazine again. *Uncle Ryke hates this one?* "Why does he hate it?" It's a great cover. Better than most of the tabloids that slap my mom and dad on the front.

"The headline."

I reread. "It says he's the best in the world."

"And he vehemently disagrees. Ryke's humility is another limb. I've tried my best to amputate it in the past, but it's never leaving."

Humility.

I blink a couple times, my eyes growing. I'm highly aware that I've been called humble multiple times. My gaze starts to narrow.

Jesus.

Christ.

How many traits do I share with him?

I just leave the magazine and sit on a leather couch. Which faces a few leather chairs in his office's lounge section. My uncle trades his desk for the chair across from me.

I pop a couple knuckles, a bad habit, but I keep eye contact with Connor. He's all about self-confidence. Eye contact. Never cowering to any adversary, and where he has employees running into cubicles or staring slack-jawed, I've never been intimidated by his godly presence.

"You know my mom was on the front page of *Celebrity Crush* this morning?" My shoulders are locked. "The headline: *Lily Calloway Goes Back to Her Old Wild Ways!* They had a photograph of her sticking her hand down my dad's pants. And Uncle Ryke is upset over a cover where he's scaling a mountain during a damn sunrise."

A bad, acidic taste drips down my throat, but I don't look away.

I meet everything head-on.

Connor barely blinks, none of this fazing him. "Ryke was ten times more upset about the tabloid yesterday than that *National Geographic* hanging in my office. That, I can assure you."

I used to look up to Ryke as a little kid.

I used to dress like him: leather jackets, fuck-if-I-care style. I used to want to *be* him. I constantly asked him to take me camping. I begged him to let me ride his motorcycle.

Then I learned about the rumors. That my mom and my dad's half-brother slept together. That I'm actually the son of Ryke Meadows.

I *don't* believe those rumors. My mom has been adamant that she's always stayed faithful to my dad. And she looks proud whenever she says, "I've never cheated on Lo." A sex addict who never cheated—it's a big deal.

My mom is strong as hell.

But there was one time where I questioned the rumors. I was twelve. I asked my dad flat-out. I asked him who's my biological father—and he said, *me*. Unequivocally, wholeheartedly. *Me*.

I believe my dad. I've seen the DNA tests, and they confirm that I'm Loren Hale's son. We've even publicized the DNA tests.

People don't like to believe facts. They want to believe the most salacious story. The one that makes you keep flipping the pages.

That story isn't always the truth.

I like the narrative where my mom and dad helped each other battle their addictions. Two addicts who used to enable one another were able to pull through together and become sober and healthy. I like my reality. My real-life parents. Who possess an unconscionable amount of strength that most people will never know and never see.

They're my heroes.

And I'm damn proud to be their son.

Recently those paternity rumors have been running rampant *again*. I want the world to know that I'm proud to be the son of Loren Hale. I want to honor my dad, and I have no idea how to do that other than to look more like him. So I dye my hair.

I need you all to know that I love him.

So damn much.

"We've got tacos!" My dad barges into the office, his light brown hair artfully styled. His daggered amber eyes rarely lose that edge, just like his voice and his jaw, but there's something so human and warm about my dad.

It's his love of the people around him.

His love for his wife and children.

His love for me. It's more powerful than anything I've ever known.

Ryke enters the office behind my dad, the walls frosted for privacy. He shuts the door—I jolt as a foiled taco lands on my lap.

My dad towers nearby, his face scrunched at me. "You look a little pissy. What'd I miss?"

I gesture from me to Connor. "We were talking about how Uncle Ryke was pretty upset over the *Celebrity Crush* issue this morning." I start peeling the taco foil, and I look up as my dad and Ryke turn to Connor. The source of the info.

Ryke glowers.

My dad's jaw sharpens. Not happy that Connor fed my frustration over Ryke and my mom's friendship.

Connor stares at me. Only me. "Context is really a beautiful thing, Moffy. Let's try not to lose that." To my dad, he says, "I was making a point that was lost in translation. And to be clear, it was poorly translated by your son."

It's true, and as my smile forms, my dad sinks on the couch beside me. Ryke takes the chair next to Connor. And they pass around food.

I look between the three of them. "Is anyone going to mention how that photograph was taken *in* the neighborhood?"

My dad and my mom were in the backyard. *Their* backyard. In the same gated neighborhood with twenty-four hour security. How Alpha let a photographer capture a shot of my parents from who-knows-where—I have no idea.

What if paparazzi are in the trees? What if they hired one of the neighbors to spy?

It's not okay.

"We're looking into it," my dad says, sifting through his paper bag of food. Off my stern expression, he adds, "Don't worry about it, Moffy."

"How can I not worry about it?" I point at him with my chicken taco. "Luna, Xander, and Kinney live there and someone is taking pictures of the house."

"I'm sorry, did you lose your name badge?" Sarcasm thick, he pretends to scan my red crewneck for the nonexistent badge. "Because…I don't think it says *Dad* on your shirt." He pats my shoulder lightly. "Pretty sure that's my job, bud."

"It says *Big Brother* on my forehead." I must've jabbed my taco towards him.

He glares. "Eat it. Don't abuse it."

Connor wears a billion-dollar grin. "Ryke's favorite motto."

They're talking about pussy.

Ryke unwraps a taco. "It's a good one but not my fucking favorite, Cobalt."

"Do tell, what's your 'fucking' favorite."

Ryke bites into a taco, sauce dripping down his unshaven jaw. He licks his thumb and says with a mouthful, "*Don't be a fucking dick.*"

My dad flashes a half-smile. "A motto we've all broken."

His brother tosses a piece of lettuce at him.

I study their interactions more than I ever do. I sense Connor scrutinizing me. Almost knowingly. He's five million steps ahead of everyone. Always.

I stop obsessing and go to eat my taco. Pausing. I notice a leak of hot sauce.

"I have yours," I say to my dad.

He checks the insides of his taco. Just cheese, chicken, and lettuce, and he swaps with me.

"You can't tell me not to worry," I say to him, back to the original topic. "I need information. Don't keep me in the dark."

He inhales a sharp breath, his jawline cutting like glass.

"I'm not a kid."

"You've been saying that since you were four. So pardon me if I just want you to be a kid." He bites into his taco and gathers his thoughts while he eats. He speaks after he sips a Fizz Life. "The security team is meeting about it this week. It's being handled. I'll let you know if anything changes. I can't give you more than that, Moffy."

Farrow can. He'll know what's happening.

Even if I didn't have Farrow as a resource, I'd nod to my dad all the same. I may push and prod a lot, but I get that he can't tell me every little damn thing. I kept the Luna tongue piercing from *him*.

And he didn't care. You know what he told me? *"I'm glad your sister has you to turn to. That's what siblings are for."*

Then he grounded her for two weeks. No comics, movies, or computers. And he took all of her cosplay costumes out of her closet.

So in the office, I nod a couple times to my dad, but another question crashes against me.

"Is she okay?" I ask firmly. "Mom. Is she alright?" One of my greatest fears is hearing and seeing bad shit from a tabloid first. I don't want to find out information from a second source.

I don't want to be whiplashed. And I can't live my life fed facts from the media. It's too warped. So that's why I push and *push* for answers.

"She's been at a great place for years, bud. She can stick her hand down my pants and be fine. She's fine." He smiles a faraway smile. Like he's recalling the moment.

I nod again. "I just hate that they're using her addiction as click-bait."

"It's fucked up," Ryke agrees.

We agree. How many times have we agreed on issues? Do we always agree? And why the fuck am I psychoanalyzing us?

The media. Maximoff Hale is just like Ryke Meadows!

I've been infected by the media. Tabloid parasites. No one notices my internal war except maybe Connor.

Ryke balls up a couple napkins and searches for another taco in the paper bag.

My dad shrugs like the foul play is just common. I recognize that we've all encountered this shit, but whenever the media touches my mom or dad's addictions, they cross a line. Incinerating all sense of morality and ethics.

"What's fucked up is this taco," my dad says. "Where are the extra hot sauce packets?" It's already dripping in orange hot sauce, but my dad would put Tabasco on everything if he could.

"You've probably burned half your taste buds in your mortal life," I tell him.

"Then you're doing well by not mimicking me."

I flip his words over and over in my head. *It's not because I wouldn't want to be like you*, I want to say. But my dad fucking knows this.

It's the world I'm concerned about.

It's you.

I stare off for a second, and Ryke throws a handful of hot sauce packets at my dad. They hit him square in the face.

My dad drills a glare between his older brother's eyes, only a year apart. Ryke is near laughter.

"I've decided you're no longer my brother," he says to Ryke.

"Who the fuck am I then?" Ryke balls up another dirty napkin.

"Just Some Guy. JSG for short."

Connor grins wider. "I've been wanting to rename him for some time. Though I'd have gone with something else."

Ryke groans. "We don't want to fucking know."

"I do," I chime in.

"Of course you do," Ryke says, tossing his wadded napkins into the paper bag. "You're always on his fucking side."

It takes him a long beat to finally look up at me. His tough brown eyes meet my steady forest-green, and I say, "I didn't know there were sides."

"There are sides." My dad stands and reaches over to Ryke's lap. "I'm always on the side with the good food." He snatches the paper bag and plops back down next to me. "Taco?" He tries to break the tension, but I'm not dropping this.

"I'm not always on Uncle Connor's side," I rebut. "He called me an idiot last week. Why would I side with that?" I try to holster a smile as I gesture at Connor who arches *one* brow. We were playing chess, and when

I lost, he told me not to worry. That I didn't have a chance with my IQ compared to *his* IQ.

Subtly, he called me an idiot. He doesn't deny or refute. And I love blunt honesty, so I actually like that memory.

"You tell me, Moffy," Ryke says. "You're the one who's been dyeing your fucking hair for a year."

The room quiets.

And he leans forward, forearms on his legs, to be closer to me. "What did I do? Just let me know, and we can fucking fix this."

I realize that I'm sitting in the exact position as him. Bent forward, forearms on my legs. I don't move. I don't blink. I just think.

I think about how Ryke Meadows may've had the greatest influence on my life. If I'm more like him than my father—isn't that the conclusion?

Does that mean I spent too much time with him? Does that mean I love him more? Will the media draw these questions—and *fuck these questions* and my mind that won't stop *turning*.

My dad raised me, and when I was twelve, I had a choice. I could either resent Ryke or I could love him as much as my dad does.

I chose to love him. As a teenager, he taught me how to ride a motorcycle. We went on annual camping trips. I created the Charity Camp-Away out of my love for hiking, camping, kayaking—and would that even exist without Ryke?

He showed me how to build a fire with flint. How to pitch a tent. How to *climb* rock faces. Outside of the Meadows family, I'm the *only* one who's ever been to their Costa Rica cabin-treehouse.

Ryke and his daughter Sulli invited me.

"Moffy," Ryke growls my name. "Did you fucking hear me?" His f-bombs come frequently but not very harshly. His gaze even softens on me. He doesn't want to hurt me.

I don't want to hurt him.

I've tried for *years* not to hurt him, but this past year—I snapped. The paternity rumors are weeds that won't die. And with the agitating

Maximoff Hale is just like Ryke Meadows! headlines, they sprout every time I blow a fuse and fight with my fists.

I should be chastised for the violence. Not be compared to my uncle out of affection.

"It's not you," I tell my uncle assuredly. "I love you. You know I love you. I'm just…" I motion to my head.

Overthinking. As always.

I just never want to be used as evidence for Loren Hale being unworthy or unfit as a father. I never want anyone to look at me and say, *Maximoff is just like Ryke, so Ryke must've raised him. He must love Ryke more. He must hate his father. What if his father abuses him? What if he's violent?*

It'd be so easy for people to draw that conclusion because of my dad's past. He's a recovering alcoholic and has been sober for over twenty years, but his own dad was an alcoholic. The media said my grandfather abused my dad. In different ways. Some are true.

Some are false.

But I don't want anyone to attach *any* ugly thing to Loren Hale. Stay back. I swear to fucking God. Stay back.

"What can I fucking do to help?" Ryke asks me. "I want to help."

I nod repeatedly, and I spit it out. "Which one of you am I most like?"

But it's my dad who answers.

"You're like all three of us, bud."

I turn to my dad.

He touches his chest. "You're sassy like me." He points at Ryke. "A hardhead like my dear brother." He nods to Connor. "And steadfast like my one true love."

Connor grins. "I couldn't agree more, darling."

I start to smile. "With which part?"

He surprises me by saying, "All of it."

I trust that they're not pacifying me with lies. I nod a few more times. Ready to change the topic to one light-years away.

"Let's talk about something else," I suggest.

My dad asks, "How are you doing with your new bodyguard?"

Dear World, are you fucking with me or what? Sincerely, a startled human.

An image pops in my head: me on top of Farrow in the backseat of my car. Since all three of them hire the bodyguards to protect their children, I'm pretty much certain they'd all hear "you're with your bodyguard" as "Farrow Keene took advantage of you"—and it's just not true.

It's why I have to lie. Sort of. "Farrow is annoying, a Grade-A know-it-all."

My dad's eyes grow teasingly. "You like him that much?"

I take a swig of water to submerge my smile. He's just joking, but Christ, it's real.

"That's it?" Ryke asks, brows knotted.

I think fast. "We're cordial. I respect him. He respects me. That's all there is to say."

"You're okay to let him handle your NDAs?" Connor asks, referring to my one-night stands.

"Sure. Yeah." I nod. "By the way, I've been meaning to ask." I set my water bottle down. "What's better, silicone-based lube or water-based?" The last word leaves my lips, and the office door cracks open. I expect Connor's assistant to peek inside.

...*Farrow* slips into the office.

What.

I rub my eyes to ensure that I'm absolutely, entirely 100% *not* fantasizing and haven't tapped into some secret superpower. Obtaining a magical ability to conjure a newly-minted boyfriend sounds more fucking believable right now.

Farrow zips up his leather jacket, a piece of his bleach-white hair brushing his dark eyelashes. His casual confidence is fucking hot, but this can't be a fantasy. Because he's not even looking at me.

He only acknowledges Connor. "Alpha asked me to check the street view from your office. Price said he sent you a text."

Connor has his phone cupped in his hand. "I saw. Do what you need to." Wait.

He's staying? My mouth falls fraction by fraction.

"Thanks," Farrow says, his eyes flitting to me for a brief second. I barely catch his lips lifting before he faces the windows and surveys the street below.

One-hundred-million-percent in earshot.

My dad pops open a Lightning Bolt! energy drink and lightly elbows my side. "Why do you want to know which lube is better?" *No.*

No

No.

Fuck.

17

MAXIMOFF HALE

I'm an upright statue. Solidified.

I hoped my earlier question would be forgotten or *die*. No one ever censors themselves in front of security. I usually wouldn't care either, but this is the very, *very* beginning of whatever is going on between us.

I don't need Farrow to know that I just asked my dad and two uncles about lube. A conversation that I had *with* Farrow—and I can't backtrack without appearing suspicious.

I have to barrel forward.

"A friend told me that silicone-based is better. I was curious what you guys thought." I stomp down the urge to glance at Farrow. I'm not about to let my dad or uncles see that I correlate *lube* with my bodyguard.

But I imagine his stretched smile and hearing him say, *so pure.*

My neck scorches. A first-time customer to Mortified-R-Us.

My dad's brows pinch. "What friend?"

I have friends that are employees and then I have family. I don't trust anyone else, and my dad is aware. I say the only possibility. "Janie."

Connor stares straight through me, his fingers to his jaw. "I'm certain my daughter knows that silicone degrades silicone." He means silicone lube destroys *sex toys.*

"She has an Asshole With Benefits," I remind them. "Nate."

"We know," they all say, not the biggest fans of Nate either. But they've never met him.

I'm the only one who meets the AWBs.

Tabloids post photos of Jane out at nightclubs with the same person. Nate is the fourth and current AWB. They also have photos of those same guys with other girls. Media and fans hesitate to call them "boyfriends" because they're not.

AWB #1 & #2 wanted his fifteen minutes of fame.

AWB #3 wanted to jump-start his acting career.

And now Nate AWB #4 wants the thousand-dollar bottles of champagne.

Janie always says their intentions don't matter because she only wants sex and they respect her in bed. Which she struggles to find. A lot more than me. It's why she can't just hookup so casually like I can. She has to hang onto the same guy for a while.

But I want Jane to be with someone who wants all of her. Not just her fame. Not just her wealth. She's one of the best people in this damn world. Beautiful inside and out. And if the guys she's sleeping with see less than that—then they're not fucking good enough for her.

Case closed.

My dad makes a scrunched face. "I'd never predict in a thousand millenniums that I'd know my niece's lube preference."

"You asked," I say.

"Regrets." He puts a hand to his heart.

"Water-based lube is fucking better," Ryke says. "Doesn't stain the sheets and feels way more natural."

Connor arches his brow and tells me, "That's if you want to listen to the one who hasn't had anal sex in two decades and counting."

I risk a glance at Farrow, and he still faces the windows. But I spot the beginning of his out-of-control smile. I tear my gaze off him quickly and look at my dad. He's not the most perceptive person in the room, and his attention is on his brother and best friend.

Ryke groans. "Fuck you, Cobalt."

Connor grins. "That's become your ineloquent way of saying *Connor Cobalt is always right.*"

Ryke gives him two middle fingers.

Connor focuses on me. "My preference depends on what I'm doing. Word of advice, silicone is preferred for anal, especially if you plan to bottom." He was with men and women before he married Rose Calloway. Whereas my dad and Ryke are straight.

I weirdly and strangely *know* that my mom's favorite position is anal because of asshole teenagers in prep school. They found the info online, and they just loved to remind me.

As I think for a second, I find a way to gain the upper-hand and maybe throw Farrow off-kilter. "I top most of the time."

Farrow pops a bubble with his gum. Drawing my gaze towards him automatically. He slightly turns his head, but he stops himself and fully faces the window.

"Are you seeing anyone?" Connor asks me.

"What?" My head swerves to my uncle. "*No.*"

My dad tries to shelter his worry, but creases line his forehead, brows cinched. He hates that I'm into one-night stands and NSA sex. In a snap second, he glances at *my bodyguard*. "Farrow."

No.

Farrow turns to us, chewing gum. "Yeah?"

"You know I'm *trusting* you to keep my son safe." My dad's glare could slaughter livestock and flocks of geese. "Whenever he brings a stranger into his room alone, he's putting himself in danger, and you're the only goddamn one who can help him—"

"Pretty sure I can help myself," I interject.

Farrow bites down on his chewing gum, smiling wide. "Listen to your dad, wolf scout. You need me."

I shake my head, trying so damn hard not to smile, too. "I need *less* of you."

He tilts his head. "Said no one ever."

"Glad I could be your first," I say dryly. The banter is pretty common between us. No one should be suspicious.

My dad relaxes back and looks between Ryke and Connor. "Not that I care if it happens, but…do you realize that all of our *eldest* children have never been in real relationships?"

"Is it a pattern or a coincidence?" Connor muses out loud, but I bet he already knows the answer.

Jane, Sulli, and me—the oldest three of each family—have the most pressure concerning who we date. It's not the only reason we all haven't been in relationships, but it's definitely added to it.

"Since you're already talking like I've evaporated," I say lightheartedly as I stand, "I need to head out. I have a meeting in a half hour." I say goodbye to everyone but Farrow. He has to follow me.

The minute we exit and walk *slowly* down the hallway, he starts laughing hard. Freeing a sound I bet he's been caging. Almost infectious.

I feel myself smiling. "Welcome to my life. Apparently you have a front row seat."

"It's entertaining as hell, but when are you going to let me behind the wheel?"

"The day I die."

He rolls his eyes at the word *die*. And then he gives me a blatant once-over. Head to toe. "You asked your dad and uncles for advice about lube. That's cute."

The way he says *cute*—it sounds sincere. But I still feel the need to defend myself. "I'm close to my family."

A warm smile appears. "I know. It's one of my favorite things about you." We exchange a heady look, my blood heating. He scans the empty hall and then whispers with his growing smile, "You top 'most of the time'." He uses air-quotes.

"Is that going to be a problem for you?" I ask.

He rolls his eyes again, like that's not where he meant for me to travel. Our shoulders brush, bodies drawing closer. We shut up as an influx of Cobalt Inc. employees meander down the hall.

We wait for the elevator in silence. Thankfully when it arrives, it's empty. We enter, and I press the lobby button. As soon as we start descending, Farrow tells me, "I'm vers." *He likes being a top and bottom.*

I look at him.

He raises his brows at me. "I want your cock in my ass."

I almost harden, but I catch him glancing at the elevator's security camera. He's aware of our surroundings. It's why we don't collide together.

Though, I risk nearing him. Only a couple feet away.

"What does *most of the time* mean for you?" he asks bluntly. "I once was with someone who didn't like any kind of penetration."

"That's definitely not me." I lick my lips, and his gaze falls to my mouth. "I like pretty much everything, but I've only bottomed twice."

His brown eyes flit up to mine, and he chews his gum slowly in thought. "You didn't like it?"

"Not with them. It's a trust thing," I say, just as the elevator dings and slides to a halt.

I don't mention how I have fantasized about Farrow behind me—his weight bearing against me, but seven out of ten times in the fantasy, I flip him around and top him.

The three other times...his erection is in me.

18

A ringing cellphone wakes me from a half-sleep. I roll onto my side and prop my body on my arm. If this is Alpha ordering me around via cellphone now, we're going to need to have a real chat.

I grab my phone that dropped to the old floorboards and first notice the time on the screen.

2:03 a.m.

Then the caller ID: *Wolf scout*

I instantly sit up, my black comforter already kicked to the edge of the mattress. On this unusually hot October night, I almost considered sleeping naked. But middle-of-the-night security emergencies basically tell me, *don't*. Unless I want to be the guy who trips over himself while putting on underwear.

And that's just not me.

I put the phone to my ear. "Maximoff."

His long pause spikes my pulse, and just before I ask what's wrong, his deep voice fills the line. "Come over."

Damn. My cock strains against my black boxer-briefs, and more heat gathers in my attic bedroom. I wonder if he intended for *come over* to sound that blistering and erotic.

I wait to jump at his command. For one reason only. "Don't you have a girl in your bed?" I found out fast that the nights where Jane and Maximoff are alone in the townhouse—no friends-with-benefits, no one-night stands—they somehow end up asleep in the same room. Same bed.

Platonically.

It's a little strange. A lot strange when I *really* sit and think about it, but I also understand how open and uninhibited these families tend to be. And how Maximoff and Jane's shared experiences from birth bond them together like fraternal twins. Much closer than just being cousins.

I've never dated a twin, and I honestly question how I'm supposed to fit into their dynamic.

Before he replies, I ask, "Have you told her about us?"

"Not yet." He plans to let her in on the secret.

I already agreed to that stipulation. See, Jane Cobalt comes first in his life, and it'll take a lot more than a five-minute ass-grab and lip-lock in his Audi to change that.

"She's asleep," Maximoff says, voice hushed. "I left her room. I'm in mine now. *Alone*." His hot impatience strokes the long length of my erection.

Aroused knot in my throat, I stand, bare feet on the floor. I use my shoulder to free my hands and push my phone to my ear. Just so I can wrap my wire around my radio and collect my holstered gun. I'm about to say *I'll be over*, but I want his voice in my ear.

"Is this your first booty call?" I ask.

"Is this your first time being propositioned by a celebrity?" he effortlessly flings back.

I smile. He's such a little smartass. "I think you mean *Harvard Dropout*."

"No, I mean *celebrity*." He could easily add: *internationally famous, overwhelming adored and revered*, but he just stops at celebrity.

I joke about Maximoff dropping out of Harvard, but I know the true reason he quit. It wasn't because he couldn't hack it. He needed three bodyguards during his first and only semester. Students bombarded him. Snapchatting. Instagraming. Taking selfies before, during, and after the lecture. The disruption his presence caused wasn't just pissing off his professors, he felt like he was ruining the education of his peers.

So he quit.

And he could've finished out his degree with online courses like Jane, but instead he threw himself into his career. It's all public knowledge.

I pull on my black cotton pants, and with my gun and radio in one hand, I'm out of my room faster than Maximoff probably thinks. Descending the narrow flight of stairs. Quietly passing the second floor where Quinn is passed-out asleep.

I reach my living room, and I open my mouth to speak. But he fills the line first.

"Try not to come before you get here," Maximoff says and then hangs up.

Damn.

I slip my phone in my pocket, my neck pricked hot. I subconsciously palm my dick, up and down twice. *I want him.*

Shit, I want him badly.

By my fireplace, I open our adjoining door.

"Walrus, you little bastard," I whisper and snatch the scampering kitten. Gently, I kick the door shut and then release Walrus in Maximoff's dark living room. No lights on.

The hot tea aroma is pungent tonight, the Earl Grey scent reminding me of him. I've seen Maximoff fill 16oz thermoses with hot tea like it's black coffee.

I quietly ascend the stairs. Careful that they don't squeak beneath my weight. I pass the second floor where Jane's room, a guest bedroom, and the only bathroom lie, and I ignore the two or three cats that stalk me.

At the very top of the staircase, I reach his door. And I enter his attic room, just as sweltering as mine—I use my leg to block two furry bastards from following.

No pussies allowed. I shut them out. Before I even look up, Maximoff says, "Lock it."

Maybe I should change his contact name to *Bossy* in my phone. I do lock the door. I'm not that big of an asshole.

I turn, and my pulse pounds in my cock. Maximoff stands in drawstring pants, hung low on his cut waist, shirtless, abs chiseled like marble, but more than that—more than the outline of his erection and his beautiful cheekbones—his unshakable, staunch demeanor overpowers the small attic room.

Basically saying, *I'm going to fuck you good.*

My blood cranks from a simmer to a boil, and I give him a slow-burning once-over. *Likewise, Maximoff.* I set my holstered gun and radio on his dresser.

In my peripheral, I survey his room out of habit: closed gray curtains, a low-standing bookshelf, all deep red brick walls, a full-sized bed and burnt-orange comforter. Tiny white lights are strung around the wooden rafters, a dim glow. No other light source but that one.

Facing one another, I comb my hair back with two hands, and his gaze trails over my tattooed abs and barbell nipple piercing.

I nearly smile. "Why are your clothes still on?"

His lips ache to rise. "Come here and take them off me."

With two lengthy steps, I bridge the distance between our strong builds—and I clutch the base of his neck, my hand running to his sharp jawline. My mouth teasingly close. Our locked gazes exhume the deepest depths, as though whispering furiously: *I know you. I know you. I know you better than most ever do.*

The intensity tightens my muscles, prolonging a kiss. I don't close my eyes. I don't look away.

Maximoff fists my hair, his other hand diving down my abs while my second palm ascends his chest. He reaches my length and massages above the cotton—he squeezes.

Good God. A rumble vibrates my throat, I throb twice as hard. Fuck, he knows what he's doing.

As my tattooed hand reaches the hollow of his neck, his eyes flit down for the first time. Watching me, his breath falls heavy.

Discovering what turns on Maximoff Hale has to be *my* greatest turn on. I want to make him come. Hard.

I lightly—very, *very* lightly—wrap my fingers around his neck. Slowly, I add pressure, faintly choking him. I study his reaction and the way his chest collapses.

I breathe against his mouth, "Do you like that?"

His groan sounds like a hollowed, wolfish growl. It's pure, raw sex.

Then his mouth meets mine, and his skillful, *sensual* tongue parts my lips. In such a languid, scorching wave. His aggression never disappearing—fisting my hair, tugging down my cotton pants. I step out and hold his jaw steady, deepening the kiss.

He walks me backwards, and my shoulders hit the brick. Our mouths don't break, and I cup his firm ass, and pull him against me, yanking down his drawstring pants. No boxer-briefs, his erection frees. I break our kiss, and my lips upturn at his size.

I'm not surprised that he has the most beautiful cock I've ever seen, thick and long. Our chests melded, our pelvises grind, and he fits his fingers in the waistband of my boxer-briefs.

His whisper warms my jaw. "That's going to be inside of you."

My head tilts back on the brick, *fuck yes*. My muscles flex, and I'm out of my boxer-briefs next. He looks down, and his reaction to my equally beautiful dick is a deep, "*Fuck*."

Yeah, you're not a winner in every arena, wolf scout. Not when I'm in contention.

With one hand, I grip the back of his neck. With the other, I stroke his shaft, my fingers tightening around him. My shoulders dig in the brick wall. He watches my hand with daggered eyes that want to roll back.

I grin as his hips buck forward, his mouth against mine again, and he takes over, aligning our erections, hot, sensitive flesh rubbing together— and he jerks both of us off with one calloused, hard hand that feels *fucking*...I groan, my parted lips falling to his jaw.

I hold his face and then nip his lip, his moan tearing through his mouth. *You liked that.* I scrape my teeth down his jaw, sucking the nape before biting lightly.

"Fuck," he breathes.

He really likes that. I rake my fingers hard down his back, and he thrusts forward, wanting to pound into me. I see that clearly. He drops his hands, and I swiftly rotate him, his back to the brick. Me facing his chest. I'm dying to watch him come.

I'm about to kneel, but he seizes my waist, his hand rising up my ribs. "Wait." His jaw tenses, and he kisses me again, slowly, and against my mouth, he whispers, "Come on me first."

Did I hear him correctly? One of the most straight-laced men I've ever met wants me to come on him?

Our eyes hit, and he sees the shock in mine. For one, I never thought he'd be *this* experienced. Despite saying that he has a lot of sex, that he loves sex—to me, he's still five years younger. Five years *less* experienced.

For another, I thought he'd be wound-tight and vanilla. But he likes to be bit. Possibly scratched and choked. Now this.

Maximoff Hale has his kinks, and they make him really vulnerable for a few seconds. Yet, he commands every action, too. I dizzy in thought, and I run my tongue over my stinging bottom lip.

He rubs my cock fast, *fuck.* I lean forward, forearm on the brick by his head. I hold his face in a tight grip. "You want me to come on you?" I ask huskily.

His head tries to arch back against the brick. He growls out a groan, "*Goddamn.*" His breath is ragged and spiked, and I'm only grasping his face.

His large hand squeezes around me—and I grit down, my muscles ablaze, my tendons pulling taut. My head thumps, blood rushing downward. I breathe hard through my nose. His hand changes speed, slower and tighter. The perfect pressure wells up inside of me, mind-numbing.

My head wants to loll back, but I remain eased forward, my forehead nearly against his forehead. He changes his pace and clutch *again.*

Fuck.

I'm going to—I jerk forward, coming by his fucking hand. His abs glisten, and with a breath knotted in my throat, I drop down to my knees.

I stroke his hard length a couple times with a skilled grip. He watches my fingers intently, and he pushes my damp hair out of my face.

I smile before I slide my tongue down him and cup his balls. He shudders and curses, "Fuck, Farrow." That *fuck* said, *stop teasing*. I try not to laugh.

I suck his tip and then wrap my mouth around him completely. I go all the way, in and out, back and forth, his cock between my lips. Gripping his shaft at times.

I love having him in my mouth, but even more than that, I'm hooked by the way he's staring deeply at me. Like I'm a fantasy. Like I'm something made of heaven and stars that he's dreamt of—and I never thought to ask what a celebrity who could have *anyone* in the fucking world fantasizes about.

And I wonder how long it's been me.

I feel myself hardening again. I clutch his ass and take him to the very back of my throat. I taste him on my tongue. He mumbles a curse, his eyes rolling back and then set into a glare at the ceiling. It's the hottest cum-face I've ever seen.

I pull back and swallow.

When I rise, we start kissing feverishly, our arms hooked around each other, and I hold his muscular back against my chest and suck the base of his neck. He moans as I bite his flesh, and then he spins. We keep wrestling for the advantage, more compatible than most would believe—like two men playing for the lead. Not fighting.

I smile wide as he guides my hand to the brick, his chest up against *my* back now. We're caked with sweat. His hands roam down my waist and ass, tracing the inked lines of my scattered tattoos.

I crane my neck over my shoulder and hold the back of his head. We kiss twice before he says, "Don't move."

Maximoff leaves to his nightstand. I lean on the brick with my forearms, almost in a relaxed lunge, watching him grab a box of condoms and lube.

"He bought my favorite," I tease.

Maximoff wears his irritated, pleasured smile like a champ. I could stare at that face all day, every day. I basically already do.

"This is your favorite?" he says, sarcasm present, breath still heavy. "I would've returned it, had I known."

I whistle. "Be careful. You're seconds away from losing your *honesty* merit badge."

He can't hide his smile, but as he comes up behind me, our gazes devour each other again. The air strains, and I don't even need to work him up. He's hard as a rock again.

Damn. He collects a condom, tosses the box aside, and tears the wrapper off with his teeth. I watch him sheath his cock, then lube himself and his fingers.

His confidence wounds a hot ball in my throat—*I want him inside of me.* Now.

I face forward, my head hanging slightly, and I relax my muscles. He clutches my waist, and then he slides one finger along me until he pushes inside.

My jaw just unhinges, the pressure enough to cage breath in my throat. He grazes against my prostate. I moan, "Fuck, *Maximoff.*"

I try to breathe full, deep breaths. He pushes another finger inside, teasing me open for a while. I glance back when he retracts his fingers.

Maximoff grips his shaft and pushes up against me. His warm breath heats my ear. "Do you need me to go slow?"

I'd smile if I weren't burning up alive. "No." I look back and seize his gaze hard. "Take me however you want." *That* idea fists my erection.

Both of us still standing, he gently eases into me, and my head turns towards the brick, my eyes nearly shutting at that body-shaking *pressure.* When I take all of him, his chest welds to my back, and he starts thrusting.

Fuck...I let out tangled, low moans. My hand in a fist on the brick. His fingers dig into my hips, his pace is deep and fast and hypnotic.

I lose myself to the rhythm. My mind floating off without my fucking body. With my free hand, I reach down and stroke myself. Only twice because his right hand drops off my waist, and *he* grips my hard shaft. Maximoff adds friction everywhere.

I extend my arm backwards and grab his ass. His muscles flex beneath my palm with each thrust deeper.

I moan and grit down. *Fuuuck*.

Our bodies buck forward with the intense rhythm, and I clench my teeth, the pleasure rippling through my red-hot veins. Barely even looking at the brick in front of me—my eyes are in the back of my head.

I come, and his groan thunders low in my ear, "*Farrow*."

His body rocks against me, milking his climax while I catch my breath. I rest my forehead on my bicep, sweaty palm on the brick.

He wraps his arm around my abs, very compassionately and comfortingly. I can honestly say that I've never been fucked that well.

Maximoff Hale is something else, and from start to finish, I can't imagine anyone else having him but me.

19

MAXIMOFF HALE

Multiply my fantasies times a fucking gazillion and that's how I'd describe last night.

It surpassed anything my mind could conjure.

Farrow set his phone alarm for 5:40 a.m. before we fell asleep in my bed. Just so he could leave before Quinn notices he's missing. Somehow we wake an hour earlier.

Must be the newness, excitement—or my idiotic brain *thanking* me repeatedly for giving into its six-year-long demands.

I lie on my side. Beneath my white sheets and orange comforter. Turned towards my bodyguard. Buck-ass naked, both of us. Farrow is propped on his elbow, and he runs his hand through my hair. Inspecting the roots.

"You need to dye it soon," he tells me.

I lick my lips, thinking. I have a routine with one-night stands. I *never* talk about myself. Never ask them anything too personal, not about to lead them on. I walk them downstairs and call a private driver to take them home safely.

I never see them again.

This is so fucking different.

Farrow's hand drops when I sit up against my headboard. He follows suit and studies my sharpened cheekbones and downcast eyes. I'm staring at my knuckles. And I realize, *I'm nervous.*

"Sore subject?" he asks.

I look at him, his stabbing gaze and neck tattoos naturally intimidating. I find comfort in all of it. "Why do you think I dye my hair?"

Farrow pauses for a millisecond. "You love your dad."

I nod, a smile trying to appear. *He knows me.* Nerves infiltrate fast. *He knows me.* I sit up straighter, my shoulders binding.

Farrow watches me closely, but neither of us speaks. He checks the time on his phone, and then he climbs out of bed. All six-foot-three of him, lean and muscular. And bare. Towering.

Christ.

He's everything I pictured and *more.*

Farrow collects his boxer-briefs from the floorboards. He pulls the elastic band to his waist. "Are we going to talk about why you're nervous?" He glances at me. "Think I didn't notice?"

I bring my legs up beneath the comforter and set my arms on my knees. "I just thought you wouldn't care."

"I care." He nods and finds his cotton pants. "I care *a lot.*"

I take a tight breath. "I know sex. I don't know *anything* else. Whatever happens after this, beyond fucking each other—it's a massive mystery to me."

He's in the midst of pulling his pants to his waist, and he smiles, his brows arching at me. "Rent a movie."

"What?"

"Rent *any* romantic movie—though the hetero ones aren't great. But just rent a movie, watch two sappy people do stupid, ordinary shit together, and there you go, Maximoff."

I growl out my irritation, but I keep repeating his words in my head. I catch myself smiling. Jesus. "It's not that fucking simple, Farrow."

"Besides the fact that I'm your bodyguard and we need to sneak around, yeah it is." He nears my side of the bed and rests a knee on the mattress. "You just like being well-informed before you do anything."

"Thank you," I say dryly.

"You're welcome." He runs his thumb over a bite mark on my shoulder. "Sorry."

"Don't be." I swallow my arousal, and he bends down and kisses me on the lips. So this is what it's like, huh? I can kiss someone the next morning. I can expect to see them in an hour.

I can do it all again and again.

Something lightens in my chest.

Feels like freedom.

Shower water rains down on me. My phone is docked in a speaker on the tiny sink. Playing a Spotify playlist that Farrow made yesterday. Full of old nineties rock. I have no clue why he likes that genre.

"Cannonball" by The Breeders blares in the bathroom, and I feel like someone is pouring gasoline straight in my bloodstream.

I squirt citrus-scented dollar shampoo on my palm. Lathering my hair with both hands. And then the door swings open. Shower glass is half permanently frosted from the waist-down. The top is just fogged, and I rub the steam with my fist.

Janie yawns sleepily at the sink, pink eye-mask on her head and blue *granny jammies* on.

"Bonjour, ma moitié!" I shout over the water and music.

"Just you and me, old chap," she yawns wider and opens the mirror's cabinet for her toothbrush.

I almost smile. Then I remember I'm hiding something from Janie. I've never hid *anything* from her, and the feeling isn't great. It's like lying to half of myself. If I can't be honest with her, then I'm never going to fully invest in whatever's going on with me and Farrow.

Just how it is.

With a mouthful of toothpaste, she shouts to me, "It's raining today, great and miserable thunderstorms!" She spits, rinses. "Chance of the media snapping photos of my frizzy hair, one-hundred percent."

I barely hear that last part over the song. *"Music off,"* I call out, and "Cannonball" abruptly stops.

"I should try to curl some pieces for the College Merit luncheon today. Try a new look…where is my…curling iron?" She digs beneath the cupboards.

"You're not supposed to join anymore charity luncheons," I say, kind of meanly. College Merit is an H.M.C. Philanthropies program, giving college financial aid to low-income students. "Aren't you shadowing a forest ranger today?"

She plugs in her curling iron. "I was, but…I mentioned the forest ranger to my brother—"

"No," I growl out, knowing where this is headed.

Janie fiddles with the buttons on the old iron. "You didn't see the way Ben looked at me when I said he could take my place. He even hugged me, and he called me *cool*, Moffy." She inspects a pimple on her chin in the nearly fogged-up mirror.

I wash shampoo out of my hair. "I'll call you *cool* every damn day for the rest of our lives. Just focus on yourself for your deadline's sake." Partly, I'm happy she'll be with me today—but it's selfish. If she graduates Princeton and still hasn't found a career path, she'll refuse to take time for herself like she is now.

Jane will say, *I'm wasting time on a fruitless search for a passion that may not even exist. My time is better spent doing charity work.*

"Tomorrow, the next day, I will," she says, but Jane's overwhelming love of her family is her greatest asset and greatest weakness. I can't predict whether that'll ever change.

I finish rinsing my hair. Unsaid things start weighing on me. I grab a bar of soap next to facial scrub and razors. "Janie?" I wipe the mist off the shower glass again.

She curls a brunette strand. "Yeah?"

"I'm seeing someone," I say, flat-out.

Jane startles, the iron slipping out of her grasp. Burning her wrist before thudding to the tiled floor. *"Merde."*

I instantly crack open the shower door, ready to help, but she raises a hand like *wait*. Jane picks up the iron, sets it aside on the sink, and then runs her reddened wrist beneath the faucet.

I wait a couple seconds. Half-hidden behind the door. I don't retreat or shut it.

When she rotates fully, Jane steeples her fingers to her pink lips. Blue eyes widened like saucers on me.

She's in shock.

"It's crazy," I agree.

"It's Farrow?" she guesses accurately. Maybe because of the massage that one time. Obviously, she sensed something between me and Farrow then. But it reminds me that I need to be more careful with Farrow.

No one can find out. Not unless we *purposefully* tell them.

"Yeah," I say. "It's Farrow."

"What changed?" she asks. "Wait, no—how long has this been going on? When did it start?" She begins to smile.

She's smiling?

My eyes start burning, overwhelmed for a hot second. "Why are you smiling?"

"You're risking so much by being with a bodyguard, and for *you* to do that…you have to like him, truly. I just want you to be happy, Moffy. Isn't that all we've ever wanted for each other?"

I nod a couple times. *She's happy for me.* Despite the consequences and the colossal secret that she'll have to keep—she's happy for me.

While she cools her wrist beneath the faucet again, I tell her, "It hasn't been long. We just *officially* fucked last night."

Her smile dimples her cheeks. "Remember when we were sixteen and you said that if you ever got head from *Farrow Redford Keene*, you'd self-combust and need CPR and an ambulance?"

"Was that me?" I joke.

"Most surely."

My lips hike up a fraction. "My sixteen-year-old virginal self would've needed a stretcher if Farrow gave me head back then—"

A light knock raps the doorframe. Yeah, the door is wide, *wide* open. And Farrow stands there.

Gun holstered, earpiece in, radio hooked to his black belt, V-neck tucked. He's ready for today and I'm naked in a shower with my cousin doing her hair three feet away. Plus, I just admitted aloud that I thought about him *sexually* at sixteen.

Great.

I add to the bathroom, "Hypothetically."

Farrow leans a shoulder on the doorframe. "You were *hypothetically* a virgin at sixteen?"

Jane snaps her curling iron at Farrow. "No virgin-shaming."

Farrow seems to just now fully register Jane's presence. He looks between us, and his gaze trails down my partially concealed, naked build. His eyes ping back to Jane, then me. "Is this a usual thing here?" he asks us.

I'm glad he drops my "hypothetical" story and fixates on my relationship with Jane.

She returns the curling iron to the cupboard. "There's only one bathroom, and it should be more peculiar for Moffy's bodyguard to see him half-naked than for me to."

Farrow tilts his head from side to side, considering the statement. "I don't think so. See, you're related—"

"Exactly." Jane is in defense mode, ready to debate her side like she's prepared with note cards, power point slides, and four-thousand word essays. "It means *nothing* to see each other naked because we're cousins, and really, if we dig deep, nudity is a social construct—"

"Okay, Cobalt," Farrow interjects. "I'll take a pass on the sociology lecture."

I hang onto the top of the shower door. *I need them to get along.* "How about we destroy the argument over which one of you is weirder for seeing me half-naked? I can think of a million other topics to debate. Like..." I toss up my hand and say the first fucking thing I can think of. "...why bananas are curved."

Jane answers, "Bananas grow towards the sun, Moffy, so as they develop against gravity, they become curved in shape." Cobalts consume trivia like water. Necessary to everyday life.

Farrow laughs. "I take it back, your relationship is cute."

Jane eyes him curiously. "You know...I can't tell if that's sarcasm."

"It's genuine," he assures.

Before I broke the whole bodyguard-client boundary, I'd call their relationship *cordial*, but to both be in my life now, they may have to form something closer to a friendship.

And if they can't...I don't know what happens.

An apocalypse?

Jane glances at Farrow and then pulls out acne medicated face wash. "Just so you realize, Moffy has told me about you two."

"I sensed that." He watches Jane. "Are you okay with keeping this secret?"

She nods. "You don't have to worry, I'd never tell anyone." Scrubbing her face, she creates suds. "If you break his heart, then you'll have to worry about me."

I smile at how blasé she says that.

Farrow tells her, "Threat noted."

She rinses her face and pats her cheeks dry with a towel. "Which one of you made the first move anyway?"

"Me," Farrow and I say in unison.

He laughs.

I scowl. "I'm one-hundred percent positive I kissed you first."

Farrow leans even more casually, his relaxed posture so damn sexy. "I'm also one-hundred percent positive I was the one who told you how I felt first."

"*Move* is an action. I took the first action," I rebut.

"If that's what you want to believe, I'm not going to stop you." His brown eyes sweep me from head to toe, and the steam in my shower feels hotter all of a sudden. *I had sex with a childhood crush.*

Five years older than me.

My bodyguard.

Blood pools south, and my cock almost rouses. Aching to be gripped. Which just means I've mentally sidelined the repercussions and accepted the full-blown attraction.

Do I crave a repeat of last night? *So damn much.* I stare off in a split-moment, picturing last night. His tattooed hand sliding up my chest. Holding my jaw, his other hand squeezing my—I blink and *blink* rapidly, catching myself in a trance.

Farrow stares at me with a knowing look.

"I can leave if you need me to," Jane says.

My head whips to her. "No, this is *your* house. Nothing's changed for you and me." I can't kick Janie out of the fucking bathroom. It's her bathroom too.

Jane contemplates this for a short second. Then her blue eyes land on my bodyguard. "Do you care if I'm here?"

"No," Farrow says quickly, the only correct answer in my mind. "Do you care if I'm here?"

"No," she says just as fast.

"Okay." Farrow nods. "Then we're cool."

She nods firmer.

I'm highly aware that they feel pressure to get along. And that pressure is coming from me. But for this to work, all three of us have to coexist.

20

"Work with me here, Farrow," Akara says over my phone that I placed in the cup holder of the Audi. Set to speaker while Maximoff speeds about twenty-five over to a gentleman & lady's charity golf tournament. "All of your daily logs are empty after 7:00 p.m."

Maximoff shoots me a narrowed look.

I mouth, *it's okay.* I'd touch him, his hand or his shoulder, but I keep a close eye on two silver SUVs that ride our bumper. I'm not sure if they have far-range camera lenses, but if one even briefly catches us in a slight embrace, we're done.

I like him too much to risk everything now just to hold hands, especially when I can grip his cock later tonight.

"I just don't see the issue," I tell Akara. "When I was on Lily's security detail, I always left gaps in the daily logs. If Alpha's not used to that by now, then that's their fucking problem. Not yours."

My "maverick" tendencies make sneaking around with Maximoff easier. *Where did your client go from 7:00 p.m. to midnight?* Blank.

No one's business but ours.

"Forget Alpha," Akara growls, switching between "boss" and "friend" too well. "This is *me* talking to *you* right now, and I'm telling you that I have two bodyguards on my Force not filling out their logs. Did I not specifically remind you that Quinn would pick up your habits?"

An annoyed noise sticks to my throat. I didn't notice he was copying me. I don't actively check everyone else's logs. It's a waste of time. "Man, it could be a good thing," I say, fixing my earpiece as muffled sound filters through. "He's learning from one of the best."

"*One* of you is enough," Akara says definitively. "We can't have two on the team."

"Let me talk to Quinn."

"No," Akara says. "Start filling out your logs. I don't care if you write one or two sentences, just show Quinn that it's a requirement. And hey, if you're *still* relenting, look down. Read your ankle."

I roll my eyes. I got a small script tattoo when I was twenty-one. Akara was with me. The ink on my ankle says: *live by your actions.* "Aye, aye captain."

He hangs up first.

Maximoff switches lanes and checks over his shoulder. "Now what's the plan? Fake a log entry? Flee the coast, fly to outerspace?" He barely looks my way; the two paparazzi SUVs have multiplied into four. "Maybe we can build a colony on Mars," he says, sarcastic. "Eat nothing but potatoes for the rest of our lives."

"You're referencing a movie I've never seen. Aren't you?"

The corner of his mouth rises. But not for long. Real concerns lie beneath his dry wit, and I'm not letting them fester.

"I'll be vague in my log," I explain, chatter growing louder in my right ear. I pull the earpiece out and increase the radio's volume. "It's very far from a grim, dark reality, so stop packing your survival kits and just trust me."

He's used to tapping into "damage control" mode. But he needs to breathe and not jump the gun here. We're just at the start of a marathon of secrecy.

Maximoff tries to turn his head to me, but he has to fixate on the paparazzi's vehicles that swarm him. "You know that I trust you more than I'd trust anyone else. We've been on the same page about all of this:

the no texting, no emails, even being careful with street cameras…and that's meant—it's meant a lot to me."

My chest inflates as my mouth pulls in a wide smile. "I'm glad you feel safe with me."

He makes a face. "Is that what I said?"

"In so many words, *yeah*."

He can't restrain his own smile, but then his lips downturn fast. His hands tighten on the steering wheel, and we go quiet as a blue sedan whips into the nearby lane. I spot the camera before the window even rolls down.

Maximoff accelerates.

I rotate and observe the SUV on our ass. From their front windshield, they point cameras at the Audi's rear window. I silently count four…five, six and now *seven* vehicles on the road. For the sole purpose of obtaining money-shots of Maximoff Hale.

"Get off 95."

"Not yet." Maximoff cuts off the blue sedan and weaves skillfully in and out of the scattered freeway traffic. Frenzied excitement blares through my earpiece's speaker, filling our concentrated silence.

"*Cobalt Empire all together,*" Oscar says.

"*Dream team,*" Donnelly sing-songs.

"*The band is about to start,*" Heidi, Eliot Cobalt's bodyguard whispers into the mic. She's on Epsilon, but Heidi is the only female bodyguard in the whole team. In her early fifties, she's been with the Cobalts since Jane was born.

Maximoff switches lanes again, and he must feel somewhat comfortable because he asks, "Wish you were there?"

My brows spike. "Do you mean with the 'Cobalt Empire' or watching Tom Cobalt and his band perform *live* publicly for the first time?"

"Either."

I keep surveillance of the speeding paparazzi SUVs. And I remember when Maximoff's seventeen-year-old cousin put together a three-person punk band when he was fourteen. Tom is the lead singer.

"I wasn't one of the bodyguards who saw Tom learn to play guitar. I didn't see him choose a band name or give my input." I roll my eyes because *Oscar* of all security members suggested the name *The Carraways*, a play off his middle name Tom Carraway Cobalt.

Tom chose The Carraways.

"And I didn't watch his rehearsals or listen to him rework songs." I crane my neck over my shoulder. I hate that SUV on our ass. "Seeing him *live* at a small venue doesn't mean that much to me."

"*Three, two,*" Donnelly whispers, "*…one.*"

Tom's deep, passionate voice and the fury of guitar, drums, and bass seep through the mic-line. I bet all nine Cobalt bodyguards are pressing their mic buttons so the rest of the security team can listen.

Maximoff smiles throughout the emo-punk song. "Tom." He shakes his head and then finds a moment to glance at me. "He was only ten when I finally told everyone that I liked girls *and* guys, and I didn't think it'd matter to him. But I stood in front of my family at Christmas, presents half-unwrapped, with goddamn *Jack Frost* playing in the background— and when everyone started hugging me and smiling, I looked over and Tom was crying."

His eyes reddened, Adam's apple bobbing.

My chest is taut with emotion. "He was happy."

"So goddamn happy." Maximoff blinks back water that wells. "Tom knew he was gay…for as long as *I* can remember, and I'm five years older than him. And when I knelt in front of him and hugged him—I felt guilty." He cringes. "For not telling him sooner. I pretty much knew I was attracted to guys by thirteen. That's two years where I could've told him."

I extend my arm over the back of his seat, acting like I'm using the seat to check behind us. I just want to be closer to Maximoff. "It's admirable how much you care," I say, "but he's lucky he has you at all." Warmly, I add, "Your compassion is showing."

He tries to hold my gaze, but he can't. Not with the paparazzi threatening to run him off the road. "Do you like compassionate guys?"

"I like you," I say without a beat.

He licks his lips, neck reddening. *He liked that.* I lean back, keeping my arm on the seat.

Maximoff glances at me. "When did you come out to your dad?"

"I was eleven," I tell him easily, "and my father asked me if there were any girls I liked at school. I said there were boys." I almost laugh at the memory. "I can still see the shock on his face, especially as I confidently said *I'm gay*, but after the initial surprise died down, he just started asking me about my crush. I came out at school around the same time."

He listens carefully. "I remember you said something about how you weren't that confused about it."

That was a brief conversation we had *years* ago when he was sixteen. Both of us at a Fourth of July party his family hosted. I'm surprised he remembered.

"Yeah," I say. "I could tell for sure when I was nine. I was at a mall, and I was attracted to the male underwear models in the poster ads. Eighteen years later, and I still have great taste." I raise my brows at him.

Maximoff smiles. "Did you just call me hot?"

"I was definitely complimenting myself there."

He's about to flip me off, but the traffic steals his attention. And then The Carraways' first song ends and chatter returns.

"*I've been reborn,*" Donnelly says.

"*Hold me,*" another bodyguard chimes in.

"*Pass the tissues.*"

"*He fucking did it.*"

"*Damn, look how good he was,*" Quinn adds.

"*Our kid is all grown up,*" Oscar says, choked up. "*Shit.*"

Maximoff has widened eyes, a bit stunned at all of their reactions.

"You didn't realize," I say, "your achievements are basically ours." Our lives are dedicated to these families, and when they succeed, there will *always* be a part of us that feels like we succeeded too.

He accelerates again. "Since you're not on a Cobalt's detail, what's your equivalent of this moment?"

I think for a short second. "The time when Luna learned to drive a car."

Maximoff nods in realization. "My mom taught my sister, so that means…"

"I was in the car, too." I notice the blue sedan the same time as Maximoff. He tenses, and we're silent. I turn off the radio so he can concentrate.

The sedan flanks our left side, and two white SUVs are on our right, one on the bumper. Maximoff is a rigid board. Constantly eyeing his rearview mirror.

"Did you know," he says, "that my dad *banned* me from teaching Luna how to drive?"

"Yeah, and I agreed. Case in point." I stretch towards him and read the speedometer. "*One-hundred-and-ten.*" I hang onto his seat and lay on his horn.

The sedan eases back, but the SUVs only squeeze closer.

"You should get off 95 now."

He tries to veer towards an exit, but paparazzi purposefully trap him. "Sit back, Farrow."

Not even a second later, all of the SUVs and sedans and every paparazzi vehicle disperses in a mad dash. Abruptly freeing us.

"*Fuck,*" he growls, knowing the cause.

Blue and red lights flicker in our rear. We're being pulled over by police.

21

MAXIMOFF HALE

When I finish a hearing at the local courthouse,
I slip on a pair of Ray Bans out of necessity. Farrow is already wearing dark aviators, and in unison, side-by-side, we push through the double doors.

Camera flashes blast in quick succession.

Reporters from prime-time news stations bounce near me. Microphones at the ready. Their questions ringing shrilly in my ears. Farrow extends his arm and bars the reporters from getting in my face.

I move forward.

No hesitating. No lingering. No wallowing or complaining. What's done is fucking done, and it's not the first time I pled my case to the court. Not the first time I said, "I take responsibility for speeding, but what's being done about the paparazzi?" They're rarely fined.

The court always replies, "Regardless of the paparazzi, you have the means to pay for a personal driver. There's no excuse for endangering the lives of other people."

I get that.

It's why I hardly argue. Before I climb into the *passenger seat* of my Audi, I catch the tail-end of a reporter speaking to a camera.

"This will be the fourth time the court has suspended Maximoff Hale's license for excessive speeding. And his license will *remain* suspended for twelve months."

I can't drive for a year.

Farrow slides into the driver's seat, shuts the door, and puts the key in the ignition. For the first time with Farrow as my bodyguard, I'm not behind the steering wheel.

I crack my knuckles and watch him adjust the side mirrors. "You're loving this."

His smile widens into James Franco territory, and he revs the car, peeling out of the courthouse. Driving with *one* hand only, but he ditches the paparazzi after a sharp turn down a narrow street. Navigating his way around Philly with ease and precision.

My cock throbs—*no*. If I could speak to my dick, I'd say *you're not allowed to be attracted to Farrow driving my car. That's my car. Mine.* He's only allowed behind it for...

I wince. A whole agonizing year.

Farrow studies my expression in a quick glance. "Realizing I'm a better driver than you?"

"Realizing doomsday just happened." I crack my knuckles again and shift in the seat. Sitting straighter. Partly to avoid a hard-on. Mostly to stop stressing about not having my feet on the gas pedal or brake. No longer the captain of my ship.

"You call everything doomsday," Farrow says, his gaze flitting to me more often.

"No I don't."

"Toaster broke last week, you said *doomsday*. You ran out of hangers, you said *doomsday*. It was raining, you said—"

"Thank you for that short summary." I have no idea what to do with myself in the passenger seat. I lean forward. I lean back. Rake my hands through my thick hair, stretch my arms over my chest—

"Just take a breath, Maximoff. I'm not going to run you off the road. I enjoy your blow jobs too much."

I break into a smile. How is he making me smile right now? I inhale and lean further back, ignoring the incessant vibrating messages on my phone. I turn my head to him.

Our eyes caress.

Farrow reaches out with his right hand, but he can't physically touch me. Just on the slim chance that *anyone* in a passing car sees and snaps a picture. Sometimes I wonder if he's silently disappointed by the lack of PDA. For me, it's all the same. I'm not missing what I never had.

But being overly cautious is what'll make this last.

Farrow commits to a safe action. He grips the back of my seat. "I bet I can distract you all the way home." His voice falls to an even huskier octave. "*Without* touching you. Hell, I bet I can make you hard without talking dirty."

"You must like to lose bets often."

Grinning, Farrow rotates the wheel with one hand. Turning onto another street. "Who and what did you fantasize about when you were a teenager?"

Fuck. I adjust in my seat, my cock constricted against my jeans. *Fuck me.*

"Hard already?" He lifts his aviators to his head, pushing back his white hair. His mannerisms, the way the corner of his mouth quirks— fucking *grips* my dick.

"Agitated, mostly."

"I can tell. It's that little grimace-smile thing." Farrow laughs as I flip him off, and he adds, "Come on, Maximoff. What'd you jerk off to?"

"Tell me your favorite gay porn categories, and maybe I'll answer."

"*Maybe* you'll answer," he says, brows raised. "Okay...my favorite gay porn..." he trails off in thought. "I like *big dick* and *rough sex*." He flicks on his blinker to take a left turn. "Have you watched any porn before?"

"Only a few times." I can see how my mom was addicted to porn, and that's partly why I think I stopped logging onto porn sites after the third session. "What'd you rub one out to as a teenager?"

"The Olympic male swim team," he says and off my knotted brows, he laughs, "I'm fucking with you. I didn't have anyone in mind specifically." Farrow evades paparazzi in the distance by driving onto a side street. His next glance is *knowing*. "Not like you."

He knows my fantasy is him.

Bluntly, Farrow emphasizes, "You can say *me*."

I give him a look. "How are you not freaked out?"

"Because I wasn't the one with the crush."

My face contorts in a series of emotions, landing on a cringe. "I could've sworn the bet was to make me *hard*, not want to push you out of the car."

Farrow laughs. "Tell me your fantasy. In detail." His gaze drips down me in a searing wave before fixing on the street. "I want to hear it."

Now his bet makes sense. He said he wouldn't have to talk dirty. Because he planned for *me* to. This shouldn't be that difficult. Every single night, we fuck in my bedroom, and then we fall asleep together. He sets his alarm for 5:40 a.m. on the dot and leaves my townhouse before Quinn wakes.

My one-night stand routine has been replaced with a Farrow Redford Keene routine—and it's better. Hotter. But it's inherently different.

Like right now, I can *verbally* describe a fantasy at noon. I'm around someone I can fuck the brains out of twenty-four-hours a day. Uninhibited, unrestricted access to the most intoxicating, euphoric experience alive. With someone I care about.

I lick my lips slowly. If I'm unleashing my fantasy to Farrow, I'm going all in. No restraint. "I have a fantasy that plays on loop."

Farrow listens, his eyes on me every other second.

"I'm in the shower," I continue, "and I've thought a ton about what that location means. So I'll save you the trouble of psychoanalyzing me and just tell you." I sit up straighter. "I never let anyone stay the morning and shower with me. I never trusted someone to linger like that, but my brain—for whatever damn reason—always, *always* lets you stay."

Farrow has this look in his eye. Like he wants to kiss me. But knows he can't. He grips my seat tighter.

Lower. I crave for that hand to drop *lower*. On me. Unzipping me. Stroking me—I shake my head once, and then just continue on, "So I'm in the shower alone, and then the door opens. And there stands…" I feign surprise. "My mortal enemy."

He rolls his eyes. "For fuck's sake. I may lose this shit bet if you keep cutting yourself off." Neither of us brings up how the bet has no stakes, no odds or payouts. Except for bragging rights.

I try to be more serious. "You're buck-ass naked."

"Getting better."

I shift somewhat in my seat, just visualizing the next part. "You enter the shower, shut the door, and you come up behind me."

Farrow goes still. "Behind you?" Maybe he expected me to bend him over and pound the fuck out of him—and while that's a good one, it's not *the* one.

"Yeah." Our breaths are heavier, my skin flush. Veins pulse in my semi-hard cock. "I'm rubbing myself, and your palm usually encases my fist on the wall. Your chest up against my back."

Farrow has to drop his hand off my seat. He rests it on his thigh by the bulge in his black pants.

I stretch my head back, my muscles flexed and burning. I keep hardening. "After that, you do different things every time. Jerking me off, kneeling down, and sometimes I have you against the wall and I take you from behind. But occasionally..." I shift again. "You're inside of me."

"Wow," Farrow breathes, "I rocked your teenage world, didn't I?"

I flash him an annoyed smile. "I'm limp now. Thank you for that."

Farrow glances at the hard outline in my jeans. "Your erection says *you're a fucking liar.*"

"Don't speak for my cock," I retort, trying not to smile. He's near-laughter, and then he drives onto our street.

We're in the garage in a matter of seconds. Closed and secure. Hidden from the public. The only threat is Quinn in the security's townhouse.

Farrow shuts off the ignition. We unbuckle our seatbelts. As we turn, our eyes collide first, unrestrained and pulsing with *want* and *need*—our lips meet. My tongue parting his, and I edge deeper. Our hands wrestling with each other's buttons and zippers.

He seizes my shaft in the *best* grip known to man. Farrow has a way with his hands that completely, utterly, massively *annihilates* me. I break the kiss just to mutter, "*Fuck.*"

He sucks the base of my neck and nips my flesh. *Yes.*

Fuck yes.

I stroke his impressive, literal mouth-watering length, pre-cum slick against my palm. I catch a glimpse of his tattooed fingers wrapped around me—my mouth opens, a guttural groan plastered in my lungs.

Fuck me.

Farrow clutches my jaw with his other hand, and he eats up my expression. *Consuming* my narrowed forest-greens that growl *fuck me*. He grits down, nose flaring. His chest rising and falling heavily.

Our pace increases, the friction like a blissful scorching hell. My head tries to loll back. *Fuckfuckfuck.* I come, and as a deep groan rumbles through Farrow, I realize that he comes by watching me hit a peak.

Both of us shirtless, pants zipped and cleaned up, I tell Farrow to wait before he climbs out of my Audi. He eases his door closed and plants his ass back on the seat. What I'm about to do— I've never done before. It seems so small and infinitesimal compared to sex, but it's not to me.

Farrow's brows furrow. "What is it?"

I gather all the confidence I own. Which is a hell of a lot. "I got you something."

"You got me something?" he repeats.

"Based on *every* romantic movie *ever*, it seemed like the right thing to do." I pop open my glove compartment, and I collect a black box about the size of a necklace case. "It's not expensive, so lower your expectations."

"Hey, I have no expectations." Farrow rubs the back of his neck and then takes the box from me. "I'm genuinely shocked right now." His mouth starts curving. "How did you even get this without me noticing?"

"There's this thing called online shopping," I say, "and they deliver the goods to your house, and then when security rifles through my mail— namely *you*—they don't touch anything postmarked *Maximoff Hale X*."

Creepy bastards send me mail under my name, so I always add the *X* to my personal purchases.

His smile expands. "Such a precious smartass." He pops the lid off the box, and he laughs. "As I was saying." He lifts up a gray and black triangular patch.

The stitched words read: *Asshole Merit Badge.*

I motion to the patch. "For the amount of awards you've given me: *valor, honesty, integrity, resourcefulness, humility*—I thought you must've been feeling lonely with *zero* of your own."

He can't stop smiling. He rubs his mouth a few times, but that smile is not vanishing any fucking time soon. He laughs and nods repeatedly. "You want me to join your little wolf scout club."

"Maybe." I breathe fully, happiness spreading across my face. Clear and free. Something light lives inside of me.

Farrow edges near, his *thank you* written all over his gaze. Even before we kiss.

I skateboard into my kitchen while dialing a number on my phone. Farrow and I split apart for lunch. He's back in his townhouse. Keeping up appearances with Quinn. Accomplishing a few other security tasks. Like filling out his logs.

I open my cabinet and grab a bag of flaxseed chips. FaceTime rings and *rings.* I have no problem calling my fourteen-year-old brother twenty or fifty more times until he fucking answers.

Right when I think the call drops, the screen switches to an image of a packed freezer.

My brows bunch. "What am I looking at?" I ask, not needing to say a greeting to Xander. If my siblings don't call me, I call *them* every day. Even if it's just for two or three minutes.

"I'm trying to find my breakfast; I just woke up."

I dump chips in a bowl. "It's two p.m."

"It's Saturday. I would've slept till four if Kinney didn't blast her screamo music in my bedroom." In the video chat, his hand shifts the frozen chicken. I can't lie—I miss being at home whenever I hear these small stories. Miss seeing them firsthand.

But that's the thing about growing up, getting older—for whatever and however much I lose, I gain something new with *someone* new.

"What are you looking for?" I ask while skateboarding to my refrigerator.

"Mom just bought more Toaster Strudles, and Luna keeps hiding them."

Toaster Strudle War is a real Hale thing. Luna thinks that Xander purposefully chomps down all of them, but he usually saves her two that just get eaten by Kinney.

Xander asks, "What are you eating?"

I flip my camera as I grab a bag of shredded cheese and skateboard to my bowl of chips. "Nachos."

All of a sudden, twenty frozen items cascade out of his freezer and thud to the floorboards. I hear our family dog scamper off in the background.

"*Fuuuuck*," Xander curses. The camera is pointed at the mess for literally a full minute while he contemplates putting it all back. "Ughhhh."

I'd clean it for him if I were there. "Just make your breakfast. Pick it up after, Summers."

My nickname for my brother is a play on his X-Men namesake: *Alexander Summers*. Likewise, my namesake is also X-Men related.

Pietro Maximoff.

As in Quicksilver.

Xander has the Strudle box in hand and heads to the toaster.

I rotate my camera back to my face and sprinkle cheese on my chips. "So I heard you haven't been outside in weeks."

"Do you blame me? No one will tell me *how* Mom and Dad ended up being photographed from the *backyard*, Moffy. The backyard, in a gated neighborhood. I'm not going out there."

I know how they were photographed.

Farrow shared the security info with me. I get why my parents would want to keep this secret from Xander. They're worried the truth will ramp up his anxiety.

I have the fucking power to unveil the curtains. And I have the power to hurt my brother. One choice. I could say, *hey, Summers, paparazzi's remote-controlled drones flew over the house. There may be more flying overhead if security doesn't catch them in enough time. There's no guarantee.*

So I set the whole truth aside and say, "I don't blame you. But you have to face the fucking world. Even if it sucks sometimes."

"All the time," he corrects and rips the plastic off his frozen pastry and puts it in the toaster. I slide my bowl of chips in my microwave.

"Flip your camera," I say.

With a sigh, Xander rotates his camera, the screen showing his face for the first time. Sharp jaw structure, messy brown hair, expressive amber eyes, and a *Hobbit* T-shirt over checkered boxers. As a child, he was lauded as a "classic beauty" and that hasn't changed.

You know Xander Hale as *the most beautiful* fourteen-year-old boy in the entire world. As said by you. You swoon over him like he's the lead singer in a boy band or a famous social media star. You covet any photos you find online and cause his name to trend weekly. You've made his money-shots worth *quadruple* what mine sell for—and in effect, paparazzi stalk him like he's the rarest, most hidden antelope of the pack. When in reality, he's an endangered, timid bird.

I know him as my little brother. An amazing human being who speaks Elfish if you hang around him long enough. Who's just trying to live in a world that's a little too big for him. Who I'll never give up on.

I just want him to be able to feel the light now and then. If I have to wrangle the sun out of the fucking sky with my bare hands, then I'll withstand the burn. I'd give it all to him if I could.

Fair warning: imagine your toes being sawed off, and that's what'll happen if you fuck with my brother.

"You look like shit," I say honestly. "You know what would help that?"

"Two more hours of sleep."

"Swimming in the backyard pool with your big brother."

Xander sighs into a glare. "Just come here and play video games with me. Stop trying to make me so..."

"Healthy, thriving, a human who goes outside—"

"Alright, alright," he says. "Jesus, you're relentless."

My microwave beeps. I pull out the bowl of chips, and when I return to my phone, I notice Xander squinting at the screen.

I give him a look. "You picking your nose?" I eat a chip.

He scratches his cellphone like he's trying to wipe a smudge off the screen. "What...what is that on your neck? Is that a *hickey*?"

I cough on my chip. *Fuck.* I drop my phone on the counter and fill a cup of water under the faucet. I down the water while Xander yells, "What, where'd you go—I need details!"

What's the chance that Farrow would be that careless and give me a grade-school hickey? *Slim.* Maybe it's not that bad.

I return to my phone and examine my neck in the screen. A dime-sized spot is faintly red. Probably because it happened recently. I doubt it'll last. "What kind of details do you want?" I ask my brother.

He contemplates my question for a long moment and he settles on this: "Is the other person alive?"

I smile. *I love my family.*

Xander explains, "Luna says that whoever you hook up with instantly *disintegrates* into astral particles. Never to be seen or heard from again."

"That's a fucking terrible superpower."

"No kidding." Xander hot-potatoes his toasted pastry. "P.S. Dad is throwing a party in honor of your license suspension today. Everyone is pretty happy."

"I saw the group-text." The party is *parents only* which is kind of bullshit since it's about me. I eat another chip. "Are you happy about it too?" I ask.

He shrugs and then looks at his pastry. Xander reaches some pretty low lows, and our parents hawk-eye him a lot. They're even more aware of his health than I can be.

Xander barely lifts his gaze to the camera. "I overheard Thatcher saying the Camp-Away's new format is 'life-threateningly' dangerous." Thatcher Moretti is his 24/7 bodyguard, but young girls bombard

Xander so often that Banks Moretti, Thatcher's identical twin, is also on my brother's detail.

"Thatcher is one of the stricter guys," I remind Xander. "He's probably overreacting."

"Yeah but…" A tense beat passes before he tells me, "I need you to live long, Moffy." He pauses, his eyes glassing a little bit. He scratches his nose and then rotates the camera to face his paper plate.

I stare hard at the phone.

My whole life, I've seen the media and nameless, faceless human beings shit on the people I love. Over and over. Clawing with no end in sight. Trying desperately to tear them apart. Ripping at the jugular. I walked on a sidewalk at ten-years-old and heard the word *rape* thrown at my mom in threat.

You wonder why I didn't become bitter at the world.

You wonder why I don't resent the world.

Because I knew I needed to become something that could withstand the world.

For my siblings, for my family, for anyone who'd grow up after me and need someone to defend them when they can't defend themselves; when they need a shoulder to cry on or a safety net to fall in—I'm here. I've been here.

I'm always here.

Strongly, I tell my brother, "I'm not going anywhere, Summers."

22

Black and orange Halloween streamers and pumpkin lanterns drape Maximoff's kitchen cupboards. I line up bottles of liquor on the countertop. Tequila, vodka, and flavored rum. I also purchased two six-packs of beer, a jug of orange juice, and a liter of Fizz.

Maximoff scowls at the haul.

I arch my brows. "You told me to buy a variety." I wave to the bottles. "This meets your requirements."

Unsaid Rule #1: *Maximoff Hale cannot, under any circumstance, purchase alcohol himself.*

Not unless he'd like a front-page headline saying he broke his sobriety. To save himself that headache, he *had* to ask me to make a liquor store run.

His grocery list said: *lots of different alcohol, Different types. & Chasers.*

I already annoyed him about his bad punctuation and random capitalization. One of my favorite things to do. And I've pointed out that for a guy who's overly *precise*, this was the vaguest list he's ever given me.

Maximoff crosses his arms over his dark-red crewneck, a domineering presence in the cramped kitchen. At the sight of his shirt, my mind drifts for a second.

I've noticed he's been ditching most of his green shirts for *red*. A deliberate, calculated change.

The public associates most of the Hales, Meadows, and Cobalts with their favorite colors.

And his dad's is *red*.

Ryke's is *green*.

I'd never tell Maximoff to not care about his dad. Hell, it'd be impossible for him to even *try* not to care. But the more he attempts to prove his dad's worth, he's essentially more and more and more like Ryke Meadows.

It's a shit Catch-22. There is no winning, and he's smart enough to have already figured this out. Maximoff is just too headstrong to let go and do nothing.

"What about whiskey or scotch or bourbon?" Maximoff asks me. "You didn't buy a single dark liquor."

I lean a hip against the counter, our bodies naturally close due to the small space. Maximoff draws even nearer, our knees knocking. We're alone in his townhouse.

For the moment, at least.

I hook two fingers in the waistband of his dark jeans. "Remind me," I say, voice husky, "what's the goal tonight?"

Maximoff stares at my long tattooed fingers, lost in his head all of a sudden. He uncrosses his arms. And he clasps my wrist.

He drives my hand down his jeans. My mouth curves, and I gladly pull us closer, chest-against-chest, and I slip my palm beneath his boxer-briefs.

His heady forest-greens rise to my mouth. His ravenous, forceful expression sears my body and contracts my muscles. I can practically see all the ways he wants to fuck me in the reflection of his eyes.

"Besides the obvious goal," I whisper. "My cum in your mouth."

He hardens beneath my firm grip, but his hand is still wrapped around my wrist. "You mean *my* cum, your mouth."

So that's how it's going to be tonight. Playing for the lead. I smile, not giving into his demands that easily. "I said what I said."

"The goal..." he remembers. "The *real* goal tonight..." Maximoff pulls my hand out of his jeans. To clear his head for a second. I comply and rest my elbows on the counter.

I help him verbalize the "real" goal. "Is to get your cousin drunk."

Maximoff scowls at the whole scenario. "Or like she said, 'I want to know what it feels like to be fucking drunk.' Which could be one beer or three or twenty vodka shots."

"Twenty shots," I repeat flatly. "We're trying to get her feel-good wasted. Not kill her."

We're not talking about Jane Cobalt.

His nineteen-year-old cousin Sullivan Meadows asked him for advice about partaking in a "quintessential adolescent party night" with booze included. Something she's never done since she dedicated her time to competing and swimming as a professional athlete.

For three hours, this was all security could talk about. Our comms convo went something like this:

Donnelly: *does Moffy know anything about booze?*

Me: *he knows vodka is clear.*

Akara: *don't get me started.*

Oscar: *someone convince Jane to convince Charlie to go so I can be there.*

Me: *or we could just have fun without you, Oliveira.*

The younger Hales, Meadows, and Cobalts all refer to Maximoff for advice, help, anything. And while the guy is great at many things, he's not great at *everything*.

Like alcohol.

Apparently his cousins and siblings don't care about good advice. Just *his* advice. It speaks volumes about their sheer love for Maximoff. And their lack of common sense.

Maximoff returns to his first point of contention. "Feel-good wasted *can* include dark liquor." He glares as my amusement brims to the surface. "What?"

"Thank God for my drunk adolescent behavior. You see, we want to start her with the basics, not level her up to a graduate degree in drinking." I count off my fingers, staring with my thumb. "No whiskey, no bourbon, no scotch, no puke."

He blinks slowly into a no-nonsense glower. "You're getting off on this."

"Getting off on what?"

"The fact that you know more than me about something."

My brows ratchet up. "Wolf scout, I know more than you about *a lot* of things. If I got an erection every time this happened, I'd be walking around with a constant hard-on."

"And I was just about to offer to help you." He gestures to my cock. "Seeing as how I would've been the cause. But now…" He places a hand on his chest. "I'm not feeling so generous."

I roll my eyes and lick my lips, smiling. "Is that right?" I sweep our builds, still pushed up against one another, my hand on his waist. His hand on my ass.

Maximoff makes a show of taking *one* step back. Our hands dropping. "All the altruism in my bones has *withered* and died."

"That's dramatic and impossible."

"Who's to say that I'm not already a selfish fucker? I sped on a freeway with you in the car. Putting your life at risk. Christ, *knowing* that Jane refused to ever ride in the same car with me if I was behind the wheel. I did that. And I'd probably still be doing it if I had my license."

He's not proud. His jaw tics, eyes darkened.

I'm used to the deep tangents. From blow jobs to life meaning. It's how Maximoff operates. Everything has greater significance to him. Every action has soul-bearing subtext that he tries to unload. His mind is fucking intriguing as hell, and I *more* than willingly follow every thread, every line of thought.

"You have your flaws," I say bluntly. "And you need to remind me and the public, the media that you're human and you're not perfect because you're so afraid to let us all down." I lean closer and whisper, "That makes you less of a selfish fucker."

Maximoff steps near, his muscular frame colliding with mine. My hand glides against the sharpness of his jaw. His deep breath mixes with mine before his warm lips nudge my mouth open. Our tongues unite, and his hand clenches my hair.

Damn, Maximoff. Heat gathers, a groan in the pit of my throat. He instinctively thrusts forward, pelvis against pelvis. He searches for harder contact on his cock. Something I notice he does often. Something that turns me into a throbbing rock.

I pin his back to the counter. Grinding my erection against his, and he breaks our hungered kiss to let out a strangled moan, "*Fuck.*"

I want him naked. Bare. Bent over the kitchen table.

I bet he wants me the same way.

I bear more of my weight on him. Maximoff curses out in a throaty groan, his daggered glare on the ceiling. His heartbeat pounds rapidly against my hard chest. I hold his jaw protectively, my fingers sliding over his mouth, down to his neck.

"Fuck," he breathes. Every look, every word he utters *fists* my dick.

Maximoff turns the tables. He grabs my ass and uses his strength to straighten up. Not letting our bodies separate, he holds us together and walks me backwards.

My spine hits the refrigerator.

He unbuckles my belt and then slides his coarse hand down my black pants. Only the thin cotton of my boxer-briefs act as a barrier. As he strokes my length, I grit down in arousal, blood pumping hot.

Fuck, I bow forward, my head spinning for a second. "Looks like you're back to being charitable," I breathe.

Maximoff removes his hand.

I almost laugh. "And then he leaves to prove a point."

"I'm checking the time, asshole." He rotates his wrist, his cheap watch-face in view. "We have ten minutes before everyone gets here. *Maybe.*"

"Only one of us is getting head then."

Neither of us forfeits that quickly for most things. Maximoff already has a solution and pulls a *coin* out of his pocket. "Let's flip for it."

"You carry quarters in your pocket?" I raise my brows at him. "What else is in there? A floppy-disk?"

"Shut up and call it." He tosses the coin.

"Heads."

He slaps the quarter on the top of his hand. Then, he lifts his palm to *heads*.

"You can't beat me at everything," I tell him.

"I'm starting to think that's your favorite phrase." He lowers to one knee, already manhandling my body by wrenching me forward—*damn.*

I lean my shoulders on the fridge, pulse in my throat. "It's definitely one of them."

In one pull, my pants are at my thighs. My fingers weave through his thick hair. Knelt before me, he still seems godly and statuesque, worthy of adoration. His hands trace the muscular curve of my waist that draw him towards my cock.

"I think I like you down there," I tease.

"Most people do." He slowly sinks my boxer-briefs down my thighs. My erection springs out, and his chest falls in a desirous breath. He looks at me once to say, "I give great head."

Great may be an understatement, but I tell him, "The amount of people that call you humble, I'm beginning to think are all liars."

"Or I am humble. Just not when it comes to sex."

That comment really stays with me for a second, and then he grips me and languidly licks my tip—*fuck.* A blistering knot builds in my throat. My head hits a fridge magnet as soon as his lips wrap around my shaft. *Fuckfuck.*

Shoulders on the fridge, my waist bowed forward, I rock into his mouth, pushing deeper. I know he can take all of me. I tighten my hold on the back of his head.

Maximoff clutches and squeezes my bare ass, and I reach back and place my hand on top of his.

He sucks and licks, doing most of the work, but my breath heavies like I'm the one running the marathon. I bite down, a groan stuck inside of me.

Fuck, I let out a heavy, strained breath. "Maximoff." His hair tangles in between my fingers. My muscles are on fire.

And then Maximoff lifts his eyes, my erection all the way in his mouth. His gaze alone nearly makes me come. He wears a look I've never seen him given anyone.

It's one that firmly.

Confidently.

And effortlessly says…

This is my kingdom.

My entire body responds, my world lit to the core. He takes my cum in his mouth, licks the remainder off my cock, and he swallows. When he eases onto his feet, like every action he just made is the most natural thing in the world, I almost harden again.

Maximoff looks utterly consumed by me. His breath heavy, gaze roaming every limb, every inch of my flesh. I pull my boxer-briefs and pants up, and he catches my hand before I zip.

One breath, he says, "I need inside of you."

Need. He's dying to come. I let go and surrender to his desires. Whatever he needs, I'd offer him. With the smallest window of time, we urgently slip into the tiny walk-in pantry.

Maximoff shuts the door and yanks my pants and boxer-briefs back down while I unbutton his jeans, freeing his erection soon after. Our hot and heavy breaths mix together.

"Condom?" I ask him.

He pulls one out of his pocket. *Of course.*

We kiss in rough, hurried waves, and I steal his condom and roll it on his shaft. Faster than he would be. He spits in his palm for lube, the image sticking in my brain. Pulsing blood in my veins.

I turn, put my forearms on a shelf next to jars of peanut butter and jam, and bend slightly over. I feel his strong grip on my waist.

His deep, edged voice kills my fortitude. "I'm going to fuck you fast."

I press my forehead to my arm, stifling a gnarled moan.

"Good," I say, choked. "Fuck me fast."

Maximoff eases into me, the pressure nerve-blistering and fucking… *fuck.* He sinks full in and starts thrusting with a quick, hungered pace.

I try to seize the wooden shelf, but my mind ascends to a place with zero common sense and just body-numbing feelings. *Good fucking God.* The pleasure wells up inside of me.

I grit my teeth, breathing hot, ragged breaths through my nose. I glance back, his gaze devouring the way his dick enters me in deep and fast repeated succession.

His satisfaction grips me in a stronger vice. Sweat coating his biceps, he quickens, holding me closer. My jaw aches, gritting down hard, and I let my lips part. A raspy groan barreling through.

"*Fuck*," Maximoff growls into a low moan. "*Farrow*." The words *I'm about to come* are all over my name. His hand shifts from my waist to my muscular shoulder.

Cords in my neck pull taut, heart rate elevated, and then a feminine voice shouts, "Moffy!"

Jane.

Dammit.

"We're home!!" she blatantly announces her presence. I assume to give us time to "collect" ourselves if we're indecent.

We are very fucking indecent.

"Finish or pull out," I tell Maximoff, voice hushed.

He's surprisingly the one who toys with the risk, staying inside of me. All for that climax—*fuck*, I swallow another moan as he rocks forward. I bear hard on my teeth again. Especially now that footsteps sound through the living room and kitchen.

Maximoff pulls out and tosses the used condom in a small trashcan beneath the shortest shelf. We both catch our breath and dress hurriedly. He's armored like he's ready for gunfire, rarely panicked. When he buttons his jeans, he turns to me.

And he fixes the wild strands of my white hair. I stand an inch taller and buckle my belt, then I tuck my V-neck into my pants and fit my earpiece back into my ear. I run my thumb against his reddened lips.

Maximoff lowers his voice. "The shade is called My Lips Against Your Lips, and it's not coming off. Stop rubbing and let's form a plan."

"I can give you a plan." I unpeel a piece of gum and pop it in my mouth. "We exit and say we were gathering food for the party." I collect a handful of shit off the shelves: peanut butter, crackers, a pack of Lightning Bolt! energy drinks.

Maximoff grabs two rolls of paper towels, and we both step forward to be the first out. We glance at one another, and then race for it. I grab the knob *first* and slip out.

I laugh when I catch sight of his scowl, and then my lips pull in a line when I notice Jane rifling through the kitchen drawers.

"There you are," she whispers, her curious blue eyes pinging to the pantry, then to us. Mainly Maximoff's hair. I flatten a few of his askew strands and then unload all the food next to the liquor bottles. I take the paper towels from Maximoff.

He gives Jane a genuine, warm smile. "Bonsoir, ma moitié." He's about to kiss her cheeks, but he freezes midway. Catching himself.

He grimaces.

Because he blew me. Very, very recently.

Jane cringes, putting the pieces together. "You should go...freshen up. I'll sort through this spread before Sulli and Akara arrive." She motions to the entire countertop.

"Thanks." Maximoff cracks two of his knuckles, and before he leaves upstairs, he asks me, "You alright?"

I frown and chew my gum slower. "Why wouldn't I be?" I read his gaze: *did I go too fast for you? Did I hurt you?* It's cute, but I'm the *last* person that needs a consoling hand. "I would've told you in the moment if I wasn't."

His shoulders noticeably unbind. And he disappears through the archway. I hear him greet Quinn, but the exchange is normal. I focus on the girl in the kitchen.

"What do you need?" I ask Jane and swivel the knob on my radio. Soft chatter returning.

She searches through a drawer, dressed in what Maximoff lovingly calls "granny jammies" for the party: flannel cat-printed pants and long-sleeve collared top. Jane checks over her shoulder and then whispers to me, "You two were almost dangerously loud. I had to send Quinn back to my car to find chocolate bonbons that I didn't even buy."

I'm more than appreciative of the cover. "Thanks, I owe you."

"Don't break Moffy's heart. That's payment enough." She shuts the drawer and opens another. "Or as my mom would say, *you break his heart; I'll break your dick.*"

I whistle and remove liquor bottles from paper bags. That was a *mild* Rose Calloway hyperbolic threat. "No chopping off my dick and flinging it at the sun?"

Jane crouches to a low cupboard. "Moffy is the one who likes grandiose, embellished warnings." She shuts the cupboard empty-handed and stands. "You can go. I know you're only lingering out of obligation to Moffy."

I'm not about to lie and say, *oh no, Jane, I'm really here for you.* I'm not. I stay in the kitchen because Maximoff would want me to. The only thing Jane Cobalt and I have in common is Maximoff Hale. Take him out of the equation, and we're a number and a letter that can't be added together.

"He wants us to get along," I tell her the truth.

She opens a nearby drawer and narrows her eyes. "Did he tell you that?"

"Not in words," I say. "But you know, Maximoff, he's so over-prepared. I'm waiting for a contract. Sign on the dotted line *I'll be friends with Jane Cobalt* type of thing."

She removes a cheese grater from the drawer, and her lips draw into a thin line as she looks at me. I said something wrong. I feel it before she even opens her mouth.

"So the only way you'd be friends with me is if Moffy made you sign a contract?"

"No," I say quickly. *Fuck.* "I'm just saying Maximoff is so practical and meticulous with everything. It was a joke." I run a hand through my hair. "Did he mention anything to you about *us?*" I motion from her to me.

"No, but I've noticed the same thing as you." She sidesteps to the fridge. "He's nervous we're not going to get along."

"And we both agree that we want to make him less nervous?" I ask.

"Of course," she says and snatches a hunk of cheddar cheese from the shelf. She kicks the fridge closed with her slipper. "There's nothing I want more than for him to be happy."

"Me too," I say holding up a hand. "See, we're already making progress here. Okay, what else do we have in common?"

Silence suddenly thickens in the room. She slices a piece of cheese slowly.

"Are you thinking?" I ask her.

"Yes, it's difficult."

"It can't be that difficult."

"Then do you have anything?" she shoots back.

"You love animals," I tell her. "And I don't hate them."

She slices a piece of cheese and lands her eyes on me. "I've heard you call Walrus a little bastard about thirty times."

"With affection," I say.

She pops the slice of cheese in her mouth. "So we have two things in common. With my calculations, we should have enough commonalities to be friends in about five-hundred and sixty-four years." She reaches for her beer, and I don't know what to say without putting my foot in my mouth.

I don't want to give up on this, but I feel the air tensing around us. Awkward silence piling on. I tap my thumb ring on the kitchen counter to fill the quiet. She watches me for a second before popping the cap of her beer on the side of the counter.

"You're supposed to disagree with that," she says casually, placing the beer to her lips.

I stop tapping my ring. "With the five-hundred and sixty-four thing?"

"Yeah," she nods and motions the bottle to me. "You're supposed to say *no, Jane, we'll be friends in a couple years.*"

"I don't have a fucking crystal ball," I say.

"Okay, then just tell me I'm wrong."

"You're wrong," I say. "Because skeletons aren't making friends in their graves."

"Wow." She shakes her head.

"Wow. What?" I can't say the right things, and correcting course is just driving myself further into a ditch.

"Wow, you want to be my friend but you can't even have any confidence that it will happen," she says. "Not in five-hundred years. Not in two years. How about ever?"

"I have confidence in myself, but friendship is a two-way street," I reply.

Her brows furrow. "So you think I'm the one not trying?"

Fucking hell.

"You're right," I say. "This is difficult."

"Agreed."

Something nags at me, and it's not going to bring us any closer since it's about Maximoff. I scratch my jaw. "So Maximoff doesn't have a license anymore," I say. "I thought the only reason you didn't ride together was because of his driving."

"It was," she replies. I pick up on the past tense.

"But it's not anymore?"

"You two don't get much time alone..." She shrugs.

I want to tell her not to worry about that. To do what she'd normally do, if I wasn't around. But *fuck*. I love my one-on-one time with Maximoff, and those car rides are a big part of it. No piece of me wants to give that up just to be nice.

My earpiece buzzes. "Akara to Farrow," Akara says through my mic. "We're driving into the garage now. Are the doors unlocked?"

I step back from Jane, realizing that this conversation went from pleasant to painful in a matter of minutes. And honestly, it's not her. I don't even know if it's me. It's just this intangible, unquantifiable thing.

23

MAXIMOFF HALE

"I don't think I brought enough chips," **Sulli** says in my kitchen beside me. The two of us fix a plate of food for everyone. She inspects the Tostitos. "What was I thinking? *One fucking bag.* Akara can eat a whole bag by himself. And why did I bring donuts? No one likes midnight donuts but me."

"Hey." I place two hands on her broad swimmer's shoulders. She's long-legged and long-armed, and barefoot, she's six-feet tall. Only a couple inches shorter than me, and we're almost eye-level.

We look like brother and sister. Not just cousins.

Our moms are sisters. We share their green eyes.

Our dads are half-brothers. We share our grandfather's dark brown hair (if I didn't dye mine).

So you know Sullivan Minnie Meadows as the *foul-mouthed*, ultra-focused Olympian who returned home with four gold medals last summer in 200 & 400-meter freestyle and individual medley. You're angry that she just retired from swimming, but some of you are too excited about the idea of Sullivan starting to date to seriously care.

I've seen your tweets about her virginity.

Back off.

And me…I know her as Sulli. My nineteen-year-old cousin who jokes crudely, loves wildly, and can outrace me on foot or water every single time. I love her like a little sister, and she has no brothers of her own.

Fair warning: I'll rip each lung out of your ribcage and grind them in a *rusted* meat processor if you fuck with her.

"Don't stress," I say, clutching her shoulders. "One bag of chips is fine. And when have you *ever* cared if no one else likes donuts?"

"It's our first Hallow Friends Eve."

I get it. Halloween is more of my dad's birthday and a giant costume get-together. Family only. Jane and Sulli have been trying to figure out a day-before-Halloween tradition for *years* that doesn't include our parents or the little kids.

Hence, *Hallow Friends Eve.* Of our cousins and siblings, we decided to only invite those who've already graduated high school. Charlie never RSVP'd. *Fucking typical.* And his twin brother Beckett just became a principal dancer at a prestigious ballet company. He'd be here for Sulli, his best friend, but he has a performance tonight.

That just leaves Jane, Sulli, and me.

"And it's my first time hosting a party," Sulli reminds me. "It has to be perfect." She inflicts pressure on herself all the time. Whenever Sullivan has a goal, in her mind it's her job to go for gold.

"Co-hosting," I correct, dropping my hands. "It's *my* house. Anything goes wrong, you can blame me." I pour her chips in an orange plastic bowl.

Sulli snorts. "That's not how this works. You can't fall on a sword for me, Mof." Quietly, she adds, "And I don't want this to be the worst party our bodyguards have ever been invited to."

My brows scrunch. "Who are you trying to impress? It's just Akara, Quinn, and Farrow." We invited them as *friends.* Off-duty. We're all staying in our townhouse all-night and watching a horror movie. They can drink alcohol, but they need to crash here.

We pushed the loveseat against the kitchen's archway. So we have to hurdle the furniture to reach the living room where we set up beanbags and sleeping bags. Like Jane, Sulli is already wearing her pajamas, cupcake boxer shorts and a turquoise tank.

"I'm trying to impress all three of them," Sulli whispers. "I've heard them talk shit about *your* pool party circa…how old were you?"

"Eighteen, and that mosquito infestation was not my fucking fault. We were *outside*. Where bugs live. Naturally."

"Hey, I'm not the one ragging on you," Sulli says. "I totally agree. It's nature's fucking fault. Not the watermelon that you cut in half."

I scowl. "You're right, they're annoying. Why'd we invite them anyway?" I'm half-serious, half-sarcastic. Even though I spend 24/7 with Farrow, this'll be the first time he's *technically* off-duty around me.

And he just loves his technicalities.

"If we didn't invite them," Sulli says, "then we'd have to call this Hallow *Family* Eve because the three of us don't have friends. Other than the people we pay to protect us."

"Jesus, we're so sad," I say, sarcasm thick.

Sulli smiles. "The fucking saddest." She grips a beer by the neck and casually takes a small sip. She cringes, nose wrinkling. Not enjoying the bitter taste.

Her dark hair is parted in the center. Splayed in waves over her broad shoulders. Sulli casts a glance to the living room.

Over the loveseat, I spot Jane entertaining Quinn, Akara, and Farrow with some elaborate story. Gesticulating madly, lemonade mixed drink in her hand.

"She's so good at that," Sulli says, wistful. "Half the time I don't know what the fuck to say to people."

"It's a Cobalt thing," I remind Sulli. "They have a harder time knowing when to shut up."

She exchanges a smile with me. We *love* our seven Cobalt cousins—our best friends are Cobalts: Beckett for her, Janie for me—but it's undeniable how different we are from them.

She nods and takes a larger swig of beer. Trying not to make a disgusted face. She succeeds. Then in a different language, she asks, "Has pensado en la ultra?" *Have you thought about the ultra?*

Ryke Meadows taught his daughters to speak Spanish. And he taught me. I'm proud to be fluent, but in the past year, being constantly compared to Ryke…I don't know.

I question everything.

"Moffy?" Sulli nudges my ribs, waking me from a stupor.

The ultra.

I grab a water bottle from the hard-shell cooler on the ground. Thinking. Sulli retired from swimming because she completed her goal. She went to the Olympics. She medaled. And she could've returned to the next summer Olympics, but she didn't want to go after more-of-the-same.

So she set her sights on doing an *ultra*-marathon in Chile. The Atacama Crossing, a 155-mile race in the desert. It's her next goal.

Her next fight for first.

And she wants me by her side.

Swimming and running go hand-in-hand. We used to condition on land by doing endurance runs together, and I'd *love* to make time for an ultra.

If she asked me a year ago, I wouldn't have hesitated like I do now.

"It's because my dad ran an ultra, isn't it?"

"Sul." I rub my sharpened jaw. "If I go, they'll compare me more to your dad than they do now."

Sulli tears at the label on her beer. "Look, I know you're not my brother—"

"I didn't mean it like that." *Goddammit.*

"Oh hey, I know. I'm fucking terrible with words." She takes a giant breath. Not giving up yet. Sulli rarely gives up on anything. "Hear me out. We started competitive swimming together, and in the grand universe of friendship and fate, maybe we should start this together too." She pauses. "And I just can't fucking imagine doing this alone. So think about it, will you?"

I nod. "For you, I will."

Sulli puts her lips to the beer rim and catches me eagle-eyeing the alcohol. She lowers the bottle. "You can stop looking at me like I've sprouted wings."

"Actually, I'm looking at you like you're cradling a lit firework."

"I know what I'm doing, Moffy," she tries to reassure me.

Our grandfather was an alcoholic.

My dad is a recovering alcoholic.

Her dad chose to stop drinking alcohol at seventeen.

Alcoholism runs in the Hale *and* Meadows bloodlines. Just because I decided to never drink alcohol doesn't mean my siblings or cousins will choose the same.

"Just be careful." I dump pretzels in another bowl.

Sulli doesn't say *I always am*. Adventure and *fearlessness* also runs deep in her blood. As a Meadows, she grew up cliff-jumping into tropical oceans, riding Ducatis, and paragliding hundreds of feet in the air.

Instead, she tells me, "I know the risk."

Sulli reaches for a bakery box that contains a dozen chocolate-covered donuts. We carry the assortment of food: pretzels, chips, buffalo poppers, Halloween candy, and a veggie tray. And we *skillfully* climb over the loveseat without spilling anything.

Akara, Quinn, and Farrow lounge on beanbags, radios set aside. So they're seriously off-duty. They face the fireplace, television mounted above the mantel. I set the food on a green sleeping bag in the middle, and Janie yanks the cord to the ceiling light.

Blanketing us in near-darkness.

Farrow leans on a black beanbag, nearest the staircase. More off on his own damn island. Akara, Quinn, and even Janie who plops down near the food are clustered much closer together.

Farrow swigs a beer, eyes dead-set on me. He's wondering what my next move is. *So am I.* I'm dying to sit beside him. But what kind of message is that sending to everyone else?

Hey, I'm fucking my bodyguard!

Or *hey, I'm just good friends with my bodyguard.*

Alright—the first one sounds like pure paranoia with a dash of overreacting. Before I step towards Farrow, Sulli places donuts next to the chips and curses, "Cumbuckets."

"What?" I ask.

"I forgot the salsa." She rests two fingers to her lips: the famous Sullivan Meadows *concentration* face. And she's using it for a *salsa* crisis.

"Sulli," I snap. "It's fine."

"Do you have anything in your fridge? I could make some." She can't offer to make a grocery run since that'd entail *needing* a sober Akara Kitsuwon.

"Forget the salsa, Sulli."

"Uncle Lo says that it's not a party until there's salsa. It's a party rule. Right?" She looks to Jane.

"Well…" Jane muses the idea for too long.

I cut in, "My dad could also eat five hot sauce packets for brunch and nothing else."

"Famous ones," Farrow calls out, and our heads turn to him. "There's *no* salsa rule for parties. Not normal."

Christ, the fact that we needed clarification from *Farrow* makes me pinch my eyes and groan. He smiles wide into his swig of beer.

"Come here, Sul." Akara waves her to sit on the green beanbag beside him, the bowl of chips on his lap.

Sitting, she holds her legs to her chest but leans towards him.

"These are perfectly fine *without* salsa." He demonstrates and tosses a corn ship in his mouth. "Delicious."

"You're just saying that," Sulli refutes.

"Am not." Akara playfully pulls the bowl against his chest. "These are mine now, thanks."

She smiles bright, and then tries to grab a chip. He hoists the bowl over her head. Teasing.

Teasing?

I dazedly walk over to Farrow. Not taking my gaze off *that* exchange, and I sink down next to him. "What's up with that?" I whisper to him.

"It's called a *buddy*-guard, wolf scout."

I've heard security use the term before. *Buddy-guard* (noun): one who protects a very-important-person while also being their close friend.

I've known that Akara understands *everything* about Sulli, her habits, her likes and dislikes—I just never really honed in on their "friendship" until...

Until I started fucking my bodyguard.

Great. Is my perception of every bodyguard-client relationship going to skew on the side of *they're copulating* now? My mind is a rabbit hole that I didn't ask to fall into.

"Lean back," Farrow says, sipping his beer.

I do, and we're shoulder-to-shoulder. But my narrowed eyes remain plastered on my cousin and her bodyguard. I lower my voice, ensuring only Farrow can hear. "Do they look super close to you? More than a buddy-guard?"

"No." He sips his beer, at total ease right now. I observe my cousin. She shoves Akara's carved bicep, laughing as he hides the bowl behind his back.

I grimace—*are they flirting?* I try not to even touch my mixed feelings. I'm a hypocrite if I dislike the mere idea of Sulli with her bodyguard, but some part of me tramples through the "Hulk-Smash Akara" territory. "You sure?"

Farrow turns his head to whisper in my ear. "I've known Akara a long time, and he'd never cross that line with Sulli. He's a security *lead.* He's too professional. And he knows Ryke Meadows would kill him."

My dad will kill you. My jaw tenses, and he must sense my sudden thought.

He whispers up against my ear again. "If your dad scared me, I wouldn't have kissed you."

That reminds me...I haven't regretted crossing a line with Farrow. Not once.

My shoulders lower a fraction, and Farrow bites into an English muffin, sandwiched with egg, bacon and cheese. Which he made at his townhouse after showering and brought it here. Even though we bought snacks for tonight.

His love of breakfast foods has no bounds. Farrow will *literally* order sunny-side up eggs and sausage seven days in a row for every meal.

Farrow extends the half-bitten sandwich to me.

"I thought you don't share."

He licks his thumb, lips lifting. "I share with you, only."

I grab the sandwich. "Because I'm your client."

"Try again."

Because I'm your... "You tell me." Are we labeling this relationship—I don't know? This is my first relationship—when do the labels come? Maybe Farrow has like a six-month minimum before he considers a person his...

I watch him survey the room out of his peripheral. Farrow being subtly alert of our surroundings—I love. I'm more obvious. Staring straight on.

Janie uses the remote to find a horror movie on Netflix. Akara and Sulli are chatting quietly, and she's stacking chips on a donut. Quinn plays with Ophelia, the white cat scurrying beneath his muscular legs.

"Maximoff." Farrow captures my gaze. He stops himself from speaking more, and I can't feel disappointed. Because I know he sees someone watching us. He stares straight ahead at the television.

I take a bite of his food before handing the sandwich back. Then I unscrew my water bottle and swig.

"What the hell is up with this one?" Quinn frowns at a calico kitten pawing at his ankle.

"It hates you, Oliveira," Farrow says into a swig of beer.

"*He,*" Janie corrects Farrow with a pointed look; when she sees me watching, she forces a smile like *we're friends; don't worry, Moffy.*

Did that convince anyone? Wallpaper, lamp, table, man on the moon—you all fucking convinced? Me neither.

"What?" Quinn says to Farrow, seeming genuinely upset at that idea. "He doesn't hate me. I'm *great* with animals. Before I boxed pro, I could've been a dog whisperer." He clucks his tongue at the kitten and makes a cooing noise.

Solo cup in hand, Akara leans towards Quinn. "Hey, you do know that's a *cat*, not a dog."

Quinn laughs with all of us. I've never seen any metaphorical jab knock him down. He sips his rum and Fizz. "I had a dog growing up."

"What kind?" Sulli asks, and Janie lands on *A Nightmare on Elm Street* and mouths to me and Farrow, *yes* or *no*.

I give her a thumbs-up.

Farrow purposefully puts his thumb-down.

I right up his fucking thumb.

He wears a self-*satisfied* expression like I just agreed to jerk him off. Not equivalent, but I am giving him a hell of a lot of attention. And he's making me aware of that.

Quinn replies to my cousin, "I had a husky."

"I had a husky too," Sulli says, and the room goes quiet. To Quinn, my cousin adds, "She died a while back."

"Yeah, I know. I saw on…" Quinn trails off and clears his throat.

"Twitter," Farrow says.

More confidently, Quinn tells Sulli, "It was actually Facebook."

If the Meadows had a fifth family member, it wouldn't be *me*. It'd be Coconut the Husky. You *loved* that dog. I loved that damn dog, and we were all sad when she finally passed from old age.

Quinn tries to pet the calico kitten, and he bites his finger. "Jane?"

"Carpenter likes vegetables. Just toss him one of those baby tomatoes."

Quinn stretches towards the veggie tray and then throws a tomato beneath the loveseat. Carpenter dashes after it.

He shakes his head. "That's not natural."

Akara motions his cup to the television. "Are we still doing the drinking game?"

"Yeah," Sulli nods repeatedly. "Jane has the rules."

"Right." Jane is busy smashing her beanbag. She's usually next to me during these kinds of things, and she's sort of off in a corner.

"Janie," I call out and motion her closer.

She mouths, *no*. And casts the briefest glance at Farrow. Like she needs to give us privacy. It's not like we're about to exchange secret hand-jobs in the fucking dark. I'm in a room with two of my cousins.

Not happening.

"Jane," Farrow calls before I have to prod further.

She hesitates for one second before dragging her pink beanbag near us. She plops a few feet from me. I reach over and slide her and the beanbag right by my side.

Jane can't hide her smile. "Hallow Friends Eve's drinking game rules," she announces to the group. "Take a sip from your drink every time Freddy Krueger appears, someone screams, and when someone says the word *nightmare, dream,* or *sleep.*"

"What about Moffy?" Sulli asks.

"I'm not playing."

"You can't *not* play," Jane replies. "And you know I'm *dreadfully* serious when I use a double negative."

Sulli bites into a donut and with a full mouth says, "Uncle Lo and my dad always have alternative rules for sober players."

Janie perks up. "Take off an article of clothing every time someone screams."

"Ce n'est pas une bonne idée," I say in French so only Jane can understand. *That's not a good idea.* Yeah, I *came* already today, and I can will-away an erection by sheer mental concentration. But not if I'm stripping beside Farrow. Look, there are some things that can't be easily hidden.

My huge, rock-hard cock is one of them.

Everyone is staring at me but Farrow. He edges away from me, and then he leaves to the kitchen with his empty beer bottle.

Jane says, "Je n'ai pas d'autre idée que celle-ci." *I have no other idea but this one.*

I glance at Sulli and remember her trepidation about the party failing. I don't want to disappoint my cousin over a boner. I shut my eyes in a long blink. Trying to scrub away that last bizarre thought.

"Alright," I say, eyes open. "Every other scream, I'll take off an article of clothing *but* I stop before my underwear." The room agrees, and Farrow returns with a new pale ale and one of Janie's pastel blue blankets. He tosses the blanket to me and sinks back down.

Just as close as before. Shoulder-to-shoulder. His presence is a furnace, boiling me from head-to-toe. *Don't get caught.* How's that mantra? If I repeat it over and over, I should be able to avoid an erection. Definitely.

Don't get fucking caught.

Janie presses play, and about ten minutes into the movie, Farrow calls out, "Akara, are you on the clock or do you just love Jane's décor?" He must've been surveying the room.

An actress suddenly shrieks. Everyone drinks, and I pull my shirt off over my head and toss the thing aside. I lean back beside Farrow. He's trying to *suppress* a smile.

That's rare.

Jane keeps the conversation alive. "Akara, you love how I decorated this place?"

"I didn't say that," he says.

"My brother likes your decorations," Quinn tells her. "He calls it Retro Granny Realness."

Janie beams.

"I think it's hella fucking cute," Sulli tells her.

"Thank you, Sullivan," Janie replies. "Will you be my new bodyguard?"

"Of course, I'll protect you to the fucking death."

"And follow me around everywhere I go?"

"Everywhere."

"Heyheyhey," Quinn cuts in, extending his arm towards Sulli. "Don't take my job. It's not for sale."

Jane beams harder. Her last, *retired* bodyguard never voiced his enjoyment of being on her detail.

"Too bad you're not in charge of transfers, Quinn," Farrow tells him. "Only Akara can decide that."

Sulli nudges Akara's arm. "What'd you say, Kits? Put me on Jane's detail?" *Kits.*

My cousin has a special nickname for her bodyguard. Off his last name Kitsuwon, but still, it's a nickname. Farrow has a nickname for me. Two plus two equals...

Huh.

My mind needs to just stop for the night. I swear I'm going to reach a new circle of hell for paranoid souls.

Akara nods to Sulli. "When you can beat me in the ring, you can take Jane's detail." He sounds serious, but maybe he knows she'd never beat him. He was trained in Muay Thai since he was six.

Sulli crinkles her nose. "But I'm a lover not a fighter."

His lips quirk. "Sorry, Sul. Gotta pass on you then. You'd make a shit bodyguard."

Jane clutches her heart. "Say it isn't so."

"Drink," Farrow calls out as the word *sleep* is said on-screen. The horror movie engrosses all of us for the next twenty minutes. I've seen everyone grab three refills.

Sulli is on her *sixth* beer.

Yeah, I'm counting.

And I have *zero* clothes left to shed. Down to my dark green boxer-briefs. The blanket was a tactical maneuver by Farrow in case I spring a boner. I'm fine. I stopped watching him swig his beer, and my brain and dick are cooperating with me for once.

Thankfully.

My phone pings a few times. I respond to my siblings. Most of whom are *pissed* they weren't invited to Hallow Friends Eve.

Kinney is the most vexed.

You turd. You don't even know what horror is — **Kinney**

We'll do a Halloween movie night at mom and dad's another time. Promise. **I reply.**

She sends a skull and cross bones emoji.

I don't want them around alcohol yet. Not when I'm hanging out with men in their twenties. My sister is *thirteen.* She can stay thirteen.

And Luna—she's walking a fragile line with our parents after the tongue piercing. I'm doing her a favor by not extending an invite.

Plus, if we invited Luna, we'd have to invite Jane's two brothers, Eliot Cobalt and Tom Cobalt. Which would probably end with *me* calling the fire department or our on-call doctor.

So that's pretty much why we made the "high school graduates only" invite stipulation.

"Sulli?" Her bodyguard's concerned voice steals my attention. He leans over my cousin and cups her cheek. "Hold on..." He stands and easily hurdles the loveseat.

Sulli hugs her legs tighter to her chest, and then she rests her forehead to her kneecaps. *She's dizzy.*

"Sulli," I start, about to stand, but Akara returns with a new box of donuts.

"Eat this." He hands Sulli a plain glazed donut. "You can kill your buzz with food." He pries the beer out of her fingers.

"Thanks," she mutters and lifts her head enough to grab the donut.

Jane strokes her black cat Lady Macbeth. "The first time I got drunk, I puked everywhere," she tells Sulli. "Moffy held my hair." She rests her cheek on my shoulder. I wrap my arm around hers.

"First time I got drunk, I passed out in my own piss," Quinn says. "Don't ask."

Farrow sets aside his empty bottle. "And now I'm going to—"

An object shatters the curtained front-window. Followed by quick, violent *pop pop pop pop...*

Pop.

24

MAXIMOFF HALE

Firecrackers

Are you fucking kidding me—I launch to my feet while all three bodyguards bolt into action.

"Farrow!" Akara yells and points to the front door, then he captures his radio off a sleeping bag. "Akara to Alpha. Akara to Alpha."

Farrow is already sprinting to the exit, and I'm not far behind with hot pinpointed eyes, seething inside-out. *Someone broke my window with the intent to harm my family. Those could've been gunshots.* It's all I feel.

And I see red.

Farrow grabs the knob, but he suddenly whips around on me. He puts his hand to my bare chest, stopping me from reaching the door. Ire blisters his vigilant gaze in a way that I've never seen directed at *me*.

"Quinn, don't near the *window*, there's glass on the ground!" Akara yells. "Take the girls and Moffy upstairs to the bathroom and lock the door!"

My raging pulse hammers in the pit of my ears.

"What *the fuck* are you doing?" Farrow sneers at me. "You *can't* follow me." I spot the briefest flash of concern, of trepidation, before his gaze mortars hard and hot again.

I clench my teeth. *I need to help. I have to fucking help.* The intrinsic need bangs at my head, my ribcage, my *heart*, and I don't know how to turn away.

I don't know how to hide in a bathroom and *wait*.

"I see him!" Quinn suddenly yells. He charges towards us. Storming through Farrow and me to fling open the door, he runs urgently into the pitch-black night. Paparazzi who've been camping out on my street awaken like dormant fireflies and hornets.

Bright in the dark. And ready to sting.

Quickly, Farrow warns me, "*Don't. Follow.*" Then he bolts outside, tracing Quinn's hurried footsteps. Farrow's caustic voice scalds my fucking ears.

He's trying to protect me. It's as simple as that.

My hands stay balled in fists, but I turn to find Jane and Sulli, to keep them safe—

"CARPENTER!" Jane screams bloody-murder, the sound lancing my heart. Everything happens fast—she tears back downstairs and out of Sulli's grasp.

"Jane!" Sulli yells, almost falling down the staircase after her, but Akara grabs Sulli by the waist. "KITS!"

"You have to stay here!" Akara shouts. "JANE!"

"MOFFY! CARPENTER!" Jane screams, alarmed tears already soaking her cheeks. I try to shut the door, keeping the cats inside, but she shrieks, "HE'S ALREADY OUTSIDE! HE'S OUTSIDE!"

Walrus, the other kitten darts past my ankles, and I reach to catch him, but he scampers into the night. I don't waste time. I chase the fucking animal down.

Running outside.

These indoor cats are her babies, and we live in the city. Where cars constantly speed by. If one dies—she'll be gutted. It's all I think.

All I know.

I fucking run. Onto the sidewalk, towards the street parking. I see Walrus scampering beneath a parked car.

And then I'm swarmed by paparazzi. Cameras in every fucking direction.

"CARPENTER!" Jane calls out, panicked. *She's outside?* My head swerves, squinting in the harsh flashes. I can hardly see in front of me.

"JANE!" I shout and then shove paparazzi to work my way towards where I think Jane went. I spot her wobbling and tripping over her bare feet but determinedly chasing after another calico kitten. *She's drunk.*

She's fucking drunk.

I forgot.

I'm the only sober one here.

"I got him! I got him, Maximoff!" a cameraman yells at me and then suddenly hands me Walrus. I have no time to express my full relief or gratitude. I nod once to him, and then set my entire damn attention on reaching Jane.

"Let him through!" paparazzi start yelling at one another. "Let him through!"

"JANE!" I shout. I push through bodies. I push through voices that yell questions. I push through groping hands.

"CARPENTER!" she wails bloody-murder. I'm barely able to see the kitten. Bounding into the goddamn *road.* And Jane runs right after him.

I body-slam my way through the fucking paparazzi. Being accidently clocked in the cheek by a hefty camera. I don't stop.

I can't stop.

My feet hit the cement road, and with Walrus in one hand, I wrap my arm around Jane's waist the same time that she has a death-clutch on her tiny calico kitten. Headlights blare at us, coming fast down our street. I rapidly steer her towards the sidewalk, and we reach the curb just in time, the car speeding past.

Jane is shaking and slightly limping. *She must've fallen.*

I try to discern where we are—I think we're twelve or fifteen houses down from ours. I guide my best friend towards our townhouse.

"Maximoff! Why are you in your underwear at eight at night?!" is the only question that snaps my attention. Reminding me that I'm nearly fucking naked on chilly October 30th.

Great.

Cameras flash in fierce frenzy, and I just fixate on getting Jane home. Getting *us* home.

"Moffy," Jane says, voice firm and wide-eyes on Carpenter and only Carpenter. "He almost…he…did you…?"

"He's alright. He's okay." I don't think she even realizes Walrus escaped too. Or that he's in my arms. She's blurry-eyed wasted, fighting to keep her heavy-lids open. I glance down. Blood seeps through the fabric of her flannel pants, both kneecaps bloodied.

My jaw locks. "Come on, Jane." I try to quicken our pace. Where there's this much commotion, there may be hecklers not long after. Although, a heckler with firecrackers started all of this—maybe he has friends coming for a round two.

Maybe he wasn't a lone wolf.

Maybe they're planning to hide in our house.

Goddammit.

Walrus squirms in my left arm. Digging his claws into my bare chest and trying to crawl up my shoulder. I yank him back down, not caring about the scratches.

Paparazzi push into my face when I wrap my right arm around Jane's shoulders. I have to let go of her just to shove them out.

"Back up!" I yell, not joking around.

A lot do shuffle backwards. And then some don't give a shit about us. Swaying drunkenly, Jane almost falls again, her legs wobbling.

"*Janie*. Hold him." I give her Walrus too.

Recognition parts her lips. That *two* cats ran outside. "Merde." We have to hope that none of the others sprinted out before Walrus and Carpenter.

Jane holds her kittens in a fiercely protective grip.

Quickly, I pick Jane up. Wrapping my arm beneath her legs, the other supporting her back. Cradling my best friend—the paparazzi go wild.

"RIGHT HERE, MAXIMOFF, JANE!! LOOK HERE!"

Fuck off.

I can move three times as fast. Jane tucks her head into my chest because of the lights. Cameras only flash hotter, more incessant.

And then…the paparazzi begin creating a path. Separating enough for a body to fit through. But not for us. For the *towering* six-foot-seven Italian-American bodyguard that bulldozes towards Jane and me.

I squint, my vision impaired from the constant flashes, but I distinguish the longish, scruffy hair, unshaven jaw and stern brown eyes of Thatcher Moretti, the lead of Security Force Epsilon.

With his massive height and strong build, he creates a barrier between us and the media. Making it ten times easier to push through the masses.

Thatcher clicks his mic on the collar of his black button-down. "I have them. Clear the street." He spots Walrus wiggling in Jane's motherly grip. Thatcher grabs the kitten and tucks Walrus protectively under his arm. Like a furry football.

By the time we reach the front stoop of my townhouse, white lights dance in my eyes. I can count on my hands the number of times I've personally used the front door.

Three.

Three fucking times.

Because this insanity happens.

As soon as the door shuts behind me, I register the sheer amount of people in my townhouse. All familiar faces from Alpha. They tape our window and sweep up glass. Speaking into mics, scouring the rest of my home for intruders.

I rest Jane on the loveseat, still pushed against the archway.

And Quinn rushes past towards the staircase. *Quinn?* "Quinn, where's Farrow?" I call out. He doesn't stop. So I chase after him, to the base of the stairs. "Quinn!"

He pauses to glance back, his nose bloodied.

What.

Happened.

Quinn opens his mouth, but Thatcher tells him, "Go, Quinn."

No. Fuck that. "Where's Farrow?!" I yell, not fucking around.

Quinn's jaw muscle tics, but he rushes upstairs. I shake my head, *pissed.* I rotate on Thatcher, but he towers near Jane while she slowly rifles through a first-aid kit. For her bloodied knees.

Thatcher barks orders, "I need eyes on all the cats!" He already places the calico kittens in their leopard-print carrier. Securing them. "We have Walrus and Carpenter. Where are Ophelia, Lady Macbeth, and Toodles?"

Jane blinks drunkenly at him. "You know their names?"

I glare at Thatcher. "Where the fuck is Farrow?"

Nothing.

No acknowledgement of my question. In the grand scheme of security, it's *unimportant* for me to be aware of my own bodyguard's where-abouts. I'm supposed to sit and let the extra security protect us. I'm not supposed to care about them.

Not even if they get hurt.

It's their job.

I spot Price by the broken window, the Alpha lead chats to a younger security member. My phone vibrates angrily on the rumpled sleeping bags. All of my family must be freaked.

My mom...

I have to call her.

Thatcher doesn't even answer Jane's question. The most strict, no-nonsense guy on the team. I swear, I liked that about him, but now I'm fucking irritated.

Thatcher holds his mic. "Jane, do you have any strays in the house?" She struggles with the gauze packet, and I go to help. He cuts me off and takes my place. Kneeling at the loveseat, he tears open the gauze.

I need to do something, but security loves to impede me from doing *anything* productive.

I could scream I'm so frustrated right now. I rub my face.

Where's Farrow?

Where's Farrow?!

Where's my... I stare fixatedly at the closed front door.

"No strays," Jane tells him, trying her hardest not to slur. "I did adopt another yesterday. Licorice. He's a four-year-old...gray, long-haired. Blue eyes."

Thatcher speaks into his mic. "There's a sixth cat—Licorice. Gray."
He presses the gauze to her knees, and Jane rips open a Band-Aid with
her teeth. Thatcher tells my best friend, "Lady Macbeth, Toodles, and
Ophelia are accounted for."

Jane nods, barely relaxing.

The door opens, and my chest rises, thinking it's Farrow. But it's not.
It's not him. It's Luna's bodyguard.

Fuck this.

I charge over to the Alpha lead. My gait is strong and determined. I've
never shied from any of these men. Not for a damn breath. Not for a
second. And they're going to *answer* me now.

"Price." My firm voice yanks his attention from the younger security
member. "I need to know where Farrow is. *Now.*"

"You should sit—"

"*No.* You fucking tell me where my bodyguard is. This isn't up for
discussion."

Price clicks his mic. "Price to security, someone give me an update
on Farrow." *Right.* Farrow never grabbed his radio before he ran outside.
Price can't contact him directly.

He stares faraway. "Price to security," he repeats. "*Someone* give me an
update on Farrow."

I cross my arms over my chest. The wait killing me. I turn slightly and
spot Akara descending the staircase.

I frown, expecting Sulli to be right behind him. The last image I have—he
was with her. I was sure he was with her. "Akara!" I call out. "Where's Sulli?"

He walks tensely over. "She left." He touches his earpiece, distracted,
then his focus returns. "She texted her dad halfway through the movie to
come pick her up. She felt a lot worse than she let on."

"Ryke was here then?"

He nods.

I'm not surprised. Sulli has a very close friendship with her dad *and*
her mom. She tells them everything. If she felt dizzy or nauseous, she
wouldn't have hesitated to call Ryke.

"He planned to stay and check on you and Jane," Akara explains, "but it got chaotic, and he needed to get Sulli out before paparazzi blocked the street."

"Why aren't you with her?"

Akara looks upset, his face cut in severe lines. "I can't officially be on her detail since I've been drinking. Someone else is with Sul." He touches his earpiece and takes a step towards the kitchen. Before he leaves, he pats my shoulder like *I'm glad you're okay, hang in there.*

"Hey," I say to him. "Thanks."

He nods. "It's just another shitty day, right?"

"*Doomsday,*" I say, and a knot is in my throat. Remembering Farrow. Price repeats that same phrase for the *fourth* time.

I'm close to searching outside for Farrow myself. Which may worsen the situation, but if no one's going to find him, I will.

"Price to security," he repeats, and then the front door opens. "There he is." I can't even relax at the news. *Is he fucking hurt?* blares in my head.

Farrow saunters inside, not casually. His muscles are taut. He locks the door behind him. And the moment he sees me, he almost rocks back, nose flared. "You went *outside?*" He hones in on my reddened cheek and my lip—I rub my mouth.

It stings. A camera must've busted my lip open.

I zero in on his *bloody* forearms. Skin scraped like he slid against pavement. All the way to his elbows.

I grimace into a cringe, my muscles turning inside out. My heart in my throat.

"Cats escaped, and Moffy went out to get them," Price explains briefly to Farrow. "We need an update."

Farrow swallows hard, his face twisting the longer he looks at me, almost pained. He takes a step towards me at the exact same time I take one towards him.

We pause. We stop.

I've never wanted to embrace someone so much in my fucking life. Something wells inside my body. An emotion that I've never experienced.

"Farrow," Price snaps.

I blink a few times, tearing my gaze off my bodyguard. Farrow combs both hands through his hair and rotates to the Alpha lead.

"Both guys are being booked tonight," Farrow says.

I go rigid. "You caught them?" I'm *stunned.* Hecklers. Harassers. People who throw shit. Who stalk us. They *rarely* ever get caught. These people are usually faceless, nameless humans. As nondescript as an anon online. I've lived my life content knowing that there'd be little retribution.

I'm fine with that.

I get it.

"A few paparazzi tripped both guys," Farrow says, more to me than to Price. "They slowed them down. I was able to tackle one guy and keep him down. Quinn grabbed the other, and then the police came. I dealt with the cops—Quinn came back here already, right?" he asks Price.

Price nods and tosses him his radio. "Keep the volume high."

Farrow attaches the radio to his belt.

"Jane has the first-aid kit," I tell Farrow and motion to the loveseat. I'm still eyeing his bloodied forearms. He's still scanning my face, even as he fits in his earpiece.

"It's all yours," Jane tells us, teetering as she stands, kneecaps bandaged. She raises her chin to meet Thatcher's gaze. "Have you located Licorice?"

His hand hovers by her hip in case she falls. "We're working on it." I hear his South Philly lilt. "Are you okay?"

"Yes." Jane blinks like she's trying to battle her drunkenness. She hiccups and says, "Thank you, Mr. Moretti." He's twenty-seven, the same age as Farrow. Not *middle-aged.*

"Thatcher is fine," he tells Jane.

Is she blushing?

Jane presses her lips together, then sways. "I should go call my parents…" Her gaze finds me. "Do you want me to call your mom, Moffy?"

"Please."

She hiccups, teeters and then with her cat carrier in hand, she tries to confidently ascend the staircase like Cinderella at a ball.

She manages to reach the second floor safely. All without tripping. I would *clap*, but I concentrate on Farrow. We both sink down onto the loveseat.

I dig through the first-aid kit, and he actually watches. Not even making a comment about how he's the doctor.

Thatcher drags the iron café chair over and sits *directly* in front of us. But he only acknowledges Farrow. "You should've grabbed your radio before you left the house."

Farrow leans back. "I'm not apologizing for that."

Thatcher glares. "You never apologize for anything."

"I caught the guy—"

"The cats escaped—"

"That has nothing to do with my fucking radio," Farrow sneers. "Drop it, Thatcher." One time I asked Farrow which guy he hated the most on security. He didn't even hesitate before saying, *Thatcher Moretti.* Now I get it.

His strictness is the antithesis of Farrow.

I rip open antiseptic wipes. "Was it a brick?" I ask Thatcher, cutting into their tension. I motion with my head to the window. Security has sufficiently taped up a piece of cardboard over the cracked hole. Glass cleaned, curtains closed.

I'm trying to visualize the projectile.

"Don't worry about it," Thatcher tells me. *Evasive.* I've been reminded tonight that Thatcher is in the camp of *Maximoff asks too many questions. Maximoff takes on too much responsibility. Maximoff isn't part of the security team. Remind him that any chance you can.*

"I'm not learning about this online tomorrow," I say firmly. "Was it a brick, a hammer, a goddamn UFO—"

"A baseball," Farrow answers.

Thatcher has a stern look that says, *he didn't need to know.* Thatcher is used to protecting Xander, who is guarded from facts that stoke his anxiety. But I'm not the same as my brother.

And I'm *eight* years older.

"I asked," I remind Thatcher.

He nods slowly. "You're right."

Farrow's brows jump and then he gestures for the antiseptic wipes. "Give me."

I hand them over, and he wipes the blood and gravel off his forearms, not even cringing. His pain tolerance has to be high. Evidence: every damn tattoo.

Thatcher sits forwards, hands cupped. Eyeing me. "The team has a few questions we need to ask you."

"Alright." My shoulders square. I rip packets of gauze open for Farrow. He seems out-of-the-loop on this pre-planned debriefing. Probably because he hasn't been tethered to a radio.

Thatcher asks, "Who bit you?"

I go completely still. "What?"

Farrow places his hand on my shoulder blade and examines my back.

Thatcher clarifies, "Who gave you the two bite marks?"

I glower. "That's *none* of your fucking business." I've never shared my sexual history with the whole security team. Not when Declan was my bodyguard. And definitely not now.

"It's online already." Thatcher passes me his cellphone, the screen popped up to *Celebrity Crush*'s homepage.

The first photograph shows me only in dark-green boxer-briefs on my street. In a second panel, they zoomed in on two reddish bite marks. One near the back of my neck. The other on my waist above the band of my underwear. The headline:

MAXIMOFF HALE CAUGHT WITH SEXY BITE MARKS! IS HE INTO KINK?!

Before I even digest this, I spot another headline, another photograph from tonight. And then a photograph from over twenty years ago. I don't blink as I read:

MAXIMOFF HALE WEARS GREEN UNDERWEAR LIKE RYKE MEADOWS!

Great.

I'd been *so* damn careful about wearing green. I didn't exactly plan to run outside in my underwear tonight. Or *ever*.

I return the phone to Thatcher, not faltering. "Regardless of the article, you don't need to know who bit me or who I'm sleeping with— *none* of that is your business."

Thatcher turns to Farrow. "Where are the NDAs of everyone he's been intimate with while you've been his bodyguard?" *Fucking Christ.* "Because you've filed zero."

"There are no NDAs." Farrow doesn't even miss a beat, taking charge of the situation. "He's been with the same girl, and he's wanted to keep it private."

"The *purpose* of an NDA is to further protect his privacy."

"Private from the security team," Farrow clarifies, maybe lying on the fly. "It's a girl his parents wouldn't approve of."

Thatcher looks to me.

I nod once. Still pissed. I want the whole security team out of my bedroom. Now. Even my fake bedroom with a fake girl that I'm fake-fucking and who's fake-biting me.

"Maximoff," Thatcher says, "if she sues you, you're in for a nightmare. Whoever this girl is, it's much better to get her to sign an NDA. Your parents are understanding."

"She won't sue me. I trust her, and that's all I have to say." I'm done. "This conversation is over. If you have something else to ask me, go ahead. If it involves sex, don't even speak."

"That was it." Thatcher stands and then stares down Farrow. "Anything happens to him. It's on you."

"Loud and clear," Farrow says, not breaking their shared glare.

It's not on Farrow. I'm responsible for my own actions. My own life. If I step into quicksand, I wouldn't blame anyone but me.

25

I finish bandaging my arms, and Maximoff goes to check on Jane and make a few family calls upstairs. We can't speak, not with security everywhere. For a full hour, I rehash tonight's events to the Tri-Force in numb detail.

Then, they let me go.

Find Maximoff. It's all I've wanted to do. *Find Maximoff. Find him. Be with him.*

I head to the staircase. Passing three Alpha bodyguards, they pat my shoulder and tell me, "Good job." Another says, "Quick hands."

They congratulate me because the guy I pinned to the cement had a handgun on him. I had to disarm him, and most of SFA believes the two guys could've easily made a U-turn to Maximoff and Jane's townhouse if they weren't caught.

I ascend the narrow staircase, my head whirling. And not because of booze. Nothing could've sobered me faster than tonight's misadventure.

I reach the second floor, the bathroom door cracked. Maximoff has a hand on the sink, his phone to his ear.

"I love you too…I know, Mom."

I lean on the doorway while he finishes his call, and his forest-greens melt against mine. His bottom lip is split. His cheekbone starts to bruise, and beneath his eye, a reddish, purple tint forms. Almost like he was punched.

My stomach twists in brutal knots, and a rock wedges in my throat. I separated the bodyguard part of myself for one moment, and it hit me full-force tonight. That I'm seriously falling for someone whose life is threatened daily. Unconscionably. More than an actor. More than most celebrities.

He's American *royalty*. Fame from birth.

A type of notoriety that incites hatred and disbelief. Where people shout, *why are they famous?!* Where people decree, *undeserving!*

Where pranks leave scars and threats verge on crimes and the cost could be lives.

And I care about him. Shit, I care whether he's hurt or in pain or if he needs me. Unfavorable opinion time: I wish he would've let the cats die.

And then I don't. Because he wouldn't be Maximoff Hale if he didn't run after the little bastards. He wouldn't be Maximoff Hale if he didn't care about Jane and his entire family.

He wouldn't be the guy I can't stop staring at. Can't stop thinking about. He'd be someone else. Someone that I would've never even thought to kiss.

"I promise," he says into his phone. "Night." He hangs up, and I slip into the bathroom. I shut and lock the door behind me.

Our eyes never detach. And our arms immediately wrap around each other. I hug him to my chest as much as he hugs me. I cup the back of his head with my hand, his palm warms my neck, and his pulse pounds against my body.

He inhales, his carriage rising. My eyes burn, but I try to breathe, deep and strong.

Two minutes must pass before we lean back. Only just slightly. I hold his sharp jaw. We kiss gently, and then we pull further back. Studying one another for a brief moment.

His eyes are bloodshot.

I wonder what it must be like to be in his head. Paranoid, I'm guessing. Thoughts moving a mile a minute. Not slowing.

For anything.

"Are you okay?" I ask him finally.

He nods once. "Are you? Because I thought something seriously fucking terrible happened to you. No one could get ahold of you, and I saw Quinn and…" He swallows hard.

"I'm okay." My brows knot. "You know what I did tonight is just part of my job?"

He licks his lips slowly. "So you don't want me to care about you—"

"No." I lower my voice. "You just need to know that I'm going to get banged up and you can't run and save me, wolf scout. You have to let it happen."

Maximoff daggers a glare to the ceiling, then the mirror. It finally sinks in for him too. That I'm allowed to protect him, but he can't protect me. Not in the same exact way.

"We can't all be heroes," I say matter-of-factly.

His glare falls to me, but his lips inch bit by bit, our arms still hooked tight around each other. "If I'm not the hero, what am I?" Maximoff is waiting for me to call him a villain. In his comic books, that's the dichotomy. Heroes versus villains.

He's very far from one.

I press my lips to his jaw, his neck, and against his ear, I whisper, "You're a prince who wants to be a knight."

26

FARROW KEENE

Maximoff swims like a bird cutting through air, graceful and effortless. Made to fly.

In a matter of seconds, he crosses the whole length of the indoor pool.

I lounge on the edge of the diving board, one leg hanging off, my other foot on the board. Water rolls off my chest, black swim shorts wet, and even though we're alone, I'd still be hooked on Maximoff if the pool were jam-packed.

I have a perfect view when he switches to the butterfly stroke. Returning to my side of the pool, his grace transforms into *power*. His strong arms extend and then dig deep into the water, pulling half his chest and head above the surface.

Damn. My cock stirs.

Maximoff is known for his great butterfly technique. He started swimming really young, competed at junior levels first, then older with regional and national competitions. Security gossips *often* about how he could've qualified for an Olympic trial. But he didn't do it.

Didn't even try.

He chose to throw himself into his career. Into charity work. Every time he swims, I'm just reminded of how big his heart is.

Maximoff reaches my end, and instead of swimming another lap, he grabs onto the side of the diving board and does a pull-up with *one* arm. He yanks off his goggles and his cap, brown hair sticking up every which way.

It's cute as fuck.

"You ready for a round five?" he asks, his chest rising and falling heavily like he ran a marathon. We've already raced *four* times. Yeah, I lost all four. No, my ego doesn't bruise that easily.

My mouth stretches. "How about you catch your breath first?"

"Afraid of losing." He smiles like he bested me.

"No," I say. "I'm afraid I'm a bad influence. *Hubris* isn't a good look on you." I also add, "And I'm still taller. Right now and *every day*."

"By *one* damn inch." He tries to hoist himself up higher—just to make a point, but I push his chest. Hard enough that he falls back into the water.

I can't stop laughing when he breaches the surface with two middle fingers. Then he captures my dangling ankle and yanks me into the pool. *Shit.*

I dunk below, the water glowing blue in the darkly lit room. I breach the surface with a growing smile. Maximoff treads water, facing me. His wet hair is darker, almost closer to his natural color.

We don't touch yet.

My gaze pings to the security cameras. We're at the Hale Co. high-rise, the offices closed for the night. He's the son of the CEO, so he has his share of perks. Like getting access to the indoor pool after-hours. It helps that H.M.C. Philanthropies' main offices are in this building.

Maximoff rarely pulls strings for himself, but whenever I see the look on his face when he dives into the water, it makes complete sense why he chooses to open the pool.

I swim to the corner of the ten-foot deep-end. The only blind-spot. I've been in Hale Co.'s security room and looked at the cam footage. I'm 100% positive.

Maximoff follows.

The second we reach the corner, we explode—his mouth crushes against my mouth, rough and strong like he saved energy for this sweltering moment. Submerged in the pool, water droplets bead and drip down our temples and jaws. Wet but hot—*so fucking hot.*

His rock-hard body screams *closer* and *more*. Bucking against me—*damn*.

Damn. This guy could fuck me all day. I grip the tiled edge and use my build to pin Maximoff to the corner. His head tilts back, arousal trying to turn his eyes. He groans with a sharp breath, "Fuck."

I whisper rough in his ear, "Did you like that?" He responds with a hard kiss, his skilled tongue parting my lips. I massage his cock above his red knee-length Speedo, his erection growing beneath my palm.

Fuck, I'm throbbing. Beneath the water, lit by a soft blue pool light, he clasps my muscular waist—and he flips us. Pinning my shoulders to the corner.

His chiseled build pushes up against mine, and my hand roams the carved ridges of his abs.

Maximoff slows down, his breath deepening, and I watch him trace one of my tattoos with his fingers. Near my collarbone, a blood-red sparrow flies through the mast of a gray-scale ship.

He's looking at me like I'm the treasured celebrity. As though I'm the most valuable one.

I skim the faint bruise on his sharpened cheekbone.

I hate seeing you hurt. And I'm not the only one. After the firecracker incident last week, all of his younger cousins and two of his siblings approached me at a family cookout. Behind Maximoff's back.

Basically, they said, "Promise us you won't let Moffy get hurt again."

His brother added, "Or die."

"He's not going to die," I said, assured of this. *I still am.*

"Then hurt," they all said in unison.

"*Promise us*," Audrey Cobalt, the youngest Cobalt of seven emphasized, a knife in her hand for a whole blood oath thing that I *declined*.

Eighteen times, I said, "I promise." Until they believed me.

And I've never carried a promise like a burden, but here, now—*remembering* the pure, unconditional love those kids have for Maximoff, I feel the fucking need to at least caution him.

I run my hand down to his smooth jaw. "You need to be more careful."

"I'm the same as I've always been." His eyes dance over my mouth and cheeks. Maximoff has one arm out of the pool. And he uses his weight to cage me, keeping our shoulders above water. "So is this my bodyguard talking or my...?" He pauses.

"Wow." My brows rise, a smile edging across my mouth. "He even can't say what we are."

"Are we...?" His chest rises in a bigger breath. Either he doesn't want to say the word first or he's not sure if it's the "normal" time for labels.

I tilt my head. "Your virginity is showing."

"Pretty sure I lost my virginity a long time ago."

"*Relationship* virginity."

In the water, his hand dips down my swim shorts, rubbing my bare ass. I bite down, my pulse hammering. I tuck him closer to my chest, even if he's the one anchoring me to the corner.

"How long is a long time ago?" I ask him. It's not public knowledge, and he hasn't really told me yet.

Maximoff stares at my lips for a long moment.

I splash water at his face.

He lets go of the edge just to wipe the water. "Thank you for that."

"Stop imagining your cock inside my mouth."

He feigns confusion. "How'd you know?"

"Wild guess."

His voice lowers to a deep whisper. "When did you have your first sexual experience with someone?" He needs me to answer first.

I don't mind. "Thirteen. I was young, and I mistook *you have a great ass* for love." Some people are into casual hookups or NSA sex, but that's not my favorite thing. I prefer getting to know the person before or during or after for a while—and I can't stand open relationships.

While you fuck me, you only fuck me.

His lips lift, but then they fall in deep contemplation, mulling over my words: *I was young, and I mistook 'you have a great ass' for love.* And then he asks, "How do you know that's not happening now?"

My brows jump. "That's assuming I'm in love with y—" I cut *myself* off, reading his stiff, rigid body language clearly. His features start padlocking. Shutting me out. *No. No.* "Hey, I'm fucking with you, Maximoff. I'm an asshole." I clutch his impassive face. My stomach twists. It's extremely hard for him to be vulnerable. *I know this.*

I shouldn't have made that joke.

"It's fine," he says, his voice void of emotion. "I get it."

"No you don't." And I tell him bluntly, assuredly, without a fucking doubt, "You're my boyfriend. And from the jump-start, this has always been more than just sex." Yeah, we wanted to fuck each other's brains out, but for Maximoff to take this risk, it had to be more than what he can get at a nightclub.

His shoulders try to loosen, and he starts to smile, water dripping off our wet hair. "Boyfriends. Are you sure that's what we are?"

"A hundred percent." I pause. "Are you?"

He nods strongly. "Yeah."

I just fucking kiss him. He deepens the embrace, his hand rising from my ass to the back of my head.

When our lips break, he finally tells me, "Seventeen. That's when I had sex for the first time."

It makes sense. I'm about to speak, but his phone *rings* by the diving board. A call. Maximoff immediately swims over to the other side, and I pull myself out of the water.

He's already sitting on the edge, phone in hand, when I reach him. "It's Luna." Concern hardens his face.

It's one a.m. on a school night, late for Luna to call.

He clicks the speakerphone button. "Hey, what's going on?"

She sniffles, and as soon as Maximoff has a mere hint of Luna crying, he stands up with the "we need to leave" face.

I grab our towels, dry clothes, my holstered gun, radio—all set. Water drips off us, creating puddles at our feet. But he won't want to waste time changing.

By the time Luna speaks, we're in the elevator descending to the parking deck.

"I just got my last test scores back before finals." Her voice cracks. "Moffy, I failed three of my classes." She starts crying. "Eliot and Tom did the calculations, and I'd...I'd have to make a hundred-and-ninety-three on my finals to even pass."

Shit. I hook my radio to my damp swim shorts and fit the earpiece in my ear.

Maximoff grips the cell hard in his hand and pushes the elevator P3 button repeatedly. "What the hell happened, Luna? I thought you were doing better."

"Hi, Luna," I greet and catch his hand so he'll stop punching the fucking button. And I keep his hand in mine for a long beat.

"Farrow, did you hear—"

"Yeah. Hang in there."

"I'm trying." Her voice shakes. "But it's my fault. I missed too many quizzes. I skipped the classes where I'd have to see Jeffra."

"What'd she do?" Maximoff almost growls.

"She made a rumor in August that I'm *so weird*, I eat shit for fun. I didn't care. She could've called me anything, and I wouldn't have cared." Luna takes a short pause. "But someone put real shit in a paper bag in my locker, and I just couldn't even look at her, it made me sick."

My jaw muscle tics.

Maximoff's eyes flash murderously. If he speaks, he may say something like, *I'm going to kill someone.*

I squeeze his hand. "It's not your fault," I tell her.

"I let her make me feel worse," Luna says. "It's my fault."

"*No,*" Maximoff growls. "It's not."

"Where was your bodyguard?" I ask. Epsilon didn't share this information with the whole team. Or else I would've known.

"He never saw. I just acted like it was my lunch and then threw it away. I didn't want him to worry Mom and Dad." Her words quiver. "Now I wish I had. Because then maybe I would've had the courage to face her in class. And I know I can repeat the school year or do homeschool like Xander, but I just wanted the cap-and-gown graduation for them. I saw how they looked at you, Moffy, when you graduated, and I wanted to give that to Mom and Dad. I wanted them to be proud of me. And I fucked it up."

Maximoff glares at the phone. "Luna, listen to me. I *love* you. I'm coming over. We'll figure out how to tell Mom and Dad then."

The elevator dings. We've reached P3.

27

We return to my townhouse at almost 4 a.m.—
Farrow and I stayed with my sister for about three hours. He would've waited at the security's house one street over, but he's closest to Luna. I was glad she wanted him there.

Luna ended up feeling comfortable enough to tell our mom and dad. Tears were shed. Hugs were given. In the end, they made a plan to speak to the principal. She may not have to repeat the whole year if they learn about the shit-in-a-bag.

I thought I was pissed, but my dad almost woke up Jeffra's parents at three a.m.—not by phone. That family lives in our gated neighborhood.

My mom spider-monkeyed his back to stop him, and he turned to complete affectionate mush in her presence.

I check my watch when I shut my bedroom door.

4:23 a.m. "I'm sorry," I tell Farrow. I turn off my harsh lamp, and the strung bulbs on the rafters cast shadows and a soft, orange glow in my small bedroom.

Farrow unlaces his boots and tugs them off. "That's the fifth time you've needlessly apologized tonight."

I pull my crew-neck over my head and toss the shirt in my wicker hamper. "Every damn time we're alone or in a conversation—actually, when we're doing *anything* at all, something in my life swoops in and cuts it off. Your pockets are overflowing with rain checks." I watch him walk to my sole window, gray curtains drawn shut. "I'm shit at this, Farrow. You should reconsider this whole thing."

He's so damn calm as he leans against the window ledge, half-sitting on it. "This whole thing?"

"Yeah, *this* whole thing." I motion from him to me, then me to him. "I can fuck. Christ, I'm good at sex—"

"Who told you that?" His lips quirk.

I don't miss a beat. "—but being someone's boyfriend is so far out of my territory. It's on another galaxy. My life can't accommodate romantic relationships. At least not the kind you deserve."

"Is that really what you think?" He frowns darkly.

"Yeah." I nod several times. "You've had *four* other boyfriends, Farrow, and I can say I'm probably without a fucking doubt your *worst*. In terms of fucking—I'm number one though, sure."

"Sure," he adds, eyeing me, still not giving anything away. Maybe he's processing everything I dumped on him. He shakes his head once. "How long have you been agonizing over this?"

"What?"

"Come on," he says, still calm. Still cool. He crosses his arms over his chest more leisurely than serious. "You're *you*. You fixate over the details, over every variable you can think of. You've most likely been wrestling with this for weeks, if not months."

He knows me well.

Millions of people know me, but not like this. Not like that. I hang onto that fact like rope on a wall that blocks my view of everything. He's how I see the other side. He's made my life *feel* freer.

He made me believe I could actually have a relationship.

He made me believe I could experience more than just this fleeting, temporary thing.

And I have.

Christ, I have, but what is this for him? I give him *halfway*. Half of a relationship. A semblance of the real thing.

"It's been on my mind," I admit. "You've experienced what it's like being with me. The *constant* interruptions that I won't ignore. The lack of privacy that won't change. The never-ending phone calls. The *zero* PDA. If you want to break things off now, I get it. Just...clean cut. You can go back to being just my bodyguard. I go back to being just your client." My chest is on fire.

"Is that what you want?" he says, those words like a sling blade.

"No." My eyes sear. "*No.* I want you." *More than I've ever wanted anyone.*

Farrow never breaks my gaze. "And you're assuming that the lack of privacy, the 'zero' PDA, and all the interruptions bother me." He shakes his head. "They don't. Would I like to touch you in the car or on the street or even in an elevator? Of course, but I get *more* by being with you than any PDA could give me."

"I don't understand."

"Maximoff," he says, "the reason why this relationship works is *because* I'm your bodyguard. I'm with you almost twenty-four hours a day, every single day. One week with you is the equivalent to three months with anyone else. You know more about me and what it's like to be with me than some of my long-term exes." He laughs at a thought. "The fact that we're sleeping together, around one another all the time, *and* not killing each other is a miracle. And it says something."

His words extinguish the toxic heat in my chest. "What?"

"We're good together. *Really* good." Farrow smiles. "And you're not a bad boyfriend. You're not the worst. Or even second-to-last-place. You're the most thoughtful, the most caring, and the media was right when they said whoever dates you would be the luckiest fucking human alive. I feel *lucky* to be with you."

I inhale, but I don't exhale yet. "I can't give you more though. I know there may be a point where a crisis in my family may conflict with whatever's happening in your life—and you're not going to like who I choose."

"You're going to choose your family because that's who you are," Farrow says strongly. "And I will love you for it."

I set my hands on the back of my neck. He's not considering all the variables. Or am I just packing sandbags around my house before it explodes? "That's not a relationship," I combat. "I *should* pick my boyfriend."

"If you keep weighing your morality with scales, you're going to lose." Farrow still sits at ease. "Just put down the hypotheticals and step away. Let go."

I don't know how. I want to give him as much as he's given me.

Farrow licks his bottom lip. "Can we agree on one thing?" he asks. "We're together. We're doing this, and neither of us wants to stop."

"Yeah."

He pushes off from the window and crosses the room. Quickly, he's in front of me, his hands on the waistband of my jeans. I hold his muscular shoulders, skin warm beneath my hands.

"One day," he tells me, his voice gravel in silk. His mouth on the base of my neck, sucking and biting up to my ear. My muscles slacken, unwinding. I edge even closer. His hot breath throbs my cock. "I'm going to be inside of you."

One day. I still like fantasizing about the idea. It's a vulnerable place I eventually want to reach with him.

Just not tonight.

I wake to the worst beeping 5:40 a.m. alarm—
too damn early. Farrow's head is on my shoulder, our muscular legs tangled. I reach over and slap the snooze on his phone.

It wouldn't be the first time he's stayed longer in my bed. We've both been lenient on this one precaution. Later, he'll return to his townhouse, hopefully without Quinn noticing anything strange.

Farrow yawns in his fist and sits up on his elbows. His white hair is a mess, his lips reddened from rough kissing barely an hour ago, and the beginnings of a know-it-all smile work their way across his mouth.

It's undeniable.

Farrow Keene is unadulterated *sex* in the morning. I have more than a small hard-on for him. Like currently. Right now. I crave him, blood rushing to my dick.

He stares at me like I'm a regular fixture to these 5:40 a.m. wake-up calls. Like no matter how tired, I'm the first face he wants to see.

Fuck me. My cock aches beneath my sheets and orange comforter.

Without saying a word, Farrow stretches to the nightstand and grabs a condom and lube. He passes the bottle to me but keeps the condom.

He tears the wrapper, and I kick down the comforter and sheets. I watch the movement of his fingers as he covers my erection. His grip is light. *Closer.*

More.

His mouth curves upwards, and he lies back on his elbows.

I lather myself while I eye the inked skull pirate on his ribcage. And the lavender sparrow nearby. I lift my gaze to his barbell nipple piercing— *fuck.* My waist arches slightly.

I turn towards Farrow, and I pull him up higher, aligning us. He drops off his elbows when I position him on his side. Not fucking gentle.

He lets out a rough, throaty noise and palms his cock twice. His round ass brushes up against me.

My mouth touches the back of his neck. I grip his thigh. Stretching his leg over my waist to spread him more. Erection grazing his hole.

His nose flares in desire. "This is the only way you're getting me to be the little spoon," he reminds me. "You better fucking enjoy it."

He turns his head back to me. Enough that I kiss him, my tongue parting his lips and sliding against his. He reaches up and holds my jaw. *Fuck me.* I ache to rock forward right now. I break the kiss early and breathe, "Trust me, I already am."

We never spoon each other at night. Neither one of us can give up that lead. Most nights while we sleep, our arms and legs end up tangling.

I clutch my shaft and *slowly* push inside of Farrow. He buries his head into his pillow, mouth opened. A garbled noise escapes.

I watch him for a second, my ass flexing. *Yes. Fuck yes.* He's pretty fucking tight for my cock. Every time I sink into him, it's top-notch, eye-rolling pressure.

My movement is unhurried. Achingly *temperate.* Trying to milk every damn second for its total worth.

"*Fuck,* Maximoff," he almost gasps, his breath shallow.

I groan, all the way in. *Yesyes.* I rock deeper into him, my arm hooked around his abs. I wrap my hand around his fucking huge erection, and I sync my thrusts with my hand.

Farrow grits down for one second before his mouth is forced open by the pleasure again. He curses into the pillow, face reddened. Holding breath. Neck muscles taut.

Fuck, holy fuck.

I thrust harder, ass flexed more. Banging up against him. My chest is welded to his strong tattooed back. Farrow reaches behind him and grips my ass. Pushing me firmer into him. *Yesyesyesyesfuckyes.* He rocks backwards into my cock when I rock forward into him.

We move together in unison. Like a slow, thundering wave.

He moans a deep, raspy moan. Like the sound was unearthed from his core. "*Fuck,*" he moans again. "*Fuckfuck.*"

"*Farrow,*" I groan, sweat built. I'm rising towards an intense peak. I quicken my pace in a final sprint—*fuckyesyesyesyesfuuuuckkk.* My orgasm ripples through me and his covers my palm. I eek the climax. Staying inside of him, slowing in and out.

In and out, my hot breath on his neck.

Farrow is trying to catch his breath in the pillow.

Then he turns his head. Watching me ease out of him completely. Then I kiss him.

Sex with Farrow is incomparable and immeasurable. I'm pretty much a goner. Totally and utterly obsessed with the before, during, and after—it's ridiculous. In the best damn way.

I sit up, discard the condom, and grab a towel from my nightstand's drawer. Tossing it to him.

Farrow leans up against the headboard. "Are you ever worried about becoming a sex addict?" He catches me off guard, and he waits for me to process.

I blink a couple times. I'm sitting on the edge of the bed, my feet cold on the hardwood. I glance back at him. "No." It's a flat *definitive* word.

"No?" Farrow seems surprised. "For how much you avoid drinking, I just thought..."

"I'm careful," I say, standing. "I don't let sex interfere with my daily life. *Ever.*" I'm highly aware of the warning signs of unhealthy behavior. *Highly aware.*

I can have a lot of sex and not be a sex addict. The minute sex ruins my relationships or my job—then it's a goddamn problem.

As far as I'm concerned, I don't have one.

"Fair enough," Farrow says, balling the towel.

He drops the topic too fast.

I rotate to face him. "Do *you* think I have a problem?" As my mom's bodyguard for three years, he was near a sex addict a lot longer than most people.

"No," Farrow says. "No, I don't, but being around you all the time, you do have addictive tendencies."

I don't ask for specifics. "I know."

"Good," he says into a nod.

28

At Superheroes & Scones, Jane places multiple boxes of pastries on a low table. Bright and neon beanbags are strewn around the loft lounge, and an *Avengers* movie plays on mounted television screens.

The place is dead at 5:00 a.m., and I sip my coffee and take a seat adjacent to Maximoff on a blue beanbag. I'm almost shoulder-to-shoulder with Quinn.

Not my first choice. But a few days ago, Quinn said to me, "I keep missing you in the mornings. Your bed is empty, too."

It didn't shake me, but I wouldn't concoct a wild, intricate lie that could unravel. I just told him, "Occasionally, I'll crash on the couch or in one of the cars. It's colder." He knows how hot my attic room can get.

Be more careful around Quinn, I agreed to Maximoff's new rule. I may've physically distanced us this morning, but I'm still consciously staring at my boyfriend. I smile into my coffee when he pretends to be more interested in an *Avengers* film on mute.

He holds a paper cup of hot tea, drinking slowly. Trying not to look at me. We all know he ranks me above Iron Man, Thor, and whatever other Avenger makes an on-screen appearance. Not just because I'm clearly better and clearly *not* fictional.

But because I'm his bodyguard. His real-life superhero.

Jane opens two pink boxes. "For the meeting, we have croissants, muffins, stuffed donuts, frosted donuts, Danishes, scones, bagels, a few waffles, but do not, under any circumstance, eat *these*." She lifts up a heart-shaped tin. "I spent two hours helping my one and only sister with math homework yesterday, and afterwards, she gave me strict orders to deliver these to Oscar Oliveira. I will complete the task."

I lean forward and grab the tin out of her hands.

"Farrow!"

"Breathe. I'm not eating Oscar's cookies." I pop the tin and inspect the perfectly heart-shaped sugar cookies, pink icing and written with *Oscar* and *I love you*.

Maximoff grimaces at Jane. "Can your twelve-year-old sister pick someone who's *not* thirty-years-old to crush on?"

What about someone five years older? I try really hard not to tease or irritate him.

"You can sheath your swords, Moffy. It's harmless," Jane says and eagle-eyes me as I pass the tin to Quinn. He snatches a cookie.

Jane glares and then yanks the entire tin out of his hands. "*Quinn.*"

I laugh. I like Quinn more and more every day.

Not hesitating, he bites into the cookie. "Oscar is my brother. I should get *one* cookie out of that. Hey, I'll be his best man or whatever at their pretend wedding."

Audrey disinvited me to that "wedding" three years ago after I told her she has bad taste in men.

Jane lowers on her beanbag and protectively clutches the tin to her lap. I've noticed the bag of peas she's been carrying around all morning and *sitting* on, and my intrigue is spilling into concern.

I have to ask now.

"Did I miss Nate coming over last night?" I motion with my coffee to the peas that she's using as an ice pack.

Jane looks genuinely surprised that I'm asking. She searches my gaze with intense curiosity. Wondering *why*—why did I ask.

Because you mean something to Maximoff.

And you're starting to mean something to me.

Maximoff's cheekbones sharpen, but he keeps his attention on the TV, not worried. I assume she must've told him the news this morning in the bathroom.

Quinn frowns at Jane. "Did Nate sneak in? You didn't tell me he was coming over—"

"He didn't," she says quickly.

"A new guy?" Quinn asks. "Then I should've been there. With an NDA."

"Not unless you'd like to try to give my sex toys an NDA." Jane smiles as realization parts Quinn's lips.

"Oh."

I arch my brows at Jane. "Not enough lube there?"

"No." She sits straighter. It's her "I'm preparing a speech" posture. "Sex is almost a family legacy. My parents were in porn."

Maximoff corrects, "Not willingly." Their tapes were leaked.

"Still," she says, "I thought perhaps, my real passion is in sex toys. I could've been a fabulous sex toy reviewer."

I rest my arm on my bent knee. "And what happened?"

"I inserted something in *terribly* wrong."

We all make a pained face.

Jane takes a deep, reassuring breath before declaring, "I've realized it's not for me."

Seriously, I say, "I know what'll make you feel better."

"What?" she wonders, a gleam in her eye.

"One of Oliveira's cookies."

Quinn laughs, and Maximoff stares between Jane and me like we're seconds from destroying a relationship we haven't really even built.

Jane tips her head to me like *touché.*

"Akara to Farrow and Quinn." The Omega lead's voice bleeds through my mic. "Sul and I are leaving now. We'll be there soon." A motorcycle revs in the background.

I stand and inspect the pastries. "Sulli and Akara are on their way," I tell Maximoff. "What do you want to eat?"

His eyes narrow like *you shouldn't speak to me in front of Quinn*.

I cock my head, smiling. *Come on*. It'd draw more attention if we were playing a silent game with one another. I trust myself to rein in the causal flirting. I'm sure he trusts himself, too. He just likes to add five padlocked chains onto a dead-bolted door.

He stands, posture stringent. "I can get my own food." It's a common phrase for him: *I can do that myself. You don't need to open my car door.* Et cetera, et cetera.

It's more endearing than he understands. I grab an egg and cheese croissant and watch him grab a blackberry scone. We sit back down at nearly the exact same time.

His attention wants to be on me so badly. He stares at my hair for a long, long beat like it's brand new.

"My hair has been blue for two weeks," I remind him, the electric-blue strands pushed back out of my face. I wanted a change. I only have one barbell in my eyebrow now. Plus, I put in my small hoop earring.

"I got that, thanks," he says, licking his lips and sipping his hot tea.

I laugh into a smile.

Quinn spreads cream cheese on his bagel with a plastic knife. "Can someone explain why there's a production meeting for *We Are Calloway* if filming doesn't start until next January?" He licks his thumb.

That's why we're all here.

A production meeting.

We Are Calloway has been an Emmy nominated and award-winning docuseries for over a decade. It's the only platform that enables the Hales, Meadows, and Cobalts to voice their opinions and tell their stories. It's to ensure their truth is heard and not twisted on social media.

When *We Are Calloway* first premiered, I was a kid, and I remember sneaking downstairs and hiding behind my father's sofa while he watched the R-rated show (for mature themes). I peeked around the armrest and saw Lily Calloway.

A twenty-something, scrawny girl that I'd one day protect. And she looked powerfully in the camera and said, "I'm always going to be a sex addict, but I'm more than just sex."

Every raw frame of the show struck a cord with me, and by the end, my father sat in silence and uttered one awed word. *Wow.*

After all these years, the families still film season after season. To humanize themselves, but also for the hundreds of people that relate to them.

Recently, the docuseries has been on a short hiatus, but it starts again next year. I only have one issue with the show.

It makes security harder.

Maximoff breaks his scone in half. "We have early production meetings because we need to talk to Jack before we do anything."

Quinn nearly chokes on his coffee. "Jack? Like *the* Jack."

I say, "The one and only Jack Highland. Take note: remember whose side you're on. One too many have fallen for his charm."

Maximoff gives me a tough look. "There are no sides."

"There are definitely sides, wolf scout." I motion to Quinn and myself. "We're in charge of protecting your private lives. And then Jack is in charge of protecting your public lives."

Still, we have to align at the end of the day and find common ground together. And almost everyone likes Jack Highland. He's hard to hate. That used to make me a little bit wary of him, but I have no real beef with Jack. He's the youngest executive producer on *We Are Calloway*, and he has an enormous amount of contact with security.

He has to. Production and security are intertwined on filming days. These meetings set up most of the prep work.

Someone knocks on the locked entrance downstairs. I stand and peer over the balcony railing. *Speaking of Jack...* "Go meet him first, Quinn."

He bites into his bagel and then jogs down the twisting iron stairs.

Maximoff has pushed aside his food and tea. He somehow sits like a board on a slouchy red beanbag, and he cracks his knuckles.

Jane shifts her bag of peas, but I see how uptight she sits too.

"What's wrong?" I ask them. Staying standing, I lean on the silver wall with a lightning bolt decal.

"It's Sulli's first production meeting," Maximoff tells me.

"It needs to go well," Jane adds.

Right.

Their cousin has never been on *We Are Calloway*. By joining the docuseries, Sulli is opening herself up to new criticism from the public.

But Maximoff and Jane have been on the show since they were little kids. Before I even met him, I watched Maximoff Hale on-screen profess his undying love for Power Rangers and excitedly say, *"I hope that if I have a brother or a sister, they'll like Power Rangers too."*

Public fact: Xander is a Power Ranger every year for Halloween.

Jane abandons her frozen peas to flip open another pastry box. "What do you want, Jack?"

Jack Highland ascends the twisting staircase. He has a quintessential "jock" look: broad, cut muscles visible through his tight black button-down, shoulder span as wide as a linebacker, and the charisma and popularity of a letter-jacket quarterback.

In any teen comedy, my "type" should hate his "type" but real people are more than just "rebel" versus "jock." Plus, we're both adults.

What I know about Jack: he wasn't a football player. He did swim in college. He's twenty-five, Filipino-American, biracial, and he has short dark brown hair, honey-brown eyes, and he's a good inch taller than me.

"Give me the blueberry muffin," he tells Jane, and she passes the baked good before gently sitting back down. Quinn slumps onto his beanbag.

Unwrapping his muffin, Jack turns to me first. "Have you reconsidered my offer?"

Maximoff's brows knit. "What offer?"

I cross my arms loosely. "Jack wants me on the show. *So fucking badly.*" I emphasize those words. "How long have you been asking me?"

"Three years." He bites into the blueberry muffin. "The more you keep turning me down, I'm going to start believing it's personal."

"Wait." Maximoff stands. He hates sitting when other people are standing, I swear. "You want *Farrow*, this Farrow"—he points at me—"on the show?"

I give Maximoff a once-over. "How many *Farrows* do you know?"

Maximoff shoots me a middle finger.

Jack is used to exchanges like these, not fazed. "I've always wanted to showcase a bodyguard on *We Are Calloway*. Farrow has a good look, there's a gif of you two..." Using one hand he scrolls on his phone and flashes me the gif first.

We've seen that one.

A Tumblr user made a gif from the footage when the court suspended Moffy's license. In the gif: Maximoff and I push through the courthouse doors, exiting with sunglasses, side-by-side, cameras flashing repeatedly.

We look hot together.

"And Farrow is good looking enough to be a model," Jack tells my boyfriend.

I raise my brows in a self-satisfied wave at Maximoff. He tries not to stare at me again. He almost has *fuck me* eyes.

By the way, Jack is straight. And I'd agree, I'm a 10 out of 10, but coming from Jack...

"That loses its meaning when I've heard you use the same compliment for forty-two different people," I say, being precise on the number because I have a great memory. So I can be precise *and* accurate.

See, Jack has a way of making people feel good. It's his job to ensure everyone in the room is comfortable. Then they can share information with him.

Even now, his eyes soften on me. "You're a gorgeous guy. Better?"

"We're getting slightly more original. But not by much," I say and return to my beanbag beside Quinn.

In a matter of seconds, we're all seated around the low table again.

Maximoff refills his tea and says to Jack, "It still doesn't make sense. If you put Farrow in the show, he'd become famous. He wouldn't be able to be my bodyguard."

"Exactly." I pick up my croissant sandwich. "Jack wants me in the show *acting* like a bodyguard. What he hasn't grasped yet is that I like my job as a real bodyguard."

Maximoff makes a concentrated effort not to look at me and draw attention. But he knows the fuller truth: I *love* my job because I'm around him.

Jack opens his notepad, slouched coolly on a yellow beanbag. "All I'm saying is one day you may want a change." He flips a page. "Before Sullivan arrives, we can start with the two of you." Pen between his fingers, he motions to Maximoff and Jane. "Next season is about big topics. Is there anything specific you want to talk about?"

29

Is there anything specific you want to talk about?
Jack always pitches this question first. My mind reels through various issues I could possibly discuss. Everything circumnavigates to one.

One topic, one plight, one goddamn annoyance.

"Yeah." I set my cup on the table. "I want to talk about my uncle."

The Superheroes & Scones loft deadens. My eyes flit to a war scene playing in *Avengers*, the Hulk smashing buildings to smithereens.

Jack skirts over the silence like it never existed. "Which uncle?"

"Ryke. Yesterday, an article compared his 'f-bombs' to mine. I don't even say *fuck* as often as him. Sulli does way more than me." I didn't plan to come in this hot and aggravated.

I sense Farrow and his at ease nature, and you know the weirdest thing? It calms me. Makes me feel like I have someone prepared to jump on my side. Right now. This moment. *Any* moment.

He's with me.

My bound shoulders unwind.

Jack isn't the type of person to just say *no*. He tries to hear people out, but he reminds me, "You talked about this last season, Moffy."

"It's been worse this year."

"But it's not going to change with this show," Jack says. "You've discussed the topic *at length* three times. We've reached the max. One more time, and the public will believe you're overcompensating for something. As a producer, I'd tell you to just go ahead and talk about it. It'll bring us ratings. But as your friend, I'm telling you not to bring it up."

Goddammit. "What about if I talk about my dad?"

"It depends." Jack twists off a cap to Ziff, a sports drink. "If you're going to just tell the audience how great of a father he is—*no*."

I rub my aching shoulder. I need to stretch. "Just tell me what I should be talking about then."

"Sex," Jack says. "It's what people want to know most about you, especially with those photos." *The bite marks.* "Who are you seeing? What kind of pressures do you deal with being the son of a sex addict? Are you more careful? Do you have insecurities?" He lists the questions rapidly.

I've heard them all before. Jack broaches the topic of *sex* almost every production meeting.

"Are you ready to talk about this stuff?" he asks.

"No," I say firmly. "Not this season. Maybe not ever. I'm sorry."

"This is a *no apology* zone, remember? Whatever content you want to share, good. Whatever you don't, that's good too. It's all up to you." Jack already jumps to a new topic. "What about your relationship with Luna? She'll be eighteen and be on her own for the first time. It'd be a great arc."

Out of my siblings, Luna is the only one who's on *We Are Calloway* with me. We've bonded a bit while filming together, and I already know she'd love a whole arc about our relationship.

So I agree.

"Jane?" Jack asks. "Any personal topics?"

Janie and I already scooted closer to one another. I stare down at my best friend who wears a cheetah-print sweater, pale yellow pants, and sequined high heels. Whatever she's about to say, she hasn't brought up with me yet.

"I'd like to discuss my weight," she says assuredly.

Our bodyguards have no idea how to react to these issues if it doesn't involve security. Even Farrow, I think. They just keep eating and drinking.

Doing their best not to appear *concerned*. It's not their job to be emotionally invested in us.

But a lot of them care, I've fucking realized.

Obviously.

One is my boyfriend. *Don't look at him.* I'm trying. Christ, I've *been* trying for the past fifteen minutes.

"More specifically?" Jack asks my best friend while jotting notes. He bites into his muffin.

I wrap my arm around Janie when she says, "That I love my body the way it is. I have tiny boobs, no ass, love-handles and a bigger belly. How *chubby* isn't a nasty word. And their hatred won't change me."

Farrow and Quinn start clapping in genuine appreciation.

Can we do take-backs?

Our bodyguards actually do know how to react. *They're our friends.*

I know. *I know.*

I squeeze Jane around the shoulders and kiss her freckled cheek. "Je t'aime, ma moitié." *I love you, my other half.*

Janie smiles warmly. "Je t'aime aussi." *I love you too.*

Jack scribbles and nods. "That'll be great. Also, you're looking lovely as ever, Jane."

"Merci."

Farrow rolls his eyes, not at Janie's comment but the producer's.

"What?" Jack asks him. "I can't give compliments to this group anymore?"

"You're almost maxed out," Farrow says.

"Then you're all ugly," Jack says with a wide grin. "How's that?"

Quinn starts a slow-clap for Jack, and Farrow, Jane, and I join in. The exec producer's smile expands.

The bell to the front door *dings* open. Akara has a key. Janie and I straighten up and exchange a look that says, *protect Sulli if it gets intense.*

The actual process of the docuseries is pretty fucking raw.

Round 1 of the Gauntlet of Over-sharing: *dump your personal story onto Jack and a hoard of bodyguards.*

Round 2: *allow production teams to invade your life for specific chunks of time.*

Round 3: *let the world watch you be vulnerable.*

Right now, I'm just fixated on round one for Sul. She'll want to complete what she starts—no matter what—but if round one makes her uncomfortable, *I'll* pull the fucking plug and call it off.

"Jack," I whisper as footsteps sound on the iron staircase. "Since this is Sulli's first meeting, can you just ease her in?"

"Sure," Jack nods, and he stands to greet my cousin. The rest of us turn and watch.

"Here, Sul." Akara takes her motorcycle helmet, already holding his.

"Thanks, Kits." Sulli unbuttons her denim jacket, dressed in denim jeans and a plain white tee. Her dark hair falls long on her chest.

Jack approaches and catches her gaze.

"You must be Jack." Sulli holds out her hand.

Akara sidesteps around them, and I spot this *long* warning look that he shoots Jack. It pretty much says, *careful with this one, or you're dead.*

Jack falters for a brief second. "Um…" He frowns and then brushes off the moment. Shaking Sulli's hand. "I'm Jack."

"Jack Highland," Sulli adds, their handshake lasting a long beat.

Janie nudges my shoulder and her brows wag as she picks apart a croissant.

I don't know what the fuck that means.

All I know is that Jack is acting weird. I can't discern whether it's because I warned him about Sulli, Akara shot him a look, or we've all been joking about his compliments.

Akara takes a seat on a beanbag between Farrow and Quinn. Security claiming their side of the low table. *Alright, there are sides.* They all observe Sulli and Jack more intently than they do most casual encounters.

"And you're Sullivan Meadows." Jack finally breaks from the handshake.

"You can call me Sulli." Then her gaze flits to Jane.

Jane waves her over and makes room for her to sit in between us. I grab a teal beanbag and set it down in the free space.

When Jack and Sulli join us at the table, he sits on his own side and picks up his notepad. Now there are three metaphorical and literal sides: *the famous, the security, the production.*

I get it.

And I watch Jack *watching* Sulli. My cousin squishes between me and Jane, and she edges up to the table. Making a plate of food.

Jack twirls his pen. "Do you want to be introduced in the show as Sulli?"

Sulli piles two waffles on a plate. "Ummm...yeah, that'd be good, right?" She looks to me, then Jane. "Fuck, I don't know. What do you two go by?"

"Jane."

"Maximoff."

She glances at Jack. "I'll go with Sullivan."

He nods.

Sulli towers *three* chocolate donuts on top of the waffles. She finds the whipped cream canister and strawberry syrup that Janie brought and squirts the waffle-donut mound.

Jack can't stop staring at her breakfast, his pen frozen on the notepad. "Would you want to talk about that?"

"About what?" She looks up, confused. "My donuts? I haven't eaten them yet. How am I supposed to talk about them?"

Farrow tilts his head at Sulli. "*Green*, the shade of newbies. It's a cute color on you."

She blushes and glances to Akara. He already throws a pillow at Farrow's chest, who rolls his eyes. I can't take in the joke or even add in a sarcastic remark. I just stay on guard for whatever's coming.

"On the show," Jack says, ignoring my bodyguard...boyfriend. *Focus.* I blink a few times. He clarifies further, "Do you want to talk about your eating habits?"

"Oh. Fuck, really?" She frowns deeply. "People would want to know about that?" Press has photographed my cousin at restaurants.

She only orders desserts. It's not like that's her breakfast, lunch, and dinner. But she's not following any nutritional food pyramid either. I only ever saw her eat healthy during intense training periods. She'd plug her nose and chug protein shakes.

"First, foremost," Jack says to Sulli, "the show is about what you want to do. The public would love to know *everything* about you. So don't feel pressured to speak about a topic that makes you uncomfortable."

Sulli nods heartily, cutting into her waffle-donuts. "I like it."

Jane flashes me a thumbs-up.

I'm not ready to rest easy. I tell Sulli, "Jack has a good perception of how the public will react to what you want to share."

"Whoa, really?" Sulli starts smiling. It's not often we find people who can ground our lives *and* trust. "So what would the public think about my breakfast?"

Security hawk-eyes Jack.

"They'll label you a picky-eater to start," Jack says, "and some will find it endearing. Other people will shit on you for it. That's a huge part of the show—you share your story and then you take the good with the bad."

Jane chimes in, "It's nice being able to have your voice out there."

Sulli stuffs her mouth and chews slowly, contemplating.

"Are you positive you want to do this?" I ask. "No one's forcing you on *We Are Calloway*. You can back out now, Sulli."

Jack studies her closely. "He's right. We'd love to have you on, but this is your choice."

"No, I need this." Sulli nods to herself now. "Look, I *need* to talk about some of this bullshit…I'm just wrapping my head around how this works."

"That's okay," Jack says, comforting. "I'll guide you through the process."

Sulli takes a bigger breath and looks to Akara. He combs his black hair back and fits on a backwards baseball cap. She asks him, "You'll be there while we film? Even if it's not a public place?"

"If you want me there," he says, "I'll be there, Sul."

"Okay, good."

Jack edges closer to the table. To her. "Hopefully," he says, drawing Sulli's gaze, "you and me will reach a place of trust where you won't need Akara in the room."

The air snaps on *the security* side of things. Jane rocks back with me, our furrowed brows on the three bodyguards.

Akara is boiling. Venom in his glare, muscles supremely flexed. Sitting completely still—that's somehow more intimidating. And *no one* intimidates me.

But you know that.

You don't know that Farrow has his fist to his mouth, jaw tensed.

Or that Quinn crosses his arms at Jack.

They're not happy that he just metaphorically banished a bodyguard from a room. Jack senses this and speaks directly to Akara.

"Why would you need to be in a secure environment?"

"Because she asked me to be," he says curtly. "Any other questions, *Jack*?"

"For Sulli, yeah," Jack says, trying to ignore the incensed bodyguards.

Sulli hesitates to eat another bite of food. "You okay, Kits?"

Jack and Akara stare each other down.

And then Akara says flat-out, "Respect security and we'll respect production."

"Sounds good, man." Jack swigs his sports drink.

Akara nods.

I'm fucking impatient. "Let's move on."

"How about," Jack says to Sulli, "you tell us what you'd like to talk about on the show. You said there's bullshit that needs to be said. What bullshit?"

Sulli uses her muscular bicep to wipe her mouth. "So the photographs from the Olympics."

My muscles bind, but she's able to meet Jack's gaze while unloading more of her feelings.

"The ones with the hair. The stupid fuckwads who keep thinking it's funny to zoom up on my bikini line need to know they are *fuckwads*."

"Agreed." I finish off my tea in one gulp.

Olympics should've been a time to *celebrate* Sulli's athletic achievements. The *entire* fucking time, the media latched onto her shaving and waxing habits. Weeks before the summer games, they photographed Sulli with stubble and hair by her bikini line.

The image went viral.

85% of the questions reporters asked at the Olympics centered on her hair—and she answered all of them with a definitive *fuck you.*

That also went viral.

"Does the topic go deeper than the Olympics?" Jack asks. I tense.

"What do you mean?" Sulli scoops a piece of waffle.

"He means when you were younger," I explain. "Did you deal with anything like that growing up?" Her forest-green eyes that match my hue just *drown* against me—because I was there. I grew up with Sulli. I saw her hit puberty earlier than most girls. Her hair is dark and grows fast.

I saw the boys after swim meets *jeer* at the hair on her arms. I shoved two in a pool when they started making gorilla noises. And then I hugged Sulli in the locker room, and we collectively said, *fuck them.*

Fuck them.

"Do I have to talk about that right now?" she whispers to me.

"No." I give Jack a serious look like *work your production magic and pivot this topic. Now.*

"Maybe you and Moffy can have a segment swimming or racing one another." *Thank you.*

I almost smile. "You mean a segment where she kicks my ass."

Sulli's lips curve, and she knocks her shoulder to mine. "I'll go easy on you."

"No you won't." I rotate to Jack. "I'll only do it if you agree to get your ass beat by her too."

Quinn coughs in his fist. *What'd I say?*

Farrow cracks his neck, silently gesturing to Akara. Who looks murderous. Not at me. At Jack.

I suggested swimming not fucking.

Jack wouldn't overstep the production-talent boundary. I would tear him limb from limb.

He knows that.

Sullivan swings her head to the exec. "You swim?" Her eyes light up. The list of people she can race on her free time is short.

"Four years at Penn." He gives her a smile and then flips a page in his notes. "Can I get personal with you for a second?"

Sulli uncaps a water. "Sure."

"Would you want to discuss your virginity on the show?"

The room cuts in a tense silence. Sulli has shared pretty much a bucket of *nothing* with the public concerning dating or sex. She's been private, and so everyone assumes she's a virgin.

Their assumption is correct. For once.

"Um..." Sulli mulls it over.

"No pressure," Jack says. "Since a lot of people talk about sex on the show, I have to ask." He pauses. "Have you watched any episodes of the series?"

"Not really." Sulli rests her hand on her squared jaw. "It's kinda weird seeing your family on TV." She's not the only one who chooses to skip it.

Her best friend Beckett Cobalt hasn't seen a single episode.

Sulli leans into Janie. "Do you talk about sex?"

Jane touches her chest. "Personally, I have to talk about sex. If another guy tries to chokehold me in bed, I will lose it."

"That's never happening again," Akara says, side-eyeing me because he knows I'll actually kill the person. I'll commit murder.

Farrow wasn't around Jane during that incident. One of the worst nights of my life—where I woke to a lamp crashing. Jane's old bodyguard started knocking down her locked door. Standing guard because she brought someone over. I charged in her bedroom before security inched inside—and I *tore* a guy twice her size off her body.

I was all rage. My mind blared three notes: *you're killing her, you're killing her, you're going to die.* My bodyguard had to restrain *me.*

Just to be clear, I'm not proud of that.

"Can I ask you something?" Sulli says to Jack. "What exactly would I say about sex? I've never had sex, the end. There's nothing more."

Jack closes his notepad. "Are you waiting to have sex until marriage or to fall in love—"

"I've been *so* focused on swimming. I just never made time for anything else, including sex or dating, and I'd do it all over again. I don't regret it."

"Have you ever been attracted to someone? Have you ever *thought* about hooking up?"

I swear they're acting like they're the only two in the room. They've blocked us out.

Sulli nods a couple times. "Definitely. A few...okay, several guys on the team were really fucking hot, but I wouldn't let that get in my way. My mom always said she regretted not waiting for someone who made her feel comfortable and loved. Like my dad. And I want that too."

He smiles. "Okay. Have you been kissed?"

She bites her lip. "No."

Wait.

I didn't know that.

I glance at Akara. And I just read his protective features really well, and I nod to myself, *he knew.*

Jack smiles more warmly. "So truth: that'll be a thing. It'll cause a lot of press, but it's up to you whether you want to share. The good: I can see a lot of girls relating. The bad: a lot of guys will..."

"Be fuckwads?"

"Yeah."

More bluntly, Farrow interjects, "Perverted fuckwads."

Sulli holds her bent leg to her chest. "It shouldn't be such a big fucking deal. So what? I haven't been kissed and I'm nineteen. Who cares?"

"So make it less of a big deal," Jack says. "Make it ordinary. Make it normal. You have that power. And it's all up to you."

30

Board meetings at eight in the morning are like an average human's ten-minute sprint. Come prepared to my table—then we'll be back in our individual offices by 8:10.

Fifteen other people sit in leather chairs. At twenty-two, I head the table. It's not just hard work that put me here. Clearly *nepotism* plays a vital role.

I don't ever forget that.

"We have three grant applications that look promising," Yara says, a longtime board member and also the COO of Cobalt Inc.

Outside of our own projects, H.M.C. Philanthropies funds local and regional nonprofit organizations, but with the amount of requests we receive every year, we need to be selective in where the money is allocated.

"Are those the ones you emailed me last night?" I ask.

"Yes."

"Approve them all," I tell her. My eyes lift to the clock on the wall. 8:05.

Farrow will pick me up at 8:10 on the dot. I'm scheduled to drop by the local animal shelter and talk about future fundraising events.

Just as I start wrapping up the meeting—the damn door blows open. Heads swing.

People freeze. Coffee cups to lips and pens raised midair. Silence invades the room like an airborne *virus*.

What the fuck is he doing here?

Charlie Cobalt stands in the doorway, all six-foot-three of him looks like he just fucked someone. No shit. White collar popped on his button-down, half-tucked into black pants. His sandy brown hair sticks up in odd places. Artfully messed.

"Sorry I'm late." He saunters inside with a commanding, oxygen-vacuuming presence. Everyone is caging their breath—everyone but *me*.

Charlie strolls past my chair and the long row of board members. Reaching the opposing head of the table. They watch.

Staring.

Like he's a reptile in the terrarium, burrowing underneath the dirt. Only exposing himself when he wants you to see him.

My phone pings on the table. I read the message without clicking in the text.

I just learned that Oscar is at the H.M.C. office. Heads up, if Charlie's not there yet. He will be. — Farrow

Just *one* minute too late, but I appreciate that Farrow tried to warn me. I look up.

Charlie stands at the other end. I shake my head a few times. He carries poise like a unique possession only he owns. His tweets go viral in under seconds. His words are like cannonballs thrown into pools.

You've seen him on *We Are Calloway*. You've watched him as long as you've watched me.

Threads about Charlie being a miniature version of his father—genius IQ, egotistical, self-serving and pretentious—swim around the internet like truths, but they're webbed from slanted perceptions.

You think you know Charlie Keating Cobalt.

But you have no fucking clue.

I know him as my cousin who turned twenty in September, just two months ago. Who skipped two grades and landed in mine. Who cheated off my science homework only because he could—not because he needed to.

As the eldest sons of two larger than life men, we both know what it's like to be shadowed by someone else's past. But for as many similarities as we share—for as many things that should bond us together—we've chosen to let them push us apart.

Fair warning: you fuck with him, it's going to make me want to defend him. So don't.

All in one swift move, he tugs back the chair, sits down, and kicks his black leather shoes onto the oak table. His yellow-green eyes cement on me. "What'd I miss?"

I temper my irritation and say easily, "What are you doing here, Charlie?"

"What does it look like I'm doing?" He spreads out his arms. "I'm attending a board meeting."

"You haven't been to a board meeting since you were *put* on this board," I remind him. I'm highly aware that fifteen other people separate me from my cousin. Fifteen people observe this interaction with keen interest that hoists my guards *tenfold*.

"There's a first for everything." Charlie waves me on, then leans an elbow on his chair. Propping his head up with a finger by his temple.

He's pissed at me.

But this is Tuesday and the sky is blue. So everything is as it should be.

I speak to the other board members. "We're done here anyway. I'll see you all next week. Thanks for coming."

They collect their things. Sending wary glances at Charlie before filing out.

When the room empties, Charlie's feet fall to the floor. He makes no move to cross the boardroom. The long empty table divides us.

I cross my arms. "How long did it take you to plan that entrance?"

"That's the problem with you," Charlie says, "you think everything has to be coordinated and premeditated. When the honest truth is: I was driving by your office. I wanted to talk to you. I stopped by. No, I didn't wait for the board meeting to be over because who the fuck cares."

260 KRISTA & BECCA RITCHIE

"*I care*," I snap. "And that's the problem with you. You can't account for anyone's feelings but your own."

"Why should I?" he combats. "You dominate the role of over-protective brother and cousin. I have no fucks to give because you've taken all of them."

"Are you really sitting there and blaming me for your own lack of empathy?" I say, dumbfounded.

"I'm making an observation," he says. "And second, I do *care*. It's why I'm here. You just can't fathom a scenario where someone else cares more about this family than you." He rolls forward to the edge of the table. "The world believes you have no ego, but you've done a bang-up job of choking it down. I'm not even sure you know it's in there." He waves a finger towards my body, my stomach. "Slowly but surely engorging."

I blow out a breath, clench my teeth. A *growl* scratches my throat, one that I won't let out.

Fighting with him leads nowhere good. Growing up, we were in plenty of fistfights, usually with his twin brother and Janie physically separating us.

We're caustic together. No matter how much we try for a better relationship, we always drive down the same road. Sometimes I think he just likes being on the opposite side of me.

I uncross my arms. "Just tell me why you're here. If this is about Jane—"

"It's not. I respect my sister enough not to intervene in your friendship," he says but has to add, "even if I think you can be a piece of shit."

"Thank you for that," I say dryly. "It's not a nutritionally *balanced* day until you've called me a piece of shit." I shut my tablet off as a notification pops up. "Why are you here?"

"The Camp-Away," he says. "I never received my invite."

You've got to be shitting me.

"I stopped sending you charity function invites a year ago," I remind him. "You usually don't show. On the occasion that you do grace us with your *larger-than-life*, peacocking presence—"

"Classy, *peacocking*."

"—you never RSVP," I say, but I'm not done. "In 365 days, you've never come to complain. So why now?"

"This is your biggest event of the year," he tells me. "I'm sincerely hurt that you wouldn't even text me about it."

"You don't text back!" I'm nearing the edge of a cliff that I want to push *him* off of. But I can't. *He's family.* "Pop up our text conversation right fucking now. There's a row of about fifty texts you've *never* responded to." I gesture from my chest to his. His to mine. "This is a two-way street."

Charlie doesn't deny that fact. "Am I invited or not?"

"*No*," I say firmly. "You're not invited because if I make the announcement to the press and you don't show, then that's on the philanthropy."

"Then don't make the announcement."

"I don't want surprise guests."

Charlie lets out a vexed breath. "You just don't want me there. And you can't admit it, like a coward." He stands.

I stand.

Someone raps the door. We quiet when it swings open, and Farrow stops himself from entering fully. He sees Charlie.

He sees me.

Farrow says to me, "Do you need me to come back later—"

"No. I'm almost done." I watch Farrow slip inside and shut the door behind him. He leans his shoulders against the wood.

My focus returns to Charlie. "You're unreliable and *erratic*. You're not invited. And I'm not joking around, Charlie. If you show up unannounced, I'll get security to escort you out." I doubt I'd actually follow through with the threat, but I need to make my point clear.

Charlie doesn't blink. "You'd use *our* security against *me*? There are only five bodyguards in Omega. One is at the door, and what would you tell them? *Treat Charlie like the enemy.*"

"*No*. You're not my enemy. You're my family, and the amount of energy I've spent *trying* to include you in the past could row a goddamn fleet of Viking ships—but you refused to jump on board. You wanted to do your own thing, and I get it. Go do your own thing. Stop fucking with mine."

Charlie sits partially on the edge of the table, hand in his pocket. He turns his head to my bodyguard. "Tell me you see how big of a self-righteous asshole he is."

Standing leisurely but on guard, Farrow says coldly, "I see how big of a prick you are."

Charlie arches a single brow. "We both could be right."

"Unlikely."

"Then you're a self-righteous asshole too." Charlie stands. "Looks like you're a perfect match for each other."

I go rigid, even though he's just referring to my bodyguard-client relationship. At that final note, Charlie exits—and I'm left hoping and praying that he'll leave the Camp-Away alone.

31

MAXIMOFF HALE

Farrow inspects my childhood bedroom like it's a relic in a museum. He wanders to the wooden dresser and picks up *The Fourth Degree* action figures. His brown eyes swing to the black-painted walls, *X-Men* chalk drawings, and all the *Batman* posters.

He's the first person outside of my family that I've ever let into my world *this* deep. And it's not a fucking fantasy. I've dreamed up Farrow Redford Keene in this bedroom a thousand damn times. And usually he's *only* on the bed.

You know—I prefer my reality. Where he's a hell of a lot more than a good fuck.

I grab a wet bone off my orange rug. Tossing the thing on Gotham's dog bed. Farrow whistles at the racks and racks of comic books and graphic novels that tower to the ceiling.

He runs his fingers down the spines.

I lean on my desk, arms crossed. "What does your old bedroom look like?"

"Messier than yours." Farrow flips through a hefty graphic novel called *Duncan the Wonder Dog* by Adam Hines. One of my favorites. "Nirvana, Blink 182 posters tacked up, school books only, an expensive surround system, and a boxing bag." He rotates the novel vertical as the panels flip. "In short, I was cooler than you."

I force an irritated smile. "It's like you want to be kicked out of my bedroom or something."

His mouth stretches. "Or something." He returns the graphic novel to its original spot and continues to meander around.

I can't stop watching him. It takes a great deal of effort to check my canvas watch. "We can't stay up here long. My parents should be home with Luna's cake any minute."

November 30th marks Luna Hale's eighteenth birthday. Time fucking flies—I remember when she was just a baby and we'd tap each other's noses and say *beep beep*.

As requested by Luna: *no big birthday parties, no surprise family guests.* Just a small dinner with immediate family, and later her best friends Eliot and Tom Cobalt will come over for a sleepover.

Farrow is here because my little sister has bad taste and has invited him to her birthdays since she was *nine*. Despite how much he aggravated *me*, Luna always liked him. Here he was, a pierced and tattooed guy who contrasted his blue-blooded clean-cut family. When you're different from the pack, it takes more guts to be yourself.

Luna is drawn to people who experience that.

"I have a watch too, wolf scout," Farrow says. "I see the time." He sinks down on my small twin-sized bed. Comforter is a Spider-Man print. His brows pinch together.

"What?"

"This is one of the most uncomfortable beds I've ever sat on." He rocks his ass on the mattress. "Fuck, it's *hard*." He leans back on his hands. "Is this why you're so stiff all the time?"

The sexual innuendos stroke my cock. "My brother probably switched out his shitty mattress with mine when I moved out." I flex my muscles and straighten up. Eyeing his lip piercing for a brief second— then his hair.

His hair is black.

He dyed the strands the other day, and I descend into this image of him—pretty much consumed. It's not just that he appears older, or that his

265 DAMAGED LIKE US

intimidation cranks to a higher newfound degree. He's attractive with any hair color, any piercing, even minus all the tattoos or add them all together.

Honestly, it's because the *first time* I ever saw this guy—he didn't have white hair. Or blue. When I first met Farrow, his hair was jet-black. Like right now.

Today.

Farrow kicks a pillow aside and props his shoulders against my headboard. I imagine joining him, and he'll pin me to the bed, then I roll him over, his stomach to the mattress.

Gripping his waist, tugging down his black pants enough to expose his *perfect* round ass, my mouth trails along his neck. And descends to the spot between his muscular shoulders—

"Maximoff." His deep voice pitches me from a fantasy.

I lift my eyes.

He smiles.

"What?" I combat.

Farrow bends a knee. "Are you thinking about the philosophical meaning of the world or are you thinking about fucking me in the ass?"

Christ. I lick my lips, wanting my mouth against his mouth. *Badly.* I near the bed. "I wasn't inside you yet."

"Yet," he repeats, his gaze sweeping my body in a boiling wave. He gestures me closer, until he stretches over and catches my wrist. He wrenches me onto the bed with him.

I'm on top of Farrow, my hands on either side of his head, but he hooks his legs around my waist and swiftly reverses me like I'm an MMA opponent. My head hits the pillow. He's on top.

Farrow brings his mouth near mine. "You may dominate in the pool, but when it comes to submission moves and grappling, I'll always have you beat."

I breathe heavily. Chest rising and falling beneath him. One night, I asked Farrow to show me a submission move. True to his nature, he didn't go easy. Not even on his *boyfriend.* I had to tap out of the chokehold in less than twenty seconds.

Farrow straddles my waist and sits up to reach into his leather jacket pocket. I'm about to say *we can't fuck here*, but I stop myself when no condom appears.

He holds a black box.

The same black box I once gave him. The *asshole merit badge* is stitched to the back of his leather jacket. So I know he's not returning my gift.

Farrow discards the box behind his back and clutches the object in a closed fist. He leans closer to me. In an affectionate, deep breath, he whispers, "Hold out your left wrist."

He's put a fucking spell on me. I never hesitate. I raise my wrist, our eyes melting against each other. Farrow opens his tattooed hand. Revealing a gray paracord bracelet, which can be unwound into rope for survival.

We watched *Mad Max: Fury Road* the other night, and I mentioned how the paracord bracelet on Tom Hardy's wrist was cool.

That feeling, one that I've only felt with him returns like a tidal wave. Welling powerfully inside my chest, and also weightless—*light enough* that I could fly.

His fingers buckle the bracelet around me. "Just so you understand, you're much hotter than Tom Hardy."

I laugh, my eyes burning with emotion.

Farrow drinks in my reaction, his chest collapsing in a strong breath. "Didn't I tell you?" he whispers, his gaze nearly glassing. "It's the little things."

This is what I missed in my life, and I can't imagine never discovering this feeling. Never having *him*. I clutch the back of his head, my mouth nudging his open. We kiss deeply, intensely—enough to raise my back off the mattress and my chest to meet his.

We part so I can whisper, "Pretty sure you called it stupid, ordinary shit. Not *the little things*."

He laughs against my mouth. "It's all the fucking same."

"MOFFY!" my brother screams from down the hall.

Fuck.

Farrow quickly climbs off me, and we're both on our feet. The second time Xander screams my name, his voice sounds less panicked. More demanding, like *get your ass over here.*

"I'm being summoned," I tell Farrow on the way out into the long hallway. His stride matches mine. I stop in front of my brother's room. A sign hangs on the ajar door and says in Elfish: *turn back you fools.*

I hear more than just my brother's voice. All three of my siblings are inside.

Before we enter, Farrow asks, "Do you want me to wait downstairs—"

"No," I cut him off. "I want you to be here." I pause. "Unless you don't want to—"

Farrow kicks the door open wider in response. We go in together, the room a mess of fantasy trade paperbacks, video games, oversized beanbags, and a six-foot-four armored knight stands next to his four-poster bed.

I zero in on Luna waving a piercing gun at our brother. She wears a crop top that says *Space Babe* and black joggers.

Xander towers above her, already six-feet at fourteen. "I said I would do it, I didn't say *you* could do it for me."

"Come on, Xander, I'm an expert now."

"*What?* You got a fucking infection in your tongue." Disbelief coats his words. He swings his head and sees me and Farrow watching. "Good. You two—tell her to back away with the weapon."

"Give it." Farrow approaches, and Luna willingly hands him the piercing gun. "Happy Birthday," he tells Luna and then inspects the actual device.

"What are you doing?" I ask Luna and motion with two hands to the piercing gun. "And Happy Birthday too."

"Thankyouthankyou." She nods to us both and then picks a star sticker off her round cheek. "And I'm celebrating my eighteenth year on this planet." She places the sticker on her eyelid. "Xander and Kinney said they'd get piercings as a birthday present to me."

Kinney lies on Xander's bed, flipping through the television channels. She shrugs. "Seemed easier than going to the mall to buy a present."

You know Kinney Hale as the Princess of Goth and all things supernatural. A lot of you worship the fuck out of her, and you hope to one day be the recipient of her insults and death glares. You've even made video compilations of her epic eye rolls and "no bitch" face. And you wish you were part of her girl squad that includes Winona Meadows, Audrey Cobalt, and Vada Abbey.

I know her as my thirteen-year-old, tough-as-nails little sister who has a soft side that she only allows family to see. And I love the hell out of her.

Fair warning: I used to change this one's diapers and feed her peas that she'd throw at me. You fuck with Kinney, I'll slit your throat and then she'll shove you to the bottom of a volcano.

Luna eyes the piercing gun in Farrow's hands, then turns to Xander. "You're still going to get your ear pierced, right?"

"Yeah." Xander sits on the edge of his bed. "But Moffy's going to do it. Not you."

Farrow tilts his head at my brother. "How is he any better than Luna?"

"Five years older than her," I defend myself.

"Tell me one body part you've ever pierced, wolf scout."

"Burn," Kinney says, still flipping TV channels.

"None."

Xander rakes a hand through his bed-head hair. "Moffy is the best at everything."

Farrow laughs hard.

"Shut the fuck up," I tell Farrow, trying not to smile as I near him and Luna.

"I'm serious," Xander says to Farrow, causing his laughter to fade. "Moffy's never been below average at anything. Every time he tries something new, he's practically a pro on the first try."

"It's magic," Luna says certainly.

"He's a demon," Kinney says. "One of the ugly ones that live in toad holes."

Farrow's smile has split his face in half. Because my sister called me a toad hole demon. He finds a way to focus, and he tells them, "I can guarantee all three of you that I'm better than your brother at everything."

They perk up.

"*Very few* things," I correct.

"*Some* things," Farrow amends.

"Maybe."

His brows jump when I concede. I'd *much* rather Farrow, who's experienced, pierce my siblings than me fuck it up. Still, I don't get why we're doing this at all.

"You seriously want to do this, Luna?" I ask. "After all the shit that your tongue piercing got you in?"

"It healed though, and I love it." She sticks her tongue out, a lime-green ball in the center. "And if all of you get piercings, we'll be linked in sibling solidarity. It's something the Cobalts would do. Don't we have that too?"

Luna stares at each of us, even Farrow, like she's mentally grouping us together as the Hale family. A band of fucking weirdos.

We're all smiling.

"Yeah, sis," Xander says and then points at Farrow and the piercing gun. "I'm trusting you, man."

"I'm not piercing you with a twelve-dollar *Claire's* gun." He turns to Luna. "You need piercing needles—"

"I bought some of those too…or really, Eliot did. His birthday gift to me."

"Get those, rubbing alcohol, cotton balls, and an apple." Farrow listing out random items shouldn't be hot. My cock is obsessed with the weirdest shit.

"Got it. Be right back." Luna darts out of the room.

"Is this gonna hurt?" Xander asks.

My brows knit. "It's a *needle*. In your ear." *Of course it's going to hurt.*

"Moffy, I'm asking the guy with real piercings."

Farrow leans on the bedpost. "Getting smarter."

I shoot my bodyguard a middle finger.

To aggravate me, he makes a point to only acknowledge Xander. "It barely hurts."

"Okay, good." Xander bites his nails, a bad habit. Any physical changes to our bodies, the media hones in on—hair color, piercings, tattoos, even bruises and cat scratches. So knowing the extra attention will come, I'm kind of surprised Xander would want a piercing. It's either out of his love for Luna or he's hoping it'll distract tabloids from his sudden growth spurt.

I check my watch. *Mom and Dad should be home any minute.*

Xander spits out his nail. "What are you getting pierced, Moffy?"

My jaw tenses. "Probably nothing."

"I told you," Kinney pipes up from the bed. "He's a prude."

Farrow pops a piece of gum, his James Franco smile at full-force right now.

"I'm not a prude," I tell my sister who looks very similar to a gangly, round-faced Luna except for the dark hair, jet-black eyeliner, mascara and lips. "And even if I were, there's nothing wrong with being a prude."

Kinney clicks the remote absentmindedly. "That's exactly what a prude would say." Then the TV lands on a tween channel, and a familiar, catchy pop song blares.

"*Shit*, no!" Xander rotates on the bed to restrain Kinney who lunges towards the television.

I already sprint over and catch Kinney around the waist. Her bony limbs flail and fight to reach the TV. She's eighty-pounds. I could easily toss her over my shoulder. But I don't.

Because she'd try to bite my ear off.

"Let. Me. Go!!" Kinney yells.

Farrow finds the remote and shuts off the commercial. She's still squirming in my arms and trying to launch herself at the TV.

Xander blocks his flat-screen. "This is brand new. You're not breaking it."

Kinney kicks out, and I tighten my hold.

Luna returns with all the piercing supplies, and our old floppy-eared basset hound follows. Gotham runs slowly to each of us and licks our legs.

Luna gapes at our sister. "Uhh…"

"Viv," I explain but also unleash the name that causes Kinney to accidentally elbow my windpipe—*fuck*. I cough hoarsely, arms slackening on Kinney. I let her go.

And she immediately spins to me, wide-eyed. "Oh hell. Moffy?"

I hold out a hand like *I'm fine*, but Farrow reaches my side, a hand on my back. I'm bent forward, palms on my thighs. *Stop coughing.* I try to straighten up and massage my neck.

"Say something," Kinney demands. "Right now."

At ease, Farrow says, "How about let him breathe first?"

Kinney sends a death glare his way.

"I'm alright." I cough one last time into my fist, my eyes watering. I pinch them, and then say to my sister. "I thought you were over Viv. It's been three months since she left for LA."

Her girlfriend moved to star in a tween show with a lot of dancing and a lot of singing, and they only split to forgo the long-distance thing.

It didn't break Kinney's heart as much as toughen it. Every time the show or song airs, she's smashed her phone. The television. She's already eaten through her entire allowance for the year.

And in her words, "Worth it."

Kinney huffs. "I am over it." She points at the TV. "That show is just crap. Not the star of the show, obviously. Viv deserves better. She's much more talented than that."

"Uh-huh," Luna nods and hands Farrow the supplies. He pulls out a Zippo lighter from his pocket.

"Maybe you should try seeing someone else?" I suggest. "Is there another girl you're interested in?"

"No," she snaps at me. "And you have no experience in dating, so you just need to chill."

Farrow grins and pops a bubble.

Being burned by my thirteen-year-old sister is nothing new. Having her bring up my lack of experience in dating *in front of* Farrow, yeah, that's priceless.

Luna tells our sister, "Tom said he'd take you to a bar to get over Viv."

"*No*," Farrow and I say in unison.

"I meant a lesbian bar," Luna clarifies.

"Still *no*," I say.

Kinney gawks at Farrow and me. "I should revoke *both* of your memberships to the Rainbow Brigade for being so unfair." She coined the *Rainbow Brigade* when she was nine, and she dubbed herself the president since she's the only lesbian. It consists of me, Tom, Farrow, Oscar, and Kinney. It's all in *spirit* since we haven't done anything as a group together yet. "I know you've both been to gay bars and clubs—"

"We're adults," Farrow says, chewing his gum slowly.

I add, "And you were twelve barely a month ago."

"I have the heart of forty-year-old," she says with complete seriousness.

Farrow rebuts, "You still have the body of a nine-year-old."

Kinney glares. "I'm *thirteen*, you turd."

"Don't call him a turd," I snap.

"And you're a turd, too."

Farrow smiles and produces a flame from the lighter, sterilizing the needle, but he doesn't get far. Gotham starts barking like the front door just opened.

My siblings, Farrow, and I pile onto the staircase.

One part of the house creates a tunnel of sound, and everything my parents say in the foyer is a megaphone to these steps.

We can't see my mom and dad yet, and Kinney extends her arm. Blocking all of us from descending to the living room.

"Let's not eavesdrop," I whisper to her.

"Shh," she hisses. "They're probably talking about something nauseatingly cute. Just wait."

Xander rests on the banister, Luna plops on a stair, and I turn to Farrow beside me. He smiles like *your family, man.* Then he passes Luna a piece of foiled gum.

I hear my dad first. "This isn't a debate." He speaks to my mom. "He's legitimately the worst character in *X-Men* lore. Period. Done. End of story."

"He's funny. *I* liked him."

"You can't say that out loud," he tells her. "One. It's ridiculous. Two. His name was *Goldballs*."

"The balls part is not why I liked him," she combats fiercely.

"I know that, Lil. Other people don't," he says. "And you're a lying liar because I know he's not even in your top ten. You're just going stand there and tell me he ranks above Sunspot, Magik, Emma Frost, Cyclops, X-23, or Hellion. Christ, we named three of our children after X-Men."

Kinney, Xander, and I all exchange a look.

Luna blows a bubble with her gum. She was named after Luna Lovegood, a *Harry Potter* character.

My dad continues, "Can you imagine if Maximoff was actually named *Goldballs*?"

I glower at Farrow like *do not speak of this, ever*. He's dying in amusement. It's palpable and all over his face.

Dear World, stop making my boyfriend who loves to fuck with me enjoy today more than he already has. Sincerely, a peeved human.

My mom groans. "Please, stop."

"Admit he's not in your top ten."

"Top twenty."

"I can live with that," my dad says.

"Good because I wasn't going to change it for you," she replies. I imagine she's grinning, lifting her chin and playfully crossing her arms. I've seen her do it a thousand times before.

"Ouch," my dad says in mock hurt. "Right in the heart, Lil."

"It's the only place I can reach," she refutes.

"I'm not sure about that…" Their voices soften. Too quiet. Which means they're lip-locked.

"Mom! Dad!" I shout, and Farrow and I reach the base of the stairs first.

A huge realization crashes into my chest right now—just as my mom swoops into view with a hearty wave and flushed cheeks.

For the first time, I'm about to have a family dinner with Farrow as my boyfriend. I get that he's *technically* here as Luna's guest. He's even off-duty as my bodyguard. But the clandestine fact grips onto me.

I thought it'd be bittersweet, not being able to share the truth with my family. Keeping my relationship a secret. *Private*.

It's not bitter at all.

I share so damn much of my life with them. With everyone. To have this space meant for only Farrow and me for a while feels *less* confining and just free. No pressure, no expectations. Just me and him.

Just us.

32

FARROW KEENE

As Lily's ex-bodyguard, I consider myself fairly versed in all things Hale. And for as many conversations I've had with Lo, her husband, I've never been apprehensive or afraid. Never broken a sweat.

But I've also never been alone in a kitchen with him, cooking an easy pasta meal for Luna's birthday. While carrying a loaded secret: *I'm not just protecting your son. I'm sleeping with him. Oh, we fucked this morning, and I even gave him the best blow job of his life. He said so.*

I manage to act casual, not cagey, but I stand on an edge I've never neared before. It's a new feeling, for sure.

I fill a pot of water.

Lo lights a gas stove. "How are you and your father getting along?"

"We're not." I shut the faucet. "I haven't talked to him in two and a half years." I place the half-full pot on the stove.

"Huh, well I think eventually he'll come around." Lo rests a comforting hand on my shoulder. Dr. Keene has been loyal to the families for a very long time. See, they hope my father and I can mend whatever we tore, but that's only going to happen if I leave security and work as a doctor.

And I'm not leaving Omega.

I'm not leaving Maximoff.

He drops his hand to pour tomato sauce in a pan.

"Dad." Maximoff enters the kitchen from the living room, where the rest of the Hale family watches a sci-fi show before dinner. "I can help with—"

"No, *no*." Lo points a spatula at the door. "Out."

This is the fifth time Lo has shooed his son out of the kitchen. Maximoff narrows a glare onto me like, *do something*.

I lean on the counter. "You can't be a part of everything, wolf scout."

"Says you," he refutes. "I say I can."

"At least now we know who's smarter."

"Me—"

"Farrow and I have this under control," his dad cuts him off. "Him and me—we're talking. Go spend time with your mom. The one who nudged you awake when you slept as a baby. All because she was afraid you weren't breathing."

"Alright." Maximoff straightens up and shoots me a look like *don't let him know we're together.*

No shit.

After he disappears, Lo asks me, "How's the security working next week with the tents?" He means at the Camp-Away. *One week left.*

I removed my radio tonight, but Donnelly has been counting down to the raffle's closing. We'll have randomly chosen the 300 entrants by midnight. Then, we all have the arduous task of vetting them in seven days. I'm of the mindset that if any fucker slips through, we'll handle it at the camp.

Preferably with no fists.

I've already had four bodyguards tell me, "Better get ready to grab Maximoff," believing I'll need to drag him out of a fight. Everything's now shaded in a new light. *I'd drag my boyfriend away from a fight.* Not just my client.

My boyfriend.

I sense an emotional current racing through my veins. At a much higher voltage.

I shake salt into the pot of water. "Since Maximoff, Jane, and Sulli are the only ones attending the Camp-Away, besides the raffle guests, we'll put most of the security on those three at night," I start explaining the sleeping arrangements to Lo.

"How?" He stirs the sauce, his concern apparent in his daggered amber eyes.

"Their personal bodyguards will be inside their tent at night—"

"So you'll be sleeping in Maximoff's tent with him?" His voice is edged. Normal for Loren Hale. But I pause, shoulders tensed up, and I study his sharp features.

Shit, I'm caging a breath right now. I never hold my breath. Not unless I'm having mind-blowing, eye-rolling sex with his son.

I comb both of my hands through my black hair. "Yeah. There'll be another bodyguard from Alpha outside of the tent. No one can unzip it unless they want a broken wrist."

Lo stirs silently and then nods several times.

"We've coordinated everything down to the tiniest detail. It's all taken care of, Lo." I sense his overwhelming parental concern. I turn to Maximoff's dad. "I promise you that I'd never let anything bad happen to him."

I'm falling in love with your son.

"I trust you, Farrow," Lo says with ease.

It simultaneously knots my stomach and relieves me. Our heads swerve as Lily slips into the kitchen, a *Star Wars* Wampa cap on her head. Three years on someone's 24/7 security detail is like a decade of time.

"Farrow." She smiles.

"Lily." I hug one of my favorite people in the world. Not bending down to her height, I straighten up, arms wrapped around her, and her feet lift off the ground.

Lily clasps my cheeks in two strong hands. "How are you? Are you eating? Have you hydrated?"

My lips rise and set her on her feet. "Hydrated, well-fed," I assure. "All is well."

Lily beams at my choice of words. "All is well—did you hear that, Lo?"

"I heard, love." He glances affectionately at his wife.

Lily claims a barstool and splays her hands on the counter. "Moffy hasn't been too stubborn, has he? He doesn't mean to be. He just likes to take on all the responsibility."

"I've noticed," I say, and right on cue, Maximoff enters and sits on a stool beside his mom.

"What are we talking about?" he asks.

"You," I say matter-of-factly.

He flashes an agitated smile. "Can't figure out any other subject?"

"Don't be mean to Farrow," Lily says, elbowing his side.

His brows pinch. "Mom, he's being an ass to *me*."

I lean on the counter. "Listen to your mom, Maximoff."

Lo dumps spaghetti in the pot. "Question, why've you only been calling him by his full name?"

"Ask your son that."

"Moffy?"

His shoulders square. "For Christ's sakes, I like my full name, and I'm not a kid."

I nod slowly, the answer finally coming. *You didn't want me to see you as a child.* He's twenty-two, but I used to only call him Moffy when he was younger.

Lo pretends to be shocked. "You're not a kid? Jesus Christ, when did that happen? Lily?"

"I didn't do it," she says. "I wanted him to be young forever. Like Peter Pan."

"Peter Pan doesn't have parents," Lo rebuts. "You're taking us out of the picture, Lil."

"A Peter Pan with parents then."

Maximoff watches their interactions with fondness, then he looks to me. *He wishes for that.* He's letting himself yearn and *long* for the soul-bearing love and admiration his parents have.

I want to give it to you. All of it.

"Farrow." Lily's voice draws my gaze. "Are you seeing anyone new?"

I force myself not to glance at Maximoff. "I am, but it's...complicated."

"Been there, done that," Lo says.

Maximoff frowns and motions to his dad. "What the hell was so complicated about you and mom? You were *best friends* who lived next door to one another."

Lo looks at his son like he's grown hooves. "We were addicts who enabled each other."

"We were doomed from the start," Lily notes.

"You persevered," Maximoff tells them strongly, wanting them to believe their worth, but Lo cautions his children about addiction by using their failures as *what not to do.* "You overcame *everything,*" Maximoff continues. "You're goddamn—"

"Lucky," Lo finishes. "Doesn't erase the hard parts, bud."

Lily stretches over the bar counter towards me. "Do you have any friends you could introduce to Moffy?"

Maximoff looks whiplashed by the abrupt topic change. "*Mom.*"

I cross my arms loosely, my smile in a laugh. I wish this could go on all night. "You don't want me to introduce you to my friends?" I ask him.

"You have friends?" he shoots back, sarcastic.

"Moffy!" Her mouth drops. "You're a Hufflepuff. *Be nice.*"

Maximoff wraps his arm around his mom. "Farrow is my exception, Mom, and he hasn't even been sorted—"

"Your mom sorted me last year." Her love for *Harry Potter* runs deep.

Lily nods firmly. "He's Gryffindor."

I blow a mocking kiss to Maximoff.

He licks his lips, trying to layer on a grimace, but he fails. Lily observes us for another second, then she asks again, "Do you know anyone that maybe would like to *date* Moffy, maybe?"

Maximoff groans and sighs heavily. "We've talked about this."

She's always wanted him to stop having one-night stands. Her past is riddled with casual sex partners, and as a sex addict, she fears a destructive path for her son. Just based on her own experiences.

Before I can speak, Lo wipes his hands with a dishtowel and asks me, "How old are your friends?"

I hang on the fringe of most "friendship circles" that I accumulated in college. I always preferred the other guys from Studio 9, but in this hypothetical scenario where he isn't my boyfriend—I know more than a few people who'd be willing to date the hottest celebrity in town.

I want to say, *he's mine.*

He's mine, and I'm not sharing him with any fucking man or woman. I grit my teeth once and play along, "Around my age, twenty-seven."

"No," Lo says flat-out. "That's too old."

My jaw tics. "It's only a five-year gap—"

"And my brother married a young girl with a *seven*-year age-gap—it comes with too many complications. Gotta nip that before it starts." He points at Maximoff. "Heed the advice, bud."

He wants *easy* for his son.

I make his everyday easier, but if we were together in front of his family and in the public, I'd be one of the most complicated choices of his life.

But I remember I'm with a steadfast, unshakable guy. Maximoff stares right at me with resilience and finality that says, *I want you.*

Only you.

33

After dinner and birthday cake, my dad asks to talk in private with me. We're on the back patio. I flick on the pool lights so we're not swamped in darkness.

I take a seat on the nearest patio chair, and he sits on the edge of a lounge chair.

"What's up?" I ask.

My dad has this severe-cut face. All sharp lines. No soft features. When he's serious or contemplative, he's even more uninviting.

I've never feared him.

Even now, as his jaw sharpens and he pours his intense focus through me.

"I haven't brought this up in a year," he begins, "because I thought you needed time to sort through things yourself. But we have to talk about your hair."

Fuck.

I run my hand through the light-brown strands. "It's getting long, yeah," I say, sarcasm thick. Dreading where this conversation may lead.

"Maximoff," my dad says, truly serious when he uses my full name. "Just explain to me what's going on. Where's your head at?"

I like that my dad does that. Asks me before going down a cavernous path assuming shit. He gives me the chance to explain my side. And I don't waste it.

Squeezing a water bottle in my tight hand, I say, "I don't want to look like Uncle Ryke. I'm so...*fucking* sick of people comparing me to him." I swallow a pit in my throat. "It's every other day, Dad. If I don't fight like him, then I'm wearing *green* underwear. It's just complete bullshit at this point." I uncap my water. "And before you say, *the rumors will never go away*, I get that. I'm not trying to convince anyone you're my dad. I have DNA evidence. That's not what this is about."

He frowns deeply. "Then what is this about?"

My chest hurts, just having to stare him in the eye and utter these words. But it's been a year, and it's time to say them.

"It's about people knowing that I love you," I say strongly. "That you're a good dad. That you raised me, and I'd be *proud* to be like you. But the more I look like *him* and act like *him*, the more they dissociate me from you."

Why can't my successes be associated with the Hale family? Is it so fucking hard for the media to believe that addicts can raise a good man? A good son?

My dad shakes his head repeatedly. Like I see the world from such a skewed lens.

"Moffy, I can't think of anything worse for you than you being more like me," he says clearly, plainly, unmistakably. A cold dagger pierces my gut. "The fact that you're more like Ryke is my greatest achievement as a father."

My nose flares. I grip my water bottle harder. Trying to restrain emotion that threatens to rock me. I don't agree with him. I can't agree, but he's sitting here telling me that I turned out okay. Maybe that's a compliment, but I just see my dad tearing himself down to build me up.

"I want to be more like you," I say. "*You're* a great person. The fact that you and the media can't see it is a goddamn problem." All they see is a recovering alcoholic. They wait for him to fail. They're shocked and surprised when he succeeds. It's fucking aggravating.

"You didn't know me at my worst," he reminds me. "The media did. And I've lived with myself too long to be disillusioned that the bad parts of me have just magically gone away. They exist inside of me, and it's a daily battle that I'm *glad* you don't share."

I pinch my burning eyes.

"So will you stop with this?" he asks.

I drop my hand and breathe in flaming determination. "It's not about what you think. It's *never* been about what you think." It's about everyone else. He may see himself as a villain, but I won't add to the demonization of Loren Hale.

It's my job to showcase the narrative where he's the hero. Where I'm the son that idolizes him, and I need everyone to see that.

His jaw cuts like a blade. His glare just as brutal. "No. No goddamn way are you changing who you are because you think the world needs to love me."

"I'm not changing who I am," I combat. "It's just hair. It's just a fucking color that I'm not wearing."

"Then why aren't you doing the ultra?" he refutes. "Give me another reason that you'd miss out on an experience like that. Go for it. I'm waiting."

Fuck.

Off my shock, he says, "Yeah, Ryke called me the other day. He said Sulli told him you're having second thoughts. All because my brother ran an ultra-marathon before. Moffy, do you see what's happening here?"

I set my intense gaze on the star-blanketed night, and I make a decision right here. "I'll do the ultra."

"And you'll stop dyeing your hair," he adds. His unspoken words: *you'll let this go completely.* Can I let go and do nothing? Can I live with myself?

I lower my gaze to my dad. "I have to keep trying."

He just stares at me and says, "One day you're going to look back and realize why you were wrong. You're going to understand. One day."

34

"What the fuck," Maximoff mutters as he inspects a box of hair dye and then he rereads the back label.

We're in my bathroom, same hellishly small size as his, but no decorations exist. See, both townhouses are currently empty. No Jane or Quinn around while they spend the night in Manhattan, visiting her twin brothers. So we have free reign of my place for today and most of tomorrow.

"Missing something?" I ask while I'm at the sink. I fit a #2 blade into my hair clippers.

"Gloves." He rummages in a plastic bag of shit he just bought at the drugstore. That outing took three hours, extra security, and my knee in a fucker's groin.

When we exited the store, a middle-aged photographer tried to grab Maximoff by the crotch. *Tried* being the key word.

The man ended up bent over in pain.

Maximoff may be used to hands all over him in massive crowds like a packed concert—people tugging at his shirt, his waist, even pulling at his hair and neck—but no way in fucking hell am I letting anyone cup his ass or grab his dick.

"More disposable ones are under the sink," I tell him and set the bladed clippers on the edge. Our eyes lock in a hot beat. And he hones in on my abs, my shirt off and tucked in my back pocket.

He licks his lips. "I can get them." Maximoff nears, then kneels and digs through the cabinet. His shoulder brushes my leg.

"You look good on your knees," I say.

"Even better than you," he rebuts.

My lips lift. "That's not what you said last night when you came in my mouth."

Maximoff shoots me a half-hearted glare. I'm going to be honest here: he's basically smiling. Gloves in hand, he straightens up—and his chest accidentally bumps into mine.

Stubbornly, we don't move.

His irritation and slow-growing smile surface with a look that says, *you're the one in my way.*

I'm definitely starting to love this whole lack of space thing. I reach up and slide my fingers through his thick hair. "So you want to match your roots then?"

Maximoff stares off a little bit as my fingers skate along his scalp. *He really likes that.* His body shifts closer, waist knocking into mine.

I rake my hand through his hair again. "It's not too late to go blue."

"What?" He blinks out of his stupor. *Where'd you go?*

He didn't hear me.

"Blue hair, wolf scout," I repeat, massaging his head.

His brows knit. "I like your black hair."

I almost laugh. I'd pay to see what he's picturing when he tunes out his surroundings. "Okay, but I didn't mean blue hair for me. I meant *for you.*"

"No way." He turns, just to grab his box of dye, but my hands drop off him. "That's something you can shelve in the *never fucking happening* category."

I lean my side on the sink. "Isn't that the category where you placed *me driving?*" I give him a look. "Seems like a flexible category."

He flips me off. "It's not."

I watch him open the box and start to mix hair dye in a plastic bowl. Maximoff always dyes his hair himself, so the whole process isn't new for him.

We share the mirror and the tight space in front of the sink. I plug in the bladed clippers.

Next to me, he tugs off his shirt. *Damn*, those abs. Maximoff throws his gray crew-neck aside.

And he suddenly asks, "You think I'm a prude?"

Maximoff. "That wasn't even on my mind." I remember what Kinney called him two days ago. "But I see it's been eating at yours."

He rubs lotion on his forehead near his hairline. Just so the dye won't stain his skin. "I'm just thinking about how I didn't get a piercing with my siblings, and I'm thinking about what that means. And maybe it says I don't love them enough to get one."

"Or it says that you're not easily peer pressured, not even by your siblings." I stare at him through the mirror. "You refused a piercing, knowing you didn't want one—that's hot."

He's smiling. And trying not to. He puts on his gloves.

I push back the top, long black strands of my hair. I'm only lightly trimming the sides. "Anyway," I say, "I don't think you're a prude. But you're definitely another 'p' word." I run the blade above my ear.

"It better be *philanthropic.*" Maximoff spreads dye in his hair like shampoo. In the mirror, he watches my hands more than he watches himself.

My smile widens. "Pure."

He blinks into a glare. "I forgot that you don't know the definition of purity."

I run my blade over the same spot. "You can have a lot of sex and still be pure." I'll always see him as being genuinely good-hearted. "And if anyone disagrees with me, I don't give a flying shit."

His throat bobs like my words just fisted his cock. He tenses, and then slicks his hair back with dark brown dye. "You know why I'm going back to my natural color?"

"I can crack a guess, but no, I don't know for sure." I didn't want to pressure him to tell me. I figured he'd open up when he was ready.

Our gazes meet through the mirror. "It felt right," he says strongly. "I didn't mind dyeing my hair lighter or wearing more red instead of green, but all it was doing was adding conflict in my family. So it felt right to go back." He combs more dye through his hair. "I'll find another way to show the world I'm proud of my dad. Just not this anymore."

I trim the other side of my head. I've always believed he's damned if he does, damned if he doesn't, and all he can do is trust his gut instinct. He once asked what I thought, and I just said, *"I'd go with the option where you're not fighting with yourself."*

Maximoff knows who he is better than most people know themselves. If something felt wrong, he'd be the first to recognize that. And I'm happy he didn't hesitate.

"You know I'll stand beside whatever you do," I say with a smile, tilting my head to run the blade further back. "Unless it's bullshit. Then I'll call you out and you'll stand beside me."

"What a turn of events," Maximoff says, no sarcasm present, "the *rebel* wants someone next to him."

"Yeah. I want your smartass." I hold his gaze. I've never spent this much time with anyone. Not even my last client. Not an ex or a friend, and if there were extra hours in the day, I'd choose to spend them with this guy.

Fuck, I'm hooked.

Maximoff holsters his *fuck me* eyes. Just to slick his hair back one last time. He snaps off his gloves, and after tossing them in the trash, he sets a ten-minute timer on his phone. "Need help?" he asks me.

No, wolf scout. I can easily cut my hair myself, but no one has ever *asked* to help me either. Hell, it's more than cute.

"Here." I pass him the clippers, and Maximoff comes up behind me, all confidence. I look at him through the mirror. "Cut from the back of my neck upward, no higher than my ear."

"Got it."

I clutch the edge of the sink. Standing in a slight lunge, head dipped, so he can reach my neck without extending his arms high.

Maximoff grips my shoulder to keep me steady. Then he runs the blade across my neck. He's doing better than a good or decent job. I'd seriously believe he's trimmed my hair a thousand times before. I remember what his brother said. How Maximoff is a pro at everything on his first try.

Okay, it's somewhat true.

His forest-greens flit to me in the mirror. *Yeah, I'm letting you help me.* It's turning him on.

I stretch my arm behind me and grab his ass, and then he steps nearer, his dick up against *my* ass. My breath cuts short, *fuck*—I can feel him hardening.

My muscles sear, veins pulsating. "Someone's excited."

"Barely," he rebuts.

I roll my eyes. "I know what your 'barely' hard cock feels like, wolf scout, and that's not it."

He tries to glower, but he has serious *kiss me, fuck me, cuddle me* eyes right now.

I grit down, my dick rousing.

I watch him turn off the clippers, finished, and I brush pieces of hair off my shoulders and into the sink basin. I check out the back of my hair that he trimmed. *Yeah, he can do that again.*

Maximoff puts away the clippers. "Good?"

"Eh, *barely.*"

He shoots me two middle fingers and straightens up. Nearing me. I lean my shoulders on the wall and give him a slow once-over. He still needs to wash out his hair dye.

Fuck, I can't stop looking at him.

My nickname for Maximoff fits him better than he realizes. He's aggressive, short-tempered and insanely protective of his pack. Like a wolf. Then he's resourceful, resilient, reliant and responsible. Able to survive any situation.

Those two words embody Maximoff Hale more than any other. And for as long as I'm alive, he'll be *wolf scout* to me.

He places a hand on the wall. Beside my shoulder. I unbutton his jeans, and his other hand already dives down the front of my black pants, stroking me—*fuck,* a groan scratches my throat.

I watch his gaze drift for the slightest second, then focuses more clearly on me.

I rub his very-far-from-barely *hard* cock. "What were you just thinking?"

He licks his lips. "That I fucking love how you smell."

This is the first I've heard this from him. "What's the scent?"

His muscles flex, as I change grip. He curses beneath his breath before he says, "Mint...fresh water and man."

I could push up against him, but the timer *beeps* and cuts us off. We retract our hands, trying to ignore the unresolved tension for right now. Within maybe a minute or two, he's buck-naked in the shower, rinsing out the hair dye.

While I wait for him, I grab a *Celebrity Crush* magazine out of the drugstore bag. He bought the tabloid to see if they mentioned the Charity Camp-Away that begins in five days.

I rest against the sink and flip through the glossy pages.

Showering, Maximoff rakes his hands through his dark brown hair, watching me while water douses him.

I look up at him and flip another page. "Something you want to say?"

"It's fucking weird seeing you with a tabloid."

He doesn't realize how often I have to search social media and tabloid comments for potential "chaos" and threats.

I turn one more page.

And I land on a Like Us article. I scan the giant photograph of Luna, Xander, and Kinney, the Hale siblings congregated at a booth inside Superheroes & Scones. A fan must've taken the photo.

The Like Us articles have been printed in this magazine for years, and they're relatively harmless. The subtitle is always the same:

The Hales, Meadows, and Cobalts—they're like us! They read books. They love movies. They go shopping!

I remember years back seeing the headline *Smart Like Us* with a photograph of Jane competing in prep school mathletes.

The one I clutch zooms in on Luna, Xander, and Kinney's new ear piercings. The title: **COOL LIKE US**

Maximoff asks, "Why are you smiling?"

"They called you *uncool*."

Maximoff rubs water out of his face and then reaches his arm out of the shower to clearly shoot me a middle finger.

I almost laugh, but my phone rings on the tiled floor. I already see the caller ID: *Alpha Asshole.*

Shit.

There's an 85% chance he's going to chew me out for shutting off my radio. Comms aren't even on me right now. So I bypass that headache and just text Price: *I'm not on SFA.*

He replies fast.

> From cams, we can tell that Moffy is home. You need to come help vet Camp-Away entrants. — **Price**

I reply even faster: I already spent six hours vetting entrants today. I purposefully signed up for a shift while Maximoff was working at the H.M.C. office.

> We need more eyes on this. You're available, so get over here. — **Price**

I could easily shut off my phone and act like I didn't just receive that fucking demand. But if the worst happens at the Camp-Away—just because I didn't take an extra three hours to vet the raffle entrants—I'd be more than pissed at myself.

I'll be there. I send that one text and slip my phone in my pocket. "Maximoff."

He cracks the shower door. "Yeah?"

"I have to go. Security needs me." I pull on my black V-neck.

Looks like he's not the only one giving out rain checks.

35

FARROW KEENE

Sprawling green fields bleed into a bright blue horizon, oak and spruce trees jutting to the sky. Leaves are orange and red as the fall season nears an end. From a hill, I spot the glittering lake and canoes stacked on a rack, inner-tubes tied to a wooden dock.

Maximoff uses the acres and acres of land from Camp Calloway, his aunt's summer camp in the Poconos Mountains, for his December Camp-Away event.

It's majestic, serene, but I'm also very much on-duty. I'm not about to be swept up by nature. Not when there are three-hundred raffle guests ranging from eighteen to forty-five in age.

And they're all playing the first group activity that Maximoff scheduled: a massive game of capture the flag.

Hundreds of people are split into four teams, denoted by red, green, blue and yellow shirts and bandanas. While they run around the field and forest, screaming out strategies and searching for other team's flags, security meanders through the crowd.

We all wear black T-shirts with *SECURITY* in bold neon-green letters.

My arms haven't uncrossed. For the past twenty-minutes, I concentrate solely on Maximoff, my guard not lowering. Earlier, I confiscated a knife that someone tried smuggling into the camp. Apparently they believed they'd be "fishing" and cleaning their own dinner.

Okay.

Sure.

My earpiece buzzes with nonstop chatter.

"I saw where Yellow Team hid their flag," Donnelly says. Even though Beckett Cobalt is his client, the Tri-Force enlisted most of the seasoned bodyguards for the event. The Meadows, Cobalts, and Hales without their regular 24/7 bodyguards have temporary ones for three days.

Akara is on the mic. "Are you really using comms to help Jane cheat?" He assumes it's Jane, but any way you toss it, Donnelly is Team Cobalt.

"I'm doin' nuthin'," Donnelly says, accent thick on the word *nothing*. I spy him circling a wooded area, blue bandana on his tattooed forearm even though he's not playing.

Maximoff sits casually on a tree stump. Stuck in blue team's "jail" until one of his red team members tags him out. I relax for a second, propping my shoulders on an oak tree.

His eyes flit briefly to me, a smile in them.

He runs his fingers through the dark brown strands of his hair. Somehow, he appears a few years older with his natural shade.

I still can't get over it.

And he found an alternative to lightening his hair. He's wearing Thor camping socks right now. Plus, he had Luna draw Spider-Man figures on his Timberland boots. It's his way of shouting *I love my dad* to paparazzi who'll take money-shots and to anyone who'll listen.

My lips begin to rise back at him.

"Quinn to security." Another voice is in my ear. "I just overheard some girls talking about dragging someone. Should I intervene?"

"Nah," Donnelly pipes in again. "That's just fandom talk."

"What?" Quinn asks.

I click my mic. "It's not a threat. Don't engage." Did I just naturally "guide" Quinn right there? Fucking hell, I've turned into a teacher.

"Ugh, I forgot my snack," Oscar complains. "Does anyone have anything on them?"

"Bro, you *just* ate," Quinn refutes. "Like fifteen pancakes."

"I don't see your point. Snacks are an essential part of life. And you know what, if you haven't learned that by now, we've encountered a real serious problem—guys, my brother needs fucking help, like a Snack Awareness Meeting."

Voices pile onto one another.

I lower the volume.

Maximoff is out of "jail" and he runs into a safe zone. He slows down as a huddle of eighteen or nineteen-year-old girls in red shirts ogle him.

I don't blame them.

He's gorgeous. And my cock definitely agrees.

I'm more hyper-aware of people here who are apathetic towards him. It means they're most likely at the Camp-Away for wrong reasons. Akara already red-marked twenty-three names for us to watch. Their motives for entering the charity event seemed suspicious.

Maximoff approaches the girls, and they squeal in glee, bouncing on their toes and grabbing onto his arms excitedly.

Easy there.

I raise the radio volume and catch the tail-end of Oscar asking for food.

I click my mic. "I have a protein bar. I'm by an oak tree."

"There are trees everywhere, Redford."

I roll my eyes. "Man, how badly do you want that snack? Because I'm not drawing you a fucking map."

"...I see you." Oscar sprints past a gaggle of green-shirted guys and then stops beside me. Curly pieces of his hair fall over a rolled blue bandana.

I grab a protein bar out of a first-aid bag. The medic stand is on the other side of the hill. So we've dropped a few emergency bags throughout the area.

"This is nuts." Oscar bites into the bar. "Legitimately stressed right now."

I shake out my crossed arms, my muscles tight. "Did you see how much money he made from the raffle?"

Oscar swigs his water. "The numbers are already in?"

"Seventy million."

"Holy shit."

Maximoff was glowing all morning. In truth, if he were stabbed in the middle of the night and wheeled into the hospital, he'd still declare this a success. Very few things can happen to where he'd call the Camp-Away a failure.

But him, being stabbed, would be my fucking nightmare.

"Quinn to security. They just said *drag her* again. And I know they're talking about Jane. That's violent."

Donnelly answers, "Still fandom language."

"I don't like it," Quinn says, making his opinion known.

"Bro." Oscar clicks his mic next to me. "Get yourself a Twitter account."

"You're not on Twitter?" Donnelly questions.

"He's only on Facebook," I tell the team, grinning.

Donnelly lets his laughter filter through the comms.

"Facebook is where it's at," Quinn rebuts.

Akara says, "This isn't the best use of the comms." He pauses, then adds, "But Facebook is better."

Oscar wolfs down the protein bar and laughs.

"They just said *Jane and Sulli are cancelled*," Quinn adds.

"They're just passionate stans," Donnelly explains.

"What the fuck is a stan?" Quinn asks and adds, "Alright, I *really* don't like this anymore. They just said Jane should go choke."

I cut in, "Go talk to them." That could be a threat. Or they could just be fans. When fandom culture comes into play, the lines blur.

Oscar knocks his arm with mine. "Look at you, helping my baby brother out." He chews the protein bar with a wide grin. "You keep that up, Tri-Force is gonna put all the green ones with you."

"Fuck," I curse.

Quinn repeats another possible threat, but Oscar and I don't bat an eye.

He tosses the protein wrapper in the red first-aid bag. "I hate how desensitized I've become to some of this shit. How do we even think that's normal?"

"I know."

I watch Maximoff depart from the huddle of girls. He lifts the corner of his red shirt and wipes sweat off his brow. Revealing his front-page-worthy abs—then he pulls the shirt up and over his head.

Damn.

Camp-goers shriek and whip out their phones. Some must be Snapchatting a video, their cameras pointed at him for a while.

A girl strolls nearby and stops dead still. Wide-eyed. "Oh. My. God."

I know.

I stretch my arm, my blood rushing down to my dick.

She whips out her phone and narrates. "He's more beautiful in person."

Accurate.

"Are you guys seeing this?!" she shrieks in glee to her video followers.

"Boners and wet pussies everywhere," Oscar whispers to me.

I shove his arm.

He laughs.

Then we both quiet and watch a redhead simultaneously sprint and gawk at Maximoff. Completely not paying attention to her feet. Like slow motion, her ankle catches on a tree root. She collapses hard with a loud *thunk.*

Maximoff saw the whole thing. And of course, he's the first one sprinting to the girl. I already grab the first-aid bag.

"Akara to Farrow. You're the closest with first aid. Doesn't look bad enough for a real doctor."

I roll my eyes and click my mic, mid-jog. "I *am* a doctor." I have an MD.

While I slow down to the girl and Maximoff, Donnelly has to chime in, "Anyone else think it's strange he *only* reminds us that he's a doctor when we say he's *not* a doctor? Any other time, he's the one telling us he can't prescribe medicine. Can't work in a hospital. Can't—"

I swivel my radio's knob. Cutting him off in my ear. I squat down beside the girl. She clutches her ankle, wincing.

Maximoff is knelt close. Me and him exchange one look in brisk greeting.

"Hey, sweetie," I say to the girl. "What's your name?"

"Ella." She winces through her teeth.

Maximoff says to me, "I think it's just a sprain,"

I tilt my head. "And what year did you graduate medical school?"

"What year did you finish that residency?"

"Still better than you."

He gives me a middle finger and a few cameras flash. #HMCCampAway has been trending on Twitter all day. Maximoff even has a link on his profile page to donate to One More Day.

I focus on Ella. She came down on her hands, then head. "Are you dizzy?"

"A little."

I slide the first-aid bag to Maximoff who is dying to do something. He's such a fixer. "Find an ice pack."

I inspect her ankle: reddened skin, not a lot of swelling. I press a few fingers on the area. "Does this hurt?" I ask, but she's already shoving my hands away.

Then she bemoans like I stabbed her throat.

Okay.

I've seen my fair share of dramatics. I can discern what's real and what's bullshit. She turns toward Maximoff. "I can't..." She tries to produce tears that don't come.

"You're going to be okay," he assures her. He wraps his arm around her shoulders in a side-hug. Then he hands me the soft ice pack.

I don't even touch the pack to her ankle before she winces.

"On a scale of one to ten," I ask, "what's your pain like?"

"Nine point five."

Okay. Sure. I felt enough of the area to know the bone's intact.

Maximoff looks seriously concerned. "Maybe we should just be safe and call an ambulance—"

"No, no, no." She raises her hands. "Really, it's not that bad. I could... walk on it...or try to."

I place the ice pack in her hand. "Use this for your head. I can wrap your ankle, and we can find you crutches if you need them. How about that?"

She nods vigorously. Then bites her lip at Maximoff. "Would you... could you stay with me for a bit?"

My brows spike.

"Of course," Maximoff says, sincere and offering another side-hug. I dig through the bag for a wrap, and then I glance up.

In earshot next to a drink station, a group of white guys in their early twenties talk shit about Jane. She's chatting to a few girls further in the forest.

"Jane Cobalt is disgusting," a guy says. His familiar angular face and aquiline nose sparks my memory. The red-marked sheet of possible threats. He's on it. His name is Tyler.

"She wants to get banged so badly. It's kind of pathetic."

"I'd fuck her. But I'd have to tie her down first."

They laugh.

My nose flares, jaw tight.

Maximoff is busy listening to Ella, but his cheekbones are sharpening. *He hears.*

I glare at them as I search through the first-aid bag.

"The BDSM shit is such a lie," a blond says. *He's also on the sheet.* Brad. "Anytime she gets shoved in this capture the flag game, she practically has an orgasm. Just watch her."

Fuck you.

Oscar starts approaching the guys. He clicks his mic. "These yellow T-shirt twats need to be watched. I'm going to keep an eye on 'em."

I turn my head and whisper into my mic so Ella can't hear. "Give them a *fuck you* from *me*."

"We're all thinking it," Oscar says.

I rip plastic off a wrap and return to the girl. "How are you feeling, Ella?" I ask before I touch her ankle.

She shrugs uncertainly.

Maximoff drops his arm off her shoulders. That was odd for him.

I set the wrap down and near him, my hand on his bicep. "Maximoff?"

He palms his collar, rubs his throat, struggling to breathe—and I know.

He's going into anaphylactic shock. I rapidly dig through the first-aid bag while he wheezes, the sound very close to someone being choked to death.

His throat is swelling closed.

He tries to say my name.

"You're okay. Stay calm," I tell him like I'm at complete ease. No care in the world.

Where's your fucking EpiPen? I touch my mic. "Get me an EpiPen." It's not in this bag.

"Oh my God, Maximoff?!" Ella almost clutches onto him, but I gently push her back. Maximoff grasps the back of my neck. His head hung, his sporadic breaths cut off short.

"You're okay."

He's not okay. I react calmly in any medical crisis, even when I know the person. Even when my heart wants to lodge in my throat. I swallow it down, and I have one mind that says, *fix this. Help him.*

Help him.

Do not leave him.

I can't leave him. In the distance, Quinn sprints urgently towards us with an EpiPen.

"He's allergic to fire ants!" Ella yells at me.

"I know." I cup his jaw. His narrowed eyes are determined to breathe when he can't. He tries to open his mouth for air.

If I could give him mine, I would.

I would in a fucking second—but his passageway is closing, tongue swelling. His blood pressure is dropping, his heart rate slowing. CPR solves nothing.

He needs epinephrine.

I should've had an EpiPen on me. It's the first week of December. We both thought there wouldn't be any fire ants.

His face reddens. He wheezes, eyes watering. I tighten my grip on his jaw. "I'm here. You're okay."

Maximoff wears no fear. He's just fighting his body to stay conscious.

"He's going to die!" she screams and bursts into tears.

"No he's not." I stare right at Maximoff. "You're not dying on me, wolf scout." *I promised you.*

Maximoff can't breathe anymore, close to passing out.

Quinn drops the EpiPen on my lap. I bite off the cap and stab Maximoff's thigh. I hear the click. A spring-loaded needle pierces through his clothing.

And he gasps a lungful of air. Like he's breaching the surface of a pool after almost drowning.

I hold the pen in place for ten seconds.

He tries to speak.

"Don't talk," I say and click my mic. "Akara, we need to call an ambulance. His vitals need to be checked at the ER." And I need to find where he was bitten.

Maximoff doesn't argue. For once.

Really, that just concerns me more.

36

FARROW KEENE

The medics check his vitals on the ambulance before driving off the property, and I find a small, reddened bite on the back of his neck. After they clear him, he jumps off the ambulance and returns to today's schedule. Barely missing a thing.

"Slow down for one second." I catch his wrist before he enters the mess hall for lunch.

Maximoff stops and checks his watch. "They're here for me and my cousins. I can't bail on anyone—"

"No one will fault you if you need to rest," I interject, taking note of his ashen complexion.

"I feel fine, or at least, good enough to eat." He stares deeper into my gaze with the same words he said the minute he could speak: *I'm glad you're here.*

Me too.

I almost reach for his hand, but a gaggle of girls and guys pass and snap photos of him.

And then a voice in my ear pulls my attention. "Akara to security."

Maximoff motions with his head to the mess hall. I nod and follow by his side.

Among the rows and rows of wooden cafeteria tables, I sit beside Jane at one of the emptiest ones.

Only one table away from Maximoff. He has a throng of people squished close. Likewise, Sulli's table is swarmed with people who want to hear stories about the Olympics.

Akara, Donnelly, and Oscar all surround her protectively.

Our earlier comms conversation stays with me.

Oscar: *how could an ant be on his neck?*

Akara: *he may've been leaning on a tree.*

Donnelly: *or someone put it there.*

Quinn: *no way.*

Me: *I would've seen it happen.*

I'm not subscribing to that conspiracy theory. No one collected fire ants just to put them on Maximoff and watch him choke to death. And even if I somehow missed a dipshit who tried to intentionally or unintentionally kill him, the person failed.

And they'll lose an arm if they try again.

Jane blows on her spoonful of chili. "Another one is coming," she tells me, and sure enough, a twenty-something brunette sits down in front of me.

This is the seventh girl that's confronted me just at lunch. During longer events, this happens frequently to the most attractive bodyguards. And let's be honest, Omega is full of sexy fuckers.

Eyes start wandering and people start noticing the guys that they can't have. The ones who are quiet in the corner with ripped muscles and a scowl. It's gotten a lot of security laid.

I've been hit on by a few men, many more women, and my answer rarely changes: *hell no.*

The girl waves to Jane like she's on the other side of the room and not right next to me. About 95% of her focus centers on me, and she begins, "My name's Tara. So my tent-mate left today, and it's just me tonight. You should stop by, check it out. I'll show you my tattoos—"

"I'm gay," I say, pausing to bite into a red apple.

She blushes. "You could've just told me you're not interested."

"I'm not interested," I say, "and I'm gay."

She quickly stands and zips back to her table.

Jane gives me a curious look.

"What?"

"You're more popular than me."

"If I were that popular, I wouldn't be security. I'd need security." And Tara won't remember my face by tomorrow.

Jane says a French word that I assume means *true*. Then I follow her gaze to Maximoff.

He hasn't been able to touch his lunch. I already grabbed him a to-go bag. And every time he goes for his hot sub sandwich, another person approaches to throw their arms around him. Most to say that they're happy he's okay. Others to share their story with him.

He listens.

He's good at that.

Some girls and guys cry as they talk, and he puts a consoling hand on their back. He focuses harder. He leans closer. Gives them encouragement and praise.

Like right now, one girl rubs her watering eyes. No older than twenty. She holds her cellphone tight. "It seems silly, but every time you post on Instagram or if I see you in the news or if a new episode of *We Are Calloway* comes out, it just makes me happy. You've always been my favorite. I've watched you since *I* was little. And I feel like we've grown up together, in this weird way."

"It's not weird," he tells her.

Tears fill her eyes, emotions gather, and where some guys may be uncomfortable, Maximoff reaches out and places a hand on her shoulder.

She continues, "I just want you to know that you've helped me through some dark times, and what you do here, for all of us—it means something."

"Can I give you a hug?" he asks her, his eyes reddening.

She smiles and wipes her tears. "Yes."

He pulls her into his arms, and she hugs back.

She's one of hundreds, but I know Maximoff will remember the moment. Her name. Everything. These interactions remind me how people find comfort in all kinds of places, with all kinds of people.

Jane's expression can only be described as sheer pride. "They love him," she says fondly. "As they should." She eats a spoonful of chili.

I bite into my red apple. I can't stop thinking about the camp-goers and all the shit they've said about Jane. Even about Sulli.

The women in these famous families have a much harder time gaining favor from the public. It makes no sense to me.

Think about it: the "fans" claim to love Maximoff to the ultimate core. Yet, they still hate Jane. If they loved him at all, they'd realize how much he'd despise anyone who spewed malice towards his best friend.

All day, my mind has been blaring *protect Jane Cobalt*.

And if anyone asked me at the start, if I had an opportunity to sit beside Maximoff or to sit next to Jane in a camp mess hall—which would I choose.

I'd never believe them if they said Jane.

And here I am.

Keeping her company. Just because I fucking feel like it.

"They could love you one day too, Jane," I say, turning my apple for another spot to bite. She has her fair share of fans online, but not very many seem to be here.

"I don't need their love." Jane stirs her chili and then meets my gaze.

We both overhear those five bastards nearby. They congregate at a table to the left of ours. Still dressed in yellow shirts from the capture the flag game. Still obnoxiously fixated on Jane.

"Do you see what she's wearing? God, it's ugly."

I take a larger, more vexed bite of apple.

Jane has on leopard pants, a frilly shirt and some sort of teal faux fur collar. And who cares what the fuck she's wearing? Jane reaches for her water, never blinking.

"Isn't her mom a fashion designer? That's just fucking sad, man."

I chew roughly and layer on a glare, about at my max. Ready to confront some bastards. Oscar's "talk" to them obviously did shit.

"It's all for attention."

Jane never flinches.

Maximoff does. Overhearing that last part as their voices escalate. His forest-greens turn to hot pinpoints.

That's it. Fingers to my mic, I tell the security team, "Don't follow me." I stand up, half-bitten apple in hand, and I turn my radio's volume to a soft chatter I can ignore.

My feet carry me to the table of five twenty-year-old bastards. I know their names by heart, but honestly, I'm not using them anymore. To me, they're just bastards and dipshits.

As soon as I tower above their table, they go absolutely quiet. Their gazes latch onto my plethora of tattoos and my T-shirt that says *SECURITY*.

"Let's talk outside," I tell all of them.

"We're not doing anything wrong," one tells me.

"I didn't say you were," I say calmly, biting my apple. I can't raise my voice. I can't raise my fists. I intimidate without inciting chaos. "Let's just go outside and have a chat. It won't take long." I nod towards the exit.

Just like that, they all agree.

For a few minutes, I lecture them about the importance of being kind and considerate. You know, the bare minimum of human decency.

They nod a lot. Whether they're really listening to me has yet to be determined.

"Sure," the blond bastard tells me, "but I think it's shitty for you to pull us aside and single us out. We paid to be here. You're taking up our time that could've been spent sitting five-feet from Jane Cobalt." He does a poor job of hiding his smile.

And his friends burst into grins.

I grit down, and off my piercing glare, they immediately stop. "Let me make this *very* fucking clear," I say. "She doesn't owe you a thing. Not her time. Not the air between your body and hers. You paid to be in a raffle.

For charity. If you choose to overstep, security will throw you the fuck out. But see, I don't want that to happen."

I pause while they hang onto my words.

And I forge past my despise, just to tell them, "You guys seem cool." *As cool as a fucking idiot.* "So the last thing I want is for you to miss out on these last couple days. Be respectful. Tone it down."

"Yeah, yeah, yeah. We get it," one says. "We'll try to be nicer or whatever."

Or whatever. Honestly.

Another one nods to me. "Thanks, man."

"No problem." Fuck, I just made friends with these dipshits.

As soon as they all leave, soft static pricks my ear. I turn up the radio.

"Did he hit them?" Oscar's voice.

"Nah, they're walking away," Donnelly replies.

"Hey, guys." I click my mic. "I've made new friends."

"Nice work," Akara tells me, genuine.

"You boys taking notes?" I ask them.

"Next time someone should be with you though," Akara adds. "That could've been five on one."

I could've taken all five of them.

"Take that note down, Farrow," Donnelly pipes in.

I roll my eyes and then watch those five bastards strut down the hill to the lake. I wish I could've just kicked them out of the camp. The publicity nightmare of sending someone home would destroy the purpose of the charity event.

So they have to stay.

37

Farrow unlocks our tent after the bonfire gathering ends. No moon out tonight, day two. I point a flashlight at the entrance and watch the way his fingers fiddle with the key and padlock. And the zipper.

Try having your bodyguard a few feet from you all day and seeing him in his element: intimidating the hell out of assholes, medically savvy, badass and smart as fuck. Now try *not* picturing his cock a million times.

Yeah, that's hard. Pun intended.

Now try *not* being able to touch him. To flash *fuck me* eyes. To clutch the back of his neck and plunge my tongue against his tongue.

I could growl I'm so pent-up. *I want him.*

All day I've wanted him, and I haven't been able to embrace him.

I'm not about to jump him like he's my sex toy. He may be exhausted. So as we both crawl into the tent, I try to hang onto other things.

Like how this is the last night of the Camp-Away, and there's been no broken bones. Not too many tears—most of them were happy. And no Charlie. It's been pretty damn good, even with the first day ant-allergy attack.

As far as *danger* goes, it's been safer than I think the entire security team predicted. After breakfast tomorrow, everyone will start packing up, last goodbyes exchanged, and we'll all go home.

I stretch my legs out on my orange sleeping bag, and Farrow padlocks the tent from the *inside*. As much as I love camping, I'm not a fan of these extra precautions. I'm so used to feeling freer in the wilderness. With this many people around and their cellphone cameras—it's practically the antithesis of why I camp.

I peel my shirt off my head. The December chill nipping my bare skin. Farrow edges back beside me, eyeing me from his peripheral while he slowly removes his earpiece and twists the cord around his radio. He places his holstered gun beneath his camping pillow.

I shut off the flashlights. No more shadows dancing along the tent.

And we're isolated from camp-goers—private but not *that* private. More security is outside. "You know," I whisper, "I've never fucked in a tent."

We haven't done anything yet because of my allergic reaction. My blood pressure has been out of whack, but I'm fine now.

His brows rise, and he pulls his black V-neck over his head. "Couldn't convince someone to have a one-night stand in a tent?"

"No." My eyes graze the inked dagger on his abs, just barely visible in the darkness. "I just didn't like the idea of only a thin sheet of canvas separating me from my bodyguard while I was fucking." Usually there's at least a *wall*.

"Understandable." Farrow watches me as I watch his fingers. He unbuttons his pants, unzips, and he kicks them off. His heady gaze sweeps me in a slow-burning once-over. And his tight black boxer-briefs suction to his muscles, ass, and his long, thick erection.

Christ.

Blood pumps harder, everywhere. Until I'm one thundering pulse.

I grab his shoulder, and he already rolls on top of me. Legs interlacing, our mouth crushing together, I clench his hair between starved fingers.

He wrestles with my pants, yanking them off my waist, down my muscular legs. Off me completely.

Yes, fuck yes.

I drop my voice to another whisper. "How far did you say the body-guards were?" Some should be standing outside all night.

As he lowers to meet my mouth again, he grinds his hard cock against mine. *Fuck me.* "I told them to give you at least a hundred yards."

Almost a football field.

"Seriously?" I whisper, my excitement and desire pooling hotter. My right hand ascends his carved muscles, and I thumb the barbell on his nipple.

His lips quirk. "Yeah, but I didn't do it so we could fuck." He rests his forearms on either side of my shoulders, and I lie beneath his weight that scorches me head-to-toe. "I did it so you could sleep."

I lick my stinging lips. Seeing that *sleep* is not on the agenda right now.

Farrow clutches my jaw, his mouth teasingly close as he breathes, "Try not to make a sound."

Fuck me. I swallow a groan, and as my cock begs for pressure, he runs his hand down my abs, and lower, he grips my length, then balls.

"Fuck," I breathe, waist arching up into him. *Fuck me, man.* I usually flip us at this point, but the weight of his build on me feels fucking good.

I yank off his boxer-briefs while he sheds mine. Buck-naked. We move more frenzied, my mouth against his mouth, his strong hand running across the back of my neck, everything sensitive. Lit up, and I stifle a groan in my throat.

Our bodies dig into each other, skin against skin. Intense friction heating us. The cold air no longer bites at me, but his teeth nip my shoulder. My mouth opens, but I cage the raspy sound.

Then I reach down and stroke him, his muscles tensing up against me. *Jesus.* His gravelly noise dies as he grits his teeth.

He jacks me off and rubs his thumb over the tip. My shoulders dig deep into the sleeping bag, my head wanting to arch back. *Fuck me.*

Fuckmefuckmefuckme—I flex, stopping myself from ejaculating. *Not happening yet.* I place a hand on his chest, and he lets go. I stretch my arm out. Patting his sleeping bag for his small duffel.

Farrow leans over and finds it. He has the lube and condoms in a flash. Setting them beside us, he kisses my jaw, sucks my neck—my breath heavies.

I squeeze his bare ass, and *fuck*, my toes curl as he rakes his teeth across the frame of my shoulder. His warm breath blistering my skin. I'm so worked up—I could easily come. But I want this to last way longer.

"Farrow," I breathe.

He studies my features, even without much light. I think he's honing in on our position. I've let him stay on top for a while, and I'm making no move to switch us yet.

Farrow runs his fingers affectionately through my hair, and his lips touch my ear. "Do you want me inside of you tonight?"

His rough but erotic voice fists my erection.

"Hmm," a groan rumbles my throat, and my muscles contract beneath his strong build.

His nose flares, his own scorching arousal hitting him hard. "Maximoff," he whispers, his hand slowly slides towards my ass.

Instantly, I catch his wrist. Stopping him. I stiffen in a different way. Like someone inside my body yelled *fire* in a crowded room.

"It's okay," he breathes, our eyes locked.

"You know I trust you. It's just…" I lick my lips. "I can't jump into that spontaneously. I want it, but…" The next part I'm about to say, I haven't told him yet. Being vulnerable is like shattering concrete on top of layers and layers of hard metal.

I lower my voice to a more hushed whisper. He's so close that he can hear me say, "The two times I've tried, I was eighteen, and I got inside my head. And it…well, it fucking hurt, and I didn't let it last long."

He cups my jaw. "Did he finger you first?"

"No."

Farrow swallows hard, his features skewing towards *pissed*. "Why wouldn't he…?" He shakes his head. "No, don't answer." He blows out a breath. "*Fuck*, I care about you, man." He kisses my temple, then my lips, an *I'm never going to hurt you* pressed powerfully against my mouth.

When we break, we're quiet for a beat.

Farrow breathes, "It's not just a trust thing then. You're nervous?"

"A little bit."

"A little bit," he repeats like I'm underscoring the truth.

"A lot," I correct.

"We'll plan nights for it. It'll be a process to work you up. Because you don't relax easily."

"I don't?" I say sarcastically. To have even his fingers inside of me, I need to be *not* nervous, not tensed, not afraid—and that could take hours or days or weeks.

I want to try. With him. Only him.

I eye his lips and his piercing. "Do you want it?"

His brows rise like I can't see what's right in front of me. "Do I want to thrust my cock inside of you?"

My breath goes shallow. "Yeah, do you want to fuck me?"

His mouth brushes my ear. "Hard and badly."

I buck up, our pelvises grinding together.

A noise catches in Farrow's throat. He speaks quietly but rapidly, "This can go two ways tonight. One: I stay on top like this, and I'll put your cock inside of me." He's a fucking power bottom. The guy pushes his ass against my dick almost every time we screw. So he'd have no problem doing the grunt work.

"Or you take me how you've fantasized me taking you."

That. My cock responds to *that.* His flexed muscles do too. I answer by pushing his chest up off mine. I'm aggressive in bed.

And every time I manhandle him, he lets out a breathy curse. An erotic *fuck* and *damn.* I kneel beside him and tear open a condom. Sheathing my erection fast.

His breath quickens, stroking his cock while watching me.

Fuck me.

We're both boiling at the delay. I reposition him. Shoving him down on all fours, his knees on the sleeping bags. Hands on the pillows.

Farrow cranes his neck over his shoulder, his mouth parted. He extends his arm behind him, gripping my ribs. I lube his hole, running my finger around the rim.

He groans as softly as he can, "Fuck." I push two fingers inside, opening him.

I replace my fingers with my erection. Slowly, slowly sinking into Farrow. *Christ, the pressure.* I growl with clenched teeth, my eyes on fire. His hand tightens on my ribs.

His gaze flitting to mine, and we share this recognition: that one day this will be him; he'll be knelt behind my ass, sinking deep, deep into me…

I'm all the way in, and I rock forward. Hands on his muscular hips. I thrust and thrust. He swings his head forward, drops his hand, needing to grip the ground. Somehow.

Closer. My body aches for contact. *Closer.*

Closer.

I want skin and friction and sweat.

I sink further into him, and he drops to his forearms, cursing a dizzying fucking curse. He bucks up into me. *Fuck me.*

My chest welds to his back, a sheen of sweat built on us both. I clutch him stronger, my biceps cut sharp.

Yes, fuck yes. The pressure, the friction, his muscular body and expression, us this close together—*everything* compounds together in a blood-pumping, mind-fucking wave.

My ass flexes with each push in. He can barely keep his head hoisted. He's pretty much flat against the sleeping bags. We're about the same size, same build, and my body cloaks his, lying on top. Pounding into him. I wrap my forearm around his collarbones. And I dig deep.

"*Fuck,*" he groans into the sleeping bag. His legs spread wide as I fuck in between them.

Farrow lifts his head, angling and his mouth meets mine. Our tongues fight for that ache. My pulse bangs my eardrums. I dig *harder.*

He breaks apart from my mouth to let out a rumbled sound that completely spins my world. Farrow buries his head in the sleeping bag, stifling his groans.

38

FARROW KEENE

Fuck.

Fuck. I'm very far gone, choked up with pleasure. Water crests the corner of my eyes. His weight bears on my body. I lie on the floor.

He lies on top of me.

This is how he wants me to fuck him. Hard and deep, and unrelenting, but also protective and sheltered. Fully connected.

He grabs onto my forearms, bracing himself so he can drive deeper— *fucking hell.* My eyes roll back, my mouth wide open.

Maximoff groans my name in the pit of my ear as an orgasm barrels through him. My muscles throb from being flexed. He slows, milking the climax, and I try to catch my breath.

When he pulls out, he flips me onto my back. And I clutch his hair while he finishes me off with his mouth. I bite down, my pulse jackhammering.

"Fuck," I curse as I hit a peak.

He swallows the last of my cum. And then we're breathing hard, staring at one another, and my eyes say what blares inside my mind, *we'll have more weeks together.*

Months.

Years.

It's not ending here.

I'm going to give him what he just gave me. I tug him down, and we end up on our backs, staring at the tent ceiling. I tangle my fingers through his hair, leisurely pushing back the damp strands.

He runs his ankle against mine.

Crickets are the only sound, and the dark bathes us. Maximoff turns his head to me, and he wears this look that says he's more than content.

He's happy.

39

♛ MAXIMOFF HALE

Akara puts his baseball cap on backwards.
"Moffy, you only have three hours until this is all over. Do you have to confront them?"

"*Yes.*" It's my only answer.

We huddle around the canoe rack by the lake's dock. Not that far away, camp-goers break down their tents and pack their bags, getting ready for the final breakfast.

Sulli and Jane stand on either side of me, our three bodyguards opposing us. Orange leaves crunch beneath our boots.

"If you heard what they said," I continue, "you'd be *pushing* me towards them."

Akara doesn't blink. "I doubt that. We're the ones who are supposed to handle this." He gestures to himself, Farrow, and Quinn.

"Not you," Farrow says for good measure, his gaze set hard on me like *no fucking way in hell are you confronting someone without me, Maximoff.*

I get that they're security. I'm the celebrity. But I can't call in reinforcements to fight all of my battles. I can't stand like a voiceless statue. Neither can Janie. Not in this instance.

"You can come with us. Farrow can come with us. Christ, bring Quinn too. But as the CEO of this charity, I'm *not* going to let this Camp-Away end without saying something to them."

Jane nods strongly in agreement.

This morning Brad, Tyler, and whatever the other three fucking guys are named—they were making lewd gestures about Jane again. Only they mentioned hogtying and *fucking* her, and I'm proud of the fact that I didn't flip out on them in the moment.

I walked away with Jane. I cooled down. We came up with a plan.

But Akara doesn't see this as *progress* on my part.

"I'm joining him," Jane reminds our bodyguards. "I need to say something too. There are hundreds of girls here, and if those guys leave thinking it's okay to say things like that—then we've failed. We can't stay silent."

Sulli stretches her arm behind me to hold Janie's hand. "If you need me, I'm there."

"Thank you." Jane breaks from my side, and the two girls share a long hug.

"And?" I ask Farrow.

He lays easy-going eyes on me. Probably because I said the magic words *come with me*. "I think that you're not going to change your mind."

Yep.

He turns to Akara. "If we approach them together, it'll seem like an attack."

Akara considers the options. "Those guys like you."

Farrow rolls his eyes but nods.

"You go with Jane and Maximoff." He leaves out Sulli. I'm guessing he doesn't want her near this altercation. Akara looks at me. "Don't get into a fistfight." To Farrow, he says, "Don't let him."

"I won't."

Akara emphasizes his point to me. "You've done good work here, Moffy. You throw a punch, and that's all the media will talk about. Not the success. Not the money you made. *Please* just stay calm while you talk to them. If you can't do that—then let Farrow, Quinn, and me handle it ourselves."

"I'll be calm."

Farrow tries not to smile. "What does that look like?"

"We're about to find out." I look to Janie who hoists her head high, shoulders pulled back, standing tall. Like the woman who raised her.

And I don't need to ask if she's ready.

Let's go kick some ass.

Civilly.

We gather Brad and his four friends by the row of log cabins that Camp Calloway uses for summer camps. Some people linger close to watch the interaction. There's no privacy, but if we brought them into the camp's office, I'm afraid I'd let my anger best me.

Janie speaks first.

"I've heard all the things you've been saying about me in particular these past few days." She adjusts the strap of a pumpkin-shaped purse that slips down her shoulder. "That's not how you should speak about another human being. Period."

Brad scratches his blond hair by the temple, *smirking*. "So...you wouldn't want to be hogtied then?"

His friends laugh.

Farrow has a hand on my shoulder, and his fingers dig into my muscle. Rage bangs at my chest. My arms stay crossed. I don't move.

"No," Jane refutes, "and that's not something you should be asking. It's not kind. It's not appropriate. If you did that to another girl—"

"Whoa." Brad holds up his hands. "I'd never say that to another chick. But you ask for it. You're always talking about BDSM on that show. I mean, you're *inviting* this shit. It's your fault."

"She talks about how she's *not* into BDSM," I snap. "Because guys like you can't seem to understand that she's not her mom."

Jane adds, "And you guys don't seem to understand the meaning of *consent.* Even if I enjoyed BDSM like my mom, you shouldn't be speaking to me or her like that. Don't be a vile person. Is it that dreadfully difficult for you?"

"Did she just compare herself to her mom?" Tyler laughs to Brad.

Brad chuckles. "I've seen Rose Calloway's sex tapes and..." He motions to Jane's body. "That's a cheap imitation." *Fuck them.*

Jane almost steps forward, but Farrow rests a hand on her shoulder now.

How is he not ready to swing? My blood is boiling. My biceps flexed, hands in fists. I swallow a thousand times to try and remind myself, *do not fight them.*

Do not move.

It solves nothing.

Farrow keeps his voice even-keeled and asks, "What's the point of saying that? They're all telling you it's hurtful. *Listen.*"

Tyler nods to Jane. "Get thicker skin."

"Fuck you," I growl. "You're a guest here."

Brad smirks, but his tone changes—hostility mounting. "No, we *won* a raffle that we paid for."

I grind my teeth. *Calm. Be calm.* I breathe out before I ask *calmly*, "Why even enter the raffle if you hate us? Why come here and take the opportunity away from other people who would've *loved* to be where you are?"

Brad extends his arms. "Free camping trip."

I have no words. Full disclosure: I don't understand them. I can't relate. I can't empathize. I don't know if it's because I stand on a platform, a pedestal too high to see from their perspective. I don't know if it's because as I try to jump down, into their shoes, I'm just flooded with *rage.*

My gaze daggers. Burning and churning, and my face is all blades. All sharp, brutal edges.

Tyler snickers. "Did you all really just pull us aside to lecture us?"

Brad snorts. "They did." He smacks his friend's chest, and they chuckle again.

Tyler shakes his head. "It's almost like they think they're so much better than us. The entitlement that you two have is honestly disgusting."

In my peripheral, I notice people filming the interaction. Phones whipping out and pointed at us. This has traveled in a direction I never thought it'd actually go.

Sometimes I can't predict what people will think. What the public thinks. Where's Jack Highland when you need him?

Jane raises her chin. "We just believe that you should be kinder. Don't tell a girl that she should be hogtied, even if it's someone you see on TV.

Even if they say they like it—they're not saying they want to be hogtied by you." She takes a deep breath. "If you consider that entitled, then… okay. I'm sorry."

"Don't fucking apologize," I tell her. They've been beating her down for three days. I'm not going to let that stand.

"Oohh," Brad says. "We've struck a cord."

I growl, "You've struck nothing, asshole."

"Maximoff," Farrow warns in the pit of my ear.

I point at these guys. "I sincerely hope that you don't ever talk to women like that in your everyday life," I growl. "Fuck it, you shouldn't talk to *anyone* like that. And if you can't see right from wrong, then remove your heads from your asses."

As soon as the words escape my mouth, phones buzz and chime and ring all around us. People whisper, casting glances our direction. Even my cell vibrates madly in my pocket. It's like someone flipped a switched and shrouded us in darkness.

What the fuck is going on?

Eyes begin to zero in on Janie and me. Like we've just undressed in the middle of the field. Naked. Bare. My pulse speeds.

Brad practically cackles, glancing from his phone, then to me, back to his phone. Then to me. "No wonder you're so defensive of Jane Cobalt," he says. "You're fucking her."

I lunge.

"Nope." Farrow grabs me around the waist. I'm all boiling wrath. I point at Brad, my feet dragging in the dirt as Farrow restrains me.

"You're a piece of *shit*," I sneer.

"You think I'm a piece of shit?" He laughs. "Dude, I'm not fucking my cousin."

"I'm not fucking her!" I scream, my lungs on fire.

"Moffy," Jane says in warning, her voice trailing ominously. She's staring haunted at her phone.

What the fuck happened?

40

Jane, Farrow, and I only have about ten minutes to talk before my parents, her parents, and our aunt and uncle show up at the camp. All six of them drove over as soon as they saw the article.

Maximoff Hale and Jane Cobalt: The Secret Love Affair!

It's fake.

You shouldn't believe it either.

Fake articles always pop up online. We process. We put out a public statement. And we deal with it. This isn't any different as far as I'm concerned.

Alright, it's a little damn different.

I've never been accused of incest. Never even thought that could be swung my way, but as soon as we tell our side of the story—everything will be as it was.

"They're waiting in there for us?" Janie asks an Alpha bodyguard who exits a camp cabin named *Green Willow*. He nods tensely, face stoic.

I climb up the short stairs with Jane, and we pause on the porch.

"Everything's fine," I remind her. "We'll deal with it like we always do. My publicist is on speed dial, and I'm sure your dad wants us to coordinate with his people."

Damage control. We're all seasoned pros.

Jane inhales a tight breath, and nods reassuringly. I glance back.

Farrow has one foot on the step and looks between us. "If you two need anything, I'll be right here." Chatter in his earpiece distracts him. His jaw tics before he touches his mic on his collar.

I can't distinguish his hushed words.

I move forward, grabbing Jane's hand.

Right when Jane and I enter the cabin, hand-in-hand, the energy shifts. Our parents and aunt and uncle grow eerily quiet all of a sudden.

We take seats on two wooden chairs. Facing a wall of bunks and some of the people we love most in our lives. The six people who've influenced us. Raised us.

Who shaped us.

And protected us.

On a top bunk bed, Uncle Ryke sits beside his wife—my Aunt Daisy, the owner of Camp Calloway and Sulli's mom: blonde hair chopped unevenly and a long scar down her cheek. She swings her legs over the side of the bunk, and her bright eyes flit to Ryke's darkened ones.

He looks pissed. But I don't know...that's his usual expression.

Below him, on the ground, my mom rests on a black trunk. Plastic baggie of trail mix on her lap, she shovels a handful in her mouth. Nervous. *She's nervous.*

My mom tugs at my dad's crew-neck shirt. Like she wants him to sit, too. He shakes his head, leaning against the post of another bunk bed. Arms crossed.

Eyes daggered.

I look to Jane's parents. Uncle Connor and Aunt Rose stand all-powerful. Side-by-side, hand-in-hand, armored for battle like a king and queen.

Only, I can't tell who they prepare to fight. I glance at each of them again. About how they positioned two chairs for us to face them.

Is this an interrogation?

"I'm glad all of you are here," I say, giving them the benefit of the doubt. "We should talk about how to deal with the article." I pause when they remain quiet.

My mom shoots her sister Rose a cagey look. *Jesus.*

Ryke is staring hard at my hand in Jane's—Jane shakes her hand out of mine. *What.*

I whip my head to each of them. Not able to glare at all six fast enough. "It's *false*. Christ, I shouldn't even have to say that."

Connor takes the reins. "We just have some questions." Jane's dad is the voice of reason. He'll be the first one to understand. Everyone else is dramatic—but still, how *the fuck* could they believe this, even for a second?

Or maybe they don't believe it.

Maybe their doubt is just my paranoia leaking into common sense. They're family. They'd never combat us.

Jane straightens, her chair creaking. "What kind of questions?"

"Nous avons besoin d'explications, mon coeur." *We need explanations, my heart.*

"No French," my dad tells him.

Rose speaks, voice icy. "We all need to be on the same page. We can't let this divide us." Her piercing yellow-green eyes drill holes into pretty much everyone. Even her husband.

"That's what we want," I say, my shoulders squared. I'm ready to resolve this and move on.

"Good." Connor nods. "Let's start with the night the cats escaped. Why were you in your underwear?"

Why the fuck would that need clarification? "We were playing a drinking game."

Jane adds, "Sober participants had to strip instead of take a sip."

"And we were using *your* rules." My gaze swings up to Uncle Ryke.

Ryke rocks back like I sucker-punched him. "*My* rules? No fucking way. You can thank Cobalt for that one."

I grimace at Uncle Connor. "You came up with the stripping rule?" He's the polished one—and he drinks. I always thought it had to be either my dad or Ryke.

"We're one question in and this is already being derailed," he says, "and *yes*, I did. Back to that same night—"

"Hallow Friends Eve," Lily clarifies.

"Such a cute name," her little sister Daisy smiles.

"You're only saying that because your daughter coined it," Rose rebuts. Daisy mock gasps.

Connor ignores the sisters, and he asks me point-blank, "Why did you have bite marks?"

My mom's eyes dart to Jane. I start shaking my head. *No.* She can't actually believe that Jane is the one who bit me. Aunt Daisy eyes us both. So does Aunt Rose.

I blink slowly like my world is starting to spin, and I'm gripping hard to hang on.

My dad's jaw sharpens with each passing beat. New uncomfortable tension vacuums the air from the cabin. I sense the shift again.

I sense the unease.

I crack my knuckles, my back achingly straight. "How much do you guys *not* believe us?" Pressure packs on my chest. "You're not just asking these questions for publicists. You're asking for yourselves, aren't you?"

Jane's hand returns to mine, and our fingers intertwine. They're all watching with suspicion.

It knives my ribcage.

"Before we make a decision, we need to hear your side of things," my dad tells me.

I disentangle my fingers from Jane. Not able to sit any longer, I stand as tall as my dad. Glowering. "You honestly *believe* I could be having sex with Jane?"

"I don't know what to think, Moffy." His eyes flash hot. "It's *incest*, for Christ's sake. That's not something you'd come to me and talk about!"

"I'm your *son*." I motion angrily at him. "You *know* me. You know me better than most people ever will. How could you even think…" My words stick to the back of my raw throat. He doesn't even look sympathetic.

He's still on guard like I'm straight up lying to his face.

I want to scream at the top of my goddamn lungs, *I'm not fucking Jane!* But I can't even unleash the words. The wind is knocked out of my chest. Stunned in the face of their doubt.

Jane's mom takes over. "When I was your age, I thought I knew my sister, but for years Lily hid her sex addiction from me," Rose tells me. "She was lying. She was sneaking around. I missed *every* sign." I hear the guilt in her voice. She wishes she'd been there for my mom earlier.

And she thinks I'm lying like my mom.

Fuck. I run my hands through my hair and growl, "I'm *not* an addict. We're not lying!" But their experiences shaped them.

They've shaped *us*. And how many times did my parents tell Rose, Connor, Ryke, and Daisy, *we're not lying*. How many times were they caught in one?

Goddammit.

"We're not lying," Jane says more clearly, less hostile. "I promise, we're not."

I nod over and over and fucking over.

"It's fucking incest, Mof," Ryke says, his rough voice strained. "Like your dad says, it's not something you're going to willingly admit."

"So then what?" I question. "You want to catch us in a lie until we're forced to admit it? Is that the goal here?"

They don't say anything.

"Jesus," I murmur.

"Here…" My mom gets up, watery eyes. "Have some trail mix."

I glare. "I don't want your trail mix, Mom." Instantly, I feel like an asshole. I don't think I've ever snapped at my mom in my life. She sinks back onto the trunk, her chin quivering. She sniffs and tries to raise her chin.

"I'll take some trail mix, love." My dad snatches her bag.

"Dad," Jane says, her voice soft and wary. "We are telling the truth."

Connor barely blinks. "I have to stick with the facts." He pauses. "And I want you two to realize the health risks if—"

"Stop." Rose covers his mouth with her hand.

My mom bursts into tears. Aunt Daisy wipes her eyes with the edge of her shirt.

"Fucking A, Cobalt," Ryke growls.

My dad looks sick.

KRISTA & BECCA RITCHIE

"We're not having sex!" I yell, veins almost protruding in my neck. I set my hands on my head, breathing hard. *Farrow.*

I almost turn to my right. Expecting him to be there. He's always next to me, but he's outside the closed door. Listening to my frustration and fury.

Ryke points to me. "Explain the fucking bite marks."

"It wasn't me," Jane says, still sitting, but confidence and power boosts her words. *The truth.*

It's the goddamn truth.

"Then who the fuck was it?" Ryke asks me.

Shit.

Shit.

Shit.

Jane, Farrow, and I already talked about *the* secret. The real one. Where I'm sleeping with my bodyguard. Jane said, "I'm not going to be the reason you two go public."

She was adamant that we not expose our secret to the world. She's intelligent and calculated and she told me, "There's no certainty the media will even believe you and Farrow were dating. They'll most likely say it's a ploy to hide our supposed love affair. The timing is suspicious. And then what, Moffy? Farrow loses his job and his privacy. You get a new bodyguard. And everyone will *still* believe we're having sex."

There's no evidence of Farrow and I hooking up. We have no texts to leak. No email thread. No photos from the past. No video footage. Us being so damn careful—I never thought that'd work against us.

Compare that load of *nothing* to the countless photographs and evidence of Jane and me together. All the times we've hugged. Where we've kissed each other's cheeks. My arms wrapped around her shoulders. Her head on my chest.

We're close.

We've always been close, but now every photograph can be twisted. Add in the hours of *We Are Calloway* footage where we both talk about how much we love each other. Platonic love—but that can be distorted too.

Even the Hallow Friends Eve is now packaged as evidence. Media posted the photo of me cradling Jane in my arms. I'm practically naked. She's in her pajamas. They say it's too close for cousins.

For the first time in my life, I feel isolated. Alone. Like Jane and I have boarded a lifeboat and been pushed out into a swelling ocean.

"Maximoff," Ryke forces. "Who bit you?"

I prepared myself to deal with tabloids, the world. Not my family. And while you may think the world would be a worse battle—it's not.

This is worse. This is *gut-wrenching*.

"Not Jane," I say strongly.

"The bite marks can't be from a one-night stand though," my dad says.

I frown, wondering how they would've drawn that conclusion.

Ryke tells me, "You haven't been going to clubs for four fucking months. I called Price, asking for the NDAs, and he doesn't have *any*."

"Which means that you haven't had any one-night stands," Connor continues, "or any random hookups. Do you follow the logic, Moffy?"

I remember the lie Farrow told the security team. "You think I'm seeing one girl."

"Price told me," Ryke says. *Price.* I shake my head repeatedly. "He said you've been sleeping with the same girl, and you refused to get an NDA because she's not someone your parents would fucking approve of."

They all look to Jane.

Dammit.

"It's not me," Jane says stiffly.

My dad gestures to my chest. "Who else would we not approve of? I can't think of one goddamn name other than your cousin."

Farrow Redford Keene.

I stare off, haunted. Morality is a demanding beast that asks me, pleads with me, *begs me* to do the right thing. What's right anymore? I'm searching for the sword that I need to fall on. I just don't want to hurt Jane or Farrow in the process.

I can't hurt him.

I can't.

Just let it slice through me.

"Maybe it's not a love affair," Ryke says. "Are you drinking? Are you having any fucking problems?"

"*No*," I say firmly.

"Are you?" Ryke turns on Jane.

"No," she says adamantly.

"We just want to help," my mom chimes in, wet tears streaking her cheeks. "If you both would be honest, we can all work this out." They think we're lying.

And I am lying.

The truth is standing just outside the door. And I remember what Farrow once said. *"You just need to know that I'm going to get banged up and you can't run and save me, wolf scout. You have to let it happen."* I'm not supposed to protect him. As much as it's killing me. As much as it's driving knots in my damn stomach.

We're supposed to stand side-by-side. And we need to take this hit together.

Go get the truth.

I turn my head.

"Do you sleep in the same bed together?" my dad asks, voice stilted.

I go rigid. The room grows hot.

My head swerves back to him. I'm not burying myself beneath another lie. "Sometimes," I say. "It's always platonic."

My mom sits on the very edge of the trunk. "But you sleep in the same bed," she says as though she needs extra confirmation. Like she didn't hear right.

"Yeah."

My mom touches her chest with two hands. "Your dad and I—we used to sleep in the same bed when we were just friends."

Oh shit.

I lick my dry lips. "You were attracted to each other. I'm not attracted to Jane."

"Likewise," Jane says, shifting in her chair. "I'm not attracted to Moffy."

"We were also liars," my dad tells me.

Right now, I am a liar, too. They spot it like blood in the water. They're sharks. I'm prey. And I'm being ripped open.

My dad keeps eye contact with me, looking broken and pained. "We love you," he tells me. "We'd love you no matter what. But we can't help you unless you're honest with us."

"I don't need help," I tell him. "I'm fine."

He nods. "I've said that one before." His words practically ice. He gives me his classic, bitter smile. "Congratulations, Maximoff, you got what you wanted. You're more like me." His disappointment is a tsunami crashing through my chest.

I stare at my dad. Right in the eyes, and I say the words that I've never wanted to utter in my damn life. It takes every ounce of power inside of me to admit this to myself and to him and to the room—and even to you.

And I tell my dad, "I'm not like you."

I would never hurt people I love with a lie, and that's what's happening now. I'm hurting him, my mom, aunts and uncles—and even Jane. I can handle the world's doubt. That's commonplace. But I can't live with theirs.

Go get the truth.

I turn to the door. And I suddenly freeze.

Farrow approaches me. Already inside the cabin, his lips rise like *I know.*

41

I heard everything from outside, and about midway through I knew what I needed to do. I feel six incredulous, confused gazes sweep my sudden presence. I don't confront them yet.

Before Maximoff repeatedly asks *are you sure you want to do this?* I catch his wrist, standing right by his side.

Very softly, I whisper, "Your morality is rubbing off on me." I feel sick putting Maximoff Hale in a place where he'd be forced to lie to these people.

His family. Who need him.

Who trust him.

Who love him.

He'd be a worse man if he trampled all over them with a lie, and he's made me a better one because I don't even hesitate to unleash the truth. I don't care about the career consequences, and we're strong enough to survive the blowback. At the end of the road, all I know is that I'm protecting and preserving the very essence of who he is.

And I'd do it five hundred times over.

I nod to Maximoff to go ahead. *Tell them.*

He fists my shirt and tugs me to his chest. In a swift, pulse-pounding moment, he has two firm hands on my neck, and his mouth meets mine.

Not wavering, not second-guessing—his pride for this second and for us lifts his carriage like he's sky-scraping tall.

He has to feel my lips rising. I can't restrain a smile. I wouldn't, even if I was ordered to. Our bodies pull together in a deeper, slower kiss, and I hook my arm around his broad shoulders. His hand slides through my black hair, his desire and hunger urging my mouth open again. Pulsating my veins and heart. All things I've felt with Maximoff before.

He went all in.

All in with me.

I recognize like everyone else has to: *this is his first kiss with an audience.* If they don't believe him now, then they're just in denial.

When we finally break the kiss, we exchange one headstrong, stubborn-as-hell look that says, *we're in this shit together, and we're going to get out together. No matter what.*

We confront his stunned family side-by-side, my arm wrapped around his lower back.

"There's the truth," Maximoff says. "And I'm not fucking lying."

His over-protective dad stakes an icy glare into me. And only me. "Either you're the best goddamn bodyguard and you're protecting him with a cover-up—or you're the shittiest bodyguard and you're sleeping with my son."

I don't miss a beat. "I'm sleeping with your son."

Lo seethes, his gaze butchering me. I expected that one, but all the respect and trust I'd built and earned with him throughout the years just rips right out of my body.

He rotates to his brother. Ryke jumps down from the top bunk before his wife can catch his shoulder.

Maximoff points angrily at them. "Farrow isn't the enemy. He's my fucking boyfriend!"

I try not to smile. *Damn, that felt good to hear.*

Connor Cobalt commands the floor with one step forward. "Let's clear the air before the overreacting begins." He raises a calming hand towards Maximoff and me. "We believe you're together, but the world won't. Not now. The media will run with the Moffy/Jane love affair story."

It's more salacious.

"Setting that aside," Connor says, "we now need to deal with the private, security issue of a bodyguard having sex with a client—"

"My *son*," Lo sneers at Connor. "I swear to God, Connor, don't treat this like it means nothing—"

"*Dad*," Maximoff interjects. "I'm an adult. We're two consenting *adults*. There's nothing wrong—"

Ryke points at me. "He's your fucking bodyguard, Moffy!"

Lily pushes through the wall of men and stands right…in front of me. Green eyes pained. I tried not to wonder what this moment would look like. Me hurting the one woman I spent years protecting.

But I was on Alpha for three years, surrounded by all six of these people—fuck, I knew how they'd react to *any* bodyguard sleeping with their children.

I knew there'd be condemnation. I knew that in their eyes, I broke a sacred rule.

"*I* matched you with my son." Her chin tries to shake, but she sucks in a breath, raises her head, and pokes my chest with a mad finger. "I trusted you, Farrow. You looked me in the eye and you promised me that you'd protect him."

"I did," I say from my core. "I am—"

"You took advantage of our son," Lo cuts me off. "That's not protecting him." I force myself not to roll my eyes. I've been there for Maximoff Hale every fucking day, and I definitely didn't coerce him into sucking my cock.

Maximoff groans into a frustrated growl. "He didn't take advantage of me. *Yes*, I'm a celebrity. *Yes,* he knows private shit about me because he's my bodyguard. Did he ever use his position to seduce me or blackmail me or hurt me? *Never.*"

Rose perches her hands on her hips. "But we hire bodyguards to *protect* our children." She sets a fiery glare on me. "Not fuck them. For your betrayal, your heart should be fed to the wolves." She extends a hand to her husband. "The knife, Richard."

Connor lowers her arm. "Let's shelve the hyperbolic murders, darling."

Maximoff tries to steal his dad's attention, but it's skewering me. "Dad, I'm twenty-two. I make my own choices, and I chose him."

"How long?" Lo asks me, ignoring his son to grill me. "Did this start before you were assigned to him—"

"*No*," I force the word.

Lo considers this for a moment before saying, "I don't trust easily. And I gave you as much as I give *family*, and you just shit on me, on Lily. For what?"

"For what?" I repeat with the shake of my head. *For what.* "I'd do anything for Maximoff. I'm here, willing to sacrifice a career for him. Because I care about him, I want to be with him. And I'm sorry that I broke your trust, but I can't lie to you or Lily. Given the opportunity, I'd do it all again."

I'm in love with him.

I haven't said those words to Maximoff yet, and he's not hearing them for the first time while I speak to his dad.

Lo stands uneasy, but they all hear what I'm saying.

"I'm telling you right now," Maximoff says firmly to the room, "you're not firing Farrow. None of you are. He's still going to be my bodyguard."

Connor speaks. "For that to happen, your relationship would need to remain secret from the public."

Ryke cuts in, "Who the fuck said he's staying in the security team and on Moffy's detail?"

"Who's going to fire him?" Maximoff rebuts. "You?"

Ryke glowers at me. Like he wants me to quit. *And just shove another bodyguard into Maximoff's arms?* Fuck no.

"I'm not quitting," I tell him. "And we're fine keeping this from the public."

"You still crossed a line," his dad says, "and there needs to be repercussions."

Maximoff motions to Lo. "Again, you're not—"

"This is a security issue," his dad declares. "We'll let security make the call. If they think Farrow isn't fit to be your bodyguard and it's too dangerous, then he's gone. And that's goddamn diplomatic of me."

Before Maximoff speaks, I tell his dad, "Fair enough."

I sound agreeable, but security has more reasons to fire me than they do to keep me. Plus, I'm betting Price and Thatcher would just love to replace me with an uptight do-gooder. Basically, someone who'd never lower their radios, argue or have sex with a client.

And I'm honestly not sure if Akara and the rest of Omega will vouch for me or turn their backs. My actions reflect poorly on SFO, and if they'd rather remain an untarnished, respectable Force, they'd transfer me.

Here's what I know: I can be fired from the whole team, just transferred to another person's detail, or they could put me on probation.

It's all up in the air.

42

FARROW KEENE

I have no gun and no radio.

Security commandeered both while they evaluate my standing on the team. I accept change better than most people, so I naturally have trouble feeling "dread" when I meet a crossroads. But I see what I may lose. Almost like a cumbersome nostalgia, staring up at a beloved college and knowing in a minute I may never step foot on campus again.

I may lose those late-night SFO meetings at Studio 9, the lighthearted jabs over comms, being kept in the loop on private issues, the overwhelming Cobalt, Meadows, and Hale pride we all share, and this tight-knit team who willingly, wholeheartedly sacrifice their time and lives to protect three families.

I zip up my leather jacket, a December wind rustling maple trees and sweeping through the Smoky Mountains. We're not at Camp Calloway anymore.

When the Camp-Away officially ended yesterday morning, Maximoff didn't want to return to Philly right away. There's only one place the families use as a sanctuary away from the media and public.

A four-story lake house hidden in the Smoky Mountains.

Fifty-miles of winding gravel and dirt reach a peaceful place the families visit for holidays and summer. The cherry roof blends into the thicket of maple trees, the leaves bright red before they fall.

334 KRISTA & BECCA RITCHIE

I've been here before. Only one mile to the east, they built another house for security. Essentially, we help keep the acres and acres of land private from the public and media—and any sightseeing cars looking to drive down random gravel roads.

I descend the house's porch stairs and hill, heading towards the lake.

Jane and Maximoff sit on the edge of the dock together. Glittering water reflects the landscape of mountains.

What's noticeable: the distance between them. It's just a weird sight.

Two bodies could squeeze in between theirs. And she's bundled alone in a quilt, not sharing with him. They're barely facing one another, but at least they're talking.

The three of us, plus Quinn, are the only ones at the lake house. The media won't stop speculating about their so-called "love affair" and Twitter even coined a name: #HaleCocest.

The actual Hale Co. is enduring a publicity nightmare. Since Maximoff's dad is the CEO, Loren Hale is combatting most of the fallout.

When I reach the dock, Jane and Maximoff are in quiet contemplation. They've been acting tough. Saying shit like, *rumors happen all the time* and *it's no different* and *we can get through anything together.*

But this is the first attack on their friendship.

Maximoff is about to stand when he sees me, but I take a seat close to him instead. Shoulder-to-shoulder, he wraps his arm around mine.

"Any news from security?" he asks.

"Not yet."

I notice his cellphone lying on the wooden dock. Black screen. With the amount of mayhem that's going on, the screen should be lit up with notifications.

I raise my brows at him. "You turned your phone off?" This is a first.

Jane tightens the quilt around her frame. "He just gave full autonomy to the COO of H.M.C. Philanthropies to make decisions, and then he powered off his phone."

"The COO has control for only two days," Maximoff clarifies. Then he speaks to his best friend. "I'm not here to work. I'm trying to be here for us, Janie—"

"We're fine. We said we're fine." She grabs a folded tabloid that she bought at a gas station and absentmindedly flips through the pages. "It means nothing."

Maximoff drops his arm off me, just to crack his knuckles. I knead his shoulders, his muscle extremely taut.

I ask, "Then what's with the five-feet of space between you two?"

Jane scoots closer, until she's only a foot away. "I still feel strange knowing our parents and some family members believed we were sleeping together. Not to mention the security team." She sighs into a tiny growl and then cringes. "Nothing has made me more embarrassed in my life…"

Maximoff's face contorts, torn to shreds. He can't fix this by physically consoling Jane. That's the problem.

I try to remind Jane, "Omega didn't believe the rumor."

Maximoff adds, "And our family believes us now."

Jane's big blue eyes lift to us. "Because you two kissed. Not because they trusted us, and we did *nothing* to lose their trust. They projected their own pasts onto us like the media always does, and they should've never doubted us. *They shouldn't have,*" she emphasizes.

"I'm sorry," I apologize as rare guilt gnaws at me. "It's my fault." For one, I could've tried not to sink my teeth so hard into him. For another, the lie I created that night fueled their parents' doubt. "The evidence they used against you—that's on me."

Maximoff gives me a look. "Pretty sure you're not the one who cradled her in your arms, kissed her cheek a thousand times, put your arm around her—"

"We all played a hand in this," Jane interjects, "but let's be terribly honest, this is the strangest situation we've ever been in, by far."

No shit.

She skims the tabloid before pushing the pages to her chest. "Have you two seen the new Like Us article?"

"No," we say together.

"Guess the title," Jane says.

Maximoff glares out at the water. "Enraged Like Us."

"I think you mean *Strange* Like Us," I tease.

Jane nearly smiles, which makes Maximoff's shoulder slacken, and then she flashes the tabloid.

DAMAGED LIKE US

The photographs show Jane and Maximoff from the Camp-Away: him carrying her in a piggyback, him kissing her cheek, Jane hugging him around the waist, smiling and laughing. All twisted to fit the headline.

I steal the magazine and throw that tabloid like a Frisbee across the lake. I hear the *plop*.

When I look back at Maximoff, he asks me, "If those pictures had been me and you, what do you think the title would've been?"

I start to smile. And I tell him the first thing that comes to me. "Lovers Like Us."

43

8:00 a.m. at the lake house, I cook bacon and constantly glance over at Maximoff. Bare-chested and dark brown hair disheveled, he cracks eggs into a bowl and tosses the shells in the nearby trashcan. His forest-greens flit back to me just as often.

There's been no news about security yet, but it's too early to care.

And I just enjoy this.

A lot.

A hell of a lot.

It's the first time we've been able to cook breakfast together. It's also the first morning where it won't matter if security or family members catch us. *They know the truth.*

Unflinchingly and resolutely, his gaze rakes down my chest and abs, to the waistband of my black cotton pants.

My smile stretches. "You just got a piece of shell in the bowl."

"Fuck." His head whips to the bowl. "...I don't see it, man." He wipes his hands on a dishtowel.

I take the bacon off the burner, and then I near Maximoff. His hand slides around my waist. Drawing me hard to his chest. *Damn.*

I cup his ass and walk him back into the edge of the counter. His gaze devours mine before our mouths press in full-bodied hunger. Heating and welding together.

Fuck, I hold his sharp jaw to control the kiss. I catch his lip between my teeth, and a shallow breath jettisons his body.

I whisper in the pit of his ear, "My clothes look good on you." He's wearing my black track pants.

Maximoff slips two fingers in my waistband. "Perks of being the same size as my boyfriend."

Hearing him say *boyfriend* out loud makes my smile widen even more.

I'd say my wardrobe doubled too, but I can't wear his clothes in public. Tabloids and fans would notice, and even with the "HaleCocest" rumor, they'd spin another story. Not letting go of the Moffy/Jane love affair, but just adding me to the equation.

Maximoff drapes his arms over my shoulders. "What happens if I get a new bodyguard?"

I won't be around you every day. "That's sweet that you like to visit these hypothetical alternate realities," I say, "but let's stick to ours, where I'm currently still your bodyguard."

Maximoff grasps the back of my head. His grip is strong as fuck, and his waist bows towards me—all of it, all of him, douses me in gasoline and lights me on fucking fire. He breathes, "Who sucks whose cock at 8:12 a.m. in our reality?"

I eye his beautiful, sharp cheekbones. "I can push you to your knees right now, but I'm thinking that you want to push me to mine."

His dark brows furrow, feigning confusion. "How'd you know?"

"You love your dick in my mouth—"

"Farrow!" That's Oscar. *Security is here.* I hear more than a few pairs of footsteps.

Maximoff straightens up, preparing for another fallout where I'm terminated from the security team. I ease casually against the counter beside him, and I wrap my arm around his lower back. My hand on his hip. While he, of course, crosses his arms, biceps flexing. Ready to put up a fight for me.

That last thought wells inside me: *he's ready to put up a fight for me.*

Oscar slips into the kitchen first, and he rolls to a dead stop, studying the scene: midway cooking breakfast together, bare-chested, and my arm is still around Maximoff.

"Redford," Oscar says, forehead wrinkling as his brows shoot up, "is he wearing your pants?"

I roll my eyes, but my smile is fucking killing me.

"We've been together for months," Maximoff says.

"In my mind it's been barely two days, and you're already wearing his—"

Maximoff cuts him off, "That's not fucking important right now."

Oscar sets a hand on the island counter. "Moffy, you're underestimating how shocked we all are. I haven't been this whiplashed in a decade." He looks to me. "You reckless motherfucker, if I hear Alpha call you a maverick one more time over comms, I'm cancelling your Netflix subscription."

"You don't have my passwords, Oliveira." I gave him my passwords at Yale so he could use my HBO, but I changed those a long time ago.

Maximoff drops his arms, about to leave and find Akara, but I catch his wrist to keep him here. My hand slips down into his.

And then Akara enters the huge kitchen, Donnelly and Quinn in tow. Those two hang back at the island bar with Oscar, and the Omega lead nears me.

"Moffy," Akara says, "you should step out—"

"No," I tell Akara. "He should hear."

Maximoff crosses his arms again.

Akara gestures to my chest. "I've spent an accumulative thirty-five hours trying to convince two men that you're worth keeping around." *Price and Thatcher.*

I fixate on the part where he tried to convince them to keep me. "You wanted me to stay? You realize that I selfishly chose a guy over the team?"

Maximoff shoots me a look like I'm digging my grave, but I can't stop staring at Akara.

"Yeah," Akara says, "and the four of us on Omega have all had the misfortune of knowing you before you ever joined security."

Donnelly blows me a middle-finger kiss. At eighteen, I met him at a tattoo shop. He was a seventeen-year-old tattoo apprentice who dropped out of high school, his parents in jail for meth. I let him do *a few* of mine. Until he became better, then he inked more, and he used to crash in my dorm at Yale and streak the hallway for shits and giggles.

Oscar, I met at Yale, and then I met his brother Quinn.

And Akara grew up two streets over from me. See, I didn't take these relationships into account. Because I broke the unbreakable rule. Don't fuck your client.

"I'm not about to stand here and praise you for an hour," Akara says. "What you did was shit, but you're far from incompetent. Alpha and Epsilon see you as a loose canon. The rest of us on Omega, we know you as a good friend."

I rub my jaw and nod more than a few times. "Thank you."

Donnelly holds out a hand to Oscar. "We got a *thank you*. Pay up."

"Fuck you, Farrow," Oscar says. "Now I owe Donnelly fifty bucks because of your gratitude."

"Told you not to take that bet, bro," Quinn says.

I almost smile, but I remember that Akara is only one vote out of three as far as transfers and firing goes. He had to convince either Thatcher or Price to let me stay on the security team and in Omega. He never said he was able to.

Maximoff stays on track. "So what's his fate?" he asks the Omega lead. "Is he being transferred or fired?"

"Price was a firm *fire you*. I'm around him a lot. He's been Daisy Calloway's bodyguard since he was in his twenties, and he just sees what you did as a violation of the parents' trust."

I sink back against the counter. "Fuck," I mutter.

Maximoff grabs his phone off the counter. "I'll talk to Thatcher and Price." He's supposed to stay out of the decision. That was his dad's stipulation. Let security decide my fate. No one in the family tries to sway or influence the team.

"You don't need to," Akara says with the start of a smile.

I shake my head in disbelief. "Thatcher would never vote to let me keep my job."

"There's one giant punishment and warning," Akara says, "but Thatcher agreed with me that you should stay on Omega and remain Maximoff's bodyguard."

Remain Maximoff's bodyguard.

The three words ring in my ears until we're both turning towards each other, and Maximoff's arms wrap around my shoulders, mine hook around his. All warmth and muscle, his pulse beats hard against my chest.

Remain Maximoff's bodyguard.

We break apart about the same time Oscar says, "Yeah, still in shock."

Donnelly hones in on Maximoff. "You wearing Farrow's pants or what?"

"Jesus Christ," he groans.

"You're wearing Jesus Christ's pants?"

Everyone laughs, but Akara is the first to speak as the humor fades. "Did you hear the part where I said there's a punishment and a warning?"

"I heard," I say. "And I'm still not sure why Thatcher would vote to keep me around either."

Akara combs a hand through his black hair. "I reminded him that you just value the privacy of your client over sharing with the team, and that, in reality, you're protecting your client in those situations. Moffy is an adult and if he told you to keep a secret, then you should've kept a secret. After a while, Thatcher acknowledged that—whereas Price wouldn't."

Damn.

"Am I going to need to send him a bottle of wine?" *What does Thatcher even like?*

"No," Oscar says and nears just to steal a piece of bacon off the pan. "Listen to this next part."

Maximoff passes his phone to his other hand. "What?" he asks Akara who now looks at him. "It's about me?"

I straighten off the counter. "What's happening?"

"Thatcher's going to be double-assigned to Maximoff and Jane's detail too."

I rake both of my hands through my hair, blown back into the counter. *Shit.*

"That sounds unnecessary," Maximoff says, "and my brother needs Thatcher. That's *his* bodyguard."

"Xander still has Banks as his 24/7 security, and after the rumor, Jane is going to need two bodyguards."

Maximoff nods in agreement.

"Hey, I want be clear here," Akara says, "this is your punishment. Thatcher thinks you'll both be less careful about hiding your relationship publicly now that you can be together privately in front of family and security. He only agreed to Farrow being Maximoff's bodyguard if he could join and make sure you're not fucking up."

I roll my eyes. "He wants to be my chaperone?"

"Basically, but for good reason."

My brows spike. "You agree?"

"This is your warning. If the media and public finds out that Maximoff is dating a bodyguard, it doesn't just hurt you two."

Maximoff frowns. "What do you mean?"

"What do you think your fans will do if they see that a bodyguard can date one of your cousins or siblings?"

Shit.

Realization washes over Maximoff too. "They'll speculate which bodyguards will be next."

"They'll pair us off," Akara nods. It's not a far stretch when there are Tumblr sites dedicated to their love lives, making predictions about future relationships and marriages. "And they'll be looking at which bodyguards are single and 'of age' and Omega is the youngest team."

"You left out attractive," I say.

"Farrow—"

"I know." *It's serious.* "None of us can become famous." Or else we can't protect our clients. It's an age-old rule that has no loophole like the one I broke.

Maximoff puts a hand on the back of his neck. "So if anyone finds out publicly that I'm dating my bodyguard, it could put the whole team at risk. You'd all lose your jobs and be replaced by older, married security."

Yeah.

We have to be extremely careful in public.

Quinn nears the fridge. "Hey, I know I haven't been in security long, but I just want to say that I fucking like this job."

"We all do," Akara says to us.

They're all letting Maximoff and me be together, and if we fuck up, it could potentially cost their careers. Fuck, I owe all of them, and I also say, "We'll be careful."

Maximoff looks to each guy. "Thank you," he says so powerfully that the kitchen goes quiet. Many of the guys nod to him.

Then the floorboards squeak in the silence, and we all turn our heads.

Sulli waves, and Maximoff starts to smile at his cousin's presence. "Security meeting over?" she asks. "We thought we'd help you all with breakfast."

"We?" Maximoff asks.

Beckett Cobalt slips into view. Darker and curlier hair than his fraternal twin brother Charlie, and his right arm tattoos are visible in a black muscle shirt. People call him *the bad boy of ballet*.

Before Maximoff speaks, Jane swoops into the kitchen wearing kitten-print pajamas.

"Sis." Beckett hugs his sister, and then to the right of their embrace, Charlie Cobalt saunters forward, yellow-green eyes only on Maximoff. I stand on guard, but Maximoff steps forward, his face solidified to marble.

"What are you doing here?" he asks Charlie.

Charlie never breaks eye contact. "Being a cousin who didn't doubt you."

Jane tears up behind him, and Beckett kisses the top of her head.

Maximoff nods repeatedly, and he extends a hand to Charlie. His cousin clasps his hand and they go in for a hug.

People start moving around, exchanging hugs and hellos—the five Omega bodyguards and their five clients haven't all been *alone* together like this in a long time. Definitely not since I've been on SFO.

Then everyone meanders around the kitchen, catching up and helping cook. I stand next to Maximoff and untwist a loaf of bread.

"More bacon," Oscar tells me as he eats all the bacon I just cooked. Donnelly already opens the freezer to grab meat and a bag of frozen biscuits. He hands them to Beckett.

Quinn has another carton of eggs and starts to help Maximoff crack them into his bowl. Sulli and Akara pull out dishes from the cabinets while Charlie and Jane chatter in French, making coffee together.

We could've detonated the security team and his family, and like a strike of perfect lightning, we've brought all ten of us closer together.

And I have the guy.

I have the guy. I extend my arm around his muscular waist, and he leans some of his weight against my side. Relaxing. I begin to smile wider and wider.

44

MAXIMOFF HALE

I hike one of my favorite mountain trails with Farrow. Not far from the lake house. Wind whistles through the towering fir and maple trees and rocky peaks. The last autumn leaves falling.

Nature has nothing on Farrow. I'm highly *distracted*. Jet-black pieces of his hair brush his lashes. His backpack buckled across his hard chest like mine. Biceps bulging in his black long-sleeve shirt.

Mainly, it's how, as we trek up the steep incline, he lengthens his pace. And we're step-for-step the whole time. Neither one of us falling behind.

I think about that a lot.

I think about how he called me pure of heart.

I think about how it'll take time for my family to see him as anything other than my bodyguard, but me and him—we've seen each other as more from the beginning.

I think about how he's helped me over a wall that I had never tried to climb.

I think about you.

And how I've been afraid to disappoint you. Maybe I still will, maybe I already have—but it'd take so much more than a wrong turn or a human mistake to ever disappoint him.

I think about how there's only one person I crave to wake up to and see before I go to sleep. The agitating know-it-all who loves to irritate the fuck out of me.

I think about him.

So when we reach a clearing on a ridge—overlooking a vast backdrop of mountains and bright blue horizon—I forget the fucking view. And I just face Farrow.

He bites the plastic waterspout from his camelbak, smiling. "Seen the view a hundred times already?" The longer he stares into my gaze, the more he sees the emotion barreling out of me. His chest rises in a deeper breath.

"I need to tell you something," I say.

He edges closer. Our hands brush and then clasp together strongly. Gazes never dropping.

Christ, let me say this right. "In hindsight, I realize that I was envisioning a kind of person I'd want to be with for more than a day, long-term. You know, something…" *fuck.* I gesture in the air for the word.

"Lasting?"

"Yeah." *Lasting.*

Something indestructible.

"I hoped for someone who wasn't afraid to put me in my place, someone who made me feel human. I hoped for someone who could be strong so I could be vulnerable, but still never make me feel weak or less than. I hoped for trust and understanding and an innate love of my family. And I realized, Farrow…"

His hand slides up my neck to my jaw, his welling eyes already caressing mine.

"I realized," I breathe, "that I was always hoping and wishing for you." *Say the words.* "I'm in love with you, and I'm the lucky one here."

He laughs into the most heartfelt smile I've seen. Both of his tattooed hands hold my face. Our chests drawn together, and he whispers, "You beat me to it."

He loves me. My face is just pure goddamn happiness. "Well, you can't be first at everything. So one guy always tells me."

"One guy," Farrow repeats.

"Some damn guy," I rephrase, my hand rising up the back of his neck.

"The guy you love," Farrow teases. Then he licks his bottom lip, and his mouth veers to my ear. Holding my head still, he whispers, deep and protective, "I love you too."

Maximoff's 16th Birthday

MAXIMOFF HALE

Dear World, I turn sixteen today. Sincerely, *an aging human.*

No big deal, you know. *Sixteen.* I'm just a year closer to adulthood, which honest-to-God couldn't come sooner. I'm ready for the responsibilities without someone saying, *just be your age, Moffy. Don't worry, Moffy.* When I was fifteen, I never felt fifteen, and I'm pretty much expecting the same at sixteen.

I'm always going to feel older. Until I am finally older.

And then, I don't know what happens. A choir starts singing the Batman theme song. Nachos will fall from the sky. The Earth will split in fucking two. That'd be my luck—once I hit adulthood, the apocalypse will strike, and I'll die. And then all this waiting for adulthood is for a big load of nothing.

I think about that.

And how I need to enjoy *now.* In case there is no later.

"Don't speed," my mom says beside me, waking me up from my head. "I know we named you after Quicksilver, but control your superpower."

I love my mom, and when going to the DMV for my road test, there was no one I wanted more with me. She's a much better driver than my dad, and she helped me reach this point. Right now, we're on two black foldout chairs at the DMV, waiting for my appointment. I finished my motorcycle permit test early (I passed with a 100%), and so we have a few minutes before the examiner should show for the road test.

Garth and Declan, our bodyguards, stand like pillars against the wall beside us.

You see me. You see my mom.

You know we're here today thanks to some *amazing* paparazzi who just so happened to tail us right out of the gated neighborhood. And I can't control that you know where I am. What I'm doing. Like I can't control how a few people try to slyly snap photos of us from their chairs at the DMV.

This is my normal.

It will always be my normal, and I'm okay with that. I have to be.

"The need for speed is at a zero, Mom," I say confidently. "My superpower is totally under control."

She smiles. "You're going to nail it, Moffy. I just know it."

I smile back, about to say *thanks* when the examiner arrives with a clipboard. She's a short forty-something lady with reddish curly hair and straightened bangs. Her hand is over her heart, starstruck at my mom.

My mom spins to me. "You have everything?"

"Yep. I'm all prepared." I stand up.

"Lily Calloway," the examiner says in awe. "I'm Patricia Clarke."

"Hi, Ms. Clarke," my mom greets, cheeks reddening. "I hope you'll take good care of my son. He's a great driver—"

"Oh of course, I will. He has nothing to worry about." She winks at my mom, and I tense. Great, I have nothing to worry about. If I hit a billion and one orange cones and run through seventeen red lights, she *still* might pass me.

She's not going to want to fail the son of Lily Calloway.

It should be comforting, but the special privileges invalidate what I want to prove to my mom.

That I'm a *safe* driver.

Christ, how will she believe that now if this examiner is biased?

So I say outright, "Ms. Clarke, don't go easy on me." *Treat me like everyone else. Please.*

"You'll be given a fair test, I assure you." She's mostly still starstruck with my mom, and my mom looks sad and guilty. Like she messed up by taking me for the test. Like she should've let Dad bring me instead. But this isn't her fault, and I don't care how much you're obsessed with her.

I want my mom with me today.

I wouldn't use a Time Turner to change that.

"Lily Calloway," Ms. Clarke says. "Do you think we could take a picture after the test?"

My mom doesn't correct her and say she's Lily Hale. It happens too often. "How about before?" My mom doesn't want to loiter at this place for longer than she has to, so she quickly takes a selfie with Ms. Clarke. "I'll see you soon, Moffy." My mom hugs me. "Remember, control the superpower."

My mom is nice enough to call speeding a superpower when we all know it's my fatal flaw. But sometimes with X-Men, superpowers and fatal flaws are one in the same.

"Controlled," I nod confidently.

Leaving my mom inside, I head outside with Ms. Clarke and my bodyguard, who goes out in front. I'm going to take the test in my mom's older BMW. Which I'm thinking she'll let me use more often now that I have my driver's license.

The examiner heads towards the newer, nicer Escalade where Declan is going.

"Uh, that's not my car, Ms. Clarke." *That's security's vehicle.* What Garth drove here with Declan, and what Declan slips inside now. My bodyguard can't be in the car with me during the road test. It just has to be me and the examiner.

"Oh?" She spins on her heels and sees me opening the driver's door to the BMW. "This is your car?"

"Yeah." I ignore her disappointment, and I slip into the old leather seat.

After she finishes examining the vehicle as part of the test, she takes the passenger seat. "Okay, let's start. Pull out of the parking lot."

I do everything she instructs. Feeling confident behind the wheel, I turn precisely. I check my mirrors. I use my blinkers. Once I'm on a three-lane road, I face more trouble.

Paparazzi.

Cars intentionally block me on either side, and Declan, in the car behind me, can't do a damn thing to help.

"Switch lanes when you can," Ms. Clarke instructs, a frown in her voice. "Those cars seem a little close to us."

"They're paparazzi."

"Really?" Shock spikes her voice. "They'll go away?"

"Maybe."

Control your superpower.

I tighten my grip on the steering wheel. Craving to outrun them. Outpace them. To not be *trapped* by them. I'm already at five-over the speed limit. Of course paparazzi match my speed—and I accelerate a little more.

Ms. Clarke grabs the door handle and repeats, "Switch lanes when you can."

I accelerate ten-over. Fifteen-over. The cars match me.

I'm twenty-five over, and I'm flying and cut into the right lane and take a sharp turn.

"I didn't say turn!" she shouts, scared.

I slow only when I know I've ditched the paparazzi, and I've successfully ditched Declan. Jesus. I'm rigid, caging breath, and I spin the wheel and take another turn, heading back to the DMV. Expecting Ms. Clarke to fail me.

I was speeding.

I did the *one* thing my mom said I shouldn't do.

Reckless driving. Endangering other people on the road. I feel like mortal shit.

"I'm sorry," I apologize to Ms. Clarke. I scared her.

"No, no—it's okay. Drive around to the back of the building. We'll finish with parallel parking."

My brows furrow. "But I—"

"You did fine under the circumstances." She clears her throat and writes on her clipboard.

I can't let her pass me. It's not fair. I shouldn't be given a license. It's not ethically *right*, but I find myself driving to the back of the building.

And partly, I want to prove she's not being biased. That this isn't a sham. I can parallel park with my eyes closed; I've practiced so damn much.

But as I spin the wheels, I purposefully drive into the line of orange cones. They bump against the BMW.

Her eyes go wide.

"Sorry," I say, less sorry this time.

"Um, try again, Maximoff."

The second attempt, I do even worse.

"Stop, stop." She swallows. "I think that's good enough. Park where we started." I drive around the DMV building and pull into the park next to Declan's SUV. She tears off her paper. "Congratulations. You passed."

"Are you sure?" *Fail me.*

Please.

"I'm sure." She smiles. "Your mom will be so proud."

"Yeah…" I have a pit in my stomach. Even as I head inside and take the photo for my temporary license (the official one will arrive in the mail)—even as I'm driving myself and my mom home.

I'm more careful this time.

I promise.

"Mom," I say. We've both been quiet on the car ride.

She finally breaks open. "Moffy, look, I'm really sorry about your examiner, I should've let your dad—"

"No, I wanted you there. I don't care about her…" Is that a lie? I don't know. I don't fucking know. I do care that Ms. Clarke was biased, but not enough to not go with my mom.

"You do care," my mom says softly, gently. "I know you care, Moffy. You don't have to pretend that you don't. It's okay."

"I'm not pretending," I whisper.

"You're my firstborn Hufflepuff. I can tell when you're upset, you know."

I smile a bit. "I know, Mom." I grip the wheel tightly. "I guess I'm just more upset that I failed."

"You have the license."

"She shouldn't have passed me."

"You don't know that."

"I do," I say strongly. "Because I did the one thing you said not to do. I sped, and I hate that I sped." I can feel her frown, and I don't have the heart to look at her disappointment.

"She still passed you, so maybe it wasn't as bad as you think."

"I didn't even successfully parallel park."

She's confused. "How? You practiced for weeks. You're better at parallel parking than even I am, you know that." Silence lingers for a moment, her eyes narrowing on me. She gasps softly in realization. "Did you try to fail on purpose? Why, Moffy?"

"I didn't deserve the license. I shouldn't have even accepted it."

"But you did," she says strongly, "because you obviously *want* to drive."

Yeah.

I really want the freedom to drive around, and my ethics, my morals—I shoved them aside. Guilt haunts me, but my mom tells me, "You already have the license, and I agree, you shouldn't have it. She should've failed you. But she didn't, and I know you're a good driver. If I didn't think you have the ability to be safe, then I wouldn't want you on the road. I wouldn't have let you take the test, Moffy."

I try to relax at her words.

Really, my shoulders are still squared. Muscles tensed. But I listen.

"Instead of trying to take it back," she continues, "why don't you just prove to yourself from now on that you aren't reckless with speeding.

Every time you get in this car, try to be the safest you can be. Can you do that?"

"I can try," I say.

But I'm not sure how big this fatal flaw of mine is. I think being behind the wheel is my means of obtaining control, but sometimes, I know, deep-down, it's controlling me.

Once I park in the driveway at home, my mom says, "Why don't you go down to Uncle Ryke's house for a little bit? Just until the afternoon-ish. Like one p.m."

"That's oddly specific," I smile.

"I know nothing!" she shouts, practically tossing herself out of the car.

I laugh.

You have no idea what my mom is planning for my 16th birthday. And neither do I. I didn't think the *no plans* were suspicious until this moment. I smell the scent of a surprise party, and I'm excited to see all my family in one place.

I'm guessing she's inviting family.

Hopefully the pool is involved. Sun is out. Sky is bright blue in July. After my road test, nothing sounds better than diving into the water.

Grabbing my skateboard, I leave the house and roll down the street in the gated neighborhood. Not needing a bodyguard around me, I end up alone at the cul-de-sac, and I kick up my board, walking up the driveway.

A sliver of the garage is cracked, and I stop at the sound of voices.

"What's the fucking problem here, Lo?" Ryke says roughly to my dad. "It's a bike, not a bomb."

"That thing could kill my kid, that's what's goddamn wrong."

"Moffy will be safe. I'll teach him how to ride fucking *safely*. And I asked you if I could get him a motorcycle for his birthday, and you said it'd be *good* since you and Lily got him a car—so what the fuck is going on?"

I back up a bit.

Shocked.

That my uncle got me a motorcycle *and* that my parents got me a car. I wasn't expecting anything, even if Janie got a blue Beetle last month for her sixteenth.

"I changed my mind."

"You're fucking scared."

"He's reckless on the road—yeah, I'm *fucking* scared."

That hurts a tiny bit.

A lotta bit.

But it's true. I know it's true. And I couldn't prove otherwise today. Maybe I'll have another chance—every day I drive and stay safe, like my mom said. Or maybe I'll keep failing.

"You could say the same thing about Daisy. And she's never wrecked."

My dad is quiet.

"He's smart, Lo. He knows what he's doing. I'll make fucking sure of it."

"You better." His voice sounds less edged.

I can feel my dad conceding, and I could ruin the surprise and show myself—but I decide not to. Instead of eavesdropping for longer, I skateboard around the neighborhood.

Ending up passing a white house with columns. A few guys in my grade at Dalton are kicking a soccer ball in the front yard.

"Maximoff!" Blake Westerfield yells as I roll along the street.

I rest my foot on the pavement. Stopping. "Hey!" I nod back in greeting. We're friendly but not really friends. I've mostly said hi to him here or there. And when he gestures me closer, I'm thinking he must want to invite me to kick the soccer ball around.

I still have some time to kill, so I might actually say, *yeah.*

He rolls the ball under his foot. His friends are smiling. "Maximoff," Carter and Henry greet, shaking my hand and patting my back in a short hug.

Blake grins, "We were actually just talking about you earlier."

I'm more on guard. *It's probably nothing.* I'm being unnecessarily paranoid. Still, I'm prepared for the worst. "Yeah?"

"Yeah," Henry says. "Have you ever looked your family up online? Like done a deep-dive? Or do you try not to look?"

It feels like a harmless, curious question, but I lick my lips and take a beat. My muscles burning as I stand stricter. "Yeah, I don't try to look." I gesture to where I came. "I've gotta go—"

"Wait, wait," Blake says fast, a hand outstretched. "So you've never read the stuff about your mom?"

I glower. "Don't talk about my mom, man."

"Why are you so defensive? Her whole life is on the internet. Like she *put it* there."

"She didn't put everything there," I combat. "And the stuff she did can be warped by media."

"Your mom's favorite sex position is anal; how can they twist that around?" Blake says. *Are you fucking kidding me?* "Unless she likes taking it in the ass from more than just your dad—"

I see red.

Skateboard is out of my hands. I drop it. And my fist is in his face. We're wrestling on the grass of his front lawn, and I lay three fast punches in his mouth before Henry and Carter pry me off their friend.

"Shit," Blake squeaks out. Blood gushing down his lips, down his chin. "You broke my tooph." He can barely say *tooth*. His front two are missing.

Henry and Carter let go of me, hands in the air. Afraid. So many damn people have been afraid of me today, and I don't love that.

"Stop talking about my mom," I growl out, "and fuck all of you." I grab my skateboard roughly, not even wanting to skate. I walk angrily home.

Blood still pumping hotly through my veins.

Halfway there, I start to cool down...and I feel a throbbing pain under my eye. I touch the stinging, swollen skin.

Awesome.

He landed a punch.

Best sixteenth birthday in the history of ever.

I reach my street and glance down at the cul-de-sac. The garage is fully open. My dad and Ryke are gone, and I see the parked motorcycle clearly. A lime green Kawasaki. It's beautiful and way too damn expensive. Something I don't really deserve, but I want to be deserving of my uncle's gift.

I swallow hard.

Gratitude floods me.

Feeling like shit for even being pissy. For throwing a punch in the first place. I have a really good life. Really great parents. Really amazing family. I know that.

I appreciate that.

I breathe in.

Pool.

Water sounds better than oxygen. Once I'm home, I veer to the backyard. Not even heading inside, I already see the commotion behind the black iron fence.

Everyone is here.

All of my family. Hales. Meadows. Cobalts. Abbeys and Stokes. And then some family friends. I smile seeing Janie place orange plastic silverware in a cup, helping my mom with the nacho table. Uncle Garrison tries to man the grill, but the chicken already looks burnt.

Luna and Xander are tying balloons to the fence. They're only eleven and eight. Kinney is pretending to ride a broom around the pool. She's six.

"Little Slytherin, no flying around bodies of water!" my dad calls out.

"But dad," Kinney whines.

"No *buts* and no flying."

She huffs and drops the broom.

I laugh.

You should know I really, *really* love my family.

And I don't make my appearance yet. I let them finish decorating in case they want this to be a full-blown surprise, and I go inside. Get my swimsuit on in my bedroom. Check out my face.

A bruise is already forming under my eye.

Come on.

I touch the spot more.

At least my eye isn't swollen closed. I'll embrace that miracle.

I consider stealing some of my mom's concealer. But I plan to swim, and I bet it'll just wash off anyway. So I end up going outside, shirtless in green swim trunks and a black-and-blue eye. Instead of making a grand entrance, I slip into the party sort of unseen.

Family greets me as soon as I pass them, and they see I'm here.

"Happy Birthday, Moffy!" is met with "What happened to your eye?"

"Battle with Thanos," I joke.

And that's that.

My mom doesn't press.

Neither do my dad or aunts and uncles. And the younger seven-year-olds and six-year-olds like when I change my story—as though it's a secret just with them—and I say, "I fought a bear and I won."

I thank everyone for coming. I thank my mom for the surprise. "You're the best mom." I wrap my arms around her, already way taller. "I'm glad I have you, seriously."

Tears brim in her eyes. She squeezes me. "Go have fun. Don't stress about anything. Today is your day."

I try to let go of the bad parts of today.

There is a whole lot of good.

And once I find myself in the water, I feel way calmer. I do a couple laps, racing Sulli, and she still outswims me at thirteen to my sixteen. Once I hang onto the edge of the deep-end, I catch sight of a family friend.

He's six-foot-something.

These beautiful tattoos scatter his fair skin, spindling down his toned calves. Disappearing up his black trunks. His black V-neck tee reveals more ink on his chest, his arms pretty damn covered. But his hands and neck are tattoo-free.

His hair is dyed jet-black, and his lip piercing is just plain hot. I wonder what it's like to kiss someone with a piercing.

You have no clue I'm bisexual. Only my family knows. I came out last Christmas, and in case my family can tell I'm staring, I do a *fantastic* job of scanning the pool and patio.

Being casual.

I can be *casual*. And cool.

Like him…

He carries himself with such damn ease. Like nothing is on his shoulders. No heartache, no hurt, no turmoil or shame. He laughs, his smile stretching from cheek to cheek, and he's speaking to a newer bodyguard that stands on the other side of the fence.

The bodyguard has a rolled bandana tied around his forehead. Curly hair hanging over. Golden-brown skin and fit build. He's in his early twenties, I think. He's assigned to protect my little cousin Ben, but I can't remember his name.

The way they're talking, they must know each other.

And then they shake hands over the fence into a hug-pat.

When he turns around to the pool, he combs his fingers through his hair with total casualness, and I could replay that motion on slo-mo for a millennium in my brain.

His shirt is kind of tight on his abs. Maybe that's the sun. The heat suctioning the fabric a bit.

Blood starts pumping south, and I flex my muscles to keep a hard-on at bay.

Jesus.

Am I staring that badly?

No.

I'm *observing*. Barely.

Almost not at all.

I glance back for another second.

I know his name.

Farrow.

Redford.

Keene.

I think he's in med school? Can't really remember exactly. Maybe he's in undergrad still. He must be back in Philly for the summer. I know he's five-years older than me. Twenty-one.

He sees my mom at the nacho table. She's piling cheese onto an orange plate, and he approaches with a genuine smile and greets her. They hug and chat, and I'm about to swim under the water to cool off and force my dick down.

How hard am I?

I adjust myself under the water.

Too damn hard.

"Moffy!" my mom calls.

I solidify. Not my dick. I instantly go limp. But the rest of my body is marble. My mom—she's waving me over to the nacho spread, and Farrow has spun around, facing me with an inching smile.

"Moffy!" she calls again like I don't understand. "Come here for a sec!"

Someone call an ambulance.

I think I fucking died.

"Coming," I say and I want to die again at my word choice.

Fuck me.

Clenching my jaw, flexing my muscles, I effortlessly pull myself out of the pool. Hoping I'm making the hottest entrance towards this guy.

Farrow is gay, and the thought that he *could* potentially find me hot in return—that does a number on my brain and cock.

Not that he knows I'm bi like my family does. Or maybe he can just tell. I don't know.

"Mom," I say first. Dripping water, I grab a nearby towel and rub my hair. I nod to Farrow. "Hey."

"Happy Birthday," he says easily, chewing a piece of gum. The way he's casually chewing that gum—I want to be that gum in his mouth.

What...the hell is wrong with me?

Trying to stay cool, confident, I nod back. "Thanks, man."

He's barely looking at me. More so smiling at my mom. My disappointment isn't strong. I'm more intrigued than anything. For as much as I want to be seen as an adult, Farrow knows me as newly *sixteen*, and he's not checking me out.

I like that more about him.

"You know Farrow," my mom says to me. "He's in medical school. I asked if he could look at your eye."

All I hear is, *Farrow* and *look at your eye*. I blink. "Mom—"

"Please, Moffy."

My face is burning. I stand rigid and catch *his* gaze. "I'm fine. It's just a bruise."

Without moving, without lifting a hand, he simply inspects my eye from a couple feet away. "Looks that way. You'll survive."

I nod a lot, wondering if he can tell I think he's hot. *I hope not.* Let me take this to my spank bank in peace.

Can he tell I'm a virgin?

I try to jump out of my useless thoughts that are burning me alive.

"Great," I say with thick sarcasm. "I was hoping to die around midnight. Guess I'll have to postpone my funeral."

"Moffy!" my mom gasps.

Farrow laughs. "You'll have to run harder into a doorknob, if you want to die."

I make a face. "I didn't run into a doorknob."

He pops a bubblegum bubble. "Man, you didn't fight some comic book villain."

"I got in a fight with a kid down the street," I admit. Why the fuck am I admitting this to him—with my mom right *here?!*

My mom actually smiles, like she's happy I finally admitted what I'm guessing was obvious. Because this isn't my first fistfight.

Farrow nods slowly. "Hope he looks worse than you."

"He does."

He slips aviators over his eyes. Sun shining brighter. The effortlessness in his action almost drips my gaze down his body. *Don't check him out.*

Don't check him out.

Not in front of my mom.

I run a hand over my tensed neck, and before I can speak, my mom says, "I can't believe you're already sixteen. It feels like yesterday you were just five, Moffy."

Farrow smiles that same cheek-to-cheek smile I saw earlier. One that seems way too entertained at my red-hot face.

More to Farrow, than to my mom, I say, "Feels like I was a hundred-and-four yesterday."

I can't see his eyes behind his aviators. His casualness feels *cocky* all of a sudden. And I want to prove that I'm way better than him.

Christ, I want to be *twenty-one*. No, I want to be *twenty-five*. Multiple years older. A thousand years older.

To my mom, I joke, "You sure I'm not a vampire?"

"I'm sure," she says assuredly, munching on a nacho chip.

Farrow smiles to my mom. "It was nice seeing you, Lily."

"I know you're busy with school, but don't be a stranger. We love seeing you when you're in town." She gives him a quick side-hug, and I try not to show disappointment in his quick departure.

Farrow nods to me. "Congrats on turning sixteen."

I grimace. Does he know how disgruntled I am at the reality of my age? His smile widens off my aggravated face. *He definitely knows.* Farrow seems like an asshole.

And I'm entertaining his asshole behavior.

I feign confusion. "Am I sixteen?"

He points to the balloons tied to the fence. The 1 and 6.

"Those are backwards. I'm sixty-one."

He lets out a laugh. "Sure." He nods again. "Take care, Moffy."

I wish he said something like, *see you around.* Or *until next time.* We might never see each other again. But that can't be true. Even if he goes to Yale, there are the summers. And he's been invited to my sister's birthday parties more than mine. Being the son of our concierge doctor and all.

I try not to watch him leave.

So I grab a plate, about to fill it up with nachos.

"You know why I'm *positive* you aren't a vampire?" my mom says to me, scooping more cheese dip on her plate.

I shake my head. "Why?"

"You love the sun way too much."

I smile.

Yeah. That's the truth.

"I guess that makes me a regular sixteen-year-old human," I tell her.

"You're still a superhero to me."

She's *my* superhero. I wouldn't be who I am without her strength and love. "Thanks, Mom." After I load my plate up with beef, chicken, and chips, I scour the pool.

Must. Find. Janie.

The need to rehash the Farrow interaction is way too damn strong, and she's the one I trust the most with *that*.

What even was *that*?

I glance back from where Farrow left.

He really is gone.

He left the party. But I can't stop staring at where he stood. I'm pretty sure he'll be making an appearance in my brain tonight. When it's just me and my hand in bed.

It's not like anything can happen in reality.

For one, I'm sixteen. Even if I wish I could be immortally old.

For another million-and-one-reasons, it just won't work. Me in a relationship with *anyone* won't work, not with the media ruining their lives because of me. I'm okay with my life and how it is. I have to be okay.

I crunch on a chip.

And I go find my best friend.

WANT MORE BONUS SCENES LIKE MAXIMOFF'S 16TH BIRTHDAY?

Join Krista & Becca's Patreon at www.patreon.com/kbritchie

Joining Krista & Becca's Patreon will give you access to all previously posted bonus scenes. Plus new content and extras release every month! Patreon is a great place for readers who love behind-the-scenes posts and all the extra goodies.

 CONNECT WITH KRISTA & BECCA
www.kbritchie.com
www.facebook.com/KBRitchie
www.instagram.com/kbmritchie

ACKNOWLEDGMENTS

To our mom, thank you for not only once again providing us with your goddess-like editing powers, but for giving us endless support. You are the most selfless human being we know, and your kindness and generosity could power a whole fleet of Viking ships.

To Lanie, Jenn, Jae, and Siiri, thank you for being the best Facebook Admins, friends, and shoulders to lean on. You ladies are a magical bunch. Thank you for always championing our books and for doing all you do to help spread the word. It's a powerful thing to meet people who just want you to succeed, who'd do anything to further your dreams. We love you all so much.

To Marie, thank you for all of your support and for all the help translating the French. Jane and Maximoff's friendship wouldn't be nearly as special without your talents.

To Kimberly, thank you for being a superhero agent. We know we constantly say this! But it's so true. We feel like the luckiest authors to have you in our corner.

To the Fizzle Force Facebook Group, we wrote this book during one of the most difficult times in our lives. Your constant, uplifting encouragement means more to us than you can possibly know. In a sea of self-doubt, other's positivity can literally be the one thing to change everything. It pushed us to keep going. To fight for the book that we wanted and thought was best. Thank you for all the love. It truly is life-changing.

And to Aisha, you've shown us what strength really means and what sunshine really looks like. We love you so very much, and your beautiful heart continues to inspire us.

To Lex, thank you for your wonderful advice and always being there to chat. Your friendship over the years has meant everything to us.

To Kennedy, meeting you will always be one of our ultimate highlights.

We admire you so much. Thank you for being such a sweet friend.

To the romance community, we are so honored to be a part of this community with such talented and amazing writers and readers. Thank you for embracing us—two very pop-culture obsessed girls—so fully.

To the bloggers and reviewers, your work is so important. Thank you for always taking the time to create and to post and to spend countless hours doing what you do—just for the sheer love of it.

To the fans of our previous novels, thank you for continuing this journey with us. Thank you for taking a chance on this new series. We know not everyone will keep reading our books, but the fact that you've stuck around is nothing short of magic.

And lastly, but definitely not least, thank you. The reader. You're a huge part of why we're still writing. Why we're still living out our dream. You picked up this book. You read it. And for that, we are so very, very grateful.